Trevlyn Hold

A Novel

by

Henry Wood

Double 9 BOOKS

Trevlyn Hold
A Novel
by Henry Wood

ISBN: 978-93-73401-45-4

Published by

DOUBLE 9 BOOKS
2/13-B, Ansari Road
Daryaganj, New Delhi – 110002
info@double9books.com
www.double9books.com
Tel. 011-40042856

ABOUT THE AUTHOR

Ellen Wood, widely known under the name Mrs. Henry Wood, was a prolific English novelist born on January 17, 1814, in England. Her literary career gained widespread popularity in both Britain and abroad, especially after the publication of her most renowned work East Lynne in 1861. Her writing style combined elements of mystery, morality, and domestic life, contributing to her lasting appeal during the Victorian period. She married Henry Wood in 1836, and they had a son named Charles Wood. After her husband's death in 1866, she supported her family through her writing and editorial work. She also managed the magazine Argosy, to which she contributed both fiction and editorial commentary. Though many of her novels are lesser known today, her stories enjoyed international readership during her lifetime and were especially well-received in the United States and Australia. In Australia, her popularity once exceeded that of Charles Dickens. Ellen Wood died in London on February 10, 1887, at the age of 73 and was buried in Highgate Cemetery. Her parents were Thomas Price and Elizabeth Price.

CONTENTS

CHAPTER I
THOMAS RYLE

The fine summer had faded into autumn, and the autumn would soon be fading into winter. All signs of harvest had disappeared. The farmers had gathered the golden grain into their barns; the meads looked bare, and the partridges hid themselves in the stubble left by the reapers.

Perched on the top of a stile which separated one field from another, was a boy of some fifteen years. Several books, a strap passed round to keep them together, were flung over his shoulder, and he sat throwing stones into a pond close by, softly whistling as he did so. The stones came out of his pocket. Whether stored there for the purpose to which they were now being put, was best known to himself. He was a slender, well-made boy, with finely-shaped features, a clear complexion, and eyes dark and earnest. A refined face; a good face—and you have not to learn that the face is the index of the mind. An index that never fails for those gifted with the power to read the human countenance.

Before him at a short distance, as he sat on the stile, lay the village of Barbrook. A couple of miles beyond the village was the large town of Barmester. But you could reach the town without taking the village *en route*. As to the village itself, there were several ways of reaching it. There was the path through the fields, right in front of the stile where that schoolboy was sitting; there was the green and shady lane (knee-deep in mud sometimes); and there were two high-roads. From the signs of vegetation around—not that the vegetation was of the richest kind—you would never suspect that the barren and bleak coal-fields lay so near. Only four or five miles away in the opposite direction—that is, behind the boy and the stile—the coal-pits flourished. Farmhouses were scattered within view, had the boy on the stile chosen to look at them; a few gentlemen's houses, and many cottages and hovels. To the left, glancing over the field and across the upper road—the road which did not lead to Barbrook, but to Barmester—on a slight eminence, rose the fine old-fashioned mansion called Trevlyn Hold. Rather to the right, behind him, was the less pretentious but comfortable dwelling called Trevlyn Farm. Trevlyn Hold, formerly the property and residence of Squire Trevlyn, had passed, with that gentleman's death, into the hands of Mr. Chattaway, who now lived in it; his wife having been the Squire's second daughter. Trevlyn Farm was tenanted by Mr. Ryle; and the boy sitting on the stile was Mr. Ryle's eldest son.

There came, scuffling along the field-path from the village, as fast as her dilapidated shoes permitted her, a wan-looking, undersized girl. She had almost reached the pond, when a boy considerably taller and stronger than the boy on the stile came flying down the field on the left, and planted himself in her way.

"Now then, little toad! Do you want another buffeting?"

"Oh, please, sir, don't stop me!" she cried, beginning to sob loudly. "Father's dying, and mother said I was to run and tell them at the farm. Please let me go by."

"Did I not order you yesterday to keep out of these fields?" asked the tall boy. "The lane and roads are open to you; how dare you come this way? I promised you I'd shake the inside out of you if I caught you here again, and now I'll do it."

"I say," called out at this juncture the lad on the stile, "keep your hands off her."

The child's assailant turned sharply at the sound. He had not seen that any one was there. For one moment he relaxed his hold, but the next appeared to change his mind, and began to shake the girl. She turned her face, in its tears and dirt, towards the stile.

"Oh, Master George, make him let me go! I'm hasting to your house, Master George. Father's lying all white upon the bed; and mother said I was to come off and tell of it."

George leaped off the stile, and advanced. "Let her go, Cris Chattaway!"

Cris Chattaway turned his anger upon George. "Mind your own business, you beggar! It is no concern of yours."

"It is, if I choose to make it mine. Let her go, I say. Don't be a coward."

"What's that you call me?" asked Cris Chattaway. "A coward? Take that!"

He had picked up a clod of earth, and dashed it in George Ryle's face. The boy was not one to stand a gratuitous blow, and Mr. Christopher, before he knew what was coming, found himself on the ground. The girl, released, flew to the stile and scrambled over it. George stood his ground, waiting for Cris to get up; he was less tall and strong, but he would not run away.

Christopher Chattaway slowly gathered himself up. He *was* a coward; and fighting, when it came to close quarters, was not to his liking. Stone-throwing, water-squirting, pea-shooting—any annoyance that might safely be carried on at a distance—he was an adept in; but hand-to-hand fighting—Cris did not relish that.

"See if you don't suffer for this, George Ryle!"

George laughed good-humouredly, and sat down on the stile as before. Cris was dusting the earth off his clothes.

"You have called me a coward, and you have knocked me down. I'll enter it in my memorandum-book, George Ryle."

"Do," equably returned George. "I never knew any *but* cowards set upon girls."

"I'll set upon her again, if I catch her using this path. There's not a more impudent little wretch in the whole parish. Let her try it, that's all."

"She has a right to use this path as much as I have."

"Not if I choose to say she sha'n't use it. *You* won't have the right long."

"Oh, indeed!" said George. "What is to take it from me?"

"The Squire says he shall cause this way through the fields to be closed."

"*Who* says it?" asked George, with marked emphasis—and the sound grated on Cris Chattaway's ear.

"The Squire says so," he roared. "Are you deaf?"

"Ah," said George. "But Mr. Chattaway can't close it. My father says he has not the power to do so."

"*Your* father!" contemptuously rejoined Cris Chattaway. "He would like his leave asked, perhaps. When the Squire says he shall do a thing, he means it."

"At any rate, it is not done yet," was the significant answer. "Don't boast, Cris."

Cris had been making off, and was some distance up the field. He turned to address George.

"You know, you beggar, that if I don't go in and polish you off it's because I can't condescend to tarnish my hands. When I fight, I like to fight with gentlefolk." And with that he turned tail, and decamped quicker than before.

"Just so," shrieked George. "Especially if they wear petticoats."

A sly shower of earth came back in answer. But it happened, every bit of it, to steer clear of him, and George kept his seat and his equanimity.

"What has he been doing now, George?"

George turned his head; the question came from one behind him. There stood a lovely boy of some twelve years old, his beautiful features set off by dark blue eyes and bright auburn curls.

"Where did you spring from, Rupert?"

"I came down by the hedge. You were calling after Cris and did not hear me. Has he been threshing you, George?"

"Threshing me!" returned George, throwing back his handsome head with a laugh. "I don't think he would try that on, Rupert. He could not thresh me with impunity, as he does you."

Rupert Trevlyn laid his cheek on the stile, and fixed his eyes on the clear blue evening sky—for the sun was drawing towards its setting. He was a sensitive, romantic, strange sort of boy; gentle and loving by nature, but given to violent fits of passion. People said he inherited the latter from his grandfather, Squire Trevlyn. Other of the Squire's descendants had inherited the same. Under happier auspices, Rupert might have learnt to subdue these bursts of passion. Had he possessed a kind home and loving friends, how different might have been his destiny!

"George, I wish papa had lived!"

"The whole parish has need to wish that," returned George. "I wish you stood in his shoes! That's what I wish."

"Instead of Uncle Chattaway. Old Canham says I ought to stand in them. He says he thinks I shall, some time, because justice is sure to come uppermost in the end."

"Look here, Rupert!" gravely returned George Ryle. "Don't go listening to old Canham. He talks nonsense, and it will do neither of you any good. If Chattaway heard a tithe of what he sometimes says, he'd turn him from the lodge, neck and crop, in spite of Miss Diana. What *is*, can't be helped, you know, Rupert."

"But Cris has no right to inherit Trevlyn over me."

"He has legal right, I suppose," answered George; "at least, he will have it. Make the best of it, Ru. There are lots of things I have to make the best of. I had a caning yesterday for another boy, and I had to make the best of that."

Rupert still looked up at the sky. "If it were not for Aunt Edith," quoth he, "I'd run away."

"You little stupid! Where would you run to?"

"Anywhere. Mr. Chattaway gave me no dinner to-day."

"Why not?"

"Because Cris carried a tale to him. But it was false, George."

"Did you tell Chattaway it was false?"

"Yes. But where's the use? He always believes Cris before me."

"Have you had no dinner?"

Rupert shook his head. "I took some bread off the tray as they were carrying it through the hall. That's all I have had."

"Then I'd advise you to make double haste home to your tea," said George, jumping over the stile, "as I am going to do to mine."

George ran swiftly across the back fields towards his home. Looking round when he was well on his way, he saw Rupert still leaning on the stile with his face turned upward.

Meanwhile the little tatterdemalion had scuffled along to Trevlyn Farm—a very moderately-sized house with a rustic porch covered with jessamine, and a large garden, more useful than ornamental, intervening between it and the high-road. The garden path, leading to the porch, was straight and narrow; on either side rose alternately cabbage-rose trees and hollyhocks. Gooseberries, currants, strawberries, raspberries, and other plain fruit-trees grew amidst vegetables of various sorts. A productive if not an elegant garden. At the side of the house the fold-yard palings and a five-barred gate separated it from the public road, and behind the house were the barns and other outdoor buildings belonging to the farm.

From the porch the entrance led direct into a room, half sitting-room, half kitchen, called "Nora's room." Nora generally sat in it; George and his brother did their lessons there; the actual kitchen being at the back of it. A parlour opening from this room on the right, whose window looked into the fold-yard, was the general sitting-room. The best sitting-room, a really handsome apartment, was on the other side of the house. As the girl scuttled up to the porch, an active, black-eyed, talkative little woman, of five or six-and-thirty saw her approaching from the window of the best kitchen. That was Nora. What with her ragged frock and tippet, broken straw bonnet, and slipshod shoes, the child looked wretched enough. Her father, Jim Sanders, was carter to Mr. Ryle. He had been at home ill the last day or two; or, as the phrase ran in the farm, was "off his work."

"If ever I saw such an object!" was Nora's exclamation. "How *can* her mother keep her in that state? Just look at Letty Sanders, Mrs. Ryle!"

Sorting large bunches of sweet herbs on a table at the back of the room was a tall, upright woman. Her dress was plain, but her manner and bearing betrayed the lady. Those familiar with the district would have recognised in her handsome but somewhat masculine face a likeness to the well-formed, powerful features of the late Squire Trevlyn. She was that gentleman's eldest daughter, and had given mortal umbrage to her family when she quitted

Trevlyn Hold to become the second wife of Mr. Ryle. George Ryle was not her son. She had only two children; Trevlyn, a boy two years younger than George; and a little girl of eight, named Caroline.

Mrs. Ryle turned, and glanced at the path and Letty Sanders. "She is indeed an object! See what she wants, Nora."

Nora, who had no patience with idleness and its signs, flung open the door. The girl halted a few paces from the porch, and dropped a curtsey.

"Please, father be dreadful bad," began she. "He be lying on the bed and don't stir, and his face is white; and, please, mother said I was to come and tell the missus, and ask her for a little brandy."

"And how dare your mother send you up to the house in this trim?" demanded Nora. "How many crows did you frighten as you came along?"

"Please," whimpered the child, "she haven't had time to tidy me to-day, father's been so bad, and t'other frock was tored in the washin'."

"Of course," assented Nora. "Everything is 'tored' that she has to do with, and never gets mended. If ever there was a poor, moithering, thriftless thing, it's that mother of yours. She has no needles and no thread, I suppose, and neither soap nor water?"

Mrs. Ryle came forward to interrupt the colloquy. "What is the matter with your father, Letty? Is he worse?"

Letty dropped several curtseys in succession. "Please, 'm, his inside's bad again, but mother's afeared he's dying. He fell back upon the bed, and don't stir nor breathe. She says, will you please send him some brandy?"

"Have you brought anything to put it into?" inquired Mrs. Ryle.

"No, 'm."

"Not likely," chimed in Nora. "Madge Sanders wouldn't think to send so much as a cracked teacup. Shall I put a drop in a bottle, and give it to her?" continued Nora, turning to Mrs. Ryle.

"No," replied Mrs. Ryle. "I must know what's the matter with him before I send brandy. Go back to your mother, Letty. Tell her I shall be going past her cottage presently, and will call in."

The child turned and scuffled off. Mrs. Ryle resumed:

"Should it be another attack of internal inflammation, brandy would be the worst thing he could take. He drinks too much, does Jim Sanders."

"His inside's like a barrel—always waiting to be filled," remarked Nora. "He'd drink the sea dry, if it ran beer. What with his drinking, and her untidiness, small wonder the children are in rags. I am surprised the master keeps him on!"

"He only drinks by fits and starts, Nora. His health will not let him do more."

"No, it won't," acquiesced Nora. "And I fear this bout may be the ending of him. That hole was not dug for nothing."

"Nonsense," said Mrs. Ryle. "How can you be so foolishly superstitious, Nora? Find Treve, will you, and get him ready."

"Treve," a young gentleman given to having his own way, and to be kept very much from school on account of "delicate health," a malady less real than imaginary, was found somewhere about the farm, and put into visiting condition. He and his mother were invited to take tea at Barbrook. In point of fact, the invitation had been for Mrs. Ryle only; but she could not bear to stir anywhere without her darling boy Trevlyn.

They had barely departed when George entered. Nora had then laid the tea-table, and was standing cutting bread-and-butter.

"Where are they all?" asked George, depositing his books upon a sideboard.

"Your mother and Treve are off to tea at Mrs. Apperley's," replied Nora. "And the master rode over to Barmester this afternoon, and is not back yet. Sit down, George. Would you like some pumpkin pie?"

"Try me," responded George. "Is there any?"

"I saved it from dinner,"—bringing forth a plate from a closet. "It is not much. Treve's stomach craves for pies as much as Jim Sanders's for beer; and Mrs. Ryle would give him all he wanted, if it cleared the larder—Is some one calling?" she broke off, going to the window. "George, it's Mr. Chattaway! See what he wants."

A gentleman on horseback had reined in close to the gate: a spare man, rather above the middle height, with a pale, leaden sort of complexion, small, cold light eyes and mean-looking features. George ran down the path.

"Is your father at home?"

"No. He is gone to Barmester."

A scowl passed over Mr. Chattaway's brow. "That's the third time I have been here this week, and cannot get to see him. Tell your father that I have had another letter from Butt, and will trouble him to attend to it. And further tell your father I will not be pestered with this business any longer. If he does not pay the money right off, I'll make him pay it."

Something not unlike an ice-bolt shot through George Ryle's heart. He knew there was trouble between his house and Mr. Chattaway; that his father was, in pecuniary matters, at Mr. Chattaway's mercy. Was this message the result of his recent encounter with Cris Chattaway? A hot flush dyed his face, and he wished—for his father's sake—that he had let Mr. Cris alone. For his father's sake he was now ready to eat humble-pie, though there never lived a boy less inclined to humble-pie in a general way than George Ryle. He went close up to the horse and raised his honest eyes fearlessly.

"Has Christopher been complaining to you, Mr. Chattaway?"

"No. What has he to complain of?"

"Not much," answered George, his fears subsiding. "Only I know he does carry tales."

"Were there no tales to carry he could not carry them," coldly remarked Mr. Chattaway. "I have not seen Christopher since dinner-time. It seems to me that you are always suspecting him of something. Take care you deliver my message correctly, sir."

Mr. Chattaway rode away, and George returned to his pumpkin pie. He had scarcely finished it—with remarkable relish, for the cold dinner he took with him to school daily was little more than a luncheon—when Mr. Ryle entered by the back-door, having been round to the stables with his horse. He was a tall, fine man, with light curling hair, mild blue eyes, and a fair countenance pleasant to look at in its honest simplicity. George delivered the message left by Mr. Chattaway.

"He left me that message, did he?" cried Mr. Ryle, who, if he could be angered by anything, it was on this very subject of Chattaway's claims against him. "He might have kept it until he saw me himself."

"He bade me tell you, papa."

"Yes; it is no matter to Chattaway how he browbeats me and exposes my affairs. He has been at it for years. Has he gone home?"

"I think so," replied George. "He rode that way."

"I'll stand it no longer, and I'll tell him so to his face," continued Mr. Ryle. "Let him do his best and his worst."

Taking up his hat, Mr. Ryle strode out of the house, disdaining Nora's invitation to tea, and leaving on the table a scarf of soft scarlet merino, which he had worn into Barmester. Recently suffering from sore throat, Mrs. Ryle had induced him to put it on when he rode out that afternoon.

"Look there!" cried Nora. "He has left his cravat on the table."

Snatching it up, she ran after Mr. Ryle, catching him half-way down the path. He took the scarf from her with a hasty movement, and went along swinging it in his hand. But he did not attempt to put it on.

"It is just like the master," grumbled Nora to George. "He has worn that warm woollen thing for hours, and now goes off without it! His throat will be bad again."

"I am afraid papa's gone to have it out with Mr. Chattaway," said George.

"And serve Chattaway right if he has," returned Nora. "It is what the master has threatened this many a day."

CHAPTER II
SUPERSTITION

Later, when George was working diligently at his lessons, and Nora was sewing—both by the help of the same candle: for an array of candles was not more indulged in than other luxuries in Mr. Ryle's house—footsteps were heard approaching the porch, and a modest knock came to the door.

"Come in," called out Nora.

A very thin woman, in a washed-out cotton gown, with a thin face and inflamed eyes, came in, curtseying. It was an honest face, a meek face; although it looked as if its owner had a meal about once a week.

"Evening, Miss Dickson; evening, Master George. I have stepped round to ask the missis whether I shall be wanted on Tuesday."

"The missis is out," said Nora. "She has been talking of putting off the wash till the week after, but I don't know that she will do so. If you sit down a bit, Ann Canham, she'll come in, perhaps."

Ann Canham seated herself respectfully on the edge of a remote chair. And Nora, who liked gossiping above every earthly thing, began to talk of Jim Sanders's illness.

"He has dreadful bouts, poor fellow!" observed Ann Canham.

"But six times out of seven he brings them on through his own fault," tartly returned Nora. "Many and many a time I have told him he'd do for himself, and now I think he has done it. This bout, it strikes me, is his last."

"Is he so ill as that?" exclaimed Ann Canham. And George looked up from his exercise-book in surprise.

"I don't know that he is," said Nora; "but—"

Nora broke suddenly off, dropped her work, and bent her head towards Ann Canham.

"We have had a strange thing happen here," she continued, her voice falling to a whisper; "and if it's not a warning of death, never believe me again. This morning—George, did you hear the dog in the night?"

"No," answered George.

"Boys sleep soundly," she remarked to Ann Canham. "You might drive a coach-and-six through their room, and not wake them. His room's at the back, too. Last night the dog got round to the front of the house, and there he was, all night long, sighing and moaning like a human creature. You couldn't call it a howl; there was too much pain in it. He was at it all night long; I couldn't sleep for it. The missis says she couldn't sleep for it. Well, this morning I was up first, the master next, Molly next; but the master went out by the back-way and saw nothing. By-and-by I spied something out of this window on the garden path, as if some one had been digging there; so out I went. It was for all the world like a grave!—a great hole, with the earth thrown up on either side of it. That dog had done it in the night!"

Ann Canham, possibly feeling uncomfortably aloof from the company when graves became the topic, drew her chair nearer the table. George sat, his pen arrested; his large wide-open eyes turned on Nora—not with fear, but merriment.

"A great hole, twice the length of our rolling-pin, and wide in proportion, all hollowed and scratched out," went on Nora. "I called the cow-boy, and asked him what it looked like. 'A grave,' said he, without a moment's hesitation. Molly came out, and they two filled it in again, and trod the path down. The marks have been plain enough all day. The master has been talking a long while of having that path gravelled, but it has not been done."

"And the hole was scratched by the dog?" proceeded Ann Canham, unable to get over the wonder.

"It was scratched by the dog," answered Nora. "And every one knows it's a sign that death's coming to the house, or to some one belonging to the house. Whether it's your own dog scratches it, or somebody else's dog, no matter; it's a sure sign that a real grave is about to be dug. It may not happen once in fifty years—no, not in a hundred; but when it does come, it's a warning not to be neglected."

"It's odd how the dogs can know!" remarked Ann Canham, meekly.

"Those dumb animals possess an instinct we can't understand," said Nora. "We have had that dog ever so many years, and he never did such a thing before. Rely upon it, it's Jim Sanders's warning. How you stare, George!"

"I may well stare, to hear you," was George's answer. "How can you put faith in such rubbish, Nora?"

"Just hark at him!" exclaimed Nora. "Boys are half heathens. I wouldn't laugh in that irreverent way, if I were you, George, because Jim Sanders's time has come."

"I am not laughing at that," said George; "I am laughing at you. Nora, your argument won't hold water. If the dog had meant to give notice that he was digging a hole for Jim Sanders, he would have dug it before his own door, not before ours."

"Go on!" cried Nora, sarcastically. "There's no profit arguing with unbelieving boys. They'd stand it to your face the sun never shone."

Ann Canham rose, and put her chair back in its place with much humility. Indeed, humility was her chief characteristic. "I'll come round in the morning, and know about the wash, if you please, ma'am," she said to Nora. "Father will be wanting his supper, and will wonder where I'm staying."

She departed. Nora gave George a lecture upon unbelief and irreverence in general, but George was too busy with his books to take much notice of it.

The evening went on. Mrs. Ryle and Trevlyn returned, the latter a diminutive boy, with dark curls and a handsome face.

"Jim Sanders is much better," remarked Mrs. Ryle. "He is all right again now, and will be at work in a day or two. It must have been a sort of fainting-fit he had this afternoon, and his wife got frightened. I told him to rest to-morrow, and come up the next day if he felt strong enough."

George turned to Nora, his eyes dancing. "What of the hole now?" he asked.

"Wait and see," snapped Nora. "And if you are impertinent, I'll never save you pie or pudding again."

Mrs. Ryle went into the sitting-room, but came back speedily when she found it dark and untenanted. "Where's the master?" she exclaimed. "Surely he has returned from Barmester!"

"Papa came home ages ago," said George. "He has gone up to the Hold."

"The Hold?" repeated Mrs. Ryle in surprise, for there was something like deadly feud between Trevlyn Hold and Trevlyn Farm.

George explained; telling of Mr. Chattaway's message, and the subsequent proceedings. Nora added that "as sure as fate, he was having it out with Chattaway." Nothing else would keep him at Trevlyn Hold.

But Mrs. Ryle knew that her easy-natured husband was not one to "have it out" with any one, even his enemy Chattaway. He might say a few words, but it was all he would say, and the interview would end almost as soon as begun. She took off her things, and Molly carried the supper-tray into the parlour.

But still there was no Mr. Ryle. Ten o'clock struck, and Mrs. Ryle grew, not exactly uneasy, but curious as to what could have become of him. What *could* be detaining him at the Hold?

"It wouldn't surprise me to hear that he has been taken too bad to come back," said Nora. "He unwound his scarlet cravat from his throat, and went away swinging it in his hand. John Pinder's waiting all this time in the kitchen."

"Have you finished your lessons, George?" asked Mrs. Ryle, perceiving that he was putting his books away.

"Every one," answered George.

"Then you shall go up to the Hold, and walk home with your father. I cannot think what is delaying his return."

"Perhaps he has gone somewhere else," said George.

"He would neither go anywhere else nor remain at Chattaway's," said Mrs. Ryle. "This is Tuesday evening."

A conclusive argument. Tuesday evening was invariably devoted by Mr. Ryle to his farm accounts, and he never suffered anything to interfere with that evening's work. George put on his cap and started on his errand.

It was a starlight night, cold and clear, and George went along whistling. A quarter of an hour's walk up the turnpike road brought him to Trevlyn Hold. The road rose gently the whole way, for the land was higher at Trevlyn Hold than at Trevlyn Farm. A white gate, by the side of a lodge, opened to the shrubbery or avenue—a dark walk wide enough for two carriages to pass, with the elm trees nearly meeting overhead. The shrubbery wound up to a lawn stretched before the windows of the house: a large, old-fashioned stone-built house, with gabled roofs, and a flight of steps leading to the entrance-hall. George ascended the steps and rang the bell.

"Is my father ready to come home?" he asked, not very ceremoniously, of the servant who answered it.

The man paused, as though he scarcely understood. "Mr. Ryle is not here, sir," was the answer.

"How long has he been gone?"

"He has not been here at all, sir, that I know of. I don't think he has."

"Just ask, will you?" said George. "He came here to see Mr. Chattaway. It was about five o'clock."

The man went away and returned. "Mr. Ryle has not been here at all, sir. I thought he had not."

George wondered. Could he be out somewhere with Chattaway? "Is Mr. Chattaway at home?" he inquired.

"Master is in bed," said the servant. "He came home to-day about five, or thereabouts, not feeling well, and he went to bed as soon as tea was over."

George turned away. Where could his father have gone to? Where to look for him? As he passed the lodge, Ann Canham was locking the gate, of which she and her father were the keepers. It was a whim of Mr. Chattaway's that the larger gate should be locked at night; but not until after ten. Foot-passengers could enter by the side-gate.

"Have you seen my father anywhere, since you left our house this evening?" he asked.

"No, I have not, Master George."

"I can't imagine where he can be. I thought he was at Chattaway's, but they say he has not been there."

"At Chattaway's! He wouldn't go there, would he, Master George?"

"He started to do so this afternoon. It's very odd! Good night, Ann."

"Master George," she interrupted, "do you happen to have heard how it's going with Jim Sanders?"

"He is much better," said George.

"Better!" slowly repeated Ann Canham. "Well, I hope he is," she added, in doubting tones. "But, Master George, I didn't like what Nora told us. I can't bear tokens from dumb animals, and I never knew them fail."

"Jim Sanders is all right, I tell you," said heathen George. "Mamma has been there, and he is coming to his work the day after to-morrow. Good night."

"Good night, sir," answered Ann Canham, as she retreated within the lodge. And George went through the gate, and stood in hesitation, looking up and down the road. But it was apparently of no use to search elsewhere in the uncertainty; and he turned towards home, wondering much.

What had become of Mr. Ryle?

CHAPTER III
IN THE UPPER MEADOW

The stars shone bright and clear as George Ryle walked down the slight descent of the turnpike-road, wondering what had become of his father. Any other night but this, he might not have wondered about it; but George could not remember the time when Tuesday evening had been devoted to anything but the farm accounts. John Pinder, who acted as a sort of bailiff, had been in the kitchen some hours with his weekly memoranda, to go through them as usual with his master; and George knew his father would not willingly keep the man waiting.

George went along whistling a tune; he was given to whistling. About half-way between Trevlyn Hold and his own house, the sound of another whistle struck upon his ear. A turn in the road brought a lad into view, wearing a smock-frock. It was the waggoner's boy at Trevlyn Hold. He ceased when he came up to George, and touched his hat in rustic fashion.

"Have you seen anything of my father, Bill?"

"Not since this afternoon, Master George," was the answer. "I see him, then, turning into that field of ours, next to where the bull be. Going up to the Hold, mayhap; else what should he do there?"

"What time was that?" asked George.

The boy considered a moment. "'Twas afore the sun set," he said at length, "I am sure o' that. He had some'at red in his hand, and the sun shone on it fit to dazzle one's eyes."

The boy went his way; George stood and thought. If his father had turned into the field indicated, there could be no doubt that he was hastening to Chattaway's. Crossing this field and the one next to it, both large, would bring one close to Trevlyn Hold, cutting off, perhaps, two minutes of the high-road, which wound round the fields. But the fields were scarcely ever favoured, on account of the bull. This bull had been a subject of much contention in the neighbourhood, and was popularly called "Chattaway's bull." It was a savage animal, and had once got out of the field and frightened several people almost to death. The neighbours said Mr. Chattaway ought to keep it under lock and key. Mr. Chattaway said he should keep it where he pleased: and he generally pleased to keep it in the field. This barred it to pedestrians; and Mr. Ryle must undoubtedly have been in hot haste to reach Trevlyn Hold to choose the route.

A hundred fears darted through George Ryle's mind. He was more thoughtful, it may be said more imaginative, than boys of his age generally are. George and Cris Chattaway had once had a run from the bull, and only saved themselves by desperate speed. Venturing into the field one day when the animal was apparently grazing quietly in a remote corner, they had not anticipated his running at them. George remembered this; he remembered the terror excited when the bull had broken loose. Had his father been attacked by the bull?—perhaps killed by it?

His heart beating, George retraced his steps, and turned into the first field. He hastened across it, glancing on all sides as keenly as the night allowed him. Not in this field would the danger be; and George reached the gate of the other, and stood looking into it.

Apparently it was quite empty. The bull was probably safe in its shed then, in Chattaway's farmyard. George could see nothing—nothing except the grass stretched out in the starlight. He threw his eyes in every direction, but could not perceive his father, or any trace of him. "What a simpleton I am," thought George, "to fear that such an out-of-the-way thing could have happened! He must—"

What was that? George held his breath. A sound, not unlike a groan, had smote upon his ear. And there it came again! "Holloa!" shouted George, and cleared the gate with a bound. "What's that? Who is it?"

A moan answered him; and George Ryle, guided by the sound, hastened to the spot. It was only a little way off, down by the hedge separating the fields. All the undefined fear George, not a minute ago, had felt inclined to treat as groundless, was indeed but a prevision of the terrible reality. Mr. Ryle lay in a narrow, dry ditch: and, but for that friendly ditch, he had probably been gored to death on the spot.

"Who is it?" he asked feebly, as his son bent over him, trying to distinguish what he could in the darkness. "George?"

"Oh, papa! what has happened?"

"Just my death, lad."

It was a sad tale. One that is often talked of in the place, in connection with Chattaway's bull. In crossing the second field—indeed, as soon as he entered it—Mr. Ryle was attacked by the furious beast, and tossed into the ditch, where he lay helpless. The people said then, and say still, that the red cravat he carried excited the anger of the bull.

George raised his voice in a shout for help, hoping it might reach the ears of the boy whom he had recently encountered. "Perhaps I can get you out, papa," he said, "though I may not be able myself to get you home."

"No, George; it will take stronger help than yours to get me out of this."

"I had better go up to the Hold, then. It is nearer than our house."

"You will not go to the Hold," said Mr. Ryle, authoritatively. "I will not be beholden to Chattaway. He has been the ruin of my peace, and now his bull has done for me."

George bent down closer. There was no room for him to get into the ditch, which was very narrow. "Papa, are you shivering with cold?"

"With cold and pain. The frost strikes keenly upon me, and my pain is great."

George instantly took off his jacket and waistcoat, and laid them gently on his father, his tears dropping silently in the dark night. "I'll run home for help," he said, speaking as bravely as he could. "John Pinder is there, and we can call up one or two of the men."

"Ay, do," said Mr. Ryle. "They must bring a shutter, and carry me home on it. Take care you don't frighten your mother, George. Tell her at first that I am a little hurt, and can't walk; break it to her so that she may not be alarmed."

George flew away. At the end of the second field, staring over the gate near the high-road, stood the boy Bill, whose ears George's shouts had reached. He was not a sharp-witted lad, and his eyes and mouth opened with astonishment to see George Ryle come flying along in his shirt-sleeves.

"What's a-gate?" asked he. "Be that bull loose again?"

"Run for your life to the second field," panted George, seizing him in his desperation. "In the ditch, a few yards along the hedge to the right, my father is lying. Go and stay by him, until I come back with help."

"Lying in the ditch!" repeated Bill, unable to collect his startled senses. "What's done it, Master George?"

"Chattaway's bull has done it. Hasten down to him, Bill. You might hear his groans all this way off, if you listened."

"Is the bull there?" asked Bill.

"I have seen no bull. The bull must have been in its shed hours ago. Stand by him, Bill, and I'll give you sixpence to-morrow."

They separated. George tore down the road, wondering how he should fulfil his father's injunction not to frighten Mrs. Ryle in telling the news. Molly, very probably looking after her sweetheart, was standing at the fold-yard gate as he passed. George sent her into the house the front way, and bade her whisper to Nora to come out; to tell her "somebody" wanted to speak to her. Molly obeyed; but executed her commission so bunglingly, that not only Nora, but Mrs. Ryle and Trevlyn came flocking to the porch. George could only go in then.

"Don't be frightened, mamma," he said, in answer to their questions. "My father has had a fall, and—and says he cannot walk home. Perhaps he has sprained his ankle."

"What has become of your jacket and waistcoat?" cried Nora, amazed to see George standing in his shirt-sleeves.

"They are safe enough. Is John Pinder still in the kitchen?" continued George, escaping from the room.

Trevlyn ran after him. "George, have you been fighting?" he asked. "Is your jacket torn to ribbons?"

George drew the boy into a dark angle of the passage. "Treve," he whispered, "if I tell you something about papa, you won't cry out?"

"No, I won't cry out," answered Treve.

"We must get a stretcher of some sort up to him, to bring him home. I am going to consult John Pinder."

"Where is papa?" interrupted Treve.

"Lying in a ditch in the large meadow. Chattaway's bull has attacked him. I am not sure but he will die."

The first thing Treve did *was* to cry out. George put his hand over his mouth. But Mrs. Ryle and Nora, who were full of curiosity, both as to George's jacketless state and George's news, had followed into the passage. Treve began to cry.

"He has dreadful news about papa, he says," sobbed Treve. "Thinks he's dead."

It was all over. George must tell now, and he could not help himself. "No, no, Treve, you should not exaggerate," he said, turning to Mrs. Ryle in his pain and earnestness. "There is an accident, mamma; but it is not so bad as that."

Mrs. Ryle retained perfect composure; very few people had seen *her* ruffled. It was not in her nature to be so, and her husband had little need to caution George as he had done. She laid her hand upon George's shoulder and looked calmly into his face. "Tell me the truth," she said in tones of quiet command. "What is the injury?"

"I do not know yet—"

"The truth, boy, I said," she sternly interposed.

"Indeed I do not yet know what it is. He has been attacked by Chattaway's bull."

It was Nora's turn now. "By Chattaway's bull?" she shrieked.

"Yes," said George. "It must have happened immediately after he left here at tea-time, and he has been lying ever since in the ditch in the upper meadow. I put my jacket and waistcoat over him; he was shivering with cold and pain."

While George was talking, Mrs. Ryle was acting. She sought John Pinder and issued her orders clearly and concisely. Men were got together; a mattress with holders was made ready; and the procession started under the convoy of George, who had been made to put on another jacket. Bill, the waggoner's boy, had been faithful, and was found by the side of Mr. Ryle.

"I'm glad you be come," was the boy's salutation. "He's been groaning and shivering awful. It set me shivering too."

As if to escape from the evil, Bill ran off, there and then, across the field, and never drew in until he reached Trevlyn Hold. In spite of his somewhat stolid propensities, he felt a sort of pride in being the first to impart the story there. Entering the house by the back, or farmyard door—for farming was carried on at Trevlyn Hold as well as at Trevlyn Farm—he passed through sundry passages to the well-lighted hall. There he seemed to hesitate at his temerity, but at length gave an awkward knock at the door of the general sitting-room.

A large, handsome room. Reclining in an easy-chair was a pretty and pleasing woman, looking considerably younger than she really was. Small features, a profusion of curling auburn hair, light blue eyes, a soft, yielding expression, and a gentle voice, were the adjuncts of a young woman, rather than of one approaching middle-age. A stranger, entering, might have taken her for a young unmarried woman; and yet she was mistress of Trevlyn Hold, the mother of that great girl of sixteen at the table, now playing backgammon and quarrelling with her brother Christopher. Mistress in name only. Although the wife of its master, Mr. Chattaway, and daughter of its late master, Squire Trevlyn; although universally called *Madam*

Chattaway—as from time immemorial it had been customary to designate the mistress of Trevlyn Hold—she was in fact no better than a nonentity in it, possessing little authority, and assuming less. She has been telling her children several times that their hour for bed has passed; she has begged them not to quarrel; she has suggested that if they will not go to bed, Maude should do so; but she may as well talk to the winds.

Miss Chattaway possesses a will of her own. She has the same insignificant features, pale leaden complexion, small, sly, keen light eyes that characterise her father. She would like to hold undisputed sway as the house's mistress; but the inclination has to be concealed; for the real mistress of Trevlyn Hold may not be displaced. She is sitting in the background, at a table apart, bending over her desk. A tall, majestic lady, in a stiff green silk dress and an imposing cap, in person very like Mrs. Ryle. It is Miss Trevlyn, usually called Miss Diana, the youngest daughter of the late Squire. You would take her to be at least ten years older than her sister, Mrs. Chattaway, but in point of fact she is that lady's junior by a year. Miss Trevlyn is, to all intents and purposes, mistress of Trevlyn Hold, and she rules its internal economy with a firm sway.

"Maude, you should go to bed," Mrs. Chattaway had said for the fourth or fifth time.

A graceful girl of thirteen turned her dark, violet-blue eyes and pretty light curls upon Mrs. Chattaway. She had been leaning on the table watching the backgammon. Something of the soft, sweet expression visible in Mrs. Chattaway's face might be traced in this child's; but in Maude it was blended with greater intellect.

"It is not my fault, Aunt Edith," she gently said. "I should like to go. I am tired."

"Be quiet, Maude!" broke from Miss Chattaway. "Mamma, I wish you wouldn't worry about bed! I don't choose Maude to go up until I go. She helps me to undress."

Poor Maude looked sleepy. "I can be going on, Octave," she said to Miss Chattaway.

"You can hold your tongue and wait, and not be ungrateful," was the response of Octavia Chattaway. "But for papa's kindness, you would not have a bed to go to. Cris, you are cheating! that was not sixes!"

It was at this juncture that the awkward knock came to the door. "Come in!" cried Mrs. Chattaway.

Either her gentle voice was not heard, for Cris and his sister were disputing just then, or the boy's modesty would not allow him to respond. He knocked again.

"See who it is, Cris," came forth the ringing voice of Miss Trevlyn.

Cris did not choose to obey. "Open the door, Maude," said he.

Maude did as she was bid: she had little chance allowed her in that house of doing otherwise. Opening the door, she saw the boy standing there. "What is it, Bill?" she asked in surprise.

"Please, is the Squire there, Miss Maude?"

"No," answered Maude. "He is not well, and has gone to bed."

This appeared to be a poser for Bill, and he stood considering. "Is Madam in there?" he presently asked.

"Who is it, Maude?" came again in Miss Trevlyn's commanding tones.

Maude turned her head. "It is Bill Webb, Aunt Diana."

"What does he want?"

Bill stepped in. "Please, Miss Diana, I came to tell the Squire the news. I thought he might be angry with me if I did not, seeing as I knowed of it."

"The news?" repeated Miss Diana, looking imperiously at Bill.

"The mischief the bull have done. He's gone and gored Farmer Ryle."

The words arrested the attention of all. They came forward, as with one impulse. Cris and his sister, in their haste, upset the backgammon-board.

"*What* do you say, Bill?" gasped Mrs. Chattaway, with white face and faltering voice.

"It's true, ma'am," said Bill. "The bull set on him this afternoon, and tossed him into the ditch. Master George found him there a short while agone, groaning awful."

There was a startled pause. "I—I—hope he is not much injured?" said Mrs. Chattaway at last, in her consternation.

"He says it's his death, ma'am. John Pinder and others have brought a bed, and be carrying of him home on it."

"What brought Mr. Ryle in that field?" asked Miss Diana.

"He telled me, ma'am, he was a-coming up here to see the Squire, and took that way to save time."

Mrs. Chattaway fell back a little. "Cris," said she to her son, "go down to the farm and see what the injury is. I cannot sleep in the uncertainty. It may be fatal."

Cris tossed his head. "You know, mother, I'd do almost anything to oblige you," he said, in his smooth accents, which had ever a false sound in them, "but I can't go to the farm. Mrs. Ryle might insult me: there's no love lost between us."

"If the accident happened this afternoon, why was it not discovered when the bull was brought to his shed to-night?" cried Miss Trevlyn.

Bill shook his head. "I dun know, ma'am. For one thing, Mr. Ryle was in the ditch, and couldn't be seen. And the bull, maybe, had gone to the top o' the field again, where the groaning wouldn't be heard."

"If I had only been listened to!" exclaimed Mrs. Chattaway, in wailing accents. "How many a time have I asked that the bull should be parted with, before he did some fatal injury. And now it has come!"

CHAPTER IV
LIFE OR DEATH?

Mr. Ryle was carried home on the mattress, and laid on the large table in the sitting-room, by the surgeon's directions. Mrs. Ryle, clear-headed and of calm judgment, had sent for medical advice even before sending for her husband. The only doctor available for immediate purposes was Mr. King, who lived about half-way between the farm and the village. He attended at once, and was at the house before his patient. Mrs. Ryle had sent also to Barmester for another surgeon, but he could not arrive just yet. It was by Mr. King's direction that the mattress was placed on the large table in the parlour.

"Better there; better there," acquiesced the sufferer, when he heard the order given. "I don't know how they'd get me up the stairs."

Mr. King, a man getting in years, was left alone with his patient. The examination over, he came forth from the room and sought Mrs. Ryle, who was waiting for the report.

"The internal injuries are extensive, I fear," he said. "They lie chiefly here"—touching his chest and right side.

"Will he *live*, Mr. King?" she interrupted. "Do not temporise, but let me know the truth. Will he live?"

"You have asked me a question I cannot yet answer," returned the surgeon. "My examination has been hasty and superficial: I was alone, and knew you were anxiously waiting. With the help of Mr. Benage, we may be able to arrive at some decisive opinion. I fear the injuries are serious."

Yes, they were serious; and nothing could be done, as it seemed, to remedy them or alleviate the pain. Mr. Ryle lay helpless on the bed, giving vent to his regret and anguish in somewhat homely phraseology. It was the phraseology of this simple farmhouse; that to which he had been accustomed; and he was not likely to change it now. Gentlemen by birth and pedigree, he and his father had been content to live as plain farmers only, in language as well as work.

He lay groaning, lamenting his imprudence, now that it was too late, in venturing within the reach of that dangerous animal. The rest waited anxiously and restlessly the appearance of the surgeon. For Mr. Benage of Barmester had a world-wide reputation, and such men seem to bring consolation with them. If any one could apply healing remedies and save his life, it was Mr. Benage.

George Ryle had taken up his station at the garden gate. His hands clasped, his head lying lightly upon them, he was listening for the sound of the gig which had been despatched to Barmester. Nora at length came out to him.

"You'll catch cold, George, out here in the keen night air."

"The air won't hurt me to-night. Listen, Nora! I thought I heard something. They might be back again by this."

He was right. The gig was bowling swiftly along, containing the well-known surgeon and messenger despatched for him. The surgeon, a little man, quick and active, was out of the gig before it had well stopped, passed George and Nora with a nod, and entered the house.

A short time, and the worst was known. There would be but a few more hours of life for Mr. Ryle.

Mr. King would remain, doing what he could to comfort, to soothe pain. Mr. Benage must return to Barmester, for he was wanted there. Refreshment was offered him, but he declined it. Nora waylaid him in the garden as he was going down.

"Will the master see to-morrow's sun, sir?"

"It's rising now; he may do so. He will not see its setting."

Can you picture to yourselves what that night was for the house and its inmates? In the parlour, gathered round the table on which lay the dying man supported by pillows and covered with blankets, were Mrs. Ryle, George and Trevlyn, the surgeon, and sometimes Nora. In the outer room was collected a larger group: John Pinder, the men who had borne him home, and Molly; with a few others whom the news of the accident had brought together.

Mrs. Ryle stood near her husband. George and Trevlyn seemed scarcely to know what to do with themselves; and Mr. King sat in a chair in the recess of the bay window. Mr. Ryle looked grievously wan, and the surgeon administered medicine from time to time.

"Come here, my boys," he suddenly said. "Come close to me."

They approached as he spoke, and leaned over him. He took a hand of each. George swallowed down his tears in the best way that he could. Trevlyn looked frightened.

"Children, I am going. It has pleased God to cut me off in the midst of my career, just when I had least thought of death. I don't know how it will be with you, my dear ones, or how it will be with the old home. Chattaway can sell up everything if he chooses; and I fear there's little hope but he will do it. If he would let your mother stay on, she might keep things together, and get clear of him in time. George will be growing into more of a man every day, and may soon learn to be useful in the farm, if his mother thinks well to trust him. Maude, you'll do your best for them? For him, as for the younger ones?"

"I will," said Mrs. Ryle.

"Ay, I know you will. I leave them all to you, and you will act for the best. I think it's well George should be upon the farm, as I am taken from it; but you and he will see to that. Treve, you must do the best you can in whatever station you may be called to. I don't know what it will be. My boys, there's nothing before you but work. Do you understand that?"

"Fully," was George's answer. Treve seemed too bewildered to give one.

"To work with all your might; your shoulders to the wheel. Do your best in all ways. Be honest and single-hearted in the sight of God; work for Him whilst you are working for yourselves, and then He will prosper you. I wish I had worked for Him more than I have done!"

A pause, broken only by George, who could no longer control his sobs.

"My days seem to have been made up of nothing but struggling, and quarrelling, and care. Struggling to keep my head above water, and quarrelling with Chattaway. The end seemed far-off, ages away, something as heaven seems. And now the end's come, and heaven's come—that is, I must set out upon the journey that leads to it. I fear the end comes to many as suddenly; cutting them off in their carelessness and their sins. Do not spend your days in quarrelling, my boys; be working on a bit for the end whilst time is given you. I don't know how it will be in the world I am about to enter. Some fancy that when once we have entered it, we shall see what is going on here, in our families and homes. For that thought, if for no other, I would ask you to try and keep right. If you were to go wrong, think how it would grieve me! I should always be thinking that I might have trained you better, and had not done so. Children! it is only when we come to lie here that we see all our shortcomings. You would not like to grieve me, George?"

"Oh, no! no!" said George, his sobs deepening. "Indeed I will try to do my best. I shall be always thinking that perhaps you are watching me."

"One greater than I is always watching you, George. And that is God. Act well in His sight; not in mine. Doctor, I must have some more of that stuff. I feel a strange sinking."

Mr. King rose, poured some drops into a wine-glass of water, and administered them. The patient lay a few moments, and then took his sons' hands, as before.

"And now, children, for my last charge to you. Reverence and love your mother. Obey her in all things. George, she is not your own mother, but you have never known another, and she has been as one to you. Listen to her always, and she will lead you aright. If I had listened to her, I shouldn't be lying where I am now. A week or two ago I wanted the character of that outdoor man from Chattaway. 'Don't go through that field,' she said before I started. 'Better keep where the bull can't touch you.' Do you remember, Maude?"

Mrs. Ryle simply bowed her head in reply. She was feeling the scene deeply, but emotion she would not show.

"I heeded what your mother said, and went up to Chattaway's, avoiding the fields," resumed Mr. Ryle. "This last afternoon, when I was going up again and had got to the field gate, I turned into it, for it cut off a few steps, and my temper was up. I thought of what your mother would say, as I swung in, but it didn't stop me. It must have been that red neckerchief that put him up, for I was no sooner over the gate than he bellowed savagely and butted at me. It was all over in a minute; I was in the ditch, and he went on, bellowing and tossing and tearing at the cloth. If you go there to-morrow, you'll see it in shreds about the field. Children, obey your mother; there'll be still greater necessity for it when I am gone."

The boys had been obedient hitherto. At least, George had been: Trevlyn was too indulged to be perfectly so. George promised that he would be so still.

"I wish I could have seen the little wench," resumed the dying man, the tears gathering on his eyelashes. "But it may be for the best that she's away, for I should hardly have borne parting with her. Maude! George! Treve! I leave her to you all. Do the best you can by her. I don't know that she'll be spared to grow up, for she's a delicate little mite: but that is as God pleases. I wish I could have stayed with you all a bit longer—if it's not sinful to wish contrary to God's will. Is Mr. King there?"

Mr. King had resumed his seat in the bay window, and was partially hidden by the curtain. He came forward. "Is there anything I can do for you, Mr. Ryle?"

"You would oblige me by writing out a few directions. I should like to write them myself, but it is impossible; you'll enter the sentences just as I speak them. I have not made my will. I put it off, and put it off, thinking I could do it at any time; but now the end's come, and it is not done. Death surprises a great many, I fear, as he has surprised me. It seems that if I could only have one day more of health, I would do many things I have left undone. You shall write down my wishes, doctor. It will do as well; for there's only themselves, and they won't dispute one with the other. Let a little table be brought, and pen, ink, and paper."

He lay quiet whilst these directions were obeyed, and then began again.

"I am in very little pain, considering that I am going; not half as much as when I lay in that ditch. Thank God for it! It might have been that I could not have left a written line, or said a word of farewell to you. There's sure to be a bit of blue sky in the darkest trouble; and the more implicitly we trust, the more blue sky we shall find. I have not been what I ought to be, especially in the matter of disputing with Chattaway—not but that Chattaway's hardness has been in fault. But God is taking me from a world of care, and I trust He will forgive all my shortcomings for our Saviour's sake. Is everything ready?"

"All is ready," said Mr. King.

"Then leave me alone with the doctor a short time, dear ones," he resumed. "We shall not keep you out long."

Nora, who had brought in the things required, held the door open for them to pass through. The pinched look that the face, lying there, was assuming, struck upon her ominously.

"After all, the boy was right," she murmured. "The scratched hole was not meant for Jim Sanders."

CHAPTER V
MAUDE TREVLYN

The sun rose gloriously, dispersing the early October frost, and brightening the world. But the sunbeams fall upon dark scenes sometimes; perhaps more often than upon happy ones.

George Ryle was leaning on the fold-yard gate. He had strolled out without his hat, and his head was bent in grief. Not that he was shedding tears now. He had shed plenty during the night; but tears cannot flow for ever, even from an aching heart.

Hasty steps were heard approaching down the road, and George raised his head. They were Mr. Chattaway's. He stopped suddenly at sight of George.

"What is this about your father? What has happened? Is he dead?"

"He is dying," replied George. "The doctors are with him. Mr. King has been here all night, and Mr. Benage has just come again from Barmester. They have sent us out of the room; me and Treve. They let my mother remain with him."

"But how on earth did it happen?" asked Chattaway. "I cannot make it out. The first thing I heard when I woke this morning was that Mr. Ryle had been gored to death by the bull. What brought him near the bull?"

"He was passing through the field up to your house, and the bull attacked him—"

"But when? when?" hastily interrupted Mr. Chattaway.

"Yesterday afternoon. My father came in directly after you rode away, and I gave him your message. He said he would go up to the Hold at once, and speak to you; and took the field way instead of the road."

"Now, how could he take it? He knew it was hardly safe for strangers. Not but that the bull ought to have known him."

"He had a red cravat in his hand, and he thinks that excited the bull. It tossed him into the ditch, and he lay there, undiscovered, until past ten at night."

"And he is badly hurt?"

"He is dying," replied George, "dying now. I think that is why they sent us from the room."

Mr. Chattaway paused in dismay. Though a hard, selfish man, who had taken delight in quarrelling with Mr. Ryle and putting upon him, he did possess some feelings of humanity as well as his neighbours; and the terrible nature of the case naturally called them forth. George strove manfully to keep down his tears; relating the circumstances was almost too much for him, but he did not care to give way before the world, especially before that unit in it represented by Mr. Chattaway. Mr. Chattaway rested his elbow on the gate, and looked down at George.

"This is very shocking, lad. I am sorry to hear it. What will the farm do without him? How shall you all get on?"

"Thinking of that has been troubling him all night," said George. "He said we might get a living at the farm, if you would let us do it. If you would not be hard," he added, determined to speak out.

"Hard, he called me, did he?" said Mr. Chattaway. "It's not my hardness that has been in fault, but his pride. He has been as saucy and independent as if he did not owe me a shilling; always making himself out my equal."

"He is your equal," said George, speaking gently in his sadness.

"My equal! Working Tom Ryle the equal of the Chattaways! A man who rents two or three hundred acres and does half the work himself, the equal of the landlord who owns them and ever so many more to them!—equal to the Squire of Trevlyn Hold! Where did you pick up those notions, boy?"

George had a great mind to say that in strict justice Mr. Chattaway had no more right to be Squire of Trevlyn Hold, or to own those acres, than his father had; not quite so much right, if it came to that. He had a great mind to say that the Ryles were gentlemen, and once owners of what his father now rented. But George remembered they were in Chattaway's power; he could sell them up, and turn them from the farm, if he pleased; and he held his tongue.

"Not that I blame you for the notions," Mr. Chattaway resumed, in the same thin, unpleasant tones—never was there a voice more thin and wiry than his. "It's natural you should have got them from Ryle, for they were his. He was always—But there! I won't say any more, with him lying there, poor fellow. We'll let it drop, George."

"I do not know how things are between you and my father," said George, "except that there's money owing to you. But if you will not press us, if you will let my mother remain on the farm, I—"

"That's enough," interrupted Mr. Chattaway. "Never trouble your head about business that's above you. Anything between me and your father, or your mother either, is no concern of yours; you are not old enough to interfere yet. I should like to see him. Do you think I may go in?"

"We can ask," answered George; some vague and indistinct idea floating to his mind that a death-bed reconciliation might help to smooth future difficulties.

He led the way through the fold-yard. Nora was coming out at the back-door as they advanced.

"Nora, do you think Mr. Chattaway may go in to see my father?" asked George.

"If it will do Mr. Chattaway any good," responded Nora, who ever regarded that gentleman in the light of a common enemy, and could with difficulty bring herself to be commonly civil to him. "It's all over; but Mr. Chattaway can see what's left of him."

"Is he dead?" whispered Mr. Chattaway; whilst George lifted his white and startled face.

"He is dead!" broke forth Nora; "and perhaps there may be some that will wish now they had been less hard with him in life. The doctors and Mrs. Ryle have just come out, and the women have gone in to put him straight and comfortable. Mr. Chattaway can go in also, if he would like it."

Mr. Chattaway, it appeared, did not like it. He turned from the door, drawing George with him.

"George, tell your mother I am grieved at her trouble, and wish that beast of a bull had been stuck before he had done this. Tell her if there's any little thing she could fancy from the Hold, to let Edith know, and she'll gladly send it to her. Good-bye, lad. You and Treve must keep up, you know."

He passed out by the fold-yard gate, as he had entered, and George leaned upon it again, with his aching heart; an orphan now. Treve and Caroline had their mother left, but he had no one. It is true he had never known a mother, and Mrs. Ryle, his father's second wife, had supplied the place of one. She had done her duty by him; but it had not been in love; nor very much in gentleness. Of her own children she was inordinately fond; she had not been so of George—which perhaps was in accordance with human nature. It had never troubled George much; but the fact now struck upon him with a sense of intense loneliness. His father had loved him deeply and sincerely: but—he was gone.

In spite of his heavy sorrow, George was awake to sounds in the distance, the everyday labour of life. The cow-boy was calling to his cows; one of the men, acting for Jim Sanders, was going out with the team. And now there came a butcher, riding up from Barmester, and George knew he had come about some beasts, all unconscious that the master was no longer here to command, or deal with. Work, especially farm work, must go on, although death may have accomplished its mission.

The butcher, riding fast, had nearly reached the gate, and George was turning away to retire indoors, when the unhappy thought came upon him—Who is to see this man? His father no longer there, who must represent him?—must answer comers—must stand in his place? It brought the fact of what had happened more practically before George Ryle's mind than anything else had done. He stood where he was, instead of turning away. That day he must rise superior to grief, and be useful; must rise above his years in the future, for his step-mother's sake.

"Good morning, Mr. George," cried the butcher, as he rode up. "Is the master about?"

"No," answered George, speaking as steadily as he could. "He will never be about again. He is dead."

The butcher thought it a boy's joke. "None of that, young gentleman!" said he, with a laugh. "Where shall I find him?"

"Mr. Cope," said George, raising his grave face—and its expression struck a chill to the man's heart—"I should not joke upon the subject of death. My father was attacked by Chattaway's bull yesterday evening, and has died of the injuries."

"Lawk-a-mercy!" uttered the startled man. "Attacked by Chattaway's bull! and—and—died of the injuries! Surely it can't be so!"

George had turned his face away; the strain was getting too much for him.

"Has Chattaway killed the bull?" was the man's next question.

"I suppose not."

"Then he is no man and no gentleman if he don't do it. If a beast of mine injured a neighbour, I'd stay him from injuring another, no matter what its value. Dear me! Mr. George, I'd rather have heard any news than this."

George's head was quite turned away now. The butcher roused himself to think of business. His time was short, for he had to be in the town again before his shop opened for the day.

"I came up about the beasts," he said. "The master as good as sold 'em to me yesterday; it was only a matter of a few shillings split us. But I'll give in sooner than not have 'em. Who is going to carry on the dealings in Mr. Ryle's place? Who can I speak to?"

"You can see John Pinder," answered George. "He knows most about things."

The man guided his horse through the fold-yard, scattering the cocks and hens, and reached the barn. John Pinder came out to him; and George escaped indoors.

It was a sad day. The excitement over, the doctors departed, the gossipers and neighbours dispersed, the village carpenter having come and taken certain measures, the house was left to its monotonous quiet; that distressing quiet which tells upon the spirits. Nora's voice was subdued, Molly went about on tiptoe. The boys wished it was over; that, and many more days to come. Treve fairly broke bounds about twelve, said he could not bear it, and went out amongst the men. In the afternoon George was summoned upstairs to the chamber of Mrs. Ryle, where she had remained since the morning.

"George, you must go to Barmester," she said. "I wish to know how Caroline bears the news, poor child! Mr. Benage said he would call and break it to her; but I cannot get her grief out of my head. You can go over in the gig; but don't stay. Be home by tea-time."

It is more than probable that George felt the commission as a relief, and he started as soon as the gig was ready. As he went out of the yard, Nora called after him to be careful how he drove. Not that he had never driven before; but Mr. Ryle, or some one else, had always been in the gig with him. Now he was alone; and it brought his loss again more forcibly before him.

He reached Barmester, and saw his sister Caroline, who was staying there on a visit. She was not overwhelmed with grief, but, on the contrary, appeared to have taken the matter coolly and lightly. The fact was, the little girl had no definite ideas on the subject of death. She had never been brought into contact with it, and could not at all realise the fact told her, that she would never see papa again. Better for the little heart perhaps that it was so; sorrow enough comes with later years; and Mrs. Ryle judged wisely in deciding to keep the child where she was until after the funeral.

When George reached home, he found Nora at tea alone. Master Treve had chosen to take his with his mother in her chamber. George sat down with Nora. The shutters were closed, and the room was bright with fire and candle; but to George all things were dreary.

"Why don't you eat?" asked Nora, presently, perceiving the bread-and-butter remained untouched.

"I'm not hungry," replied George.

"Did you have tea in Barmester?"

"I did not have anything," he said.

"Now, look you here, George. If you are going to give way to—Mercy on us! What's that?"

Some one had entered hastily. A lovely girl in a flowing white evening dress and blue ribbons in her hair. A heavy shawl fell from her shoulders to the ground, and she stood panting, as one who has run quickly, her fair curls falling, her cheeks crimson, her dark blue eyes glowing. On the pretty arms were coral bracelets, and a thin gold chain was on her neck. It was Maude Trevlyn, whom you saw at Trevlyn Hold last night. So out of place did she look in that scene, that Nora for once was silent, and could only stare.

"I ran away, Nora," said Maude, coming forward. "Octave has a party, but they won't miss me if I stay only a little time. I have wanted to come all day, but they would not let me."

"Who would not?" asked Nora.

"Not any of them. Even Aunt Edith. Nora, is it *true*? Is it true that he is dead?" she reiterated, her pretty hands clasped with emotion, her great blue eyes cast upwards at Nora, waiting for the answer.

"Oh, Miss Maude! you might have heard it was true enough up at the Hold. And so they have a party! Some folk in Madam Chattaway's place might have had the grace to put it off, when their sister's husband was lying dead!"

"It is not Aunt Edith's fault. You know it is not, Nora. George, you know it also. She has cried very much to-day; and she asked long and long ago for the bull to be sent off. But he was not sent. Oh, George, I am so sorry! I wish I could have seen him before he died. There was no one I liked so well as Mr. Ryle."

"Will you have some tea?" asked Nora.

"No, I must not stay. Should Octave miss me she will tell of me, and then I should be punished. What do you think? Rupert displeased Cris in some way, and Miss Diana sent him to bed away from all the pleasure. It is a shame!"

"It is all a shame together, up at Trevlyn Hold—all that concerns Rupert," said Nora, not, perhaps, very judiciously.

"Nora, where did he die?" asked Maude, in a whisper. "Did they take him up to his bedroom when they brought him home?"

"They carried him in there," said Nora, pointing to the sitting room door. "He is lying there now."

"I want to see him," she continued.

Nora received the intimation dubiously.

"I don't know whether you had better," said she, after a pause.

"Yes, I must, Nora. What was that about the dog scratching a grave before the porch?"

"Who told you anything about that?" asked Nora, sharply.

"Ann Canham came up to the Hold and spoke about it. Was it so, Nora?"

Nora nodded. "A hole, Miss Maude, nearly big enough to lay the master in. Not that I thought it a token for *him*! I thought only of Jim Sanders. And some folk laugh at these warnings!" she added. "There sits one," pointing to George.

"Well, never mind it now," said George, hastily. Never was a boy less given to superstition; but, with his father lying where he was, he somehow did not care to hear much about the mysterious hole.

Maude moved towards the door. "Take me in to see him," she pleaded.

"Will you promise not to be frightened?" asked Nora. "Some young people can't bear the sight of death."

"What should I fear?" returned Maude. "He cannot hurt me."

Nora rose in acquiescence, and took up the candle. But George laid his hand on the girl.

"Don't go, Maude. Nora, you must not let her go in. She might regret it. It would not be right."

Now, of all things, Nora disliked being dictated to, especially by those she called children. She saw no reason why Maude should not look upon the dead if she wished to do so, and gave a sharp word of reprimand to George, in an undertone. How could they speak aloud, entering that presence?

"Maude, Maude!" he whispered. "I would advise you not to go in."

"Let me go!" she pleaded. "I should like to see him once again. I did not see him for a whole week before he died. The last time I ever saw him was one day in the copse, and he got down some hazel-nuts for me. I never thanked him," she added, tears in her eyes. "In a hurry to get home, I never stayed to thank him. I shall always be sorry for it. George, I must see him."

Nora was already in the room with the candle. Maude advanced on tiptoe, her heart beating with awe. She halted at the foot of the table and looked eagerly upwards.

Maude Trevlyn had never seen the dead, and her heart gave a bound of terror, and she fell back with a cry. Before Nora knew well what had occurred, George had her in the other room, his arms wound about her with a sense of protection. Nora came out and closed the door, vexed with herself for having allowed her to enter.

"You should have told me you had never seen any one dead before, Miss Maude," cried she, testily. "How was I to know? And you ought to have come right up to the top before looking."

Maude was clinging tremblingly to George, sobbing hysterically. "Don't be angry with me," she whispered. "I did not think he would look like that."

"Oh, Maude, I am not angry; I am only sorry," he said soothingly. "There's nothing really to be frightened at. Papa loved you very much; almost as much as he loved me."

"Shall I take you back, Maude?" said George, when she was ready to go.

"Yes, please," she eagerly answered. "I should not dare to go alone now. I should be fancying I saw—it—looking out at me from the hedges."

Nora folded her shawl well over her again, and George drew her closer to him that she might feel his presence as well as see it. Nora watched them down the path, right over the hole the restless dog had favoured the house with a night or two ago.

They went up the road. An involuntary shudder shook George's frame as he passed the turning which led to the fatal field. He seemed to see his father in the unequal conflict. Maude felt the movement.

"It is never going to be out again," she whispered.

"What?" he asked, his thoughts buried deeply just then.

"The bull. I heard Aunt Diana talking to Mr. Chattaway. She said it must not be set at liberty again, or we might have the law down upon Trevlyn Hold."

"Yes; that's all Miss Trevlyn and he care for—the law," returned George, in tones of pain. "What do they care for the death of my father?"

"George, he is better off," said she, in a dreamy manner, her face turned towards the stars. "I am very sorry; I have cried a great deal over it; and I wish it had never happened; I wish he was back with us; but still he is better off; Aunt Edith says so. You don't know how she has felt it."

"Yes," answered George, his heart very full.

"Mamma and papa are better off," continued Maude. "Your own mother is better off. The next world is a happier one than this."

George made no rejoinder. Favourite though Maude was with George Ryle, those were heavy moments for him. They proceeded in silence until they turned in at the great gate by the lodge: a round building, containing two rooms upstairs and two down. Its walls were not very substantial, and the sound of voices could be heard within. Maude stopped in consternation.

"George, that is Rupert talking!"

"Rupert! You told me he was in bed."

"He was sent to bed. He must have got out of the window again. I am sure it is his voice. Oh, what will be done if it is found out?"

George Ryle swung himself on to the very narrow ledge under the window, contriving to hold on by his hands and toes, and thus obtained a view of the room.

"Yes, it is Rupert," said he, as he jumped down. "He is sitting talking to old Canham."

But the slightness of structure which allowed voices to be heard within the lodge also allowed them to be heard without. Ann Canham came hastening to the door, opened it a few inches, and stood peeping. Maude took the opportunity to slip past her into the room.

But no trace of her brother was there. Mark Canham was sitting in his usual invalid seat by the fire, smoking a pipe, his back towards the door.

"Where has he gone?" cried Maude.

"Where's who gone?" roughly spoke old Canham, without turning his head. "There ain't nobody here."

"Father, it's Miss Maude," interposed Ann Canham, closing the outer door, after allowing George to enter. "Who be you taking the young lady for?"

The old man, partly disabled by rheumatism, put down his pipe, and contrived to turn in his chair. "Eh, Miss Maude! Why, who'd ever have thought of seeing you to-night?"

"Where is Rupert?" asked Maude.

"Rupert?" composedly returned old Canham. "Is it Master Rupert you're asking after? How should we know where he is, Miss Maude?"

"We saw him here," interposed George Ryle. "He was sitting on that bench, talking to you. We both heard his voice, and I saw him."

"Very odd!" said the old man. "Fancy goes a great way. Folks is ofttimes deluded by it."

"Mark Canham, I tell you—"

"Wait a minute!" interrupted Maude. She opened the door leading into the inner room, and stood looking into its darkness. "Rupert!" she called; "it is only George and I. You need not hide."

It brought forth Rupert; that lovely boy, with his large blue eyes and auburn curls. There was a great likeness between him and Maude; but Maude's hair was lighter.

"I thought it was Cris," he said. "He is learning to be as sly as a fox: though I don't know that he was ever anything else. When I am ordered to bed before my time, he has taken to dodging into the room every ten minutes to see that I am safe in it. Have they missed me, Maude?"

"I don't know," she answered. "I also came away without their knowing it. I have been down to Aunt Ryle's, and George has brought me home again."

"Will you be pleased, to sit down, Miss, Maude?" asked Ann Canham, dusting a chair.

"Eh, but that's a pretty picture!" cried old Canham, gazing at Maude, who had slipped off her heavy shawl, and stood warming her hands at the fire.

Mark Canham was right. A very pretty picture. He extended the hand that was not helpless towards her.

"Miss Maude, I mind me seeing your mother looking just as you look now. The Squire was out, and the young ladies at the Hold thought they'd give a dance, and Parson Dean and Miss Emily were invited to it. I don't know that they'd have been asked if the Squire had been at home, matters not being smooth between him and parson. She was older than you be; but she was dressed just as you be now; and I could fancy, as I look at you, that it was her over again. I was in the rooms, helping to wait. It doesn't seem so long ago! Miss Emily was the sweetest-looking of 'em all present; and the young heir seemed to think so. He opened the ball with Miss Emily in spite of his sisters; they wanted him to choose somebody grander. Ah, me! and both of 'em lying low so soon after, leaving you two behind 'em!"

"Mark!" cried Rupert, throwing his eyes on the old man—eyes sparkling with excitement—"if they had lived, papa and mamma, I should not have been sent to bed to-night because there's another party at Trevlyn Hold."

Mark's only answer was to put up his hands with an indignant gesture. Ann Canham was still offering the chair to Maude. Maude declined it.

"I cannot stay, Ann. They will miss me if I don't return. Rupert, you will come?"

"To be boxed up in my bedroom, whilst the rest of you are enjoying yourselves," cried Rupert. "They would like to take the spirit out of me; have been trying at it a long time."

Maude wound her arm within his. "Do come, Rupert!" she whispered coaxingly. "Think of the disturbance if Cris should find you here and tell!"

"And tell!" repeated Rupert, mockingly. "*Not* to tell would be impossible to Cris Chattaway. It's what he'd delight in more than in gold. I wouldn't be the sneak Cris Chattaway is for the world."

But Rupert appeared to think it well to depart with his sister. As they were going out, old Canham spoke to George.

"And Mrs. Ryle, sir—how does she bear it?"

"She bears it very well, Mark," answered George, as the tears rushed to his eyes unbidden. The old man marked them.

"There's one comfort for ye, Master George," he said, in low tones: "that he has took all his neighbours' sorrow with him. And as much couldn't be said if every gentleman round about here was cut off by death."

The significant tone was not needed to tell George that he alluded to Mr. Chattaway. The master of Trevlyn Hold was, in fact, no greater favourite with old Canham than he was with George Ryle.

"Mind how you get in, Master Rupert, so they don't fall upon you," whispered Ann Canham, as she held open the lodge door.

"I'll mind," was the boy's answer. "Not that I should care much if they did," he added. "I am getting tired of it."

She stood and watched them up the dark walk until a turn in the road hid them from view, and then closed the door. "If they don't take to treat him kinder, I misdoubt me but he'll do something desperate, as the dead-and-gone heir, Rupert, did," she remarked, sitting down near her father.

"Like enough," was the old man's reply, taking up his pipe again. "He has the true Trevlyn temper, have young Rupert."

"Maude," began Rupert, as they wound their way up the dark avenue, "don't they know you came out?"

"They would not have let me come if they had known it," replied Maude. "I have been wanting to go down all day, but Aunt Diana and Octave kept me in. I begged to go down last night when Bill Webb brought the news; and they were angry with me."

"Do you know what I should have done in Chattaway's place, George?" cried the boy, impulsively. "I should have loaded my gun the minute I heard of it, and shot the beast between the eyes. Chattaway would, if he were half a man."

"It is of no use talking of it, Rupert," answered George, in sadly subdued tones. "That would not mend the evil."

"Only fancy their having this rout to-night, while Mr. Ryle is lying dead!" indignantly resumed Rupert. "Aunt Edith ought to have interfered for once, and stopped it."

"Aunt Edith did interfere," spoke up Maude. "She said it must be put off. But Octave would not hear of it, and Miss Diana said Mr. Ryle was no real rela—"

Maude dropped her voice. They were now in view of the house and its lighted windows; and some one, probably hearing their footsteps, came bearing down upon them with a fleet step. It was Cris Chattaway. Rupert stole into the trees, and disappeared: Maude, holding George's arm, bore bravely on, and met him.

"Where have you been, Maude? The house has been searched for you. What brings *you* here?" he roughly added to George.

"I came because I chose to come," was George's answer.

"None of your insolence," returned Cris. "We don't want you here to-night. Just be off from this."

Was Cris Chattaway's motive a good one, under his rudeness? Did he feel ashamed of the gaiety going on, whilst Mr. Ryle, his uncle by marriage, was lying dead, under circumstances so unhappy? Was he anxious to conceal the unseemly proceeding from George? Perhaps so.

"I shall go back when I have taken Maude to the hall-door," said George. "Not before."

Anything that might have been said further by Cris, was interrupted by the appearance of Miss Trevlyn. She was standing on the steps.

"Where have you been, Maude?"

"To Trevlyn Farm," was Maude's truthful answer. "You would not let me go during the day, so I have been now. It seemed to me that I must see him before he was put underground."

"See *him*!" cried Miss Trevlyn.

"Yes. It was all I went for. I did not see my aunt. George, thank you for bringing me home," she continued, stepping in. "Good-night. I would have given all I possess for it never to have happened."

She burst into a flood of tears as she spoke—the result, no doubt, of her previous fright and excitement, as well as her sorrow for Mr. Ryle's unhappy fate. George wrung her hand, and lifted his hat to Miss Trevlyn as he turned away.

But ere he had well plunged into the dark avenue, there came swift and stealthy steps behind him. A soft hand was laid upon him, and a soft voice spoke, broken by tears:

"Oh, George, I am so sorry! I have felt all day as if it would almost be my death. I think I could have given my own life to save his."

"I know, I know! I know how *you* will feel it," replied George, utterly unmanned by the true and unexpected sympathy.

It was Mrs. Chattaway.

CHAPTER VI
THE ROMANCE OF TREVLYN HOLD

It is impossible to go on without a word of retrospect. The Ryles, gentlemen by a long line of ancestry, had once been rich men, but they were open-handed and heedless, and in the time of George's grandfather, the farm (not called the farm then) passed into the possession of the Trevlyns of the Hold, who had a mortgage on it. They named it Trevlyn Farm, and Mr. Ryle and his son remained on as tenants where they had once been owners.

After old Mr. Ryle's death, his son married the daughter of the curate of Barbrook, the Reverend George Berkeley, familiarly known as Parson Berkeley. In point of fact, the parish knew no other pastor, for its Rector was an absentee. Mary Berkeley was an only child. She had been petted, and physicked, and nursed, after the manner of only children, and grew up sickly as a matter of course. A delicate, beautiful girl in appearance, but not strong. People (who are always fond, you know, of settling everybody else's business for them) deemed that she made a poor match in marrying Thomas Ryle. It was whispered, however, that he himself might have made a greater match, had he chosen—no other than Squire Trevlyn's eldest daughter. There was not so handsome, so attractive a man in all the country round as Thomas Ryle.

Soon after the marriage, Parson Berkeley died—to the intense grief of his daughter, Mrs. Ryle. He was succeeded in the curacy and parsonage by a young clergyman just in priest's orders, the Reverend Shafto Dean. A well-meaning man, but opinionated and self-sufficient in the highest degree, and before he had been one month at the parsonage, he and Squire Trevlyn were at issue. Mr. Dean wished to introduce certain new fashions and customs into the church and parish; Squire Trevlyn held to the old. Proud, haughty, overbearing, but honourable and generous, Squire Trevlyn had known no master, no opposer; *he* was lord of the neighbourhood, and was bowed down to accordingly. Mr. Dean would not give way, the Squire would not give way; and the little seed of dissension grew and spread. Obstinacy begets obstinacy. That which a slight yielding on either side, a little mutual good-feeling, might have removed at first, became at length a terrible breach, the talk of a county.

Meanwhile Thomas Ryle's fair young wife died, leaving an infant boy—George. In spite of her husband's loving care, in spite of having been shielded from all work and management, so necessary on a farm, she died. Nora Dickson, a humble relative of the Ryle family, who had been partially brought up on the farm, was housekeeper and manager. She saved all trouble to young Mrs. Ryle: but she could not save her life.

The past history of Trevlyn Hold was a romance in itself. Squire Trevlyn had five children: Rupert, Maude, Joseph, Edith and Diana. Rupert, Maude and Diana were imperious as their father; Joseph and Edith were mild, yielding, and gentle, as had been their mother. Rupert was of course regarded as the heir: but the property was not entailed. An ancestor of Squire Trevlyn's coming from some distant part—it was said Cornwall—bought it and settled down upon it. There was not a great deal of grass land on the estate, but the coal-mines in the distance made it very valuable. Of all his children, Rupert, the eldest, was the Squire's favourite: but poor Rupert did not live to come into the estate. He had inherited the fits of passion characteristic of the Trevlyns; was of a thoughtless, impetuous nature; and he fell into trouble and ran away from his country. He embarked for a distant port, which he did not live to reach. And Joseph became the heir.

Very different, he, from his brother Rupert. Gentle and yielding, like his sister Edith, the Squire half despised him. The Squire would have preferred him passionate, haughty, and overbearing—a true Trevlyn. But the Squire had no intention of superseding him in the succession of Trevlyn Hold. Provided Joseph lived, none other would be its inheritor. *Provided*. Joseph—always called Joe—appeared to have inherited his mother's constitution; and she had died early, of decline.

Yielding, however, as Joe Trevlyn was naturally, on one point he did not prove himself so—that of his marriage. He chose Emily Dean; the pretty and lovable sister of Squire Trevlyn's *bête noire*, the obstinate parson. "I would rather you took a wife out of the parish workhouse, Joe," the Squire said, in his anger. Joe said little in reply, but he held to his choice; and one fine morning the marriage was celebrated by the obstinate parson himself in the church at Barbrook.

The Squire and Thomas Ryle were close friends, and the former was fond of passing his evenings at the farm. The farm was not a productive one. The land, never of the richest, had become poorer and poorer: it wanted draining and nursing; it wanted, in short, money laid out upon it; and that money Mr. Ryle did not possess. "I shall have to leave it, and try and take a farm in better condition," he said at length to the Squire.

The Squire, with all his faults and his overbearing temper, was generous and considerate. He knew what the land wanted; money spent on it; he knew Mr. Ryle had not the money to spend, and he offered to lend it him. Mr. Ryle accepted it, to the amount of two thousand pounds. He gave a bond for the sum, and the Squire on his part promised to renew the lease upon the present terms, when the time of renewal came, and not raise the rent. This promise was not given in writing: but none ever doubted the word of Squire Trevlyn.

The first of Squire Trevlyn's children to marry had been Edith: some years before she had married Mr. Chattaway. The two next to marry had been Maude and Joseph. Joseph, as you have heard, married Emily Dean; Maude, the eldest daughter, became the second wife of Mr. Ryle. A twelvemonth after the death of his fair young wife Mary, Miss Trevlyn of the Hold stepped into her shoes, and became the step-mother of the little child, George. The youngest daughter Diana, never married.

Miss Trevlyn, in marrying Thomas Ryle, gave mortal offence to some of her kindred. The Squire himself would have forgiven it; nay, perhaps have grown to like it—for he never could do otherwise than like Thomas Ryle—but he was constantly incited against it by his family. Mr. Chattaway, who had no great means of living of his own, was at the Hold on a long, long visit, with his wife and two little children, Christopher and Octavia. They were always saying they must leave; but they did *not* leave; they stayed on. Mr. Chattaway made himself useful to the Squire on business matters, and whether they ever would leave was a question. She, Mrs. Chattaway, was too gentle-spirited and loving to speak against her sister and Mr. Ryle; but Chattaway and Miss Diana Trevlyn kept up the ball. In point of fact, they had a motive—at least, Chattaway had—for making permanent the estrangement between the Squire and Mr. Ryle, for it was thought that Squire Trevlyn would have to look out for another heir.

News had come home of poor Joe Trevlyn's failing health. He had taken up his abode in the south of France on his marriage: for even then the doctors had begun to say that a more genial climate than this could alone save the life of the heir to Trevlyn. Bitterly as the Squire had felt the marriage, angry as he had been with Joe, he had never had the remotest thought of disinheriting him. He was the only son left: and Squire Trevlyn would never, if he could help it, bequeath Trevlyn Hold to a woman. A little girl, Maude, was born in due time to Joe Trevlyn and his wife; and not long after this, there arrived the tidings that Joe's health was rapidly failing. Mr. Chattaway, selfish, mean, sly, covetous, began to entertain hopes that *he* should be named the heir; he began to work on it in stealthy determination. He did not forget that, were it bequeathed to the husband of one of the daughters, Mr. Ryle, as the husband of the eldest, might be considered to possess most claim to it. No wonder then that he did all he could, secretly and openly, to incite the Squire against Mr. Ryle and his wife. And in this he was joined by Miss Diana Trevlyn. She, haughty and imperious, resented the marriage of her sister with one of inferior position, and willingly espoused the cause of Mr. Chattaway as against Thomas Ryle. It was whispered about, none knew with what truth, that Miss Diana made a compact with Chattaway, to the effect that she should reign jointly at Trevlyn Hold with him and enjoy part of its revenues, if he came into the inheritance.

Before the news came of Joe Trevlyn's death—and it was some months in coming—Squire Trevlyn had taken to his bed. Never did man seem to fade so rapidly as the Squire. Not only his health, but his mind failed him; all its vigour seemed gone. He mourned poor Joe excessively. In rude health and strength, he would not have mourned him; at least, would not have shown that he did so; never a man less inclined than the Squire to allow his private emotions to be seen: but in his weakened state he gave way to lamentation for his heir (his *heir*, note you, more than his son) every hour in the day. Over and over again he regretted that the little child, Maude, left by Joe, was not a boy. Nay, had it not been for his prejudice against her mother, he would have willed the estate to her, girl though she was. Now was Mr. Chattaway's time: he put forth in glowing colours his own claims, as Edith's husband; he made golden promises; he persuaded the poor Squire, in his wrecked mind, that black was white—and his plans succeeded.

To the will which had bequeathed the estate to the eldest son, dead Rupert, the Squire added a codicil, to the effect that, failing his two sons, James Chattaway was the inheritor. But all this was kept a profound secret.

During the time the Squire lay ill, Mr. Ryle went to Trevlyn Hold, and succeeded in obtaining an interview. Mr. Chattaway was out that day, or he had never accomplished it. Miss Diana Trevlyn was out. All the Squire's animosity departed the moment he saw Thomas Ryle's long-familiar face. He lay clasping his hand, and lamenting their estrangement; he told him he should cancel the two-thousand-pound bond, giving the money as his daughter's dowry; he said his promise of renewing the lease of the farm to him on the same terms would be held sacred, for he had left a memorandum to that effect amongst his papers. He sent for a certain box, in which the bond for the two thousand pounds had been placed, and searched for it, intending to give it to him then; but the bond was not there, and he said that Mr. Chattaway, who managed all his affairs now, must have placed it elsewhere. But he would ask him for it when he came in, and it should be destroyed before he slept. Altogether, it was a most pleasant and satisfactory interview.

But strange news arrived from abroad ere the Squire died. Not strange, certainly, in itself; only strange because it was so very unexpected. Joseph Trevlyn's widow had given birth to a boy! On the very day that little Maude was twelve months old, exactly three months after Joe's death, this little fellow was born. Mr. Chattaway opened the letter, and I will leave you to judge of his state of mind. A male heir, after he had made everything so safe and sure!

But Mr. Chattaway was not a man to be thwarted. *He* would not be deprived of the inheritance if he could by any possible scheming retain it, no matter what wrong he dealt out to others. James Chattaway had as little conscience as most people. The whole of that day he never spoke of the news; he kept it to himself; and the next morning there arrived a second letter, which rendered the affair a little more complicated. Young Mrs. Trevlyn was dead. She had died, leaving the two little ones, Maude and the infant.

Squire Trevlyn was always saying, "Oh, that Joe had left a boy; that Joe had left a boy!" And now, as it was found, Joe *had* left one. But Mr. Chattaway determined that the fact should never reach the Squire's ears to gladden them. Something had to be done, however, or the little children would be coming to Trevlyn. Mr. Chattaway arranged his plans, and wrote off hastily to stop their departure. He told the Squire that Joe's widow had died, leaving Maude; but he never said a word about the baby boy. Had the Squire lived, perhaps it could not have been kept from him; but he did not live; he went to his grave all too soon, never knowing that a male heir was born to Trevlyn.

The danger was over then. Mr. Chattaway was legal inheritor. Had Joe left ten boys, they could not have displaced him. Trevlyn Hold was his by the Squire's will, and could not be wrested from him. The two children, friendless and penniless, were brought home to the Hold. Mrs. Trevlyn had lived long enough to name the infant "Rupert," after the old Squire and the heir who had run away and died. Poor Joe had always said that if ever he had a boy, it should be named after his brother.

There they had been ever since, these two orphans, aliens in the home that ought to have been theirs; lovely children, both of them; but Rupert had the passionate Trevlyn temper. It was not made a systematically unkind home to them; Miss Diana would not have allowed that; but it was a very different home from that they ought to have enjoyed. Mr. Chattaway was at times almost cruel to Rupert; Christopher exercised upon him all sorts of galling and petty tyranny, as Octave Chattaway did upon Maude; and the neighbourhood, you may be quite sure, did not fail to talk. But it was known only to one or two that Mr. Chattaway had kept the fact of Rupert's birth from the Squire.

He stood tolerably well with his fellow-men, did Chattaway. In himself he was not liked; nay, he was very much disliked; but he was owner of Trevlyn Hold, and possessed sway in the neighbourhood. One thing, he could not get the title of Squire accorded to him. In vain he strove for it;

he exacted it from his tenants; he wrote notes in the third person, "Squire Chattaway presents his compliments," etc.; or, "the Squire of Trevlyn Hold desires," etc., etc., all in vain. People readily accorded his wife the title of Madam—as it was the custom to call the mistress of Trevlyn Hold—she was the old Squire's daughter, and they recognised her claim to it, but they did not give that of Squire to her husband.

These things had happened years ago, for Maude and Rupert were now aged respectively thirteen and twelve, and all that time James Chattaway had enjoyed his sway. Never, never; no, not even in the still night when the voice of conscience in most men is so suggestive; never giving a thought to the wrong dealt out to Rupert.

And it must be mentioned that the first thing Mr. Chattaway did, after the death of Squire Trevlyn, was to sue Mr. Ryle upon the bond; which he had *not* destroyed, although ordered to do so by the Squire. The next thing he did was to raise the farm to a ruinous rent. Mr. Ryle, naturally indignant, remonstrated, and there had been ill-feeling between them from that hour to this; but Chattaway had the law on his own side. Some of the bond was paid off; but altogether, what with the increased rent, the bond and its interest, and a succession of ill-luck on the farm, Mr. Ryle had scarcely been able to keep his head above water. As he said to his wife and children, when the bull had done its work—he was taken from a world of care.

CHAPTER VII
MR. RYLE'S LAST WILL AND TESTAMENT

Etiquette, touching the important ceremonies of buryings and christenings, is much more observed in the country than in towns. To rural districts this remark especially applies. In a large town people don't know their next-door neighbours, don't care for their neighbours' opinions. In a smaller place the inhabitants are almost as one family, and their actions are chiefly governed by that pertinent remark, "What will people say?" In these narrow communities, numbers of which are scattered about England, it is considered necessary on the occasion of a funeral to invite all kith and kin. Omit to do so, and it would be set down as a slight; affording the parish a theme of gossip for weeks afterwards. Hence Mr. Chattaway, being a connection—brother-in-law, in fact, of the deceased gentleman's wife—was invited to follow the remains of Thomas Ryle to the grave. In spite of the bad terms they had been on; in spite of Mrs. Ryle's own bitter feelings against Chattaway and Trevlyn Hold generally; in spite of Mr. Ryle's death having been caused by Chattaway's bull—Mr. Chattaway received a formal invitation to attend as mourner the remains to the grave. And it would never have entered into Mr. Chattaway's ideas of manners to decline it.

An inquest had been held at the nearest inn. The verdict returned was "Accidental Death," with a deodand of five pounds upon the bull. Which Mr. Chattaway had to pay.

The bull was already condemned. Not to annihilation; but to be taken to a distant fair, and there sold; whence he would be conveyed to other pastures, where he might possibly gore somebody else. It was not consideration for the feelings of the Ryle family which induced Mr. Chattaway to adopt this step, and so rid the neighbourhood of the animal; but consideration for his own pocket. Feeling ran high in the vicinity; fear also; the stoutest hearts could feel no security that the bull might not have a tilt at them: and Chattaway, on his part, was as little certain that an effectual silencer would not be dealt out to the bull some quiet night. Therefore he resolved to part with him. Apart from his misdoings, he was a valuable animal, worth a great deal more than Mr. Chattaway cared to lose; and the bull was dismissed.

The day of the funeral arrived, and those bidden to it began to assemble about one o'clock: that is, the undertaker's men, the clerk, and the bearers. Of the latter, Jim Sanders made one. "Better he had gone than his master," said Nora, in a matter-of-fact, worldly spirit of reasoning, as her thoughts went back to the mysterious hole she had gratuitously, and the reader will say absurdly, coupled with Jim's fate. A table was laid out in the entrance-room groaning under an immense cold round of beef, bread-and-cheese, and large supplies of ale. To help to convey a coffin to church without being first regaled with a good meal, was a thing Barbrook had never heard of, and never wished to hear of. The select members of the company were shown to the drawing-room, where the refreshment consisted of port and sherry, and "pound" cake. These were the established rules of hospitality at all well-to-do funerals: wine and cake for the gentry; cold beef and ale for the men. They had been observed at Squire Trevlyn's; at Mr. Ryle's father's; at every substantial funeral within the memory of Barbrook. Mr. Chattaway, Mr. Berkeley (a distant relative of Mr. Ryle's first wife), Mr. King the surgeon, and Farmer Apperley comprised the assemblage in the drawing-room.

At two o'clock, after some little difficulty in getting it into order, the sad procession started. It had then been joined by George and Trevlyn Ryle. A great many spectators had collected to view and attend it. The infrequency of a funeral in the respectable class, combined with the circumstances attending the death, drew them together: and before the church was reached, where it was met by the clergyman, it had a train half-a-mile long after it; chiefly women and children. Many dropped a tear for the premature death of one who had lived amongst them as a good master and kind neighbour.

They left him in his grave, by the side of his long-dead wife, Mary Berkeley. As George stood at the head of his father's coffin, during the ceremony in the churchyard, the gravestone with its name was in front of him; his mother's name: "Mary, the wife of Thomas Ryle, and only daughter of the Rev. George Berkeley." None knew with what feeling of loneliness the orphan boy turned from the spot, as the last words of the minister died away.

Mrs. Ryle, in her widow's weeds, was seated in the drawing-room on their return, as the gentlemen filed into it. In Barbrook custom, the relatives of the deceased, near or distant, were expected to assemble together for the remainder of the day; or for a portion of it. The gentlemen would sometimes smoke, and the ladies in their deep mourning sat with their hands folded in their laps, resting on their snow-white handkerchiefs. The conversation was only allowed to run on family matters, future prospects, and the like; and the voices were amicable and subdued.

As the mourners entered, they shook hands severally with Mrs. Ryle. Chattaway put out his hand last, and with perceptible hesitation. It was many a year since his hand had been given in fellowship to Mrs. Ryle, or had taken hers. They had been friendly once, and in the old days he had called her "Maude": but that was over now.

Mrs. Ryle turned from the offered hand. "No," she said, speaking in quiet but decisive tones. "I cannot forget the past sufficiently for that, James Chattaway. On this day it is forcibly present to me."

They sat down. Trevlyn next his mother, called there by her. The gentlemen disposed themselves on the side of the table facing the fire, and George found a chair a little behind them; no one seemed to notice him. And so much the better; the boy's heart was too full to bear much notice then.

On the table was placed the paper which had been written by the surgeon, at the dictation of Mr. Ryle, the night when he lay in extremity. It had not been unfolded since. Mr. King took it up; he knew that he was expected to read it. They were waiting for him to do so.

"I must premise that the dictation of this is Mr. Ryle's," he said. "He expressly requested me to write down his *own words*, just as they came from his lips. He—"

"Is it a will?" interrupted Farmer Apperley, a little man, with a red face and a large nose. He had come to the funeral in top boots, which constituted his idea of full dress.

"You can call it a will, if you please," replied Mr. King. "I am not sure that the law would do so. It was in consequence of his not having made a will that he requested me to write down these few directions."

The farmer nodded; and Mr. King began to read.

"In the name of God: Amen. I, Thomas Ryle.

"First of all, I bequeath my soul to God: trusting that He will pardon my sins, for the sake of Jesus Christ our Saviour. Amen.

"It's a dreadful blow, this meeting my death by Chattaway's bull. The more so, that I am unable to leave things straightforward for my wife and children. They know—at least, my wife knows, and all the parish knows—the pressure that has been upon me, through Chattaway coming down upon me as he has done. I have been as a bird with its wings clipped. As soon as I tried to get up, I was pulled down again.

"Ill luck has been upon me besides. Beasts have died off, crops have failed. The farm's not good for much, for all the money that has been laid out upon it, and I alone know the labour it has cost. When you think of these things, my dear wife and boys, you'll know why I do not leave you better provided for. Many and many a night have I lain awake upon my bed, fretting, and planning, and hoping, all for your sakes. Perhaps if that bull had spared me to old age, I might have left you better off.

"I should like to bequeath the furniture and all that is in the house, the stock, the beasts, and all that I die possessed of, to my dear wife, Maude—but it's not of any use, for Chattaway will sell up—except the silver tankard, and that should go to Trevlyn. But for having 'T.R.' upon it, it should go to George, for he is the eldest. T.R. stood for my father, and T.R. has stood for me, and T.R. will stand for Trevlyn. George, though he is the eldest, won't grudge it him, if I know anything of his nature. And I give to George my watch, and I hope he'll keep it for his dead father's sake. It is only a silver one; but it's a very good one, and George can have his initials engraved on the shield. The three seals, and the gold key, I give to him with it. The red cornelian has our arms on it. For we had arms once, and my father and I have generally sealed our letters with them: not that they have done him or me any good. And let Treve keep the tankard faithfully, and never part with it. And remember, my dear boys, that your poor father would have left you better keepsakes had it been in his power. You must prize these for the dead giver's sake. But there! it's of no use talking, for Chattaway will sell up, watch and tankard, and all.

"And I should like to leave that bay foal to my dear little Caroline. It will be a pretty creature when it's bigger. You must let it have the run of the three cornered paddock, and I should like to see her on it, sweet little soul!—but Chattaway's bull has stopped it. And don't grudge the cost of a little saddle for her; and Roger can break it in; and mind you are all true and tender with my dear little girl. You are good lads—though Treve is hasty when his temper's put out—and I know you'll be to her what brothers ought to be. I always meant that foal for Carry, since I saw how pretty it was likely to grow, though I didn't say so; and now I give it to her. But where's the use? Chattaway will sell up.

"If he does sell up, to the last stick and stone, he won't get his debt in full. Perhaps not much above half of it; for things at a forced sale don't bring their value. You have put down 'his debt,' I suppose; but it is not his debt. I am on my death-bed, and I say that the two thousand pounds was made a present of to me by the Squire on *his* death-bed. He told me it was made all right with Chattaway; that Chattaway understood the promise given to me, not to raise the rent; and that he'd be the same just landlord to me that the Squire had been. The Squire could not lay his hand on the bond, or he would have given it me then; but he said Chattaway should burn it as soon as he entered, which would be in an hour or two. Chattaway knows whether he has acted up to this; and now his bull has done for me.

"And I wish to tell Chattaway that if he'll act a fair part as a man ought, and let my wife and the boys stop on the farm, he'll stand a much better chance of getting the money, than he would if he turns them out of it. I don't say this for their sakes more than for his; but because from my heart I believe it to be the truth. George has his head on his shoulders the right way, and I would advise his mother to keep him on the farm; he will be getting older every day. Not but that I wish her to use her own judgment in all things, for her judgment is good. In time, they may be able to pay off Chattaway; in time they may be able even to buy back the farm, for I cannot forget that it belonged to my forefathers, and not to the Squire. That is, if Chattaway will be reasonable, and let them stop on it, and not be hard and pressing. But perhaps I am talking nonsense, for he may turn them off and do for them, as his bull has done for me.

"And now, my dear George and Treve, I repeat it to you, be good boys to your mother. Obey her in all things. Maude, I have left all to you in preference to dividing it between you and them, for which there is no time; but I know you'll do the right thing by them: and when it comes to your turn to leave—if Chattaway don't sell up—I wish you to bequeath to them in equal shares what you die possessed of. George is not your son, but he is mine, and—But perhaps I'd better not say what I was going to say. And, my boys, work while it's day. In that Book which I have not read so much as I ought to have read, it says, 'The night cometh when no man can work.' When we hear that read in church, or when we get the Book out on a Sunday evening and read it to ourselves, that night seems a long, long way off. It seems so far off that it can hardly ever be any concern of ours; and it is only when we are cut off suddenly that we find how very near it is. That night has come for me; and that night will come for you before you are aware of it. So, *work*—and score that, doctor. God has placed us in this world to work, and not to be ashamed of it; and to work for Him as well as for ourselves. It was often in my mind that I ought to work more for God—that I ought to think more of Him; and I used to say, 'I will do so when a bit of this bother's off my mind.' But the bother was always there, and I never did it. And now the end's come; and I can see things would have been made easier to me if I *had* done it—score it again, doctor—and I say it as a lesson to you, my children.

"And I think that's about all; and I am much obliged to you, doctor, for writing this. I hope they'll be able to manage things on the farm, and I would ask my neighbour Apperley to give them his advice now and then, for old friendship's sake, until George shall be older, and to put him in a way of buying and selling stock. If Chattaway don't sell up, that is. If he does, I hardly know how it will be. Perhaps God will put them in some other way, and take care of them. And I would leave my best thanks to Nora, for she has been a true friend to us all, and I don't know how the house would have got on without her. And now I'm growing faint, doctor, and I think the end is coming. God bless you all, my dear ones. Amen."

A deep silence fell on the room as Mr. King ceased. He folded the paper, and laid it on the table near Mrs. Ryle. The first to speak was Farmer Apperley.

"Any help that I can be of to you and George, Mrs. Ryle, and to all of you, is heartily at your service. It will be yours with right goodwill at all times and seasons. The more so, that you know if I had been cut off in this way, my poor friend Ryle would have been the first to offer to do as much for my wife and boys, and have thought no trouble of it. George, you can come over and ask me about things, just as you would ask your father; or send for me up here to the farm; and whatever work I may be at at home, though it was putting out a barn on fire, I'd come."

"And now it is my turn to speak," said Mr. Chattaway. "And, Mrs. Ryle, I give you my promise, in the presence of these gentlemen, that if you choose to remain on the farm, I will put no hindrance upon it. Your husband thought me hard—unjust; he said it before my face and behind my back. My opinion always has been that he entirely mistook Squire Trevlyn in that last interview he had with him. I do not think it was ever the Squire's intention to cancel the bond; Ryle must have misunderstood him altogether: at any rate, I heard nothing of it. As successor to the estate, the bond came into my possession; and in my wife and children's interest I could not consent to destroy it. No one but a soft-hearted man—and that's what Ryle was, poor fellow—would have thought of asking such a thing. But I was willing to give him every facility for paying it, and I did do so. No! It was not my hardness that was in fault, but his pride and nonsense, and his thinking I ought not to ask for my own money—"

"If you bring up these things, James Chattaway, I must answer them," interrupted Mrs. Ryle. "I would prefer not to be forced to do it to-day."

"I do not want to bring them up in any unpleasant spirit," answered Mr. Chattaway; "or to say it was his fault or my fault. We'll let bygones be bygones. He is gone, poor man; and I wish that savage beast of a bull had been in four quarters before he had done the mischief! All I would now say, is, that I'll put no impediment to your remaining on the farm. We will not go into business details this afternoon, but I will come in any day you like to appoint, and talk it over. If you choose to keep on the farm at its present rent—it is well worth it—to pay me interest for the money owing, and a yearly sum towards diminishing the debt, you are welcome to do it."

Just what Nora had predicted! Mr. Chattaway loved money far too much to run the risk of losing part of the debt—as he probably would do if he turned them from the farm. Mrs. Ryle bowed her head in cold acquiescence. She saw no way open to her but that of accepting the offer. Mr. Chattaway probably knew there was no other.

"The sooner things are settled, the better," she remarked. "I will name eleven o'clock to-morrow morning."

"Very good; I'll be here," he answered. "And I am glad it is decided amicably."

The rest of those present also appeared glad. Perhaps they had feared some unpleasant recrimination might take place between Mrs. Ryle and James Chattaway. Thus relieved, they unbent a little, and crossed their legs as if inclined to become more sociable.

"What shall you do with the boys, Mrs. Ryle?" suddenly asked Farmer Apperley.

"Treve, of course, will go to school as usual," she replied. "George—I have not decided about George."

"Shall I have to leave school?" cried George, looking up with a start.

"Of course you will," said Mrs. Ryle.

"But what will become of my Latin; my studies altogether?" returned George, in tones of dismay. "You know, mamma—"

"It cannot be helped, George," she interrupted, speaking in the uncompromising, decisive manner, so characteristic of her; as it was of her sister, Diana Trevlyn. "You must turn your attention to something more profitable than schooling, now."

"If a boy of fifteen has not had schooling enough, I'd like to know when he has had it?" interposed Farmer Apperley, who neither understood nor approved of the strides education and intellect had made since he was a boy. Substantial people in his day had been content to learn to read and write and cipher, and deem that amount of learning sufficient to grow rich upon. As did the Dutch professor, to whom George Primrose wished to teach Greek, but who declined the offer. He had never learned Greek; he had lived, and ate, and slept without Greek; and therefore he did not see any good in Greek. Thus was it with Farmer Apperley.

"What do you learn at school, George?" questioned Mr. Berkeley.

"Latin and Greek, and mathematics, and—"

"But, George, where will be the good of such things to you?" cried Farmer Apperley, not allowing him to end the catalogue. "Latin and Greek and mathematics! What next, I wonder!"

"I don't see much good in giving a boy that sort of education myself," put in Mr. Chattaway, before any one else had time to speak. "Unless he is to take up a profession, the classics only lie fallow in the mind. I hated them, I know that; I and my brother, too. Many and many a caning we have had over our Latin, until we wished the books at the bottom of the sea. Twelve months after we left school we could not have construed a page, had it been put before us. That's all the good Latin did for us."

"I shall keep up my Latin and Greek," observed George, very independently, "although I may have to leave school."

"Why need you keep it up?" asked Mr. Chattaway, turning full upon George.

"Why?" echoed George. "I like it, for one thing. And a knowledge of the classics is necessary to a gentleman."

"Necessary to what?" cried Mr. Chattaway.

"To a gentleman," repeated George.

"Oh," said Mr. Chattaway. "Do you think of being one?"

"Yes, I do," repeated George, in tones as decisive as any ever used by his step-mother.

This bold assertion nearly took away the breath of Farmer Apperley. Had George Ryle announced his intention of becoming a convict, Mr. Apperley's consternation had been scarcely less. The same word bears different constructions to different minds. That of "gentleman" in the mouth of George, could only bear one to the simple farmer.

"Hey, lad! What wild notions have ye been getting into your head?" he asked.

"George," said Mrs. Ryle almost at the same moment, "are you going to give me trouble at the very outset? There is nothing for you to look forward to but work. Your father said it."

"Of course I look forward to work," returned George, as cheerfully as he could speak that sad afternoon. "But that will not prevent my being a gentleman."

"George, I fancy you may be somewhat misusing terms," remarked the surgeon, who was an old inhabitant of that rustic district, and a little more advanced than the rest. "What you meant to say was, that you would be a good man, honourable and upright; nothing mean about you. Was it not?"

"Yes," said George, after an imperceptible hesitation. "Something of that sort."

"The boy did not express himself clearly, you see," said Mr. King, looking round on the rest. "He means well."

"Don't you ever talk about being a gentleman again, my lad," cried Farmer Apperley, with a sagacious nod. "It would make the neighbours think you were going in for bad ways. A gentleman is one who follows the hounds in white smalls and scarlet coat, goes to dinners and drinks wine, and never puts his hands to anything, but leads an idle life."

"That is not the sort of gentleman I meant," said George.

"It is to be hoped not," replied the farmer. "A man may do this if he has a good fat balance at his banker's, but not else."

George made no remark. To have explained how very different his ideas of a gentleman were from those of Farmer Apperley might have involved him in a long conversation. His silence was looked suspiciously upon by Mr. Chattaway.

"Where idle and roving notions are taken up, there's only one cure for them!" he remarked, in short, uncompromising tones. "And that is hard work."

But that George's spirit was subdued, he might have hotly answered that he had taken up neither idle nor roving notions. As it was, he sat in silence.

"I doubt whether it will be prudent to keep George at home," said Mrs. Ryle, speaking generally, but not to Mr. Chattaway. "He is too young to do much on the farm. And there's John Pinder."

"John Pinder would do his best, no doubt," said Mr. Chattaway.

"The question is—if I do resolve to put George out, what can I put him to?" resumed Mrs. Ryle.

"My father thought it best I should remain on the farm," interposed George, his heart beating a shade faster.

"He thought it best that I should exercise my own judgment in the matter," corrected Mrs. Ryle. "The worst is, it takes money to place a lad out," she added, looking at Farmer Apperley.

"It does that," replied the farmer.

"There's nothing like a trade for boys," said Mr. Chattaway, impressively. "They earn a living, and are kept out of mischief. It appears to me that Mrs. Ryle will have expense enough upon her hands, without the cost and keep of George added to it. What good can so young a boy do the farm?"

"True," mused Mrs. Ryle, agreeing for once with Mr. Chattaway. "He could not be of much use at present. But the cost of placing him out?"

"Of course he could not," repeated Mr. Chattaway, with an eagerness which might have betrayed his motive, but that he coughed it down. "Perhaps I may be able to put him out for you without cost. I know of an eligible place where there's a vacancy. The trade is a good one, too."

"I am not going to any trade," said George, looking Mr. Chattaway full in the face.

"You are going where Mrs. Ryle thinks fit to send you," returned Mr. Chattaway, in his hard, cold tones. "If I can get you into the establishment of Wall and Barnes without premium, it will be a first-rate thing for you."

All the blood in George Ryle's body seemed to rush to his face. Poor though they had become, trade had been unknown in their family, and its sound in George's ears, as applied to himself, was something terrible. "That is a retail shop!" he cried, rising from his seat.

"Well?" said Mr. Chattaway.

They remained gazing at each other. George with his changing face flushing to crimson, fading to paleness; Mr. Chattaway with his composed leaden features. His light eyes were sternly directed to George, but he did not glance at Mrs. Ryle. George was the first to speak.

"You shall never force me there, Mr. Chattaway."

Mr. Chattaway rose from his seat, took George by the shoulder, and turned him towards the window. The view did not take in much of the road to Barbrook; but a glimpse of it might be caught sight of here and there, winding along in the distance.

"Boy! Do you remember what was carried down that road this afternoon—what you followed next to, with your younger brother? *He* said that you were not to oppose your mother, but obey her in all things. These are early moments to begin to turn against your father's dying charge."

George sat down, heart and brain throbbing. He did not see his duty very distinctly before him then. His father certainty had charged him to obey his mother's requests; he had left him entirely subject to her control; but George felt perfectly sure that his father would never have placed him in a shop; would not have allowed him to enter one.

Mr. Chattaway continued talking, but the boy heard him not. He was bending towards Mrs. Ryle, enlarging persuasively upon the advantages of the plan. He knew that Wall and Barnes had taken a boy into their house without premium, he said, and he believed he could induce them to waive it in George's case. He and Wall had been at school together; had passed many an impatient hour over the Latin previously spoken of; had often called in to have a chat with him in passing. Wall was a ten-thousand-pound man now; and George might become the same in time.

"How would you like to place Christopher at it, Mr. Chattaway?" asked George, his heart beating rebelliously.

"Christopher!" indignantly responded Mr. Chattaway. "Christopher's heir to Trev—Christopher isn't you," he concluded, cutting his first retort short. In the presence of Mrs. Ryle it might not be altogether prudent to allude to the heirship of Cris to Trevlyn Hold.

The sum named conciliated the ear of Mr. Apperley, otherwise he had not listened with any favour to the plan. "Ten thousand pounds! And Wall hardly a middle-aged man! That's worth thinking of, George."

"I could never live in a shop; the close air, the confinement, the pettiness of it, would stifle me," said George, with a groan, putting aside for the moment his more forcible objections.

"You'd rather live in a thunder-storm, with the rain coming down on your head in bucketfuls," said Mr. Chattaway, sarcastically.

"A great deal," said George.

Farmer Apperley did not detect the irony of Mr. Chattaway's remark, or the bitterness of the answer. "You'll say next, boy, that you'd rather turn sailor, exposed to the weather night and day, perched midway between sky and water!"

"A thousand times," was George's truthful answer. "Mother, let me stay at the farm!" he cried, the nervous motion of his hands, the strained countenance, proving how momentous was the question to his grieved heart. "You do not know how useful I should soon become! And my father wished it."

Mrs. Ryle shook her head. "You are too young, George, to be of use. No."

George seemed to turn white. He was approaching Mrs. Ryle with an imploring gesture; but Mr. Chattaway caught his arm and pushed him towards his seat again. "George, if I were you, I would not, on this day, cross my mother."

George glanced at her. Not a shade of love, of relenting, was there on her countenance. Cold, haughty, self-willed, it always was; but more cold, more haughty, more self-willed than usual now. He turned and left the room, crossed the kitchen, and passed into the room whence his father had been carried only two hours before.

"Oh, father! father!" he sobbed; "if you were only back again!"

CHAPTER VIII
REBELLION

Borne down by the powers above him, George Ryle could only succumb to their will. Persuaded by the eloquence of Mr. Chattaway, Mrs. Ryle became convinced that placing George in the establishment of Wall and Barnes was the most promising thing that could be found for him. The wonder was, that she should have brought herself to listen to Chattaway at all, or have entertained for a moment any proposal emanating from him. There could have been but one solution to the riddle: that of her own anxiety to get George settled in something away from home. Deep down in the heart of Mrs. Ryle, there was seated a keen sense of injury—of injustice—of wrong. It had been seated there ever since the death of Squire Trevlyn, influencing her actions, warping her temper—the question of the heirship of Trevlyn. Her father had bequeathed Trevlyn Hold to Chattaway; and Chattaway's son was now the heir; whereas, in her opinion, it was her son, Trevlyn Ryle, who should be occupying that desirable distinction. How Mrs. Ryle reconciled it to her conscience to ignore the claims of young Rupert Trevlyn, she best knew.

Ignore them she did. She gave no more thought to Rupert in connection with the succession to Trevlyn, than if he had not existed. He had been barred from it by the Squire's will, and there it ended. But, failing heirs to her two dead brothers, it was *her* son who should have come in. Was she not the eldest daughter? What right had that worm, Chattaway, to have insinuated himself into the Squire's home? into—it may be said—his heart? and so willed over to himself the inheritance?

A bitter fact to Mrs. Ryle; a fact which rankled in her heart night and day; a turning from the path of justice which she firmly intended to see turned back again. She saw not how it was to be accomplished; she knew not by what means it could be brought about; she divined not yet how she should help in it; but she was fully determined that it should be Trevlyn Ryle eventually to possess Trevlyn Hold. Never Cris Chattaway.

A determination immutable as the rock: a purpose in the furtherance of which she never swerved or faltered; there it lay in the archives of her most secret thoughts, a part and parcel of herself, not the less indulged because never alluded to. It may be that in the death of her husband she saw her way to the end somewhat more clearly; his removal was one impediment taken from the path. She had never but once given utterance to her ambitious hopes for Trevlyn: and that had been to her husband. His reception of them was a warning never to speak of them again to him. No son of his, he said, should inherit Trevlyn Hold whilst the children of Joseph Trevlyn lived. If Chattaway chose to wrest their rights from them, make his son Cris usurper after him, he, Thomas Ryle, could not hinder it; but his own boy Treve should never take act or part in so crying a wrong. So long as Rupert and Maud Trevlyn lived, he could never recognise other rights than theirs. From that time forward Mrs. Ryle kept silence with her husband, as she did with others; but the roots of the project grew deeper and deeper in her heart, overspreading all its healthy fibres.

With this destiny in view for Treve, it will readily be understood why she did not purpose bringing him up to any profession, or sending him out in the world. Her intention was, that Treve should live at home, as soon as his school-days were over; should be master of Trevlyn Farm, until he became master of Trevlyn Hold. And for this reason, and this alone, she did not care to keep George with her. Trevlyn Farm might be a living for one son; it would not be for two; neither would two masters on it answer, although they were brothers. It is true, a thought at times crossed her whether it might not be well, in the interests of the farm, to retain George. He would soon become useful; would be trustworthy; her interests would be his; and she felt dubious about confiding all management to John Pinder. But these suggestions were overruled by the thought that it would not be desirable for George to acquire a footing on the farm as its master, and be turned from it when the time came for Treve. As much for George's sake as for Treve's, she felt this; and she determined to place George at something away, where his interests and Treve's would not clash with each other.

Wall and Barnes were flourishing and respectable silk-mercers and linen-drapers; their establishment a large one, the oldest and best conducted in Barmester. Had it been suggested to Mrs. Ryle to place Treve there, she would have retorted in haughty indignation. And yet there she was sending George.

What Mr. Chattaway's precise object could be in wishing to get George away from home, he alone knew. That he had such an object, there could be no shadow of doubt about; and Mrs. Ryle's usual clear-sightedness must have been just then obscured not to perceive it. Had his own interests or pleasure not been in some way involved, Chattaway would have taken no more heed as to what became of George than he did of a clod of earth in that miserable field just rendered famous by the ill-conditioned bull. It was Chattaway who did it all. He negotiated with Wall and Barnes; he brought news of his success to Mrs. Ryle; he won over Farmer Apperley.

Wall and Barnes had occasionally taken a youth without premium—the youth being expected to perform an unusual variety of work for the favour, to be at once an apprentice and a general factotum, at the beck and call of the establishment. Under those concessions, Wall and Barnes had been known to forego the usual premium; and this great boon was, through Mr. Chattaway, offered to George Ryle. Chattaway boasted of it; enlarged upon his luck to George; and Mrs. Ryle—accepted it.

And George? Every pulse in his body coursed on in fiery indignation against the measure, every feeling of his heart rebelled. But of opposition he could make none: none that served him. Chattaway quietly put him down; Mrs. Ryle met all remonstrances with the answer that she had *decided*; and Farmer Apperley laboured to convince him that it was a slice of good fortune, which any one (under the degree of a gentleman who rode to cover in a scarlet coat and white smalls) might jump at. Was not Wall, who had not yet reached his five-and-fortieth year, a ten-thousand pound man? Turn where George would, there appeared to be no escape for him. He must give up all the dreams of his life—not that the dreams had been as yet particularly defined—and become what his mind revolted at, what he knew he should ever dislike bitterly. Had he been a less right-minded boy, he would have defied Chattaway, and declined to obey Mrs. Ryle. But that sort of rebellion George did not enter upon. The injunction of his dead father lay on him all too forcibly—"Obey and reverence your mother." And so the agreement was made, and George Ryle was to go to Wall and Barnes, to be bound to them for seven years.

He stood leaning out of the casement window the night before he was to enter; his aching brow bared to the cold air, cloudy as the autumn sky. Treve was fast asleep, in his own little bed in the far corner, shaded and sheltered by its curtains; but there was no such peaceful sleep for George. The thoughts he was indulging were not altogether profitable; and certain questions which arose in his mind had been better left out of it.

"What *right* have they so to dispose of me?" he soliloquised, alluding, it must be confessed, to the trio, Chattaway, Mrs. Ryle, and Apperley. "They *know* that if my father had lived, they would not have dared to urge my being put to it. I wonder what it will end in? I wonder whether I shall have to be at it always? It is *not* right to put a poor fellow to what he hates most of all in life, and will hate for ever and for ever."

He gazed out at the low stretch of land lying under the night sky, looking as desolate as he. "I'd rather go for a sailor!" broke from him in his despair; "rather—"

A hand on his shoulder caused him to start and turn. There stood Nora.

"If I didn't say one of you boys was out of bed! What's this, George? What are you doing?—trying to catch your death at the open window."

"As good catch my death, for all I see, as live in the world, now," was George's answer.

"As good be a young simpleton and confess it," retorted Nora, angrily. "What's the matter?"

"Why should they force me to that horrible place at Barmester?" cried George, following up his thoughts, rather than answering Nora. "I wish Chattaway had been a thousand miles away first! What business has he to interfere about me?"

"I wish I was queen at odd moments, when work seems coming in seven ways at once, and only one pair of hands to do it," quoth Nora.

George turned from the window. "Nora, look here! You know I am a gentleman born and bred: *is* it right to put me to it?"

Nora evaded an answer. She felt nearly as much as the boy did; but she saw no way of escape for him, and therefore would not oppose it.

There was no way of escape. Chattaway had decided it, Mrs. Ryle had acquiesced, and George was conducted to the new house, and took up his abode in it, rebellious feelings choking his heart, rebellious words rising to his lips.

But he did his utmost to beat down rebellion. The charge of his dead father was ever before him, and George was mindful of it. He felt as one crushed under a weight of despair; as one who had been rudely thrust from his proper place on earth: but he constantly battled with himself and his wrongs, and strove to make the best of it. How bitter the struggle, none save himself knew: its remembrance would never die out from memory.

The new work seemed terrible; not for its amount, though that was great; but from its nature. To help make up this parcel, to undo that; to take down these goods, to put up others. He ran to the post with letters—and that was a delightful phase of his life, compared with the rest—he carried out brown paper parcels. He had to stand behind the counter, and roll and unroll goods, and measure tapes and ribbons. You will readily conceive what all this was to a proud boy. George might have run away from it altogether, but that the image of that table in the sitting-room, and of him who lay upon it, was ever before him, whispering to him not to shrink from his duty.

Not a moment's idleness was George allowed; however the shopmen might enjoy leisure intervals when customers were few, there was no such interval for him. He was the new scapegoat of the establishment; often doing the work that of right did not belong to him. It was perfectly well known to the young men that he had entered as a working apprentice; one who was not to be particular in work he did, or its quantity; and therefore he was not spared. He had taken his books with him, classics and others; he soon found he might as well have left them at home. Not one minute in the twenty-four hours could he devote to them. His hands were full of work until bed-time; and no reading was permitted in the chambers. "Where is the use of my having gone to school at all?" he would sometimes ask himself. He would soon become as oblivious of Latin and Greek as Mr. Chattaway could wish; and his prospects of adding to his stock of learning were such as would have gladdened Farmer Apperley's heart.

One Saturday, when George had been there about three weeks, and the day was drawing near for the indentures to be signed, binding him to the business for years, Mr. Chattaway rode up in the very costume that was the subject of Farmer Apperley's ire, when worn by those who ought not to afford to wear it. The hounds had met that day near Barmester, had found their fox, and been led a round-about chase, the fox bringing them back to their starting-point to resign his brush; and the master of Trevlyn Hold, on his splashed hunter, in his scarlet coat, white smalls and boots, splashed also, rode through Barmester on his return, and pulled up at the door of Wall and Barnes. Giving his horse to a street boy to hold, he entered the shop, whip in hand.

The scarlet coat, looming in unexpectedly, caused a flutter in the establishment. Saturday was market-day, and the shop was unusually full. The customers looked round in admiration, the shopmen with envy. Little chance thought those hard-worked, unambitious young men, that they should ever wear a scarlet coat, and ride to cover on a blood hunter. Mr. Chattaway, of Trevlyn Hold, was an object of consideration just then. He shook hands with Mr. Wall, who came forward from some remote region; then turned and shook hands condescendingly with George.

"And how does he suit?" blandly inquired Mr. Chattaway. "Can you make anything of him?"

"He does his best," was the reply. "Awkward at present; but we have had others who have been as awkward at first, I think, and who have turned out valuable assistants in the long run. I am willing to take him."

"That's all right then," said Mr. Chattaway. "I'll call in and tell Mrs. Ryle. Wednesday is the day he is to be bound, I think?"

"Wednesday," assented Mr. Wall.

"I shall be here. I am glad to take this trouble off Mrs. Ryle's hands. I hope you like your employment, George."

"I do not like it at all," replied George. And he spoke out fearlessly, although his master stood by.

"Oh, indeed!" said Mr. Chattaway, with a false-sounding laugh. "Well, I did not suppose you would like it too well at first."

Mr. Wall laughed also, a hearty, kindly laugh. "Never yet did an apprentice like his work too well," said he. "It's their first taste of the labour of life. George Ryle will like it better when he is used to it."

"I never shall," thought George. But he supposed it would not quite do to say so; neither would it answer any end. Mr. Chattaway shook hands with Mr. Wall, nodded to George, and he and his scarlet coat loomed out again.

"Will it last for ever?—will this dreadful slavery last throughout my life?" broke from George Ryle's rebellious heart.

CHAPTER IX
EMANCIPATION

On the following day, Sunday, George walked home: Mrs. Ryle had told him to come and spend the day at the Farm. All were at church except Molly, and George went to meet them. Several groups were coming along; and presently he met Cris Chattaway, Rupert Trevlyn, and his brother Treve, walking together.

"Where's my mother?" asked George.

"She stepped indoors with Mrs. Apperley," answered Treve. "Said she'd follow me on directly."

"How do you relish linen-drapering?" asked Cris Chattaway, in a chaffing sort of manner, as George turned with them. "Horrid, isn't it?"

"There's only about one thing in this world more horrid," answered George.

"My father said you expressed fears before you went that you'd find the air stifling," went on Cris, not asking what the one exception might be. "Is it hopelessly so?"

"The black hole in Calcutta must have been cool and pleasant in comparison with it," returned George.

"I wonder you are alive," continued Cris.

"I wonder I am," said George, equably. "I was quite off in a faint one day, when the shop was at the fullest. They thought they must have sent for you, Cris; that the sight of you might bring me to again."

"There you go!" exclaimed Treve Ryle. "I wonder if you *could* let each other alone if you were bribed to do it?"

"Cris began it," said George.

"I didn't," said Cris. "I *should* like to see you at your work, though, George! I'll come some day. The Squire paid you a visit yesterday afternoon, he told us. He says you are getting to be quite the counter cut; one can't serve out yards of calico without it, you know."

George Ryle's face burnt. He knew Mr. Chattaway had ridiculed him at Trevlyn Hold, in connection with his new occupation. "It would be a more fitting situation for you than for me, Cris," said he. "And now you hear it."

Cris laughed scornfully. "Perhaps it might, if I wanted one. The master of Trevlyn won't need to go into a linen-draper's shop."

"Look here, Cris. That shop is horrid, and I don't mind telling you that I find it so; not an hour in the day goes over my head but I wish myself out of it; but I would rather bind myself to it for twenty years than be master of Trevlyn Hold, if I came to it as you will come to it—by wrong."

Cris broke into a shrill, derisive whistle. It was being prolonged to an apparently interminable length, when he found himself rudely seized from behind.

"Is that the way you walk home from church, Christopher Chattaway? Whistling!"

Cris looked round and saw Miss Trevlyn. "Goodness, Aunt Diana! are you going to shake me?"

"Walk along as a gentleman should, then," returned Miss Trevlyn.

She went on. Miss Chattaway walked by her side, not deigning to cast a word or a look to the boys as she swept past. Gliding up behind them, holding the hand of Maude, was gentle Mrs. Chattaway. They all wore black silk dresses and white silk bonnets: the apology for mourning assumed for Mr. Ryle. But the gowns were not new; and the bonnets were the bonnets of the past summer, with the coloured flowers removed.

Mrs. Chattaway slackened her pace, and George found himself at her side. She seemed to linger, as if she would speak with him unheard by the rest.

"Are you pretty well, my dear?" were her first words. "You look taller and thinner, and your face is pale."

"I shall look paler before I have been much longer in the shop, Mrs. Chattaway."

Mrs. Chattaway glanced her head timidly round with the air of one who fears she may be heard. But they were alone now.

"Are you grieving, George?"

"How can I help it?" he passionately answered, feeling that he could open his heart to Mrs. Chattaway as he could to no one else in the wide world. "Is it a proper thing to put me to, dear Mrs. Chattaway?"

"I said it was not," she murmured. "I remarked to Diana that I wondered Maude should place you there."

"It was not my mother so much as Mr. Chattaway," he answered, forgetting possibly that it was Mr. Chattaway's wife to whom he spoke. "At times, do you know, I feel as though I would almost rather be—be—"

"Be what, dear?"

"Be dead, than remain there."

"Hush, George!" she cried, almost with a shudder. "Random figures of speech never do any good! I have learnt it. In the old days, when—"

She suddenly broke off and glided forward without further notice. As she passed she caught up the hand of Maude, who was then walking by the side of the boys. George looked round for the cause of desertion, and found it in Mr. Chattaway. That gentleman was coming along with a quick step, one of his younger children in his hand.

The Chattaways turned off towards Trevlyn Hold, and George walked on with Treve.

"Do you know how things are going on at home, Treve, between my mother and Chattaway?" asked George.

"Chattaway's a miserable screw," was Treve's answer. "He'd like to grind down the world, and doesn't let a chance escape him. Mamma says it's a dreadful sum he has put upon her to pay yearly, and she does not see how the farm will do it, besides keeping us. I wish we were clear of him! I wish I was as big as you, George! I'd work my arms off, but I'd get together the money to pay him!"

"I'm not allowed to work," said George. "They have thrust me away from the farm."

"I wish you were back at it; I know that! Nothing goes on as it used to, when you were there and papa was alive. Nora's cross, and mamma's cross; and I have not a soul to speak to. What do you think Chattaway did this week?"

"Something mean, I suppose!"

"Mean! We killed a pig, and while it was being cut up, Chattaway marched in. 'That's fine meat, John Pinder,' said he, when he had looked at it a bit; 'as fine as ever I saw. I should like a bit of this meat; I think I'll take a sparerib; and it can go against Mrs. Ryle's account with me.' With that, he laid hold of a sparerib, the finest of the two, called a boy who was standing by, and sent him up with it at once to Trevlyn Hold. What do you think of that?"

"Think! That it's just the thing Chattaway would do every day of his life, if he could. Mamma should have sent for the meat back again."

"And enrage Chattaway! It might be all the worse for us if she did."

"Is it not early to begin pig-killing?"

"Yes. John Pinder killed this one on his own authority; never so much as asking mamma. She was so angry. She told him, if ever he acted for himself again, without knowing what her pleasure might be, she should discharge him. But it strikes me John Pinder is fond of doing things on his own head," concluded Treve, sagaciously; "and will do them, in spite of everyone, now there's no master over him."

The day soon passed. George told his mother how terribly he disliked being where he was placed; worse than that, how completely unsuited he was to the business. Mrs. Ryle coldly said we all had to put up with what we disliked, and he would grow reconciled to it in time. There was evidently no hope for him; and he returned to Barmester at night, feeling there was not any.

On the following afternoon, Monday, some one in deep mourning entered the shop of Wall and Barnes, and asked if she could speak to Mr. Ryle. George was at the upper end of the shop. A box of lace had been accidentally upset on the floor, and he had been called to set it straight. Behind him hung two shawls, and, hidden by those shawls, was a desk, belonging to Mr. Wall. The visitor approached George and saluted him.

"Well, you *are* busy!"

George lifted his head at the well-known voice—Nora's. Her attention appeared chiefly attracted by the lace.

"What a mess it is in! And you don't go a bit handy to work, towards putting it tidy."

"I shall never be handy at this sort of work. Oh, Nora! I cannot tell you how I dislike it!" he exclaimed, with a burst of feeling that betrayed its own pain. "I would rather be with my father in his coffin!"

"Don't talk nonsense!" said Nora.

"It is not nonsense. I shall never care for anything again in life, now they have put me here. It was Chattaway's doing; you know it was, Nora. My mother never would have thought of it. When I remember that my father would have objected to this for me just as strongly as I object to it myself, I can hardly *bear* my thoughts. I think how he will grieve, if he can see what goes on in this world. You know he said something about that when he was dying—the dead retaining their consciousness of what is passing here."

"Have you objected to be bound?"

"I have not objected. I don't mean to object. My father charged me to obey Mrs. Ryle, and not cross her—and I won't forget that; therefore I shall remain, and do my duty to the very best of my power. But it was a cruel thing to put me to it. Chattaway has some motive for getting me off the farm; there's no doubt about it. I shall stay if—if—"

"Why do you hesitate?" asked Nora.

"Well, there are moments," he answered, "when a fear comes over me whether I *can* bear and stay on. You see, Nora, it is Chattaway and my mother's will balancing against all the hopes and prospects of my life. I know that my father charged me to obey my mother; but, on the other hand, I know that if he were alive he would be pained to see me here; would be the first to take me away. When these thoughts come forcibly upon me, I doubt whether I can remain."

"You must not encourage them," said Nora.

"I don't encourage them; they come in spite of me. The fear comes; it is always coming. Don't say anything at home, Nora. I have made up my mind to stop, and I'll try hard to do it. As soon as I am out of my time I'll go off to India, or somewhere, and forget the old life in the new one."

"My goodness!" uttered Nora. But having no good arguments at hand, she thought it as well to leave him, and took her departure.

The day arrived on which George was to be bound. It was a gloomy November day, and the tall chimneys of Barmester rose dark and dismal against the outlines of the grey sky. The previous night had been hopelessly wet, and the mud in the streets was ankle-deep. People who had no urgent occasion to be abroad, drew closer to their comfortable fire-sides, and wished the dreary month of November was over.

George stood at the door of the shop, having snatched a moment to come to it. A slender, handsome boy, with his earnest eyes and dark chestnut hair, looking far too gentlemanly to belong to that place. Belong to it! Ere the stroke of another hour should have been told on the dial of the church clock of Barmester, he would be irrevocably bound to it—have become as much a part and parcel of it as the silks displayed in its windows, the shawls exhibited in their gay and gaudy colours. As he stood there, he was feeling that no fate on earth was ever so hopelessly dark as his: feeling that he had no friend either in earth or heaven.

One, two; three, four! chimed out over the town through the leaden atmosphere. Half-past eleven! It was the hour fixed for signing the indentures which would bind him to servitude for years; and he, George Ryle, looked to the extremity of the street, expecting the appearance of Mr. Chattaway.

Considering the way in which Mr. Chattaway had urged on the matter, George had thought he would be half-an-hour before the time, rather than five minutes behind it. He looked eagerly to the extremity of the street, at the same time dreading the sight he sought for.

"George Ryle!" The call came ringing in sharp, imperative tones, and he turned in obedience to it. He was told to "measure those trimmings, and card them."

An apparently interminable task. About fifty pieces of ribbon-trimmings, some scores of yards in each piece, all off their cards. George sighed as he singled out one and began upon it—he was terribly awkward at the work.

It advanced slowly. In addition to the inaptitude of his fingers for the task, to his intense natural distaste for it—and so intense was that distaste, that the ribbons felt as if they burnt his fingers—in addition to this, there were frequent interruptions. Any of the shopmen who wanted help called to George Ryle; and once he was told to open the door for a lady who was departing.

As she walked away, George leaned out, and took another gaze. Mr. Chattaway was not in sight. The clocks were then striking a quarter to twelve. A feeling of something like hope, but vague and faint and terribly unreal, dawned over his heart. Could the delay augur good for him?—was it possible that there could be any change?

How unreal it was, the next moment proved. There came round that far corner a horseman at a hand-gallop, his horse's hoofs scattering the mud in all directions. It was Mr. Chattaway. He reined up at the private door of Wall and Barnes, dismounted, and consigned his horse to his groom, who had followed at the same pace. The false, faint hope was over; and George walked back to his cards and his trimmings, as one from whom all spirit has gone out.

A message was brought to him almost immediately by one of the house servants: Squire Chattaway waited in the drawing-room. Squire Chattaway had sent the message himself, not to George, to Mr. Wall; but Mr. Wall was engaged at the moment with a gentleman, and sent the message on to George. George went upstairs.

Mr. Chattaway, in his top boots and spurs, stood warming his hands over the fire. He had not removed his hat. When the door opened, he raised his hand to do so; but seeing it was only George who entered, he left it on. He was much given to the old-fashioned use of boots and spurs when out riding.

"Well, George, how are you?"

George went up to the fireplace. On the centre table, as he passed it, lay an official-looking parchment rolled up, an inkstand by its side. George had not the least doubt that the parchment was no other than that formidable document, his Indentures.

Mr. Chattaway had taken up the same opinion. He extended his riding whip towards the parchment, and spoke in a significant tone, turning his eye on George.

"Ready?"

"It is no use attempting to say I am not," replied George. "I would rather you had forced me to become one of the lowest boys in your coal-mines, Mr. Chattaway."

"What's this?" asked Mr. Chattaway.

He was pointing now to the upper part of the sleeve of George's jacket. Some ravellings of cotton had collected there unnoticed. George took them off, and put them in the fire.

"It is only a badge of my trade, Mr. Chattaway."

Whether Mr. Chattaway detected the bitterness of the words—not the bitterness of sarcasm, but of despair—cannot be told. He laughed pleasantly, and before the laugh was over, Mr. Wall came in. Mr. Chattaway removed his hat now, and laid it with his riding-whip beside the indentures.

"I am later than I ought to be," observed Mr. Chattaway, as they shook hands. "The fact is, I was on the point of starting, when my colliery manager came up. His business was important, and it kept me the best part of an hour."

"Plenty of time; plenty of time," said Mr. Wall. "Take a seat."

They sat down near the table. George, apparently unnoticed, remained standing on the hearth-rug. A few minutes were spent conversing on different subjects, and then Mr. Chattaway turned to the parchment.

"These are the indentures, I presume?"

"Yes."

"I called on Mrs. Ryle last evening. She requested me to say that should her signature be required, as the boy's nearest relative and guardian—as his only parent, it may be said, in fact—she should be ready to affix it at any given time."

"It will not be required," replied Mr. Wall, in a clear voice. "I shall not take George Ryle as an apprentice."

A stolid look of surprise struggled to Mr. Chattaway's leaden face. At first, he scarcely seemed to take in the full meaning of the words. "Not take him?" he rejoined, staring helplessly.

"No. It is a pity these were made out," continued Mr. Wall, taking up the indentures. "It has been so much time and parchment wasted. However, that is not of great consequence. I will be at the loss, as the refusal comes from my side."

Mr. Chattaway found his tongue—found it volubly. "Won't he do? Is he not suitable? I—I don't understand this."

"Not at all suitable, in my opinion," answered Mr. Wall.

Mr. Chattaway turned sharply upon George, a strangely evil look in his dull grey eye, an ominous curl in his thin, dry lip. Mr. Wall likewise turned; but on his face there was a reassuring smile.

And George? George stood there as one in a dream; his face changing to perplexity, his eyes strained, his fingers intertwined with the nervous grasp of emotion.

"What have you been guilty of, sir, to cause this change of intentions?" shouted Mr. Chattaway.

"He has not been guilty of anything," interposed Mr. Wall, who appeared to be enjoying a smile at George's astonishment and Mr. Chattaway's discomfiture. "Don't blame the boy. So far as I know and believe, he has striven to do his best ever since he has been here."

"Then why won't you take him? You *will* take him," added Mr. Chattaway, in a more agreeable voice, as the idea dawned upon him that Mr. Wall had been joking.

"Indeed, I will not. If Mrs. Ryle offered me a thousand pounds premium with him, I should not take him."

Mr. Chattaway's small eyes opened to their utmost width. "And why not?"

"Because, knowing what I know now, I believe that I should be committing an injustice upon the boy; an injustice which nothing could repair. To condemn a youth to pass the best years of his life at an uncongenial pursuit, to make the pursuit his calling, is a cruel injustice wherever it is knowingly inflicted. I myself was a victim to it. My boy," added Mr. Wall, laying his hand on George's shoulder, "you have a marked distaste to the mercery business. Is it not so? Speak out fearlessly. Don't regard me as your master—I shall never be that, you hear—but as your friend."

"Yes, I have," replied George.

"You think it a cruel piece of injustice to have put you to it: you will never more feel an interest in life; you'd as soon be with poor Mr. Ryle in his coffin! And when you are out of your time, you mean to start for India or some out-of-the-world place, and begin life afresh!"

George was too much confused to answer. His face turned scarlet. Undoubtedly Mr. Wall had overheard his conversation with Nora.

Mr. Chattaway was looking red and angry. When his face did turn red, it presented a charming brick-dust hue. "It is only scamps who take a dislike to what they are put to," he exclaimed. "And their dislike is all pretence."

"I differ from you in both propositions," replied Mr. Wall. "At any rate, I do not think it the case with your nephew."

Mr. Chattaway's brick-dust grew deeper. "He is no nephew of mine. What next will you say, Wall?"

"Your step-nephew, then, to be correct," equably rejoined Mr. Wall. "You remember when we left school together, you and I, and began to turn our thoughts to the business of life? Your father wished you to go into the bank as clerk, you know; and mine—"

"But he did not get his wish, more's the luck," again interposed Mr. Chattaway, not pleased at the allusion. "A poor start in life that would have been for the future Squire of Trevlyn Hold."

"Pooh!" rejoined Mr. Wall, in a good-tempered, matter-of-fact tone. "You did not expect then to be exalted to Trevlyn Hold. Nonsense, Chattaway! We are old friends, you know. But, let me continue. I overheard a certain conversation of this boy's with Nora Dickson, and it seemed to bring my own early life back to me. With every word he spoke, I had a fellow-feeling. My father insisted that I should follow the business he was in; this one. He carried on a successful trade for years, in this very house, and nothing would do but I must succeed to it. In vain I urged my repugnance to it, my dislike; in vain I said I had formed other views for myself; I was not listened to. In those days it was not the fashion for sons to run counter to their fathers' will; at least, such was my experience; and into the business I came. I have reconciled myself to it by dint of time and habit; liked it, I never have; and I have always felt that it was—as I heard this boy express it—a cruel wrong to force me into it. You cannot, therefore, be surprised that I decline so to force another. I will never do it knowingly."

"You decline absolutely to take him?" asked Mr. Chattaway.

"Absolutely and positively. He can remain in the house a few days longer if it will suit his convenience, or he can leave to-day. I am not displeased with you," added Mr. Wall, turning to George, and holding out his hand. "We shall part good friends."

George seized it and grasped it, his countenance glowing, a whole world of gratitude shining from his eyes as he lifted them to Mr. Wall. "I shall always think you have been the best friend I ever had, sir, next to my father."

"I hope it will prove so. I trust you will find some pursuit in life more congenial to you than this."

Mr. Chattaway took up his hat and whip. "This will be fine news for your mother, sir!" cried he, severely.

"It may turn out well for her," replied George, boldly. "My belief is the farm never would have got along with John Pinder as manager."

"You think you would make a better?" said Mr. Chattaway, his thin lip curling.

"I can be true to her, at any rate," said George. "And I can have my eyes about me."

"Good morning," resumed Mr. Chattaway to Mr. Wall, putting out unwillingly the tips of two fingers.

Mr. Wall laughed. "I do not see why you should be vexed, Mr. Chattaway. The boy is no son of yours. For myself, all I can say is, that I have been actuated by motives of regard for his interest."

"It remains to be proved whether it will be for his interest," coldly rejoined Mr. Chattaway. "Were I his mother, and this check were dealt out to me, I should send him off to break stones on the road. Good morning, Wall. And I beg you will not bring me here again upon a fool's errand."

George went into the shop, to get from it some personal trifles he had left there. He deemed it well to depart at once, and carry the news home to Mrs. Ryle himself. The cards and trimmings lay in the unfinished state he had left them. What a change, that moment and this! One or two of the employés noticed his radiant countenance.

"Has anything happened?" they asked.

"Yes," answered George. "I have been suddenly lifted into paradise."

He started on his way, leaving his things to be sent after him. His footsteps scarcely touched the ground. Not a rough ridge of the road felt he; not a sharp stone; not a hill. Only when he turned in at the gate did he remember there was his mother's displeasure to be met and grappled with.

Nora gave a shriek when he entered the house. "*George!* What brings you here?"

"Where's my mother?" was George's only answer.

"In the best parlour," said Nora. "And I can tell you she's not in the best of humours just now, so I'd advise you not to go in."

"What about?" asked George, taking it for granted she had heard the news about himself, and that was the grievance. But he was agreeably undeceived.

"It's about John Pinder. He has been having two of the meads ploughed up, and he never asked the missis first. She *is* angry."

"Has Chattaway been here to see my mother, Nora?"

"He came up on horseback in a desperate hurry half-an-hour ago; but she was out on the farm, so he said he'd call again. It was through going out this morning that she discovered what they were about with the fields. She says she thinks John Pinder must be going out of his mind, to take things upon himself in the way he is doing."

George bent his steps to the drawing-room. Mrs. Ryle was seated before her desk, writing a note. The expression of her face as she looked up at George between the white lappets of her widow's cap was resolutely severe. It changed to astonishment.

Strange to say, she was writing to Mr. Wall to stop the signing of the indentures, or to desire that they might be cancelled if signed. She could not do without George at home, she said; and she told him why she could not.

"Mamma," said George, "will you be angry if I tell you something that has struck me in all this?"

"Tell it," said Mrs. Ryle.

"I feel quite certain Chattaway has been acting with a motive; he has some private reason for wishing to get me away from home. That's what he has been working for; otherwise he would never have troubled himself about me. It is not in his nature."

Mrs. Ryle gazed at George steadfastly, as if weighing his words, and presently knit her brow. George could read her countenance tolerably well. He felt sure she had arrived at a similar conclusion, and that it irritated her. He resumed.

"It looks bad for you, mother; but you must not think I say this selfishly. Twenty minutes I have asked myself the question, Why does he wish me away? And I can only think that he would like the farm to go to rack and ruin, so that you may be driven from it."

"Nonsense, George."

"Well, what else can it be?"

"If so, he is defeated," said Mrs. Ryle. "You will take your place as master of the farm from to-day, George, under me. Deferring to me in all things, you understand; giving no orders on your own responsibility, taking my pleasure upon the merest trifle."

"I should not think of doing otherwise," replied George. "I will do my best for you in all ways, mother. You will soon see how useful I can be."

"Very well. But I may as well mention one thing to you. When Treve shall be old enough, it is he who will be master here, and you must resign the place to him. It is not that I wish to set the younger of your father's sons unjustly above the head of the elder. This farm will be a living but for one of you; barely that; and I prefer that Treve should have it; he is my own son. We will endeavour to find a better farm for you before that time shall come."

"Just as you please," said George, cheerfully. "Now that I am emancipated from that dreadful nightmare, my prospects look very bright to me. I'll do the best I can on the farm, remembering that I do it for Treve's future benefit; not for mine. Something else will turn up for me, no doubt, before I'm ready for it."

"Which will not be for some years to come," said Mrs. Ryle, feeling pleased with the boy's acquiescent spirit. "Treve will not be old enough for—"

Mrs. Ryle was interrupted. The door had opened, and there appeared Mr. Chattaway, showing himself in. Nora never affected to be too courteous to that gentleman; and on his coming to the house to ask for Mrs. Ryle a second time, she had curtly answered that Mrs. Ryle was in the best parlour (the more familiar name for the drawing-room in the farmhouse), and allowed him to find his own way to it.

Mr. Chattaway looked surprised at seeing George; he had not bargained for his arriving home so soon. Extending his hand towards him, he turned to Mrs. Ryle.

"There's a dutiful son for you! You hear what he has done?—returned on your hands as a bale of worthless goods."

"Yes, I hear that Mr. Wall has declined to take him," was her composed answer. "It has happened for the best. When he arrived just now, I was writing to Mr. Wall requesting that he might *not* be bound."

"And why?" asked Mr. Chattaway in considerable amazement.

"I find I am unable to do without him," said Mrs. Ryle, her tone harder and firmer than ever; her eyes, stern and steady, thrown full on Chattaway. "I have tried the experiment, and it has failed. I cannot do without one by my side devoted to my interests; and John Pinder cannot get on without a master."

"And do you think you'll find what you want in him!—in that inexperienced schoolboy?" burst forth Mr. Chattaway.

"I do," replied Mrs. Ryle, her tone so significantly decided, as to be almost offensive. "He takes his standing from this day as master of Trevlyn Farm; subject only to me."

"I wish you joy of him!" angrily returned Chattaway. "But you must understand, Mrs. Ryle, that your having a boy at the head of affairs will oblige me to look more keenly after my interests."

"My arrangements with you are settled," she said. "So long as I fulfil my part, that is all that concerns you, James Chattaway."

"You'll not fulfil it, if you put him at the head of things."

"When I fail you can come here and tell me of it. Until then, I prefer that you should not intrude on Trevlyn Farm."

She rang the bell sharply as she spoke, and Molly, who was passing along the passage, immediately appeared. Mrs. Ryle extended her hand imperiously, the forefinger pointed.

"The door for Mr. Chattaway."

CHAPTER X
MADAM'S ROOM

Leading out of Mrs. Chattaway's dressing-room was a comfortable apartment, fitted up as a sitting-room, with chintz hangings and maple-wood furniture. It was called in the household "Madam's Room," and here Mrs. Chattaway frequently sat. Yes; the house and the neighbourhood accorded her readily the title which usage had long given to the mistress of Trevlyn Hold: but they would not give that of "Squire" to her husband. I wish particularly to repeat this. Strive for it as he would, force his personal servants to observe the title as he did, he could not get it recognised or adopted. When a written invitation came to the Hold—a rare event, for the old-fashioned custom of inviting verbally was chiefly followed there—it would be worded, "Mr. and Madam Chattaway," and Chattaway's face would turn green as he read it. No, never! He enjoyed the substantial good of being proprietor of Trevlyn Hold, he received its revenues, he held sway as its lord and master; but its honours were not given to him. It was so much gall and wormwood to Chattaway.

Mrs. Chattaway stood at this window on that dull morning in November mentioned in the last chapter, her eyes strained on the distance. What was she gazing at? Those lodge chimneys?—The dark, almost bare trees that waved to and fro in the wintry wind?—The extensive landscape stretching out in the distance, not fine to-day, but dull and cheerless?—Or on the shifting clouds in the grey skies? Not on any of these; her eyes, though apparently bent on all, in reality saw nothing. They were fixed on vacancy; buried, like her thoughts.

She wore a muslin gown, with dark purple spots upon it; her collar was fastened with a bow of black ribbon, her sleeves were confined with black ribbons at the wrist. She was passing a finger under one of these wrist-ribbons, round and round, as if the ribbon were tight; in point of fact, it was only a proof of her abstraction. Her smooth hair fell in curls on her fair face, and her blue eyes were bright as with a slight touch of inward fever.

Some one opened the door, and peeped in. It was Maude Trevlyn. Her frock was of the same material as Mrs. Chattaway's gown, and a sash of black ribbon encircled her waist. Mrs. Chattaway did not turn, and Maude came forward.

"Are you well to-day, Aunt Edith?"

"Not very, dear." Mrs. Chattaway took the pretty young head within her arm as she answered, and fondly stroked the bright curls. "You have been crying, Maude!"

Maude shook back her curls with a smile, as if she meant to be brave; make light of the accusation. "Cris and Octave went on so shamefully, Aunt Edith, ridiculing George Ryle; and when I took his part, Cris hit me a sharp blow. It was stupid of me to cry, though."

"Cris did?" exclaimed Mrs. Chattaway.

"I know I provoked him," candidly acknowledged Maude. "I'm afraid I flew into a passion; and you know, Aunt Edith, I don't mind what I say when I do that. I told Cris that he would be placed at something not half as good as a linen-draper's some time, for he'd want a living when Rupert came into Trevlyn Hold."

"Maude! Maude! hush!" exclaimed Mrs. Chattaway in tones of terror. "You must not say that."

"I know I must not, Aunt Edith; I know it is wrong; wrong to think it, and foolish to say it. It was my temper. I am very sorry."

She nestled close to Mrs. Chattaway, caressing and penitent. Mrs. Chattaway stooped and kissed her, a strangely marked expression of tribulation, shrinking and hopeless, upon her countenance.

"Oh, Maude! I am so ill!"

Maude felt awed; and somewhat puzzled. "Ill, Aunt Edith?"

"There is an illness of the mind worse than that of the body, Maude. I feel as though I should sink under my weight of care. Sometimes I wonder why I am kept on earth."

"Oh, Aunt Edith!"

A knock at the room door, followed by the entrance of a female servant. She did not observe Mrs. Chattaway; only Maude.

"Is Miss Diana here, Miss Maude?"

"No. Only Madam."

"What is it, Phœbe?" asked Mrs. Chattaway.

"Master Cris wants to know if he can take the gig out, ma'am?"

"I cannot tell anything about it. You must ask Miss Diana. Maude, see; that is your Aunt Diana's step on the stairs now."

Miss Trevlyn came in. "The gig?" she repeated. "No; Cris cannot take it. Go and tell him so, Maude. Phœbe, return to your work."

Maude ran away, and Phœbe went off grumbling, not aloud, but to herself; no one dared grumble in the hearing of Miss Trevlyn. She had spoken in sharp tones to Phœbe, and the girl did not like sharp tones. As Miss Trevlyn sat down opposite Mrs. Chattaway, the feverish state of that lady's countenance arrested her attention.

"What is the matter, Edith?"

Mrs. Chattaway buried her elbow on the sofa-cushion, and pressed her hand to her face, half covering it, before she spoke. "I cannot get over this business," she answered in low tones. "To-day—perhaps naturally—I am feeling it more than is good for me. It makes me ill, Diana."

"What business?" asked Miss Trevlyn.

"This apprenticing of George Ryle."

"Nonsense," said Miss Diana.

"It is not the proper thing for him, Diana; you admitted so yesterday. The boy says it is the blighting of his whole future life; and I feel that it is nothing less. I could not sleep last night for thinking about it. Once I dozed off, and fell into an ugly dream," she shivered. "I thought Mr. Ryle came to me, and asked whether it was not enough that we had heaped care upon him in life, and then sent him to his death, but must also pursue his son."

"You always were weak, you know, Edith," was the composed rejoinder of Miss Trevlyn. "Why Chattaway should be interfering with George Ryle, I cannot understand; but it surely need not give concern to you. The proper person to put a veto on his being placed at Barmester, as he is being placed, was Mrs. Ryle. If she did not think fit to do it, it is no business of ours."

"It seems to me as if he had no one to stand up for him. It seems," added Mrs. Chattaway, with more passion in her tone, "as if his father must be looking down at us, and condemning us."

"If you will worry yourself over it, you must," was the rejoinder of Miss Trevlyn. "It is very foolish, Edith, and it can do no earthly good. He is bound by this time, and the thing is irrevocable."

"Perhaps that is the reason—because it is irrevocable—that it presses upon me to-day with greater weight. It has made me think of the past, Diana," she added in a whisper. "Of that other wrong, which I cheat myself sometimes into forgetting; a wrong—"

"Be silent!" imperatively interrupted Miss Trevlyn, and the next moment Cris Chattaway bounded into the room.

"What's the reason I can't have the gig?" he began. "Who says I can't have it?"

"I do," said Miss Trevlyn.

Cris insolently turned from her, and walked up to Mrs. Chattaway. "May I not take the gig, mother?"

If there was one thing irritated the sweet temper of Mrs. Chattaway, it was being appealed to against any decision of Diana's. She knew that she possessed no power; was a nonentity in the house; and though she bowed to her dependency, and had no resource but to bow to it, she did not like it brought palpably before her.

"Don't apply to me, Cris. I know nothing about things downstairs; I cannot say one way or the other. The horses and vehicles are specially the things that your father will not have meddled with. Do you remember taking out the dog-cart without leave, and the result?"

Cris looked angry; perhaps the reminiscence was not agreeable. Miss Diana interfered.

"You will *not* take out the gig, Cris. I have said it."

"Then see if I don't walk! And if I am not home to dinner, Aunt Diana, you can just tell the Squire the thanks are due to you."

"Where do you wish to go?" asked Mrs. Chattaway.

"I am going to Barmester. I want to wish that fellow joy of his indentures," added Cris, a glow of triumph lighting up his face. "He is bound by this time. I wonder the Squire is not back again!"

The Squire was back again. As Cris spoke, his tread was heard on the stairs, and he came into the room. Cris was too full of his own concerns to note the expression of his face.

"Father, may I take out the gig? I want to go to Barmester, to pay a visit of congratulation to George Ryle."

"No, you will not take out the gig," said Mr. Chattaway, the allusion exciting his anger almost beyond bearing.

Cris thought he might have been misunderstood. Cris deemed that his proclaimed intention would find favour with Mr. Chattaway.

"I suppose you have been binding that fellow, father. I want to go and ask him how he likes it."

"No, sir, I have not been binding him," thundered Mr. Chattaway. "What's more, he is not going to be bound. He has left it, and is at home again."

Cris gave a blank stare of amazement, and Mrs. Chattaway let her hands fall silently upon her lap and heaved a gentle sigh, as though some great good had come to her.

CHAPTER XI
RUPERT

None of us can stand still in life. Everything rolls on its course towards the end of all things. In noting down a family's or a life's history, its periods will be differently marked. Years will glide quietly on, giving forth few events worthy of record; again, it will happen that occurrences, varied and momentous, will be crowded into an incredibly short space of time. Events, sufficient to fill up the allotted life of man, will follow one another in rapid succession in the course of as many months; nay, of as many days.

Thus it was with the Trevlyns, and those connected with them. After the lamentable death of Mr. Ryle, the new agreement touching money-matters between Mr. Chattaway and Mrs. Ryle, and the settling of George Ryle into his own home, it may be said in his father's place, little occurred for some years worthy of note. Time seemed to pass uneventfully. Girls and boys grew into men and women; children into girls and boys. Cris Chattaway lorded it in his own offensive manner as the Squire's son—as the future Squire; his sister Octavia was not more amiable than of yore, and Maude Trevlyn was governess to Mr. and Mrs. Chattaway's younger children. Miss Diana Trevlyn had taken care that Maude should be well educated, and she paid the cost of it out of her own pocket, in spite of Mr. Chattaway's sneers. When Maude was eighteen years of age, the question arose, What shall be done with her? "She shall go out and be a governess," said Mr. Chattaway. "Of what profit her fine education, if it's not to be made use of?" "No," dissented Miss Diana; "a Trevlyn cannot be sent out into the world to earn her own living: our family have not come to that." "I won't keep her in idleness," growled Chattaway. "Very well," said Miss Diana; "make her governess to your girls, Edith and Emily: it will save the cost of schooling." The advice was taken; and Maude for the past three years had been governess at Trevlyn Hold.

But Rupert? Rupert was found not to be so easily disposed of. There's no knowing what Chattaway, in his ill-feeling, might have put Rupert to, had he been at liberty to place him as he pleased. If he had not shown any superfluous consideration in placing out George Ryle—or rather in essaying to place him out—it was not likely he would show it to one whom he hated as he hated Rupert. But here Miss Diana again stepped in. Rupert was a

Trevlyn, she said, and consequently could not be converted into a chimney-sweep or a shoe-black: he must get his living at something befitting his degree. Chattaway demurred, but he knew better than run counter to any mandate issued by Diana Trevlyn.

Several things were tried for Rupert. He was placed with a clergyman to study for the Church; he went to an LL.D. to read for the Bar; he was consigned to a wealthy grazier to be made into a farmer; he was posted off to Sir John Rennet, to be initiated into the science of civil engineering. And he came back from all. As one venture after the other was made, so it failed, and a very short time would see Rupert return as ineligible to Trevlyn Hold. Ineligible! Was he deficient in capacity? No. He was only deficient in that one great blessing, without which life can bring no enjoyment—health. In his weakness of chest—his liability to take cold—his suspiciously delicate frame, Rupert Trevlyn was ominously like his dead father. The clergyman, the doctor, the hearty grazier, and the far-famed engineer, thought after a month's trial they would rather not take charge of him. He had a fit of illness—it may be better to say of weakness—in the house of each; and they, no doubt, one and all, deemed that a pupil predisposed to disease—it may be almost said to death—as Rupert Trevlyn appeared to be, would bring with him too much responsibility.

So, times and again, Rupert was returned on the hands of Mr. Chattaway. To describe that gentleman's wrath would take a pen dipped in gall. Was Rupert *never* to be got rid of? It was like the Eastern slippers which persisted in turning up. And, in like manner, up came Rupert Trevlyn. The boy could not help his ill-health; but you may be sure Mr. Chattaway's favour was not increased by it. "I shall put him in the office at Blackstone," said he. And Miss Diana acquiesced.

Blackstone was the locality where Mr. Chattaway's mines were situated. An appropriate name, for the place was black enough, and stony enough, and dreary enough for anything. A low, barren, level country, its flatness alone broken by signs of the pits, its uncompromising gloom enlivened only by ascending fires which blazed up at night, and illumined the country for miles round. The pits were not all coal: iron mines and other mines were scattered with them. On Chattaway's property, however, there was coal alone. Long rows of houses, as dreary as the barren country, were built near: occupied by the workers in the mines. The overseer or manager for Mr. Chattaway was named Pinder, a brother to John Pinder, who was on Mrs. Ryle's farm: but Chattaway chose to interfere very much with the executive himself, and may almost have been called his own overseer. He had an office near the pits, in which accounts were kept, the men paid, and other business items transacted: a low building, of one storey only, consisting of three or four rooms. In this office he kept one regular clerk, a young man named Ford, and into this same office he put Rupert Trevlyn.

But many and many and many a day was Rupert ailing; weak, sick, feverish, coughing, and unable to go to it. But for Diana Trevlyn, Chattaway might have driven him there ill or well. Not that Miss Diana possessed any extraordinary affection for Rupert: she did not keep him at home out of love, or from motives of indulgence. But hard, cold, and imperious though she was, Miss Diana owned somewhat of the large open-handedness of the Trevlyns: she could not be guilty of trivial spite, or petty meanness. She ruled the servants with an iron hand; but in case of their falling into sickness or trouble, she had them generously cared for. So with respect to Rupert. It may be that she regarded him as an interloper; that she would have been better pleased were he removed elsewhere. She had helped to deprive him of his birthright, but she did not treat him with personal unkindness; and she would have been the last to say he must go out to his daily occupation, if he felt ill or incapable of it. She deplored his ill-health; but, ill health upon him, Miss Diana was not one to ignore it, to reproach him with it, or put hindrances in the way of his being nursed.

It was a tolerably long walk for Rupert in a morning to Blackstone. Cris Chattaway, when he chose to go over, rode on horseback; and Mr. Cris did not infrequently choose to go over, for he had the same propensity as his father—that of throwing himself into every petty detail, and interfering unwarrantably. In disposition, father and son were alike—mean, stingy, grasping. To save a sixpence, Chattaway would almost have sacrificed a miner's life. Improvements which other mine owners had introduced into their pits, into the working of them, Chattaway held aloof from. In his own person, however, Cris was not disposed to be saving. He had his horse, and he had his servant, and he favoured an extensive wardrobe, and was given altogether to various little odds and ends of self-indulgence.

Yes, Cris Chattaway rode to Blackstone; with his groom behind him sometimes, when he chose to make a dash; and Rupert Trevlyn walked. Better that the order of travelling had been reversed, for that walk, morning and evening, was not too good for Rupert in his weakly state. He would feel it particularly in an evening. It was a gradual ascent nearly all the way from Blackstone to Trevlyn Hold, almost imperceptible to a strong man, but sufficiently apparent to Rupert Trevlyn, who would be fatigued with the day's work.

Not that he had hard work to do. But even sitting on the office stool tired him. Another thing that tired him—and which, no doubt, was excessively bad for him—was the loss of his regular meals. Excepting on Sundays, or on days when he was not well enough to leave Trevlyn Hold, he had no dinner: what he had at Blackstone was only an apology for one. The clerk, Ford, who lived at nearly as great a distance from the place as Rupert, used to cook himself a chop or steak at the office grate. But that the coals were lying about in heaps and cost nothing, Chattaway might have objected to the fire being used for such a purpose. Rupert occasionally cooked himself some meat; but he more frequently dined upon bread and cheese, or scraps brought from Trevlyn Hold. It was not often that Rupert had the money to buy meat or anything else, his supply of that indispensable commodity, the current coin of the realm, being very limited. Deprived of his dinner, deprived of his tea—tea being generally over when he got back to the Hold—that, of itself, was almost sufficient to bring on the disease feared for Rupert Trevlyn. One sound in constitution, revelling in health and strength, might not have been much the worse in the long-run; but Rupert did not come under the head of that favoured class of humanity.

It was a bright day in that mellow season when summer is merging into autumn. A few fields of the later grain were lying out yet, but most of the golden store had been gathered into barns. The sunlight glistened on the leaves of the trees, lighting up their rich tints of brown and red—tints which never come until the season of passing away.

Halting at a stile which led to a field white with stubble, were two children and a young lady. Not very young children, either, for the younger of the two must have been thirteen. Pale girls both, with light hair, and just now a disagreeable expression of countenance. They were insisting upon crossing that stile to pass through the field: one of them, in fact, had already mounted, and they did not like to be thwarted in their wish.

"You cross old thing!" cried she on the stile. "You always object to our going where we want to go. What dislike have you to the field, pray, that we may not cross it?"

"I have no dislike to it, Emily. I am only obeying your father's injunctions. You know he has forbidden you to go on Mrs. Ryle's lands."

She spoke in calm tones; a sweet, persuasive voice. She had a sweet and gentle face, too, with delicate features, and large blue eyes. It is Maude Trevlyn. Eight years have passed since you last saw her, and she is twenty-one. In spite of her girlish, graceful figure, which scarcely reaches middle height, she bears a look of the Trevlyns. Her head is well set upon her shoulders, thrown somewhat back, as you may see in Miss Diana Trevlyn. She wears a grey flowing cloak, and pretty blue bonnet.

"The lands are not Mrs. Ryle's," retorted the girl on the stile. "They are papa's."

"They are Mrs. Ryle's as long as she rents them. It is all the same. Mr. Chattaway has forbidden you to cross them. Come down from the stile, Emily."

"No. I shall jump over it."

It was ever thus. Except in the presence of Miss Diana Trevlyn, the girls were openly rude and disobedient to Maude. Expected to teach them, she was denied the ordinary authority vested in a governess. And Maude could not emancipate herself: she must suffer and submit.

Emily Chattaway put her foot over the top bar of the stile, preparatory to jumping over it, when the sound of a horse was heard, and she turned her head. Riding along the lane at a quick pace was a gentleman of some three or four-and-twenty years: a tall man, as far as could be seen, who sat his horse well. He reined in when he saw them, and bent down a pleasant face, with a pleasant smile upon it. The sun shone into his fine dark eyes, as he stooped to shake hands with Maude.

Maude's cheeks had turned crimson. "Quite well," she stammered, in answer to his greeting, somewhat losing her self-possession. "When did you return home?"

"Last night. I was away two days only, instead of the four anticipated. Emily, you'll fall backwards if you don't mind."

"No, I sha'n't," said Emily. "Why did you not stay longer?"

"I found Treve away when I reached Oxford, so I came back again, and got home last night—to Nora's discomfiture."

Maude looked into his face with a questioning glance. She had quite recovered her self-possession. "Why?" she asked.

George Ryle laughed. "Nora had turned my bedroom inside out, and accused me, in her vexation, of coming back on purpose."

"Where did you sleep?" asked Emily.

"In Treve's room. Take care, Edith!"

Maude hastily drew back Edith Chattaway, who had gone too near the horse. "How is Mrs. Ryle?" asked Maude. "We heard yesterday she was not well."

"She is suffering from a cold. I have scarcely seen her. Maude," leaning down and whispering, "are things any brighter than they were?"

Again the soft colour came into her face, and she threw him a glance from her dark blue eyes. If ever glance spoke of indignation, hers did. "What change can there be?" she breathed. "Rupert is ill again," she added in louder tones.

"Rupert!"

"At least, he is not well, and is at home to-day. But he is better than he was yesterday—"

"Here comes Octave," interrupted Emily.

George Ryle gathered up his reins. Shaking hands with Maude, he said a hasty good-bye to the other two, and cantered down the lane, lifting his hat to Miss Chattaway, who was coming up from a distance.

She was advancing quickly across the common, behind the fence on the other side of the lane. A tall, thin young woman, looking her full age of four or five-and-twenty, with the same leaden complexion as of yore, and the disagreeably sly grey eyes. She wore a puce silk paletot, and a brown hat trimmed with black lace; an unbecoming costume for one so tall.

"That was George Ryle!" she exclaimed, as she came up. "What brings him back already?"

"He found his brother away when he reached Oxford," was Maude's reply.

"I think he was very rude not to stop and speak to you, Octave," observed Emily Chattaway. "He saw you coming."

Octave made no reply. She mounted the stile and gazed after the horseman, apparently to see what direction he would take on reaching the end of the lane. Patiently watching, she saw him turn into another lane, which branched off to the left. Octave Chattaway jumped over the stile, and went swiftly across the field.

"She's gone to meet him," was Emily's comment.

It was precisely what Miss Chattaway *had* gone to do. Passing through a copse after quitting the field, she emerged from it just as George was riding quietly past. He halted and stopped to shake hands, as he had done with Maude.

"You are out of breath, Octave. Have you been hastening to catch me?"

"I need not have done so but for your gallantry in riding off the moment you saw me," she answered, resentfully.

"I beg your pardon. I did not know you wanted me. And I am in a hurry."

"It seems so—stopping to speak so long to the children and Maude," she returned, with irony. And George Ryle's laugh was a conscious one.

Latent antagonism was seated in the minds of both, and a latent consciousness of it running through their hearts. When George Ryle saw Octave hastening across the common, he knew she was speeding to reach him ere he should be gone; when Octave saw him ride away, a voice whispered that he did so to avoid meeting her; and each felt that their secret thoughts and motives were known to the other. Yes, there was constant antagonism between them; if the word may be applied to Octave Chattaway, who had learnt to value the society of George Ryle more highly than was good for her. Did he so value hers? Octave wore out her heart, hoping for it. But in the midst of her unwise love for him, her never-ceasing efforts to be in his presence, near to him, there constantly arose the bitter conviction that he did not care for her.

"I wished to ask you about the book you promised to get me," she said. "Have you procured it?"

"No; and I am sorry to say that I cannot meet with it," replied George. "I thought of it at Oxford, and went into nearly every bookseller's shop in the place, unsuccessfully. I told you it was difficult to find. I must get them to write to London for it from Barmester."

"Will you come to the Hold this evening?" she asked, as he was riding away.

"Thank you. I am not sure that I can. My day or two's absence has made me busy."

Octave Chattaway drew back under cover of the trees and halted: never retreating until every trace of that fine young horseman had passed out of sight.

CHAPTER XII
UNANSWERED

It is singular to observe how lightly the marks of Time occasionally pass over the human form and face. An instance of this might be seen in Mrs. Chattaway. It was strange that it should be so in her case. Her health was not good, and she certainly was not a happy woman. Illness was frequently her portion; care ever seemed to follow her; and it is upon these sufferers in mind and body that Time is fond of leaving his traces. He had not left them on Mrs. Chattaway; her face was fair and fresh as it had been eight years ago; her hair fell in its mass of curls; her eyes were still blue, and clear, and bright.

And yet anxiety was her constant companion. It may be said that remorse never left her. She would sit at the window of her room upstairs—Madam's room—for hours, apparently contemplating the outer world; in reality seeing nothing.

As she was sitting now. The glories of the bright day had faded into twilight; the sun no longer lit up the many hues of the autumn foliage; all the familiar points in the landscape had faded to indistinctness; old Canham's lodge chimneys were becoming obscure, and the red light from the mines and works was beginning to show out on the right in the extreme distance. Mrs. Chattaway leaned her elbow on the old-fashioned armchair, and rested her cheek upon her hand. Had you looked at her eyes, gazing out so upon the fading landscape, you might have seen that they were deep in the world of thought.

That constitutional timidity of hers had been nothing but a blight to her throughout life. Reticence in a woman is good; but not that timid, shrinking reticence which is the result of fear; which dare not speak up for itself, even to oppose a wrong. Every wrong inflicted upon Rupert Trevlyn—every unkindness shown him—every pang, whether of mind or body, which happier circumstances might have spared him, was avenged over and over again in the person of Mrs. Chattaway. It may be said that she lived only in pain; her life was one never-ending sorrow—sorrow for Rupert.

In the old days, when her husband had chosen to deceive Squire Trevlyn as to the existence of Rupert, she had not dared to avow the truth, and say to her father, "There is an heir born." She dared not fly in the face of her husband, and say it; and, it may be, that she was too willingly silent for her husband's sake. It would seem strange, but that we know what fantastic tricks our passions play us, that pretty, gentle Edith Trevlyn should have *loved* that essentially disagreeable man, James Chattaway. But so it was. And, while deploring the fact of the wrong dealt out to Rupert—it may almost be said *expiating* it—Mrs. Chattaway never visited that wrong upon her husband, even in thought, as it ought to have been visited. None could realise more intensely its consequences than she realised them in her secret heart. Expiate it? Ay, she expiated it again and again, if her sufferings could only have been reckoned as atonement.

But they could not. *They* were enjoying Trevlyn Hold and its advantages, and Rupert was little better than an outcast on the face of the earth. Every dinner put upon their table, every article of attire bought for their children, every honour or comfort their position brought them, seemed to rise up reproachfully before the face of Mrs. Chattaway, and say, "The money to procure all this is not yours and your husband's; it is stolen from Rupert." And she could do nothing to remedy it; could only wage ever-constant battle with the knowledge, and the sting it brought. No remedy existed. They had not come into the inheritance by legal fraud; had succeeded to it fairly and openly, according to the will of Squire Trevlyn. If the whole world ranged itself on Rupert's side, pressing that the property should be resigned to him, Mr. Chattaway had only to point to the will, and say, "You cannot act against that."

It may be that this very fact brought remorse home with greater force to Mrs. Chattaway. It may be that incessantly dwelling upon it caused a morbid state of feeling, which increased the malady. Certain it is, that night and day the wrongs of Rupert pressed on her mind. She loved him with that strange intensity which brings an aching to the heart. When the baby orphan was brought home to her from its foreign birthplace, with its rosy cheeks and its golden curls—when it put out its little arms to her, and gazed at her with its large blue eyes, her heart went out to it there and then, and she caught it to her with a love more passionate than any ever given to her own children. The irredeemable wrong inflicted on the unconscious child, fixed itself on her conscience in that hour, never to be lifted from it.

If ever a woman lived a dual life, that woman was Mrs. Chattaway. Her true aspect—that in which she saw herself as she really was—was as different from the one presented to the world as light from darkness. Do not blame her. It was difficult to help it. The world and her own family saw in Mrs. Chattaway a weak, gentle, apathetic woman, who did not take upon herself even the ordinary authority of the head of a household. They little imagined that that weak woman, remarkable for nothing but indifference, passed her days in sadness, in care, in thought. The hopeless timidity (inherited from her mother) which had been her bane in former days, was her bane still. She had not dared to rise up against her husband when the wrong was inflicted upon Rupert Trevlyn; she did not dare openly rise up now against the petty tyrannies daily dealt out to him. There may have been a latent consciousness in her mind that if she did interfere it would not change things for the better, and might make them worse for Rupert. Probably it would have done so.

There were many things she could have wished for Rupert, and went so far as to hint some of them to Mr. Chattaway. She wished he could be altogether relieved from Blackstone; she wished greater indulgences for him at home; she wished he might be transported to a warmer climate. A bare suggestion she dropped, once in a way, to Mr. Chattaway, but they fell unheeded on his ear. He replied to the hint of the warmer climate with a prolonged stare and a demand as to what romantic absurdity she could be thinking of. Mrs. Chattaway had never mentioned it again. In these cases of constitutional timidity, a rebuff, be it ever so slight, is sufficient to close the lips for ever. Poor lady! she would have sacrificed her own comfort to give peace and comfort to the unhappy Rupert. He was miserably put upon; treated with less consideration than the servants; made to feel his dependent state daily and hourly by petty annoyances; and yet she could not openly interfere!

Even now, as she sat watching the deepening shades, she was dwelling on this; resenting it in her heart, for his sake. It was the evening of the day when the girls had met George Ryle in the lane. She could hear sounds of merriment downstairs from her children and their visitors, and felt sure Rupert did not make one of them. It had long been the pleasure of Cris and Octave to exclude Rupert from the evening gatherings of the family, as far as they could do so; and if, through the presence of herself or Miss Diana, they could not absolutely deny his entrance, they treated him with studied indifference. She sat on, revolving these bitter thoughts in the gloom, until roused by the entrance of an intruder.

It was Rupert himself. He approached Mrs. Chattaway, and she fondly threw her arm round him, and drew him down to a chair by her side. Only when they were alone could she show him these marks of affection, or prove to him that he did not stand in the world entirely isolated from all love.

"Do you feel better to-night, Rupert?"

CHAPTER XIII
OPINIONS DIFFER

The nights were chilly in the early autumn, and a blazing fire lighted up the drawing-room at Trevlyn Farm. On a comfortable sofa, drawn close to it, sat Mrs. Ryle, a warm shawl thrown over her black silk gown—soft cushions heaped around her. A violent cold had made an invalid of her for some days past, but she was recovering. Her face was softened by a white cap of delicate lace; but its lines had grown haughtier and firmer with her years. She wore well, and was handsome still.

Trevlyn Farm had prospered. It was a lucky day for Mrs. Ryle when she decided upon her step-son's remaining on it. He had brought energy and goodwill to bear on his work; a clear head and calm intelligence; and time had contributed judgment and experience. Mrs. Ryle knew that she could not have been more faithfully served, and gradually grew to feel his value. Had they been really mother and son, they could not have been better friends. In the beginning she was inclined to discountenance sundry ways and habits George favoured. He did not turn himself into a *working* farmer, as his father had done, and as Mrs. Ryle thought he ought to do. George objected. A man who worked on his own farm must give it a less general supervision, he urged: and after all, it was only the cost of an additional day-labourer. His argument carried reason with it; and keen and active Farmer Apperley, who deemed idleness the greatest sin (next, perhaps, to hunting) a young farmer could commit, nodded approval. George did not put aside his books; his classics, and his studies in general literature; quite the contrary. In short, George Ryle appeared to be going in for a gentleman—as Cris Chattaway chose to term it—a great deal more than Mrs. Ryle considered would be profitable for him or for her. But George had held on his course, in a quiet, undemonstrative way; and Mrs. Ryle had at length fallen in with it. Perhaps she now saw its wisdom. That he was essentially a gentleman, in person and manners, in mind and conduct, she could only acknowledge, and she felt a pride in him she had never dreamed she should feel for any one but Treve.

Could she feel pride in Treve? Not much, with all her partiality. Trevlyn Ryle was not turning out quite satisfactorily. There was nothing very objectionable to be urged against him; but Mrs. Ryle was accustomed to measure by a high standard of excellence; and of that Treve fell exceedingly short. She had not deemed it well that George Ryle should be too much of a gentleman, but she had determined Trevlyn should be one. Upon the completion of his school life, he was sent to Oxford. The cost might have been imprudently heavy for Mrs. Ryle, had she borne it unassisted; but Trevlyn had gained a scholarship at Barmester Grammar School, and the additional cost was light. Treve, once at Oxford, did not get on quite so fast as he might have done. Treve spent; Treve seemed to have plenty of wild-oats to sow; Treve thought he should like a life of idleness better than farming. His mother had foolishly whispered the fond hope that he might some time be owner of Trevlyn Hold, and Treve reckoned upon its fulfilment more confidently than was good for him. Meanwhile, until the lucky chance arrived which should give him the inheritance (though by what miracle the chance was to fall was at present hidden in the womb of mystery), Treve, upon leaving college, was to assume the mastership of Trevlyn Farm, in accordance with the plan originally decided upon by Mrs. Ryle. He would not be altogether unqualified for this: having been about the farm since he was a child, and seen how it should be worked. Whether he would give sufficient personal attention to it was another matter.

Mrs. Ryle expressed herself as not being too confident of him—whether of his industry or qualifications she did not state. George had given one or two hints that when Treve came home for good, he must look out for something else; but Mrs. Ryle had waived away the hints as if they were unpleasant to her. Treve must prove what metal he was made of, before assuming the management, she briefly said. And George suffered the subject to drop.

Treve had now but one more term to keep at the university. At the conclusion of the previous term he had not returned home: remaining on a visit to a friend, who had an appointment in one of the colleges. But Treve's demand for money had become somewhat inconvenient to Mrs. Ryle, and she had begged George to pay Oxford a few days' visit, that he might see how Treve was really going on. George complied, and proceeded to Oxford, where he found Treve absent—as in the last chapter you heard him say to Maude Trevlyn.

Mrs. Trevlyn sat by the drawing-room fire, enveloped in her shawl, and supported by her pillows. The thought of these things was bringing a severe look to her proud face. She had scarcely seen George since his return; had not exchanged more than ten words with him. But those ten words had not been of a cheering nature; and she feared things were not going on satisfactorily with Treve. With that hard look on her features, how wonderfully her face resembled that of her dead father!

Presently George came in. Mrs. Ryle looked up eagerly at his entrance.

"Are you better?" he asked, advancing, and bending with a kindly smile. "It is long since you had such a cold as this."

"I shall be all right in a day or two," she answered. "Yesterday I thought I was going to have a long illness, my chest was so painful. Sit down, George. What about Treve?"

"Treve was not at Oxford. He had gone to London."

"You told me so. What had he gone there for?"

"A little change, Ferrars said. He had been gone a week."

"A little change? In plain English, a little pleasure, I suppose. Call it what you will, it costs money."

George had seated himself opposite to her, his arm resting on the centre table, and the red blaze lighting up his frank, pleasant face. In figure he was tall and slight; his father, at his age, had been so before him.

"Why did you not follow him to London?" resumed Mrs. Ryle. "It would have been less than a two hours' journey from Oxford."

George turned his large dark eyes upon her, some surprise in them. "How was I to know where to look for him, if I had gone?"

"Could Mr. Ferrars not give you his address?"

"No. I asked him. Treve had not told him where he should put up. In fact, Ferrars did not think Treve knew himself. Under these circumstances, my going to town would have been only waste of time and money."

"It is of no use your keeping things from me," resumed Mrs. Ryle, after a pause. "Has Treve contracted fresh debts at Oxford?"

"I fancy he has. A few."

"A 'few'—and you 'fancy!' George, tell me the truth. That you know he has, and that they are not a few."

"That he has, I believe to be true: I gathered as much from Ferrars. But I do not think they are serious; I do not indeed."

"Why did you not inquire? I would have gone to every shop in the town, in order to ascertain. If he is contracting more debts, who is to pay them?"

George was silent.

"When shall we be clear of Chattaway?" she abruptly resumed. "When will the last payment be due?"

"In a month or two's time. Principal and interest will all be paid off then."

"It will take all your efforts to make up the sum."

"It will be ready, mother. It shall be."

"I don't doubt it. But it will not be ready, George, if a portion is to be taken from it for Treve."

George knit his brow. He was falling into thought.

"I *must* get rid of Chattaway," she resumed. "He has been weighing us down all these years like an incubus; and now that emancipation has nearly come, were anything to delay it, I should—I think I should go mad."

"I hope and trust nothing will delay it," answered George. "I am more anxious to get rid of Chattaway than, I think, even you can be. As to Treve, his debts must wait."

"But it would be more desirable that he should not contract them."

"Of course. But how are we to prevent his contracting them?"

"He ought to prevent it himself. *You* did not contract debts."

"I!" he rejoined, in surprise. "I had no opportunity of doing so. Work and responsibility were thrown upon me before I was old enough to think of pleasure: and they kept me steady."

"You were not naturally inclined to spend, George."

"There's no knowing what I might have acquired, had I been sent out into the world, as Treve has," he rejoined.

"It was necessary that Treve should go to college," said Mrs. Ryle, quite sharply.

"I am not saying anything to the contrary," George quietly answered. "It was right that he should go—as you wished it."

"I shall live—I hope I shall live—I pray that I may live—to see Trevlyn lawful possessor of the Hold. A gentleman's education was essential to him: hence I sent him to Oxford."

George made no reply. Mrs. Ryle felt vexed. She knew George disapproved her policy in regard to Trevlyn, and charged him with it now. George would not deny it.

"What I think unwise is your having led Treve to build hopes upon succeeding to Trevlyn Hold," he said.

"Why?" she haughtily asked. "He will come into it."

"I do not see how."

"He has far more right to it than he who is looked upon as its successor—Cris Chattaway," she said, with flashing eyes. "You know that."

George could have answered that neither of them had a just right to it, whilst Rupert Trevlyn lived; but Rupert and his claims had been so completely ignored by Mrs. Ryle, as by others, that his advancing them would have been waived away as idle talk. Mrs. Ryle resumed, her voice unsteady. It was most rare that she suffered herself to speak of these past grievances; but when she did, her vehemence mounted to agitation.

"When my boy was born, the news that Joe Trevlyn's health was failing had come home to us. I knew the Squire would never leave the property to Maude, and I expected that my son would inherit. Was it not natural that I should do so?—was it not his right?—I was the Squire's eldest daughter. I had him named Trevlyn; I wrote a note to my father, saying he would not now be at fault for a male heir, in the event of poor Joe's not leaving one—"

"He did leave one," interrupted George, speaking impulsively.

"Rupert was not born then, and his succession was afterwards barred by my father's will. Through deceit, I grant you: but I had no hand in that deceit. I named my boy Trevlyn; I regarded him as the heir; and when the Squire died and his will was opened, it was found he had bequeathed all to Chattaway. If you think I have ever once faltered in my hope—my resolve—to see Trevlyn some time displace the Chattaways, you do not know much of human nature."

"I grant what you say," replied George; "that, of the two, Trevlyn has more right to it than Cris Chattaway. But has it ever occurred to you to ask, *how* Cris is to be displaced?"

Mrs. Ryle did not answer. She sat beating her foot upon the ottoman, as one whose mind is not at ease. George continued:

"It appears to me the wildest possible fallacy, the bare idea of Trevlyn's being able to displace Cris Chattaway in the succession. If we lived in the barbarous ages, when inheritances were wrested by force of arms, when the turn of a battle decided the ownership of a castle, then there might be a chance that Cris might lose Trevlyn Hold. As it is, there is none. There is not the faintest shadow of a chance that it can go to any one beside Cris. Failing his death—and he is strong and healthy—he *must* succeed. Why, even were Rupert—forgive my alluding to him again—to urge *his* claims, there would be no hope for him. Mr. Chattaway legally holds the estate; he has willed it to his son; and that son cannot be displaced by others."

Her foot beat more impatiently; a heavier line settled on her brow. Often and often had the arguments now stated by her step-son occurred to her aching brain. George spoke again.

"And therefore, the improbability—I may say the impossibility—of Treve's ever succeeding renders it unwise that he should have been taught to build upon it. Far better, mother, the thought had never been so much as whispered to him."

"Why do you look at it in this unfavourable light?" she cried angrily.

"Because it is the correct light. The property is Mr. Chattaway's—legally his, and it cannot be taken from him. It will be Cris's after him. It is simply madness to think otherwise."

"Cris may die," said Mrs. Ryle sharply.

"If Cris died to-morrow, Treve would be no nearer succession. Chattaway has daughters, and would will it to each in turn rather than to Treve. He can will it away as he pleases. It was left to him absolutely."

"My father was mad when he made such a will in favour of Chattaway! He could have been nothing less. I have thought so many times."

"But it was made, and cannot now be altered. Will you pardon me for saying that it would have been better had you accepted the state of affairs, and endeavoured to reconcile yourself to them?"

"*Better?*"

"Yes; much better. To rebel against what cannot be remedied can only do harm. I would a great deal rather Treve succeeded to Trevlyn Hold than Cris Chattaway: but I know Treve never will succeed: and, therefore, it is a pity it was ever suggested to him. He might have settled down more steadily had he never become possessed of the idea that he might some time supersede Cris Chattaway."

"He *shall* supersede him—"

The door opened to admit a visitor, and he who entered was no other than Rupert Trevlyn. Ignore his claims as she would, Mrs. Ryle felt it would not be seemly to discuss before him Treve's chance of succession. She had in truth completely put from her all thought of the claims of Rupert. He had been deprived of his right by Squire Trevlyn's will, and there was an end to it. Mrs. Ryle rather liked Rupert; or, it may be better to say, she did not *dis*like him; really to like any one except Treve, was not in her nature. She liked Rupert in a negative sort of way; but would not have helped him to his inheritance by lifting a finger. In the event of her possessing no son to be jealous for, she might have taken up the wrongs of Rupert—just to thwart Chattaway.

"Why, Rupert," said George, rising, and cordially shaking hands, "I heard you were ill again. Maude told me so to-day."

"I am better to-night. Aunt Ryle, they said you were in bed."

"I am better, too, Rupert. What has been the matter with you?"

"Oh, my chest again," said Rupert, pushing the waving hair from his bright and delicate face. "I could hardly breathe this morning."

"Ought you to have come out to-night?"

"I don't think it matters," carelessly answered Rupert. "For all I see, I am as well when I go out as when I don't. There's not much to stay in for, there."

Painfully susceptible to cold, he edged himself closer to the hearth with a slight shiver. George took the poker and stirred the fire, and the blaze went flashing up, playing on the familiar objects of the room, lighting up the slender figure, the well-formed features, the large blue eyes of Rupert, and bringing out all the signs of constitutional delicacy. The transparent fairness of complexion and the bloom of the cheeks, might have whispered a warning.

"Octave thought you were going up there to-night, George."

"Did she?"

"The two Beecroft girls are there, and they turned me out of the drawing-room. Octave said 'I wasn't wanted.' Will you play chess to-night, George?"

"If you like; after supper."

"I must be home by half-past ten, you know. I was a minute over the half-hour the other night, and one of the servants opened the door for me. Chattaway pretty nearly rose the roof off, he was so angry; but he could not decently turn me out again."

"Chattaway is master of Trevlyn Hold for the time being," remarked Mrs. Ryle. "Not Squire; never Squire"—she broke off, straying abruptly from her subject, and as abruptly resuming it. "You will do well to obey him, Rupert. When I make a rule in this house, I *never permit it to be broken.*"

A valuable hint, if Rupert had only taken it for guidance. He meant well: he never meant, for all his light and careless speaking, to disobey Mr. Chattaway's mandate. And yet it happened that very night!

The chess-board was attractive, and the time slipped on to half-past ten. Rupert said a hasty good night, snatched up his hat, tore through the entrance-room and made the best speed his lungs allowed him to Trevlyn Hold. His heart was beating as he gained it, and he rang that peal at the bell which had sent its echoes through the house; through the trembling frame and weak heart of Mrs. Chattaway.

He rang—and rang. There came back no sign that the ring was heard. A light shone in Mrs. Chattaway's dressing-room; and Rupert took up some gravel, and gently threw it against the window. No response was accorded in answer to it; not so much as the form of a hand on the blind; the house, in its utter stillness, might have been the house of the dead. Rupert threw up some more gravel as silently as he could.

He had not to wait very long this time. Cautiously, slowly, as though the very movement feared being heard, the blind was drawn aside, and the face of Mrs. Chattaway appeared looking down at him. He could see that she had not begun to undress. She shook her head; raised her hands and clasped them with a gesture of despair; and her lips formed themselves into the words, "I may not let you in."

He could not hear the words, but read the expression of the whole all too clearly—Chattaway would not suffer him to be admitted. Mrs. Chattaway, dreading possibly that her husband might cast his eyes within her dressing-room, quietly let the blind fall again, and removed her shadow from the window.

What was Rupert to do? Lie on the grass that skirted the avenue, and take his night's rest under the trees in the freezing air and night dews? A strong frame, revelling in superfluous health, might possibly risk that; but not Rupert Trevlyn.

A momentary thought come over him that he would go back to Trevlyn Farm, and ask for a night's shelter there. He would have done so, but for the recollection of Mrs. Ryle's stern voice and sterner face when she remarked that, as he knew the rule made for his going in, he must not break it. Rupert had never got on too cordially with Mrs. Ryle. He remembered shrinking from her haughty face when he was a child; and somehow he shrank from it still. No; he would not knock them up at Trevlyn Farm.

What must he do? Should he walk about until morning? Suddenly a thought came to him—were the Canhams in bed? If not, he could go there, and lie on their settle. The Canhams never went to bed very early. Ann Canham sat up to lock the great gate—it was Chattaway's pleasure that it should not be done until after ten o'clock; and old Canham liked to sit up, smoking his pipe.

With a brisk step, now that he had decided on his course, Rupert walked down the avenue. At the first turning he ran against Cris Chattaway, who was coming leisurely up it.

"Oh, Cris! I am so glad! You'll let me in. They have shut me out to-night."

"Let you in!" repeated Cris. "I can't."

Rupert's blue eyes opened in the starlight. "Have you not your latch-key?"

"What should hinder me?" responded Cris. "*I'm* going in; but I can't let you in."

"Why not?" hotly asked Rupert.

"I don't choose to fly in the Squire's face. He has ordered you to be in before half-past ten, or not to come in at all. It has gone half-past ten long ago: is hard upon eleven."

"If you can go in after half-past ten, why can't I?" cried Rupert.

"It's not my affair," said Cris, with a yawn. "Don't bother. Now look here. It's of no use following me, for I shall not let you in."

"Yes you will, Cris."

"*I will not,*" responded Cris, emphatically. Rupert's temper was getting up.

"Cris, I wouldn't show myself such a hangdog sneak as you to be made king of England. If every one had their rights, Trevlyn Hold would be mine, to shut you out of it if I pleased. But I wouldn't please. If only a dog were turned out of his kennel at night, I would let him into the Hold for shelter."

Cris put his latch-key into the lock. "*I* don't turn you out. You must settle that question with the Squire. Keep off. If he says you may be let in at eleven, well and good; but I'm not going to encourage you in disobeying orders."

He opened the door a few inches, wound himself in, and shut it in Rupert's face. He made a great noise in putting up the bar, which was not in the least necessary. Rupert had given him his true appellation—that of sneak. He was one: a false-hearted, plausible, cowardly sneak. As he stood at a table in the hall, and struck a match to light his candle, his puny face and dull light eyes betrayed the most complaisant enjoyment.

He went upstairs smiling. He had to pass the angle of the corridor where his mother's rooms were situated. She glided silently out as he was going by. Her dress was off, and she had apparently thrown a shawl over her shoulders to come out to Cris: an old-fashioned spun-silk shawl, with a grey border and white centre: not so white, however, as the face of Mrs. Chattaway.

"Cris!" she said, laying her hand upon his arm, and speaking in the most timid whisper, "why did you not let him in?"

"I thought we had been ordered not to let him in," returned he of the deceitful nature. "*I* have been ordered, I know that."

"You might have done it just for once, Cris," his mother answered. "I know not what will become of him, out of doors this sharp night."

Cris disengaged his arm, and continued his way up to his room. He slept on the upper floor. Maude was standing at the door of her chamber when he passed—as Mrs. Chattaway had been.

"Cris—wait a minute," she said, for he was hastening by. "I want to speak a word to you. Have you seen Rupert?"

"Seen him and heard him too," boldly avowed Cris. "He wanted me to let him in."

"Which, of course, you would not do?" answered Maude, bitterly. "I wonder if you ever performed a good-natured action in your life?"

"Can't remember," mockingly retorted Cris.

"Where is Rupert? What is he going to do?"

"You know where he is as well as I do: I suppose you could hear him. As to what he is going to do, I didn't ask him. Roost in a tree with the birds, perhaps."

Maude retreated into her room and closed the door. She flung herself into a chair, and burst into a passionate flood of tears. Her heart ached for her brother with pain that amounted to agony: she could have forced down her proud spirit and knelt to Mr. Chattaway for him: almost have sacrificed her own life to bring comfort to Rupert, whom she loved so well.

He—Rupert—stamped off when the door was closed against him, feeling he would like to stamp upon Cris himself. Arrived in front of the lodge, he stood and whistled, and presently Ann Canham looked from the upper casement in her nightcap.

"Why, it's never you, Master Rupert!" she exclaimed, in intense surprise.

"They have locked me out, Ann. Can you manage to come down and open the door without disturbing your father? If you can, I'll lie on the settle for to-night."

Once inside, there ensued a contest. In her humble way, begging pardon for the presumption, Ann Canham proposed that Master Rupert should occupy her room, and she'd make herself contented with the settle. Rupert would not hear of it. He threw himself on the narrow bench they called the settle, and protested that if Ann said another word about giving up her room, he would go out and spend the night in the avenue. So she was fain to go back to it herself.

A dreary night on that hard bench; and the morning found him cold and stiff. He was stamping one foot on the floor to stamp life into it, when old Canham entered, leaning on a crutch. Ann had told him the news, and the old man was up before his time.

"But who shut you out, Master Rupert?" he asked.

"Chattaway."

"Ann says Mr. Cris went in pretty late last night. After she had locked the big gate."

"Cris came up whilst I was ringing to be let in. He went in himself, but would not let me enter."

"He's a reptile," said old Canham in his anger. "Eh me!" he added, sitting down with difficulty in his armchair, and extending the crutch before him, "what a mercy it would have been if Mr. Joe had lived! Chattaway would never have been stuck up in authority then. Better the Squire had left Trevlyn Hold to Miss Diana."

"They say he would not leave it to a woman."

"That's true, Master Rupert. And of his children there were but his daughters left. The two sons had gone. Rupert the heir first: he died on the high seas; and Mr. Joe next."

"Mark, why did Rupert the heir go to sea?"

Old Canham shook his head. "Ah, it was a bad business, Master Rupert, and it's as well not to talk of it."

"But *why* did he go?" persisted Rupert.

"It was a bad business, I say. He, the heir, had fallen into wild ways, got to like bad company, and that. He went out one night with some poachers—just for the fun of it. It wasn't on these lands. He meant no harm, but he was young and random, and he went out and put a gauze over his face as they did,—just, I say, for the fun of it. Master Rupert, that night they killed a gamekeeper."

A shiver passed through Rupert's frame. "*He* killed him?—my uncle, Rupert Trevlyn?"

"No, it wasn't he that killed him—as was proved a long while afterwards. But you see at the time it wasn't known exactly who had done it: they were all in league together, all in a mess, as may be said. Any way, the young heir, whether in fear or shame, went off in secret, and before many months had gone over, the bells were tolling for him. He had died far away."

"But people never could have believed that a Trevlyn killed a man?" said Rupert, indignantly.

Old Canham paused. "You have heard of the Trevlyn temper, Master Rupert?"

"Who hasn't?" returned Rupert. "They say I have a touch of it."

"Well, those that believed it laid it to that temper, you see. They thought the heir had been overtook by a fit of passion, and might have done the mischief in it. In those fits of passion a man is mad."

"Is he?" abstractedly remarked Rupert, falling into a reverie. He had never before heard this episode in the history of the uncle whose name he bore—Rupert Trevlyn.

CHAPTER XIV
NO BREAKFAST

Old Canham stood at the door of his lodge, gazing after one who was winding through the avenue, in the direction of Trevlyn Hold, one whom old Canham delighted to patronise and make much of in his humble way; whom he encouraged in all sorts of vain and delusive notions—Rupert Trevlyn. Could Mr. Chattaway have divined the treason talked against him nearly every time Rupert dropped into the lodge, he might have tried hard to turn old Canham out of it. Harmless treason, however; consisting of rebellious words only. There was neither plotting nor hatching; old Canham and Rupert never glanced at that; both were perfectly aware that Chattaway held his place by a tenure which could not be disturbed.

Many years ago, before Squire Trevlyn died, Mark Canham had grown ill in his service. In his service he had caught the cold which ended in an incurable rheumatic affection. The Squire settled him in the lodge, then just vacant, and allowed him five shillings a week. When the Squire died, Chattaway would have undone this. He wished to turn the old man out again (but it must be observed in a parenthesis that, though universally styled old Canham, the man was less old in years than in appearance), and place some one else in the lodge. I think, when there is no love lost between people, as the saying runs, each side is conscious of it. Chattaway disliked Mark Canham, and had a shrewd suspicion that Mark returned the feeling with interest. But he found he could not dismiss him from the lodge, for Miss Trevlyn put her veto upon it. She openly declared that Squire Trevlyn's act in placing his old servant there should be observed; she promised Mark he should not be turned out of it as long as he lived. Chattaway had no resource but to bow to it; he might not cross Diana Trevlyn; but he did succeed in reducing the weekly allowance. Half-a-crown a week was all the regular money enjoyed by the lodge since the time of Squire Trevlyn. Miss Diana sometimes gave him a trifle from her private purse; and the gardener was allowed to make an occasional present of vegetables in danger of spoiling: at the beginning of winter, too, a load of wood would be stacked in the shed behind the lodge, through the forethought of Miss Diana. But it was not much altogether to keep two people upon; and Ann Canham was glad to accept a day's hard work offered her at any of the neighbouring houses, or do a little plain sewing at home. Very fine sewing she could not do, for she suffered from weak eyes.

Old Canham watched Rupert until the turnings of the avenue hid him from view, and then drew back into the room. Ann was busy with the breakfast. A loaf of oaten bread and a basin of skim milk, she had just heated, was placed before her father. A smaller cup served for her own share: and that constituted their breakfast. Three mornings a week Ann Canham had the privilege of fetching a quart of skim milk from the dairy at the Hold. Chattaway growled at the extravagance of the gift, but he did no more, for it was Miss Diana's pleasure that it should be supplied.

"Chattaway'll go a bit too far, if he don't mind," observed old Canham to his daughter, in relation to Rupert. "He must be a bad nature, to lock him out of his own house. For the matter of that, however, he's a very bad one; and it's known he is."

"It is not his own, father," Ann Canham ventured to retort. "Poor Master Rupert haven't no right to it now."

"It's a shame but he had. Why, Chattaway has no more moral right to that fine estate than I have!" added the old man, holding up his left hand in the heat of argument. "If Master Rupert and Miss Maude were dead,—if Joe Trevlyn had never left a child at all,—others would have a right to it before Chattaway."

"But Chattaway has it, father, and nobody can't alter it, or hinder it," sensibly returned Ann. "You'll have your milk cold."

The breakfast hour at Trevlyn Hold was early, and when Rupert entered, he found most of the family downstairs. Rupert ran up to his bedroom, where he washed and refreshed himself as much as was possible after his weary night. He was one upon whom only a night out of bed would tell seriously. When he went down to the breakfast-room, they were all assembled except Cris and Mrs. Chattaway. Cris was given to lying in bed in a morning, and the self-indulgence was permitted. Mrs. Chattaway also was apt to be late, coming down generally when breakfast was nearly over.

Rupert took his place at the breakfast-table. Mr. Chattaway, who was at that moment raising his coffee-cup to his lips, put it down and stared at him. As he might have stared at some stranger who had intruded and sat down amongst them.

"What do you want?" asked Mr. Chattaway.

"Want?" repeated Rupert, not understanding. "My breakfast."

"Which you will not get here," calmly and coldly returned Mr. Chattaway. "If you cannot come home to sleep at night, you shall not have your breakfast here in the morning."

"I did come home," said Rupert; "but I was not let in."

"Of course you were not. The household had retired."

"Cris came home after I did, and was allowed to enter," objected Rupert again.

"That is no business of yours," said Mr. Chattaway. "All you have to do is to obey the rules I lay down. And I will have them obeyed," he added, more sternly.

Rupert sat on. Octave, who was presiding at the table, did not give him any coffee; no one attempted to hand him anything. Maude was seated opposite to him, and he could see that the unpleasantness was agitating her painfully; her colour went and came; she toyed with her breakfast, but could not swallow it: least of all, dared *she* interfere to give even so much as bread to her ill-fated brother.

"Where did you sleep last night, pray?" inquired Mr. Chattaway, pausing in the midst of helping himself to some pigeon-pie, as he looked at Rupert.

"Not in this house," curtly replied Rupert. The unkindness seemed to be changing his very nature. It had continued long and long; had been shown in many and various forms.

The master of Trevlyn Hold finished helping himself to the pie, and began eating it with apparent relish. He was about half-way through the plateful when he again stopped to address Rupert, who was sitting in silence, nothing but the table-cloth before him.

"You need not wait. If you stop there until mid-day you'll get no breakfast. Gentlemen who sleep outside do not break their fasts in my house."

Rupert pushed back his chair, and rose. Happening to glance across at Maude, he saw that her tears were dropping silently. It was a most unhappy home for both! He crossed the hall to the door: and thought he might as well depart at once for Blackstone. Fine as the morning was, the air, as he passed out, struck coldly upon him, and he turned back for an overcoat.

It was in his bedroom. As he came down with it on his arm, Mrs. Chattaway was crossing the corridor, and she drew him inside her sitting-room.

"I could not sleep," she murmured. "I was awake nearly all night, grieving and thinking of you. Just before daylight I dropped into a sleep, and then dreamt you were running up to the door from the waves of the sea, which were rushing onwards to overtake you. I thought you were knocking at the door, and we could not get down to it in time, and the waters came on and on. Rupert, darling, all this is telling upon me. Why did you not come in?"

"I meant to be in, Aunt Edith; indeed I did; but I was playing chess with George Ryle, and did not notice the time. It was only just turned half-past when I got here; Mr. Chattaway might have let me in without any great stretch of indulgence," he added, bitterly. "So might Cris."

"What did you do?" she asked.

"I got in at old Canham's, and lay on the settle. Don't repeat this, or it may get the Canhams into trouble."

"Have you breakfasted?"

"I am not to have any."

The words startled her. "Rupert!"

"Mr. Chattaway ordered me from the table. The next thing, I expect, he will order me from the house. If I knew where to go I wouldn't stop in it another hour. I would not, Aunt Edith."

"Have you had nothing—nothing?"

"Nothing. I would go round to the dairy and get some milk, but I should be reported. I'm off to Blackstone now. Good-bye."

Tears were filling her eyes as she lifted them in their sad yearning. He stooped and kissed her.

"Don't grieve, Aunt Edith. You can't make it better for me. I have got the cramp like anything," he carelessly observed as he went off. "It is through lying on the cold, hard settle."

"Rupert! Rupert!"

He turned back, half in alarm. The tone was one of wild, painful entreaty.

"You will come home to-night, Rupert?"

"Yes. Depend upon me."

She remained a few minutes longer watching him down the avenue. He had put on his coat, and went along with slow and hesitating steps; very different from the firm, careless steps of a strong frame, springing from a happy heart. Mrs. Chattaway pressed her hands to her brow, lost in a painful vision. If his father, her once dearly-loved brother Joe, could look on at the injustice done on earth, what would he think of the portion meted out to Rupert?

She descended to the breakfast-room. Mr. Chattaway had finished his breakfast and was rising. She kissed her children one by one; sat down patiently and silently, smiling without cheerfulness. Octave passed her a cup of coffee, which was cold; and then asked her what she would take to eat. But she said she was not hungry that morning, and would eat nothing.

"Rupert's gone away without his breakfast, mamma," cried Emily. "Papa would not let him have it. Serve him right! He stayed out all night."

Mrs. Chattaway stole a glance at Maude. She was sitting pale and quiet; her air that of one who has to bear some long, wearing pain.

"If you have finished your breakfast, Maude, you can be getting ready to take the children for their walk," said Octave, speaking with her usual assumption of authority—an assumption Maude at least might not dispute.

Mr. Chattaway left the room, and ordered his horse to be got ready. He was going to ride over his land for an hour before proceeding to Blackstone. Whilst the animal was being saddled, he rejoiced his eyes with his rich stores; the corn in his barns, the hay-ricks in his yard. All very satisfactory, very consoling to the covetous master of the Hold.

He went out, riding hither and thither. Half-an-hour afterwards, in the lane skirting Mrs. Ryle's lands on the one side and his on the other, he saw another horseman before him. It was George Ryle. Mr. Chattaway touched his horse with the spur, and rode up to him. George turned his head and continued his way. Chattaway had been better pleased had George stopped.

"Are you hastening on to avoid me, Mr. Ryle?" he called out, sullenly. "You might have seen that I wished to speak to you, by the pace at which I urged my horse."

George reined in, and turned to face Mr. Chattaway. "I saw nothing of the sort," he answered. "Had I known you wanted me, I should have stopped; but it is no unusual circumstance to see you riding fast about your land."

"Well, what I have to say is this: that I'd recommend you not to get Rupert Trevlyn to your house at night, and keep him there to unreasonable hours."

George paused. "I don't understand you, Mr. Chattaway."

"Don't you?" retorted that gentleman. "I'm not talking Dutch. Rupert Trevlyn has taken to frequenting your house of late; it's not altogether good for him."

"Do you fear he will get any harm in it?" quietly asked George.

"I think it would be better that he should stay away. Is the Hold not sufficient for him to spend his evenings in, but he must seek amusement elsewhere? I shall be obliged to you not to encourage his visits."

"Mr. Chattaway," said George, his face full of earnestness, "it appears to me that you are labouring under some mistake, or you would certainly not speak to me as you are now doing. I do not encourage Rupert to my mother's house, in one sense of the word; I never press for his visits. When he does come, I show myself happy to see him and make him welcome—as I should do by any other visitor. Common courtesy demands this of me."

"You do press for his visits," said Mr. Chattaway.

"I do not," firmly repeated George. "Shall I tell you why I do not? I have no wish but to be open in the matter. An impression has seated itself in my mind that his visits to our house displease you, and therefore I have not encouraged them."

Perhaps Mr. Chattaway was rather taken back by this answer. At any rate, he made no reply to it.

"But to receive him courteously when he does come, I cannot help doing," continued George. "I shall do it still. If Trevlyn Farm is to be a forbidden house to Rupert, it is not from our side the veto shall come. As long as Rupert pays us these visits of friendship—and what harm you can think they do him, or why he should not pay them, I am unable to conceive—so long he will be met with a welcome."

"Do you say this to oppose me?"

"Far from it. If you look at the case in an unprejudiced light, you may see that I speak in accordance with the commonest usages of civility. To close the doors of our house to Rupert when there exists no reason why they should be closed—and most certainly he has given us none—would be an act we might blush to be guilty of."

"You have been opposing me all the later years of your life. From that time when I wished to place you with Wall and Barnes, you have done nothing but act in opposition to me."

"I have forgiven that," said George, pointedly, a glow rising to his face at the recollection. "As to any other opposition, I am unconscious of it. You have given me advice occasionally respecting the farm; but the advice has not in general tallied with my own opinion, and therefore I have not taken it. If you call that opposing you, Mr. Chattaway, I cannot help it."

"I see you have been mending that fence in the three-cornered paddock," remarked Mr. Chattaway, passing to another subject, and speaking in a different tone. Possibly he had had enough of the last.

"Yes," said George. "You would not mend it, and therefore I have had it done. I cannot let my cattle get into the pound. I shall deduct the expense from the rent."

"You'll not," said Mr. Chattaway. "I won't be at the cost of a penny-piece of it."

"Oh yes, you will," returned George, equably. "The damage was done by your team, through your waggoner's carelessness, and the cost of making it good lies with you. Have you anything more to say to me?" he asked, after a pause. "I am very busy this morning."

"Only this," replied Mr. Chattaway significantly. "That the more you encourage Rupert Trevlyn, by making a companion of him, the worse it will be for him."

George lifted his hat in salutation. The master of Trevlyn Hold replied by an ungracious nod, and turned his horse back down the lane. As George rode on, he met Edith and Emily Chattaway—the children, as Octave had styled them—running towards him. They had seen their father, and were hastening after him. Maude came up more leisurely. George stopped to shake hands with her.

"You look pale and ill, Maude," he said, his low voice full of sympathy, his hand retaining hers. "Is it about Rupert?"

"Yes," she replied, striving to keep back her tears. "He was not allowed to come in last night, and has been sent away without breakfast this morning."

"I know all about it," said George. "I met Rupert just now, and he told me. I asked him if he would go to Nora for some breakfast—I could not do less, you know," he added musingly, as if debating the question with himself. "But he declined. I am almost glad he did."

Maude was surprised. "Why?" she asked.

"Because I have had an idea—have felt it for some time—that any attention shown to Rupert, no matter by whom, only makes his position worse with Chattaway. And Chattaway has now confirmed it by telling me so."

Maude's eyelids drooped. "How sad it is!" she exclaimed with emotion—"and for one in his weak state! If he were only strong as the rest of us are, it would matter less. I fear—I do fear he must have slept under the trees in the avenue," she continued. "Mr. Chattaway inquired where he had passed the night, and Rupert answered—"

"I can so far relieve your fears, Maude," interrupted George, glancing round, as if to make sure no ears were near. "He was at old Canham's."

Maude gave a deep sigh in her relief. "You are certain, George?"

"Yes, yes. Rupert told me so just now. He said how hard he found the settle. Here come your charges, Maude; so I will say good-bye."

She suffered her hand to linger in his, but her heart was too full to speak. George bent lower.

"Do not make the grief weightier than you can bear, Maude. It is real grief; but happier times may be in store for Rupert—and for you."

He released her hand, and cantered down the lane; and the two girls came up, telling Maude they should go home now, for they had walked long enough.

CHAPTER XV
TORMENTS

There appeared to be no place on earth for Rupert Trevlyn. Most people have some little nook they can fit themselves into and call their own; but he had none. He was only on sufferance at the Hold, and was made to feel more of an interloper in it day by day.

What could be the source of this ill-feeling towards Rupert? Did some latent dread exist in the heart of Mr. Chattaway, and from thence reach that of Cris, whispering that he, Rupert, the true heir of Trevlyn Hold, might at some future day, through some unforeseen and apparently impossible chance, come into his rights? No doubt it was so. There are no other means of accounting for it. It may be, they deemed, that the more effectually he was kept under, treated as an object to be despised, lowered from his proper station, the less chance would there be of that covert dread growing into a certainty. Whatever its cause, Rupert was shamefully put upon. It is true that he sat at their table, occupied the same sitting-room. But at table he was placed below the rest, was served last, and from the plainest dish. Mrs. Chattaway's heart would ache; it had ached for many a year; but she could not alter it. In their evenings, when the rest were gathered round the fire, Rupert would be left out in the cold. Nothing in the world did he so covet as a warm seat near the fire. It had been sought by his father when he was Rupert's age, and perhaps Miss Diana remembered this, for she would call Rupert forward, and sharply rebuke those who would have kept him from it.

But Miss Diana was not always in the room; not often, in fact. She had her own sitting-room upstairs, as Mrs. Chattaway had hers; and both ladies more frequently retired to them in an evening, leaving the younger ones to enjoy themselves, with their books and work, their music and games, unrestrained by their presence. And poor Rupert was condemned to remote quarters, where no one noticed him.

From that point alone, the cold, it was a severe trial. Of weakly constitution, a chilly nature, warmth was to Rupert Trevlyn almost an essential of existence. And it was what he rarely had at Trevlyn Hold. No wonder he was driven out. Even old Canham's wood fire, that he might get right into if he pleased, was an improvement upon the drawing-room at the Hold.

After parting with George Ryle, Maude Trevlyn, in obedience to the imperious wills of her pupils, turned her steps homewards. Emily was a boisterous, troublesome, disobedient girl; Edith was more gentle and amiable, in looks and disposition resembling her mother; but the example of her sisters was infectious, and spoiled her. There was another daughter, Amelia, older than they were, and at school at Barmester: a very disagreeable girl indeed.

"What was George Ryle saying to you, Maude?" somewhat insolently asked Emily.

"He was talking of Rupert," she incautiously answered, her mind buried in thought.

When they reached the Hold, Mr. Chattaway's horse was being led about by a groom, waiting for its master, who had returned, and was indoors. As they crossed the hall, they met him coming out of the breakfast-room. Octave was with him, talking.

"Cris would have waited, no doubt, papa, had he known you wanted him. He ate his breakfast in a hurry, and went out. I suppose he has gone to Blackstone."

"I particularly wanted him," grumbled Mr. Chattaway, who was never pleasant at the best of times, but would be unbearable if put out. "Cris knew I should want him this morning. First Rupert, and then Cris! Are you all going to turn disobedient?"

He made a halt at the door, putting on his riding-glove. They stood grouped around him—Octave, Maude, and Emily. Edith had run out, and was near the horse.

"I would give a crown-piece to know what Mr. Rupert did with himself last night," he savagely uttered. "John," exalting his voice, "have you any idea where Rupert Trevlyn hid himself all night?"

The locking-out had been known to the household, and afforded considerable gossip. John had taken part in it; joined in its surmises and comments; therefore he was not at fault for a ready answer.

"I don't know nothing certain, sir. It ain't unlikely he went down to the Sheaf o' Corn, and slept there."

"No, no, he did not," involuntarily burst from Maude.

It was an unlucky admission, for its tone was decisive, implying that she knew where he did sleep. She spoke in the moment's impulse. The Shear of Corn was the nearest public-house; notorious for its irregular doings; and

Maude felt shocked at the bare suggestion that Rupert would enter such a place.

Mr. Chattaway turned to her. "Where *did* he sleep? What do you know about it?" Maude's face grew hot and cold. She opened her lips to answer, but closed them again without speaking, the words dying away in her uncertainty and hesitation.

Mr. Chattaway may have felt surprised. He knew perfectly well that Maude had held no communication with Rupert that morning. He had seen Rupert come in and go out; and Maude had not stirred from his presence. He bent his cold grey eyes upon her.

"From whom have you been hearing of Rupert's doings?"

It is very probable that Maude would have been at a loss for an answer, but she was saved a reply, for Emily spoke up before she had time to give one, ill-nature in her tone and words.

"Maude must have heard it from George Ryle. You saw her talking to him, papa. She said he had been speaking of Rupert."

Mr. Chattaway did not ask another question. It would have been superfluous to do so, in the conclusion he had come to. He believed Rupert had slept at Trevlyn Farm. How else could George Ryle have become acquainted with his movements?

"They'll be hatching a plot to try to over-throw me," he muttered to himself as he went out to his horse: for his was one of those mean, suspicious natures that are always fancying the world is antagonistic to them. "Maude Ryle has been wanting to get me out of Trevlyn Hold ever since I came into it. From the very hour she heard the Squire's will read, and found I had inherited, she has been planning and plotting for it. She would rather see Rupert in it than me; and rather see her pitiful Treve in it than anyone. Yes, yes, Mr. Rupert, we know what you frequent Trevlyn Farm for. But it won't answer. It's waste of time. They must change England's laws before they can upset Squire Trevlyn's will. But it's not less annoying to know that my tenure is constantly being hauled over and peered into, to see if they can't find a flaw in it, or insert one of their own making."

It was strange that these fears should continually trouble the master of Trevlyn Hold. A man who legally holds an estate, on which no shade of a suspicion can be cast, need not dread its being wrested from him. It was in Squire Trevlyn's power to leave the Hold and its revenues to whom he would. Had he chosen to bequeath it to an utter stranger, it was in his power to do so: and he had bequeathed it to James Chattaway. Failing direct male heirs, it may be thought that Mr. Chattaway had as much right to it as anyone else. At any rate, it had been the Squire's pleasure to bequeath it to him, and there the matter ended. That the master of Trevlyn Hold was ever conscious of a dread his tenure was to be some time disturbed, was indisputable. He never betrayed it to any living being by so much as a word; he strove to conceal it even from himself; but there it was, deep in his secret heart. There it remained, and there it tormented him; however unwilling he might have been to acknowledge the fact.

Could it be that a prevision of what was really to take place was cast upon him?—a mysterious foreshadowing of the future? There are people who tell us such warnings come.

The singularity of the affair was, that no grounds could exist for this latent fear. Whence then should it arise? Why, from that source whence it arises in many people—a bad conscience. It was true the estate had been legally left to him; but he knew that his own handiwork, his deceit, had brought it to him; he knew that when he suppressed the news of the birth of Rupert, and suffered Squire Trevlyn to go to his grave uninformed of the fact, he was guilty of nothing less than a crime in the sight of God. Mr. Chattaway had heard of that inconvenient thing, retribution, and his fancy suggested that it might possibly overtake *him*.

If he had only known that he might have set his mind at rest as to the plotting and planning, he would have cared less to oppose Rupert's visits to the Farm. Nothing could be further from the thoughts of Rupert, or George Ryle, than any plotting against Chattaway. Their evenings, when together, were spent in harmless conversation, in chess, without so much as a reference to Chattaway. But that gentleman did not know it, and tormented himself accordingly.

He mounted his horse, and rode away. As he was passing Trevlyn Farm, buried in unpleasant thoughts, he saw Nora Dickson at the fold-yard gate, and turned his horse's head towards her.

"How came your people to give Rupert Trevlyn a bed last night? They must know it would very much displease me."

"Give Rupert Trevlyn a bed!" repeated Nora, regarding Mr. Chattaway with the uncompromising stare she was fond of according to that gentleman. "He did not sleep here."

"No!" replied Mr. Chattaway.

"No," reiterated Nora. "What should he want with a bed here? Has he not his own at Trevlyn Hold? A bed there isn't much for him, when he ought to have owned the whole place; but I suppose he can at least count upon that."

Mr. Chattaway turned his horse short round, and rode away without another word. He always got the worst of it with Nora. A slight explosion of his private sentiments with regard to her was given to the air, and he again became absorbed on the subject of Rupert.

"Where, then, *did* he pass the night?"

CHAPTER XVI
MR. CHATTAWAY'S OFFICE

It was Nora's day for churning. The butter was made twice a week at Trevlyn Farm, and the making fell to Nora. She was sole priestess of the dairy. It was many and many a long year since any one else had interfered in it: except, indeed, in the actual churning. One of the men on the farm did that for her in a general way; but to-day they were not forthcoming.

When Nora was seen at the fold-yard gate by Mr. Chattaway, idly staring up and down the road, she was looking for Jim Sanders, to order him in to churn. Not the Jim Sanders mentioned in the earlier portion of our history, but Jim's son. Jim the elder was dead: he had brought on rather too many attacks of inflammation (a disease to which he was predisposed) by his love of beer; and at last one attack worse than the rest came, and proved too much for him. The present Jim, representative of his name, was a youth of fourteen, not over-burdened with brains, but strong and sound, and was found useful on the farm, where he was required to be willing to do any work that came first to hand.

Just now he was wanted to churn. The man who usually performed that duty was too busy to be spared to-day; therefore it fell to Jim. But Jim could not be seen anywhere, and Nora returned indoors and commenced the work herself.

The milk at the right temperature—for Nora was too experienced a dairy-woman not to know that if she attempted to churn at the wrong one, it would be hours before the butter came—she took out the thermometer, and turned the milk into the churn. As she was doing this, the servant, Nanny, entered: a tall, stolid girl, remarkable for little except height.

"Is nobody coming in to churn?" asked she.

"It seems not," answered Nora.

"Shall I do it?"

"Not if I know it," returned Nora. "You'd like to quit your work for this pastime, wouldn't you? Have you the potatoes on for the pigs?"

"No," said Nanny.

"Then go and see about, it. You know it was to be done to-day. And I suppose the fire's burning away under the furnace."

Fanny stalked out of the dairy. Nora churned away steadily, and turned her butter on to the making-up board in about three-quarters of an hour. As she was proceeding with it, she saw George ride into the fold-yard, and leave his horse in the stable. Another minute and he came in.

"Has Mr. Callaway not come yet, Nora?"

"I have seen nothing of him, Mr. George."

George took out his watch: the one bequeathed him by his father. It was only a silver one—as Mr. Ryle had remarked—but George valued it as though it had been set in diamonds. He would wear that watch and no other as long as he lived. His initials were engraved on it now: G. B. R. standing for George Berkeley Ryle.

"If Callaway cannot keep his appointment better than this, I shall beg him not to make any more with me," he remarked. "The last time he kept me waiting three-quarters of an hour."

"Have you seen Jim Sanders this morning?" asked Nora.

"I saw him in the stables as I rode out."

"I should like to find him!" said Nora. "He is skulking somewhere. I have had to churn myself."

"Where's Roger?"

"Roger couldn't hinder his time indoors to-day. Mr. George, what's up at Trevlyn Hold again about Rupert?" resumed Nora, turning from her butter to glance at George.

"Why do you ask?"

"Chattaway rode by an hour ago when I was outside looking after Jim Sanders. He stopped his horse and asked how we came to give Rupert a bed last night, when we knew that it would displease him. Like his insolence!"

"What answer did you make?" said George, after a pause.

"I gave him one," replied Nora, significantly. "Chattaway needn't fear not getting an answer when he comes to me. He knows that."

"But what did you say about Rupert?"

"I said that he had not slept here. If Chattaway—"

Nora was interrupted by the entrance of Mr. Chattaway's daughter, Octave. She had come to the farm, and, attracted by the sound of voices in the dairy, made her way to it. Miss Chattaway had taken it into her head lately to be friendly, to honour the farm with frequent visits. Mrs. Ryle neither encouraged nor repulsed her. She was civilly indifferent: but the young lady chose to take that as a welcome. Nora did not show her much greater favour than she was in the habit of showing her father. She bent her head over her butter-board, as if unaware that any one had entered.

George removed his hat which he had been wearing, as she stepped on to the cold floor of the dairy, and took the hand held out to him.

"Who would have thought of seeing you at home at this hour?" she exclaimed, in the winning manner which she could put on at times, and always did put on for George Ryle.

"And in Nora's dairy, watching her make up the butter!" he answered, laughing. "The fact is, I have an appointment with a gentleman this morning, and he is keeping me waiting, and making me angry. I can't spare the time."

"You look angry!" exclaimed Octave, laughing at him.

"Looks go for nothing," returned George.

"Is your harvest nearly in?"

"If this fine weather only lasts four or five days longer, it will be all in. We have had a glorious harvest this year. I hope every one's as thankful as I am."

"You have some especial cause for thankfulness?" she observed.

"I have."

She had spoken lightly, and was struck by the strangely earnest answer. George could have said that but for that harvest they might not quite so soon have discharged her father's debt.

"When shall you hold your harvest home?"

"Next Thursday; this day week," replied George. "Will you come to it?"

"Thank you," said Octave. "Yes, I will."

Had it been to save his life, George Ryle could not have helped the surprise in his eyes, as he turned them on Octave Chattaway. He had asked the question in the careless gaiety of the moment; really not intending it as an invitation. Had he proffered it in all earnestness, he never would have supposed it one to be accepted by Octave. Mr. Chattaway's family were not in the habit of visiting at Trevlyn Farm.

"In for a penny, in for a pound," thought George. "I don't know what Mrs. Ryle will say to this; but if *she* comes, some of the rest shall come also."

It almost seemed as if Octave had divined part of his thoughts. "I must ask my aunt Ryle whether she will have me. By way of bribe, I shall tell her that I delight in harvest-homes."

"We must have you all," said George. "Your sisters and Maude. Treve will be home I expect, and the Apperleys will be here."

"Who else?" asked Octave. "But I don't know about my sisters and Maude."

"Mr. and Mrs. Freeman. They and the Apperleys always come."

"Our starched old parson!" uttered Octave. "He is not a favourite with us at the Hold."

"I think he is with your mother."

"Oh, mamma's nobody. Of course we are civil to the Freemans, and exchange dull visits with them occasionally. You must be passably civil to the parson you sit under."

There was a pause. Octave advanced to Nora, who had gone on diligently with her work, never turning her head, or noticing Miss Chattaway by so much as a look. Octave drew close and watched her.

"How industrious you are, Nora!—just as if you enjoyed the occupation. I should not like to soil my hands, making up butter."

"There are some might make it up in white kid gloves," retorted Nora. "The butter wouldn't be any the better for it, Miss Chattaway."

At this juncture Mrs. Ryle's voice was heard, and Octave left the dairy in search of her. George was about to follow when Nora stopped him.

"What is the meaning of this new friendship—these morning calls and evening visits?" she asked; her eyes thrown keenly on George's face.

"How should I know?" he carelessly replied.

"If you don't, I do," she said. "Can you take care of yourself, George?"

"I believe I can."

"Then do," said Nora, with an emphatic nod. "And don't despise my caution: you may want it."

He laughed in his light-heartedness: but he did not tell Nora how unnecessary her warning was.

Later in the day, George Ryle had business which took him to Blackstone. It was not an inviting ride. The place, as he drew near, had that dreary aspect peculiar to the neighbourhood of mines. Rows of black, smoky huts were to be seen, the dwellings of the men who worked in the pits; and little children ran about with naked legs and tattered clothing, their thin faces white and squalid.

"Is it the perpetual dirt they live in makes these children look so unhealthy?" thought George—a question he had asked himself a hundred times. "I believe the mothers never wash them. Perhaps think it would be superfluous, where even the very atmosphere is black."

Black, indeed! Within George's view at that moment might be seen high chimneys congregating in all directions, throwing out volumes of smoke and flame. Numerous works were around, connected with iron and other rich mines abounding in the neighbourhood. Valuable areas for the furtherance of civilisation, the increase of wealth; but not pleasant to the eye, as compared with green meadows and blossoming trees.

The office belonging to Mr. Chattaway's colliery stood in a particularly dreary offshoot from the main road. It was a low but not very small building, facing the road on one side, looking to those tall chimneys and the dreary country on two of the others. On the fourth was a sort of waste ground, which appeared to contain nothing but various heaps of coal, a peculiar description of barrow, and some round shallow baskets. The building looked like a great shed; it was roofed over, and divided into partitions.

As George rode by, he saw Rupert standing at the narrow entrance door, leaning against it, as if in fatigue or idleness. Ford, the clerk, a young man accustomed to taking life easily, and to give himself little concern as to how it went, was standing near, his hands in his pockets. To see them doing nothing was sufficient to tell George that Chattaway was not about, and he rode up to the office.

"You look tired, Rupert."

"I am tired," answered Rupert. "If things are to go on like this, I shall grow tired of life altogether."

"Not yet," said George, cheeringly. "You may talk of that some fifty years hence."

Rupert made no answer. The sunlight fell on his fair features and golden hair. There was a haggardness in those features, a melancholy in the dark blue eyes, George did not like to see. Ford, the clerk, who was humming the verse of a song, cut short the melody, and addressed George.

"He has been in this gay state all the afternoon, sir. A charming companion for a fellow! It's a good thing I'm pretty jolly myself, or we might get consigned to the county asylum as two cases of melancholy. I hope he won't make a night of it again, that's all. Nothing wears out a chap like a night without bed, and no breakfast at the end of it."

"It isn't that," said Rupert. "I'm sick of it altogether. There has been nothing but a row here all day, George—ask Ford. Chattaway has been on at all of us. First, he attacked me. He demanded where I slept, and I wouldn't tell him. Next, he attacked Cris—a most unusual thing—and Cris hasn't got over it yet. He has gone galloping off, to gallop his ill-temper away."

"Chattaway has?"

"Not Chattaway; Cris. Cris never came here until one o'clock, and Chattaway wanted him, and a row ensued. Next, Ford came in for it: he had made a mistake in his entries. Something had uncommonly put out Chattaway—that is certain. And to improve his temper, the inspector of collieries came to-day and found fault, ordering things to be done that Chattaway says he won't do."

"Where's Chattaway now?"

"Gone home. I wish I was there, without the trouble of walking," added Rupert. "Chattaway has been ordering a load of coals to the Hold. If they were going this evening instead of to-morrow morning, I protest I'd take my seat upon them, and get home that way."

"Are you so very tired?" asked George.

"Dead beat."

"It's the sitting up," put in Ford again. "I don't think much of that kind of thing will do for Mr. Rupert Trevlyn."

"Perhaps it wouldn't do for you," grumbled Rupert.

George prepared to ride away. "Have you had any dinner, Rupert?" he asked.

"I made an attempt, but my appetite had gone by. Chattaway was here till past two o'clock, and after that I wasn't hungry."

"He tried some bread-and-cheese," said Ford. "I told him if he'd get a chop I'd cook it for him; but he didn't."

"I must be gone," said George. "You will not have left in half-an-hour's time, shall you, Rupert?"

"No; nor in an hour either."

George rode off over the stony ground, and they looked after him. Then Ford bethought himself of a message he was charged to deliver at one of the pits, and Rupert went indoors and sat down to the desk on his high stool.

Within the half-hour George Ryle was back again. He rode up to the door, and dismounted. Rupert came forward, a pen in hand.

"Are you ready to go home now, Rupert?"

Rupert shook his head. "Ford went to the pit and is not back yet; and I have a lot of writing to do. Why?"

"I thought we would have gone home together. You shall ride my horse, and I'll walk; it will tire you less than going on foot."

"You are very kind," said Rupert. "Yes, I should like to ride. I was thinking just now, that if Cris were worth anything, he'd let me ride his horse home. But he's not worth anything, and would no more let me ride his horse and walk himself, than he'd let me ride him."

"Has Cris not gone home?"

"I fancy not. Unless he has gone by without calling in. Will you wait, George?"

"No. I must walk on. But I'll leave you the horse. You can leave it at the Farm, Rupert, and walk the rest of the way."

"I can ride on to the Hold, and send it back."

George hesitated a moment. "I would rather you left it at the Farm, Rupert. It will not be far to walk after that."

Rupert acquiesced. Did he wonder why he might not ride the horse to the Hold? George would not say, "Because even that slight attention must, if possible, be kept from Chattaway."

He fastened the bridle to a hook in the wall, where Mr. Chattaway often tied his horse, where Cris sometimes tied his. There was a stable near; but unless they were going to remain in the office or about the pits, Mr. Chattaway and his son seldom put up their horses.

George Ryle walked away with a quick step, and Rupert returned to his desk. A quarter-of-an-hour passed on, and the clerk did not return. Rupert grew impatient for his arrival, and went to the door to look out for him. He did not see Ford; but he did see Cris Chattaway. Cris was approaching on foot, at a snail's pace, leading his horse, which was dead lame.

"Here's a nice bother!" called out Cris. "How I am to get back home, I don't know."

"What has happened?" returned Rupert.

"Can't you see what has happened? How it happened, I am unable to tell you. All I know is, the horse fell suddenly lame, and whined like a child. Something must have run into his foot, I conclude. Whose horse is that? Why, it's George Ryle's," Cris exclaimed as he drew sufficiently near to recognise it. "What brings his horse here?"

"He has lent it to me, to save my walking home," said Rupert.

"Where is he? Here?"

"He has gone home on foot. I can't think where Ford's lingering," added Rupert, walking into the yard, and mounting one of the smaller heaps of coal for a better view of the road by which Ford might be expected to arrive. "He has been gone this hour."

Cris was walking off in the direction of the stable, carefully leading his horse. "What are you going to do with him?" asked Rupert. "To leave him in the stable?"

"Until I can get home and send the groom for him. *I'm* not going to cool my heels, dragging him home," retorted Cris.

Rupert retired indoors, and sat down on the high stool. He still had some accounts to make up. They had to be done that evening; and as Ford did not come in to do them, he must. Had Ford been there, Rupert would have left him to do it, and gone home at once.

"I wonder how many years of my life I am to wear out in this lively place?" thought Rupert, after five minutes of uninterrupted attention given to his work, which slightly progressed in consequence. "It's a shame that I should be put to it. A paid fellow at ten shillings a week would do it better than I. If Chattaway had a spark of good feeling in him, he'd put me into a farm. It would be better for me altogether, and more fitting for a Trevlyn. Catch him at it! He wouldn't let me be my own master for—"

A sound as of a horse trotting off interrupted Rupert's cogitations. He came down from his stool. A thought crossed him that George Ryle's horse might have got loose, and be speeding home riderless, at his own will and pleasure.

It was George Ryle's horse, but not riderless. To Rupert's intense astonishment, he saw Mr. Cris mounted on him, and leisurely riding away.

"Halloa!" called Rupert, speeding after the horse and his rider. "What are you going to do with that horse, Cris?"

Cris turned his head, but did not stop. "I'm going to ride him home. His having been left here just happens right for me."

"You get off," shouted Rupert. "The horse was lent to me, not to you. Do you hear, Cris?"

Cris heard, but did not stop: he was urging the horse on. "*You* don't want him," he roughly said. "You can walk, as you always do."

Further remonstrance, further following, was useless. Rupert's words were drowned in the echoes of the horse's hoofs, galloping away in the distance. Rupert stood, white with anger, impotent to stop him, his hands stretched out on the empty air, as if their action could arrest the horse and bring him back again. Certainly the mortification was bitter; the circumstance precisely one of those likely to affect an excitable nature; and Rupert was on the point of going into that dangerous fit known as the Trevlyn passion, when its course was turned aside by a hand laid upon his shoulder.

He turned, it may almost be said, savagely. Ford was standing there out of breath, his good-humoured face red with the exertion of running.

"I say, Mr. Rupert, you'll do a fellow a service, won't you? I have had a message that my mother's taken suddenly ill; a fit, they say, of some sort. Will you finish what there is to do here, and lock up for once, so that I can go home directly?"

Rupert nodded. In his passionate disappointment, at having to walk home when he expected to ride, at being treated as of no moment by Cris Chattaway, it seemed of little consequence to him how long he remained, or what work he had to do: and the clerk, waiting for no further permission, sped away with a fleet foot. Rupert's face was losing its deathly whiteness—there is no whiteness like that born of passion or of sudden terror; and when he sat down again to the desk, the hectic flush of reaction was shining in his cheeks and lips.

Well, oh, well for him, could these dangerous fits of passion have been always arrested on the threshold, as this had been arrested now! The word is used advisedly: they brought nothing less than danger in their train.

But, alas! this was not to be.

CHAPTER XVII
DEAD BEAT

Nora was at some business or other in the fold-yard, when the servant at Trevlyn Hold more especially devoted to the service of Cris Chattaway entered the gate with George Ryle's horse. As he passed Nora on his way to the stables, she turned, and the man spoke.

"Mr. Ryle's horse, ma'am. Shall I take it on?"

"You know the way," was Nora's short answer. She did not regard the man with any favour, reflecting upon him, in her usual partial fashion, the dislike she entertained for his master and Trevlyn Hold in general. "Mr. Trevlyn has sent it, I suppose."

"Mr. Trevlyn!" repeated the groom, betraying some surprise.

Now, it was a fact that at Trevlyn Hold Rupert was never called "Mr. Trevlyn." That it was his proper title was indisputable; but Mr. Chattaway had as great a dislike to hear Rupert called by it as he had a wish to hear himself styled "the Squire." At the Hold, Rupert was "Mr. Rupert" only, and the neighbourhood generally had fallen into the same familiar mode when speaking of him. Nora supposed the man's repetition of the name had insolent reference to this; as much as to say, "Who's Mr. Trevlyn?"

"Yes, Mr. Trevlyn," she resumed in sharp tones of reprimand. "He is Mr. Trevlyn, Sam Atkins, and you know he is, however some people may wish it forgotten. He is not Mr. Rupert, and he is not Mr. Rupert Trevlyn, but he is Mr. Trevlyn; and if he had his rights, he'd be Squire Trevlyn. There! you may go and tell your master that I said so."

Sam Atkins, a civil, quiet young fellow, was overpowered with astonishment at Nora's burst of eloquence. "I'm not saying naught against it, ma'am," cried he, when he had sufficiently recovered. "But Mr. Rupert didn't send me with the horse at all. It was young Mr. Chattaway."

"What had he to do with it?" resentfully asked Nora.

"He rode it home from Blackstone."

"*He* rode it? Cris Chattaway!"

"Yes," said the groom. "He has just got home now, and told me to bring the horse back at once."

Nora desired the man to take the horse to the stable, and went indoors. She could not understand it. When George returned home on foot, and she inquired what he had done with his horse, he told her that he had left it at Blackstone for Rupert Trevlyn. To hear now that Cris had reaped the benefit of it, and not Rupert, excited Nora's indignation. But the indignation would have increased fourfold had she known that Mr. Cris had ridden the horse hard and made a *détour* of some five miles out of his way, to transact a private matter of business of his own. She went straight to George, who was seated at tea with Mrs. Ryle.

"Mr. George, I thought you told me you had left your horse at Blackstone for Rupert Trevlyn, to save his walking home?"

"So I did," replied George.

"Then it's Cris Chattaway who has come home on it. I'd see *him* far enough before he should have the use of my horse!"

"It can't be," returned George. "You must be mistaken, Nora; Cris had his own horse there."

"You can go and ask for yourself," rejoined Nora, crustily, not at all liking to be told she was mistaken. "Sam Atkins is putting the horse in the stable, and says Cris Chattaway rode it from Blackstone."

George did go and ask for himself. He could not understand it at all; and he had no more fancy for allowing Cris Chattaway the use of his horse than Nora had. He supposed they had exchanged steeds; though why they should do so, he could not imagine.

Sam Atkins was in the stable, talking to Roger, one of the men about the farm. George saw at a glance that his horse had been ridden hard.

"Who rode this horse home?" he inquired, as the groom touched his hat to him.

"Young Mr. Chattaway, sir."

"And Mr. Rupert: what did he ride?"

"Mr. Rupert, sir? I don't think he is come home."

"Where's Mr. Cris Chattaway's own horse?"

"He left it at Blackstone, sir. It fell dead lame, he says. I be going for it now."

George paused. "I lent my horse to Mr. Rupert," he said. "Do you know why he did not use it himself?"

"I don't know nothing about it, sir. Mr. Cris came home just now on your horse, told me to bring it down here, go on to Blackstone for his, and mind I led it gently home. He never mentioned Mr. Rupert."

Considerably later—in fact, it was past nine o'clock—Rupert Trevlyn appeared. George Ryle was leaning over the gate at the foot of his garden in a musing attitude, the bright stars above him, the slight frost of the autumn night rendering the air clear, though not cold, when he saw a figure slowly winding up the road. It was Rupert Trevlyn. The same misfortune seemed to have befallen him that had befallen the horse, for he limped as he walked.

"Are you lame, Rupert?" asked George.

"Lame with fatigue; nothing else," answered Rupert in that low, half-inaudible voice which a very depressed physical state will induce. "Let me come in and sit down half-an-hour, George, or I shall never get to the Hold."

"How came you to let Cris Chattaway ride my horse home? I left it for you."

"*Let* him! He mounted and galloped off without my knowing—the sneak! I should be ashamed to be guilty of such a trick. I declare I had half a mind to ride his horse home, lame as it was. But that the poor animal is evidently in pain, I would have done so."

"You are very late."

"I have been such a time coming. The truth is, I sat down when I was half-way here, so dead tired I couldn't stir a step further; and I dropped asleep."

"A wise proceeding!" cried George, in pleasant though mocking tones. He did not care to say more plainly how *un*wise it might be for Rupert Trevlyn. "Did you sleep long?"

"Pretty well. The stars were out when I awoke; and I felt ten times more tired when I got up than I had felt when I sat down."

George placed him in a comfortable armchair, and got him a glass of wine, Nora brought some refreshment, but Rupert could not eat.

"Try it," urged George.

"I can't," said Rupert; "I am completely done up."

He leaned back in the chair, his fair hair falling on the cushions, his bright face—bright with a touch of inward fever—turned upwards to the light. Gradually his eyelids closed, and he dropped into a calm sleep.

George sat watching him. Mrs. Ryle, who was still poorly, had retired to her chamber for the night, and they were alone. Very unkindly, as may be thought, George woke him soon, and told him it was time to go.

"Do not deem me inhospitable, Rupert; but it will not do for you to be locked out again to-night."

"What's the time?" asked Rupert.

"Considerably past ten."

"I was in quite a nice dream. I thought I was being carried along in a large sail belonging to a ship. The motion was pleasant and soothing. Past ten! What a bother! I shall be half dead again before I get to the Hold."

"I'll lend you my arm, Ru, to help you along."

"That's a good fellow!" exclaimed Rupert.

He got up and stretched himself, and then fell back in his chair, like a leaden weight. "I'd give five shillings to be there without the trouble of walking," quoth he.

"Rupert, you will be late."

"I can't help it," returned Rupert, folding his arms and leaning back again in the chair. "If Chattaway locks me out again, he must. I'll sit down in the portico until morning, for I sha'n't be able to stir another step from it."

Rupert was in that physical depression which reacts upon the mind. Whether he got in or not, whether he passed the night in a comfortable bed, or under the trees in the avenue, seemed of very little moment in his present state of feeling. Altogether he was some time getting off; and they heard the far-off church clock at Barbrook chime the half-past ten before they were half-way to the Hold. The sound came distinctly to their ears on the calm night air.

"I was somewhere about this spot when the half-hour struck last night, for your clocks were fast," remarked Rupert. "I ran all the way home after that—with what success, you know. I can't run to-night."

"I'll do my best to get you in," said George. "I hope I sha'n't be tempted, though, to speak my mind too plainly to Chattaway."

The Hold was closed for the night. Lights appeared in several of the windows. Rupert halted when he saw the light in one of them. "Aunt Diana must have returned," he said; "that's her room."

George Ryle rang a loud, quick peal at the bell. It was not answered. He rang again, a sharp, urgent peal, and shouted with his stentorian voice; a prolonged shout that could not have come from the lungs of Rupert; and it brought Mr. Chattaway to the window of his wife's dressing-room in surprise. One or two more windows in different parts of the house were thrown up.

"It is I, Mr. Chattaway. I have been assisting Rupert home. Will you be good enough to have the door opened?"

Mr. Chattaway was nearly struck dumb with the insolence of the demand, coming from the quarter it did. He could scarcely speak at first, even to refuse.

"He does not deserve your displeasure to-night," said George, in his clear, ringing tones, which might be heard distinctly ever so far off. "He could scarcely get here from fatigue and illness. But for taking a rest at my mother's house, and having the help of my arm up here, I question if he would have got as far. Be so good as to let him in, Mr. Chattaway."

"How dare you make such a request to me?" roared Mr. Chattaway, recovering himself a little. "How dare you come disturbing the peace of my house at night, like any house-breaker—except that you make more noise about it!"

"I came to bring Rupert," was George's answer. "He is waiting to be let in; tired and ill."

"I will not let him in," raved Mr. Chattaway. "How dare you, I ask?"

"What *is* all this?" broke from the amazed voice of Miss Diana Trevlyn. "What does it mean? I don't comprehend it in the least."

George looked up at her window. "Rupert could not get home by the hour specified by Mr. Chattaway—half-past ten. I am asking that he may be admitted now, Miss Trevlyn."

"Of course he can be admitted," said Miss Diana.

"Of course he sha'n't," retorted Mr. Chattaway.

"Who says he couldn't get home in time if he had wanted to come?" called out Cris from a window on the upper story. "Does it take him five or six hours to walk from Blackstone?"

"Is that you, Christopher?" asked George, falling back a little that he might see him better. "I want to speak to you. By what right did you take possession of my horse at Blackstone this afternoon, and ride him home?"

"I chose to do it," said Cris.

"I lent that horse to Rupert, who was unfit to walk. It would have been more generous—though you may not understand the word—had you left it for him. He was not in bed last night; has gone without food to-day—you were more capable of walking home than he."

Miss Diana craned forth her neck. "Chattaway, I must inquire into this. Let that front-door be opened."

"I will not," he answered. And he banged down his window with a resolute air, as if to avoid further colloquy.

But in that same moment the lock of the front-door was turned, and it was thrown open by Octave Chattaway.

CHAPTER XVIII
AN OLD IMPRESSION

It was surely a scene to excite some interest, if only the interest of curiosity, that was presented at Trevlyn Hold that night. Octave Chattaway in evening dress—for she had not begun to prepare for bed, although some time in her chamber—standing at the hall-door which she had opened; Miss Diana pressing forward from the back of the hall in a hastily assumed dressing gown; Mr. Chattaway in a waistcoat; Cris in greater déshabille; and Mrs. Chattaway dressed as was Octave.

Rupert came in, coughing with the night air, and leaning on the arm of George Ryle. There was no light, except such as was afforded by a candle carried by Miss Trevlyn; but she stepped forward and lighted the lamp.

"Now then," said she. "What is all this?"

"It is this," returned the master of Trevlyn Hold: "that I make rules for the proper regulation of my household, and a beardless boy chooses to break them. I should think"—turning shortly upon Miss Diana—"that you are not the one to countenance that."

"No," said she; "when rules are made they must be kept. What is your defence, Rupert?"

Rupert had thrown himself upon a bench against the wall in utter weariness of mind and body. "I don't care to make any defence," said he, in his apathy, as he leaned his cheek upon his hand, and fixed his blue eyes on Miss Trevlyn; "I don't know that there's much defence to make. Mr. Chattaway orders me to be in by half-past ten. I was at George Ryle's last night, and I a little exceeded the time, getting here five minutes or so after it, so I was locked out. Cris let himself in with his latch-key, but he would not let me in."

Miss Diana glanced at Cris, but said nothing. Mr. Chattaway interrupted. George, erect, fearless, was standing opposite the group, and it was to him that Chattaway turned.

"What I want to know is this—by what right *you* interfere, George Ryle?"

"I am not aware that I have interfered—except by giving Rupert my arm up the hill, and asking you to admit him. No very unjustifiable interference, surely, Mr. Chattaway."

"But it is, sir. And I ask why you presume to do it?"

"Presume? I saw Rupert to-night, accidentally, as he was coming from Blackstone. It was about nine o'clock. He appeared terribly tired, and wished to come into the house and rest. There he fell asleep. I awoke him in time, but he seemed too weary to get here himself, and I came with him to help him along. He walked slowly—painfully I should say; and it made him later than he ought to have arrived. Will you be so good, Mr. Chattaway, as to explain what part of this was unjustifiable interference? I do not see that I could have done less."

"You will see that you do less in future," growled Mr. Chattaway. "I will have no interference of yours between the Hold and Rupert Trevlyn."

"You may make yourself perfectly easy," returned George, some sarcasm in his tone. "Nothing could be farther from my intention than to interfere in any way with you, or with the Hold, or with Rupert in connection with you and the Hold. But, as I told you this morning, until you show me good and sufficient reason for the contrary, I shall observe common courtesy to Rupert when he comes in my way."

"Nonsense!" interposed Miss Diana. "Who says you are not to show courtesy to Rupert? Do you?" wheeling sharply round on Chattaway.

"There's one thing requires explanation," said Mr. Chattaway, turning to Rupert, and drowning Miss Diana's voice. "How came you to stop at Blackstone till this time of night? Where had you been loitering?"

Rupert answered the questions mechanically, never lifting his head. "I didn't leave until late. Ford wanted to go home, and I had to stop. After that I sat down on the way and dropped asleep."

"Sat down on your way and dropped asleep!" echoed Miss Diana. "What made you do that?"

"I don't know. I had been tired all day. I had no bed, you hear, last night. I suppose I can go to mine now?" he added, rising. "I want it badly enough."

"You can go—for this time," assented the master of Trevlyn Hold. "But you will understand that it is the last night I shall suffer my rules to be set at naught. You shall be in to time, or you do not come in at all."

Rupert shook hands with George Ryle, spoke a general "Good night" to the rest collectively, and went towards the stairs. At the back of the hall, lingering there in her timidity, stood Mrs. Chattaway. "Good night, dear Aunt Edith," he whispered.

She gave no answer: only laid her hand upon his as he passed: and so momentary was the action that it escaped unobserved, except by one pair of eyes—those of Octave Chattaway.

George was the next to go. Octave put out her hand to him. "Does Caroline come to the harvest-home?" she inquired.

"Yes, I think so. Good night."

"Good night," replied Octave, amiably. "I am glad you took care of Rupert."

"She's as false as her father," thought George, as he went down the avenue.

They were all dispersing. There was nothing now to remain up for. Chattaway was turning to the staircase, when Miss Diana stepped inside one of the sitting-rooms, carrying her candle, and beckoned to him.

"What do you want, Diana?" he asked, not in pleasant tones, as he followed her in.

"Why did you shut out Rupert last night?"

"Because I chose to do it!"

"But suppose I chose that he should not be shut out?"

"Then we shall split," angrily rejoined the master of Trevlyn Hold. "I say that half-past ten is quite late enough for Rupert. He is younger than Cris; you and Edith say he is not strong; *is* it too early?"

Mr. Chattaway was so far right. It was a sufficiently late hour; and Miss Diana, after a pause, pronounced it to be so. "I shall talk to Rupert," she said. "There's no harm in his going to spend an hour or two with George Ryle, or with any other friend, but he must be home in good time."

"Just so; he must be home in good time," acquiesced Chattaway. "He shall be home by half-past ten. And the only way to insure that, is to lock him out at first when he transgresses. Therefore, Diana, I shall follow my own way in this, and I beg you not to interfere."

Miss Diana went up to Rupert's room. He had taken off his coat, and thrown himself on the bed, as if the fatigue of undressing were too much for him.

"What's that for?" asked Miss Diana, as she entered. "Is that the way you get into bed?"

Rupert rose and sat down on a chair. "Only coming upstairs seems to tire me," he said in tones of apology. "I should not have lain a minute."

Miss Diana threw back her head a little, and looked at Rupert: the determined will of the Trevlyns shining out in every line of her face.

"I have come to ask where you slept last night. I mean to know, Rupert."

"I don't mind your knowing," replied Rupert; "I have told Aunt Edith. I decline to tell Chattaway, and I hope that no one else will tell him."

"Why?"

"Because he might lay blame where no blame is due. Chattaway turned me from the door, Aunt Diana, and Cris, who came up just after, turned me from it also. I went down to the lodge, and Ann Canham let me in; and I lay part of the night on their hard settle, and part of the night I sat upon it. That's where I was. But if Chattaway knew it, he'd turn old Canham and Ann from the lodge, as he turned me from the door."

"Oh no, he wouldn't," said Miss Diana, "if it were my pleasure to keep them in it. Do you feel ill, Rupert?"

"I feel middling. It is that I am tired, I suppose. I shall be all right in the morning."

Miss Diana descended to her own room. Waiting there for her was Mrs. Chattaway. In spite of a shawl thrown over her shoulders, she seemed to be shivering. She slipped the bolt of the door—what was she afraid of?—and turned to Miss Trevlyn, her hands clasped.

"Diana, this is killing me!" she wailed. "Why should Rupert be treated as he is? I know I am but a poor creature, that I have been one all my life—a very coward; but sometimes I think that I must speak out and protest against the injustice, though I should die in the effort."

"Why, what's the matter?" uttered Miss Diana, whose intense composure formed a strange contrast to her sister's agitated words and bearing.

"Oh, you know!—you know! I have not dared to speak out much, even to you, Diana; but it's killing me—it's killing me! Is it not enough that we despoiled Rupert of his inheritance, but we must also—"

"Be silent!" sharply interrupted Miss Diana, glancing around and lowering her voice to a whisper. "Will you never have done with that folly, Edith?"

"I shall never have done with its remembrance. I don't often speak of it; once, it may be, in seven years, not more. Better for me that I could speak of it; it would prey less upon my heart!"

"You have benefited by it as much as any one has."

"I cannot help myself. Heaven knows that if I could retire to some poor hut, and live upon a crust of bread, and benefit by it no more, I should do so—oh, how willingly! But there's no escape. I am hemmed in by its consequences; we are all hemmed in by them—and there's no escape."

Miss Diana looked at her. Steadfastly, keenly; not angrily, but searchingly and critically, as a doctor looks at a patient supposed to be afflicted with mania.

"If you do not take care, Edith, you will become insane upon this point, as I believe I have warned you before," she said, with calmness. "I am not sure but you are slightly touched now!"

"I do not think I am," replied poor Mrs. Chattaway, passing her hand over her brow. "I feel confused enough sometimes, but there's no fear that madness will really come. If thinking could have turned me mad, I should have gone mad years ago."

"The very act of your coming here in this excited state, when you should be going to bed, and saying what you do say, must be nothing less than a degree of madness."

"I would go to bed, if I could sleep," said Mrs. Chattaway. "I lie awake night after night, thinking of the past; of the present; thinking of Rupert and of what we did for him; the treatment we deal out to him now. I think of his father, poor Joe; I think of his mother, Emily Dean, whom we once so loved; and I—I cannot sleep, Diana!"

There really did seem something strange in Mrs. Chattaway to-night. For once in her life, Diana Trevlyn's heart beat a shade faster.

"Try and calm yourself, Edith," she said soothingly.

"I wish I could! I should be more calm if you and my husband would allow it. If you would only allow Rupert to be treated with common kindness—"

"He is not treated with unkindness," interrupted Miss Diana.

"It appears to me that he is treated with nothing but great unkindness. He—"

"Is he beaten?—is he starved?"

"The system pursued towards him is altogether unkind," persisted Mrs. Chattaway. "Indulgences dealt out to our own children are denied to him. When I think that he might be the true master of Trevlyn Hold—"

"I will not listen to this," interrupted Miss Diana. "What has come to you to-night?"

A shiver passed over the frame of Mrs. Chattaway. She was sitting on a low toilette chair covered with white drapery, her head bent on her hand. By her reply, which she did not look up to give, it appeared that she took the question literally.

"I feel the pain more than usual; nothing else. I do feel it so sometimes."

"What pain?" asked Miss Diana.

"The pain of remorse: the pain of the wrong dealt out to Rupert. It seems greater than I can bear. Do you know," raising her feverish eyes to Miss Diana, "that I scarcely closed my eyelids last night? All the long night through I was thinking of Rupert: fancying him lying outside on the damp grass; fancying—"

"Stop a minute, Edith. Are you seeking to blame your husband to me?"

"No, no; I don't wish to blame any one. But I wish it could be altered."

"If Rupert knows the hour for coming in—and it is not an unreasonable hour—it is he who is to blame if he exceeds it."

Mrs. Chattaway could not gainsay this. In point of fact, though she found things grievously uncomfortable, wrong altogether, she had not the strength of mind to say *where* the fault lay, or how it should be altered. On this fresh agitation, the coming in at half-past ten, she could only judge as a vacillating woman. The hour, as Miss Diana said, was not unreasonable, and Mrs. Chattaway would have fallen in with it, and approved her husband's judgment, if Rupert had only obeyed the mandate. If Rupert did not obey it—if he somewhat exceeded its bounds—she would have liked the door to be still open to him, and no scolding given. It was the discomfort that worried her; mixing itself up with the old feeling of the wrong done to Rupert, rendering things, as she aptly expressed it, more miserable than she could bear.

"I'll talk to Rupert to-morrow morning," said Miss Diana. "I shall add my authority to Chattaway's, and tell him that he *must* be in."

It may be that a shadow of the future was casting itself over the mind of Mrs. Chattaway, dimly and vaguely pointing to the terrible events hereafter to arise—events which would throw their consequences on the remainder of Rupert's life, and which had their origin in this new and ill-omened order, touching his coming home at night.

"Edith," said Miss Diana, "I would recommend you to become less sensitive on the subject of Rupert. It is growing into a morbid feeling."

"I wish I could! It does grow upon me. Do you know," sinking her voice and looking feverishly at her sister, "that old impression has come again! I thought it had worn itself out. I thought it had left me for ever."

Miss Diana almost lost patience. Her own mind was a very contrast to her sister's; the two were as opposite in their organisation as the poles. Fanciful, dreamy, vacillating, weak, the one; the other strong, practical, matter-of-fact.

"I don't know what you mean by the 'old impression,'" she rejoined, with a contempt she did not seek to disguise. "Is it not some new folly?"

"I told you of it in the old days, Diana. I used to feel certain—certain—that the wrong we inflicted on Rupert would avenge itself—that in some way he would come into his inheritance, and we should be despoiled of it. I felt so certain of it, that every morning of my life when I got up I seemed to expect its fulfilment before the day closed. But the time went on and on, and it never came. It went on so long that the impression wore itself out, I say, and now it has come again. It is stronger than ever. For some weeks past it has been growing more present with me day by day, and I cannot shake it off."

"The best thing you can do now is to go to bed, and try and sleep off your folly," cried Miss Trevlyn, with the stinging contempt she allowed herself at rare times to show to her sister. "I feel more provoked with you than I can express. A child might be pardoned for indulging in such absurdities; a woman, never!"

Mrs. Chattaway rose. "I'll go to bed," she meekly answered, "and get what sleep I can. I remember that you ridiculed this feeling of mine in the old days—"

"Pray did anything come of it then?" interrupted Miss Diana, sarcastically.

"I have said it did not. And the impression left me. But it has come again. Good night, Diana."

"Good night, and a more sensible frame of mind to you!" was the retort of Miss Diana.

Mrs. Chattaway crept softly along the corridor to her own dressing-room, hoping that her husband by that time was in bed and asleep. What was her surprise, then, to see him sitting at the table when she entered, not undressed, and as wide awake as she was.

"You have business late with Diana," he remarked.

Mrs. Chattaway felt wholly and entirely subdued; she had felt so since the previous night, when Rupert was denied admittance. The painful shyness, clinging to her always, seemed partially to have left her for a time. It was as though she had not strength left to be timid; almost as Rupert felt in his weariness of body, she was past caring for anything in her utter weariness of mind. Otherwise, she might not have spoken to Miss Diana as she had just done: most certainly she could never have spoken as she was about to speak to Mr. Chattaway.

"What may your business with her have been?" he resumed.

"It was not much, James," she answered. "I was saying how ill I felt."

"Ill! With what?"

"Ill in mind, I think," said Mrs. Chattaway, putting her hand to her brow. "I was telling her that the old fear had come upon me; the impression that used to cling to me always that some change was at hand regarding Rupert. I lost it for a great many years, but it has come again."

"Try and speak lucidly, if you can," was Mr. Chattaway's answer. "What has come again?"

"It seems to have come upon me in the light of a warning," she resumed, so lucidly that Mr. Chattaway, had he been a few steps lower in social grade, might have felt inclined to strike her. "I have ever felt that Rupert would in some manner regain his rights—I mean what he was deprived of," she hastily added, condoning the word which had slipped from her. "That he will regain Trevlyn Hold, and we shall lose it."

Mr. Chattaway listened in consternation, his mouth gradually opening in bewilderment. "What makes you think that?" he asked, when he found his voice.

"I don't exactly *think* it, James. Think is not the right word. The feeling has come upon me again within the last few weeks, and I cannot shake it off. I believe it to be a presentiment; a warning."

Paler and paler grew Mr. Chattaway. He did not understand. Like Miss Diana Trevlyn, he was very matter-of-fact, comprehending nothing but what could be seen and felt; and his wife might as well have spoken in an unknown tongue as of "presentiments." He drew a rapid conclusion that some unpleasant fact, bearing upon the dread *he* had long felt, must have come to his wife's knowledge.

"What have you heard?" he gasped.

"I have heard nothing; nothing whatever. I—"

"Then what on earth are you talking about?"

"Did you understand me, James? I say the impression was once firmly seated in my mind that Rupert would somehow be restored to what—to what"—she scarcely knew how to frame her words with the delicacy she deemed due to her husband's feelings—"to what would have been his but for his father's death. And that impression has now returned to me."

"But you have not heard anything? Any plot?—any conspiracy that's being hatched against us?"

"No, no."

Mr. Chattaway stared searchingly at his wife. Did he fancy, as Miss Diana had done, that her intellect was becoming disordered?

"Then, what do you mean?" he asked, after a pause. "Why should such an idea arise?"

Mrs. Chattaway was silent. She could not tell him the truth; could not say she believed it was the constant dwelling upon the wrong and injustice, which had first suggested the notion that the wrong would inevitably recoil on its workers. They had broken alike the laws of God and man; and those who do so cannot be sure of immunity from punishment in this world. That they had so long enjoyed unmolested the inheritance gained by fraud, gave no certainty that they would enjoy it to the end. She felt it, if her husband and Diana Trevlyn did not. Too often there were certain verses of Holy Writ spelling out their syllables upon her brain. "Remove not the old landmark; and enter not into the fields of the fatherless; for their Redeemer is mighty; he shall plead their cause with thee."

All this she could not say to Mr. Chattaway. She could give him no good reason for what she had said; he did not understand imaginative fancies, and he went to rest after bestowing upon her a sharp lecture for indulging them.

Nevertheless, in spite of her denial, the master of Trevlyn Hold could not divest himself of the impression that she must have picked up some scrap of news, or heard a word dropped in some quarter, which had led her to say what she did. And it gave him terrible discomfort.

Was the haunting shadow, the latent dread in his heart, about to be changed into substance? He lay on his bed, turning uneasily from side to side until the morning, wondering from what quarter the first glimmer of mischief would come.

CHAPTER XIX
A FIT OF AMIABILITY

Rupert came down to breakfast the next morning. He was cold, sick, shivery; little better than he had felt the previous night; his chest sore, his breathing painful. A good fire burnt in the grate of the breakfast-room—Miss Diana was a friend to fires, and caused them to be lighted as soon as the heat of summer had passed—and Rupert bent over it. He cared for it more than for food; and yet it was no doubt having gone without food the previous day which was causing the sensation of sickness within him now.

Miss Diana glided in, erect and majestic. "How are you this morning?" she asked of Rupert.

"Pretty well," he answered, as he warmed his thin white hands over the blaze. "I have the old pain here a bit"—touching his chest. "It will go off by-and-by, I dare say."

Miss Diana had her eyes riveted on him. The extreme delicacy of his countenance—its lines of fading health—struck upon her greatly. Was he looking worse? or was it that her absence from home for three weeks had caused her to notice it more than she had done when seeing him daily? She asked herself the question, and could not decide.

"You don't look very well, Rupert."

"Don't I? I have not felt well for this week or two. I think the walking to Blackstone and back is too much for me."

"You must have a pony," she continued after a pause.

"Ah! that would be a help to me," he said, his countenance brightening. "I might get on better with what I have to do there. Mr. Chattaway grumbles, and grumbles, but I declare, Aunt Diana, that I do my best. The walk there seems to take away all my energy, and, by the time I sit down, I am unfit for work."

Miss Diana went nearer to him, and spoke in lower tones. "What was the reason that you disobeyed Mr. Chattaway with regard to coming in?"

"I did not do it intentionally," he replied. "The time slipped on, and it got late without my noticing it. I think I told you so last night, Aunt Diana."

"Very well. It must not occur again," she said, peremptorily and significantly. "If you are locked out in future, I shall not interfere."

Mr. Chattaway came in, with a discontented gesture and a blue face. He was none the better for his sleepless night, and the torment which had caused it. Rupert drew away from the fire, leaving the field clear for him: as a schoolboy does at the entrance of his master.

"Don't let us have this trouble repeated," he roughly said to Rupert. "As soon as you have breakfasted, make the best of your way to Blackstone: and don't lag on the road."

"Rupert's not going to Blackstone to-day," said Miss Diana.

Mr. Chattaway turned upon her: no very pleasant expression on his countenance. "What's that for?"

"I shall keep him at home for a week, and have him nursed. After that, I dare say he'll be stronger, and can attend better to his duty in all ways."

Mr. Chattaway could willingly have braved Miss Diana, if he had only dared. But he did not dare. He strode to the breakfast-table and took his seat, leaving those who liked to follow him.

It has been remarked that there was a latent antagonism ever at work in the hearts of George Ryle and Octave Chattaway; and there was certainly ever constant and visible antagonism between the actions of Mr. Chattaway and Miss Diana Trevlyn, as far as they related to the ruling economy of Trevlyn Hold. She had the open-heartedness of the Trevlyns—he, the miserly selfishness of the Chattaways. She was liberal on the estate and in the household—he would have been niggardly to the last degree. Miss Diana, however, was the one to reign paramount, and he was angered every hour of his life by seeing some extravagance—as he deemed it—which might have been avoided. He could indemnify himself at the mines; and there he did as he pleased.

Breakfast over, Mr. Chattaway went out. Cris went out. Rupert, as the day grew warm and bright, strolled into the garden, and basked on a bench in the sun. He very much enjoyed these days of idleness. To sit as he was doing now, feeling that no exertion whatever was required of him; that he might stay where he was for the whole day, and gaze up at the blue sky as he fell into thought; or watch the light fleecy clouds that rose above the horizon, and form them into fantastic pictures—constituted one of the pleasures of Rupert Trevlyn's life. Not for the bright blue of the sky, the ever-changing clouds, the warm sunshine and balmy air—not for all these did he care so much as for the *rest*. The delightful consciousness that he might be as quiet as he pleased; that no Blackstone or any other far-off place would demand him; that for a whole day he might be at *rest*—there lay the charm. Nothing could possibly have been more suggestive of his want of strength—as anyone might have guessed possessed of sufficient penetration.

No. Mr. Chattaway need not have feared that Rupert was hatching plots against him, whenever he was out of his sight. Had poor Rupert possessed the desire, he lacked the energy.

The dinner hour at Trevlyn Hold, nominally early, was frequently regulated by the will or movements of the master. When he said he could only be home at a given hour—three, four, five, six, as the case might be—the cook had her orders accordingly. To-day it was fixed for four o'clock. At two (the more ordinary dinner hour) Cris came in.

Strictly speaking, it was ten minutes past two, and Cris burst into the dining-room with a heated face, afraid lest he should come in for the end of the meal. Whatever might be the hour fixed, dinner had to be on the table to the minute; and it generally was so. Miss Diana was an exacting mistress. Cris burst in, hair untidy, hands unwashed, desperately afraid of losing his share.

He drew a long face. Not a soul was in the room, and the dining-table showed its bright mahogany. Cris rang the bell.

"What time do we dine to-day?" he asked sharply of the servant who answered it.

"At four, sir."

"What a nuisance! And I am as hungry as a hunter. Get me something to eat. Here—stop—where are they all?"

"Madam's at home, sir; and I think Miss Octave's at home. The rest are out."

Cris muttered something which was not heard, which perhaps he did not intend should be heard; and when his luncheon was brought in, he sat down to it with great satisfaction. After he had finished, he went to the stables, and by-and-by came in to find his sister.

"Octave, I want to take you for a drive. Will you go?"

The unwonted attention on her brother's part quite astonished Octave. Before now she had asked him to drive her out, and been met with a rough refusal. Cris was of that class of young men who see no good in overpowering their sisters with attention.

"Get your things on at once," said Cris.

Octave felt dubious. She was writing letters to some particular friends with whom she kept up a correspondence, and did not care to be interrupted.

"Where is it to go, Cris?"

"Anywhere. We can drive through Barmester, and so home by the cross-roads. Or we'll go down the lower road to Barbrook, and go on to Barmester that way."

The suggestion did not offer sufficient attraction to Octave. "No," said she, "I am busy, and shall not go out this afternoon. I don't care to drive out when there's nothing to go for."

"You may as well come. It isn't often I ask you."

"No, that it is not," returned Octave, with emphasis. "You have some particular motive in asking me now, I know. What is it, Cris?"

"I want to try my new horse. They say he goes beautifully in harness."

"What! that handsome horse you took a fancy to the other day?—that papa said you should not buy?"

Cris nodded. "They let me have him for forty-five pounds."

"Where did you get the money?" wondered Octave.

"Never you mind. I have paid ten pounds down, and they'll wait for the rest. Will you come?"

"No," said Octave. "I sha'n't go out to-day."

The refusal perhaps was somewhat softened by the dashing up to the door of the dog-cart with the new purchase in it; and Cris ran out. A handsome animal certainly, but apparently restive. Mrs. Chattaway came through the hall, dressed for walking. Cris seized upon her.

"Mother, dear, you'll go for a drive with me," cried he, caressingly. "Octave won't—ill-natured thing!"

It was so unusual a circumstance to find herself made much of by her son, spoken to affectionately, that Mrs. Chattaway, in surprise and gratitude, forthwith ascended the dog-cart. "I am glad to accompany you, dear," she softly said. "I was only going to walk in the garden."

But before Cris had gathered the reins in his hand and taken his place beside her, George Ryle came up, and somewhat hindered the departure.

"I have been to Barmester to see Caroline this morning, Mrs. Chattaway, and have brought you a message from Amelia," he said, keeping his hold on the dog-cart as he spoke—as much as he could do so, for the restive animal.

"That she wants to come home, I suppose?" said Mrs. Chattaway, smiling.

"The message I was charged with was, that she *would* come home," he said, smiling in answer. "The fact is, Caroline is coming home for a few days: and Amelia thinks she will be cruelly used unless she is allowed holiday also."

"Caroline is coming to the harvest-home?"

"Yes. I told Amelia—"

Holding on any longer became impossible; and George drew back, and took a critical survey of the new horse. "Why, it is the horse Allen has had for sale!" he exclaimed.

"What brings him here, Cris?"

"I have bought him," shortly answered Cris.

"Have you? Mrs. Chattaway, I would advise you not to venture out behind that horse. He has not been broken in for driving."

"He has," returned Cris. "You mind your own business. Do you think I should drive him if he were not safe? He's only skittish. I understand horses, I hope, as well as you do."

George turned to Mrs. Chattaway. "Do not go with him," he urged. "Let Cris try him first alone."

"I am not afraid, George," she said, in loving accents. "It is not often Cris finds time to drive me. Thank you all the same."

Cris gave the horse its head, and the animal dashed off. George stood watching until a turn in the avenue hid them from view, and then gave utterance to an involuntary exclamation:

"Cris has no right to risk the life of his mother."

Not very long afterwards, the skittish horse was flying along the road, with nothing of the dog-cart left behind him, but its shafts.

CHAPTER XX
AN INVASION AT THE PARSONAGE

On the lower road, leading from Trevlyn Farm to Barbrook, stood Barbrook Rectory. A pretty house, covered with ivy, standing in the midst of a flourishing garden, and surrounded by green fields. An exceedingly pretty place for its size, that parsonage—it was never styled anything else—but very small. Fortunately the parsons inhabiting it had none of them owned large families, or they would have been at fault for room.

The present occupant was the Reverend John Freeman. Occupant of the parsonage house, but not incumbent of the living. The living, in the gift of a neighbouring cathedral, was held by one of the chapter; and he delegated his charge (beyond an occasional sermon) to a curate. It had been so in the old time when Squire Trevlyn flourished, and it was so still. Whispers were abroad that when the death of this canon should take place—a very old man, both as to years and occupancy of his prebendal stall—changes would be made, and the next incumbent would have to reside on the living. But this has nothing to do with us, and I don't know why I have alluded to it.

Mr. Freeman had been curate of the place for more than twenty years. He succeeded the Reverend Shafto Dean, of whom you have heard. Mr. Dean had remained at Barbrook only a very short time after his sister's marriage to Joe Trevlyn. That event had not tended to allay the irritation existing between Trevlyn Hold and the parsonage, and on some promotion being offered to Mr. Dean he accepted it. The promotion given him was in the West Indies: he would not have chosen a residence there under happier auspices; but he felt sick of the ceaseless contention of Squire Trevlyn. Mr. Dean went out to the West Indies, and died of fever within six months of his arrival. Mr. Freeman had succeeded him at Barbrook, and Mr. Freeman was there still: a married man, without children.

The parsonage household was very modest. One servant only was kept; and if you have the pleasure of making both ends meet at the end of the year upon the moderate sum of one hundred pounds sterling, you will wonder how even that servant could be retained. But a clergyman has advantages in some points over the rest of the world: at least this one had; his house was rent-free, and his garden supplied more vegetables and fruit than his household could consume. Some of the choicer fruit he sold. His superfluous vegetables he gave away; and many and many a cabbage leaf full of gooseberries and currants did the little parish children look out for, and receive. He was a quiet, pleasant little man of fifty, with a fair face and a fat double chin. Never an ill word had he had with any one in the parish since he came into it. His wife was pleasant, too, and talkative; and would as soon be caught by visitors making puddings in the kitchen, or shelling peas for dinner, as sitting in state in the drawing-room.

At the back of the house, detached from it, was a room called the brewhouse, where sundry abnormal duties, quite out of the regular routine of things, were performed. A boiler was in one corner, a large board or table which would put up or let down at will was under the casement, and the floor was paved. On the morning of the day when Mr. Cris Chattaway contrived to separate his dog-cart from its shafts, or to let his new horse do it for him, of which you will hear more presently, this brewhouse was so filled with steam that you could not see across it. A tall, strong, rosy-faced woman, looking about thirty years of age, was standing over a washing-tub; and in the boiler, bubbling and seething, white linen heaved up and down like the waves of a small sea.

You have seen the woman before, though the chances are you have forgotten all about her. It is Molly, who once lived at Trevlyn Farm. Some five years ago she came to an issue with the ruling potentates, Mrs. Ryle and Nora, and the result was a parting. Since then Molly had been living at the parsonage, and had grown to be valued by her master and mistress. She looks taller than ever, but wears pattens to keep her feet from the wet flags.

Molly was rubbing vigorously at her master's surplice—which shared the benefits of the wash with more ignoble things, when the church-clock striking caused her to pause and glance up through the open window. She was counting the strokes.

"Twelve o'clock, as I'm alive! I knew it must have gone eleven, but never thought it was twelve yet! And nothing out but a handful o' coloured things and the flannels! If missis was at home, she'd say I'd been wasting all my morning gossiping."

An accusation Mrs. Freeman might have made with great truth. There was not a more inveterate gossip than Molly in the parish; and her propensity had lost her her last place.

She turned to the boiler, seized the rolling-pin, and poked down the rising clothes with a fierceness which seemed to wish to make up for the lost hours. Then she dashed open the little iron door underneath, threw on a shovel of coals, and shut it again.

"This surplice is wearing as thin as anything in front," soliloquised she, recommencing at the tub. "I'd better not rub it too much. But it's just in the very place where master gets 'em most dirty. If I were missis, I should line 'em in front. His other one's going worse. They must cost a smart penny, these surplices. Now, who's that?"

Molly's interjection was caused by a flourishing knock at the front-door. It did not please her. She was too busy to answer useless visitors; unless because her master and mistress were out.

"I won't go to the door," decided she, in her vexation. "Let 'em knock again, or go away."

The applicant preferred the former course, for a second knock, louder than the first, echoed through the house. Molly brought her wet arms out of the water, dried them, and went on her way grumbling.

"It's that bothering Mother Hurnall, I know! And ten to one but she'll walk in, under pretence of resting, and poke her nose into my brewhouse, and see how my work's getting on. An interfering, mischief-making old toad, and if she *does* come in, I'll—"

Molly had opened the door, and her words came to an abrupt conclusion. Instead of the interfering mischief-maker, there stood a gentleman; a stranger: a tall, oldish man, with a white beard and white whiskers, jet-black eyes, a kindly but firm expression on his sallow face, a carpet-bag in one hand, a large red umbrella in the other.

Molly dropped a dubious curtsey. Beards were not much in fashion in that simple country place, neither were red umbrellas, and her opinion vacillated. Was the gentleman before her some venerable, much-to-be-respected patriarch; or one of those conjurers who frequented fairs in a caravan? Molly had had the gratification of seeing the one perform who came to the last fair, and he wore a white beard.

"I have been directed to this house as the residence of the Reverend Mr. Freeman," began the stranger. "Is he at home?"

"No, sir, he's not," replied Molly, dropping another and more assured curtsey. There was something about the stranger's voice and straightforward glance which quieted her fears. "My master and mistress are both gone out for the day, and won't be home till night."

This seemed a poser for the stranger. He looked at Molly, and Molly looked at him. "It is very unfortunate," he said at length. "I have come a great many hundred miles, and reckoned very much upon seeing my old friend Freeman. I shall be leaving England again in a few days."

Molly opened her eyes. "Come a great many hundred miles, all to see master!" she exclaimed.

"Not to see him," answered the stranger, with a smile at Molly's simplicity—not that he looked like a smiling man in general, but a very sad one. "I had to come to England on business, and I travelled a long way to get here, and shall have to travel the same long way to get back again. I have come from London on purpose to see Mr. Freeman. It is many years since we met, and I thought, if quite agreeable, I would sleep a couple of nights here. Did you ever happen to hear him mention an old friend of his, named Daw?"

The name struck on Molly's memory: it was a somewhat peculiar one. "Well, yes, I have, sir," she answered. "I have heard him speak of a Mr. Daw to my mistress. I think—I think—he lived somewhere over in France, that Mr. Daw. And he was a clergyman. My master lighted upon a lady's death a short time ago in the paper, while I was in the parlour helping my missis with some bed-furniture, and he exclaimed and said it must be Mr. Daw's wife."

"Right—right in all," said the gentleman. "I am Mr. Daw."

He took a small card-case from his pocket, and held out one of its cards to Molly; deeming it well, no doubt, that the woman should be convinced he was really the person he professed to be. "I can see but one thing to do," he said, "you must give me house-room until Mr. Freeman comes home this evening."

"You are welcome, sir. But my goodness! there's nothing in the house for dinner, and I'm in the midst of a big wash."

He shook his head as he walked into the parlour—a sunny apartment, redolent of mignonette, boxes of which stood outside the windows. "I don't in the least care about dinner," he carelessly observed. "A crust of bread, a little fresh butter, and a cup of milk, will do as well for me as anything more substantial."

Molly left him, to see what she could do in the way of entertainment, and take counsel with herself. "If it doesn't happen on purpose!" she ejaculated. "Anything that upsets the order of the house is sure to come on washing day! Well, it's no good worrying. The wash must go. If I can't finish to-day, I must finish to-morrow. I think he's what he says he is; and I've heard them red umbrellas is used in France."

She carried in a tray of refreshment—bread, butter, cheese, milk, and honey, and had adjusted the sleeves of her gown, straightened her hair, put on a clean apron, and taken off her pattens. Mr. Daw detained her whilst he helped himself, asking divers questions; and Molly, nothing loth, ever ready for a gossip, remembered not her exacting brewhouse.

"There is a place called Trevlyn Hold in this neighbourhood, is there not?"

"Right over there, sir," replied Molly, extending her hand. "You might see its chimneys but for them trees."

"I suppose the young master of Trevlyn has grown into a fine man?"

Molly turned up her nose, never supposing but the question alluded to Cris, and Cris was no favourite of hers: a prejudice possibly imbibed during her service at Trevlyn Farm.

"I don't call him so," said she, shortly. "A weazened-face fellow, with an odd look in his eyes as good as a squint! He's not much liked about here, sir."

"Indeed! That's a pity. Is he married? I suppose not though, yet. He is young."

"There's many a one gets married younger than he is. But I don't know who'd have him," added Molly, in her prejudice. "I wouldn't, if I was a young lady."

"Who has acted as his guardian?" resumed Mr. Daw.

Molly scarcely understood the question. "A guardian, sir? That's somebody that takes care of a child's money, who has no parents, isn't it? *He* has no guardian that I ever heard of, except it's his father."

Mr. Daw laid down his knife. "The young master of Trevlyn has no father," he exclaimed.

"Indeed he has, sir," returned Molly. "What should hinder him?"

"My good woman, you cannot know what I am talking about. His father died years and years ago. I was at his funeral."

Molly opened her mouth in very astonishment. "His father is alive now, sir, at any rate," cried she, after a pause. "I saw him ride by this house only yesterday."

They stared at each other, as people at cross-purposes often do. "Of whom are you speaking?" asked Mr. Daw, at length.

"Of Cris Chattaway, sir. You asked me about the young master of Trevlyn Hold. Cris will be its master after his father. Old Chattaway's its master now."

"Chattaway? Chattaway?" repeated the stranger, as if recalling the name. "I remember. It was he who—Is Rupert Trevlyn dead?" he hastily asked.

"Oh, no, sir."

"Then why is he not master of Trevlyn Hold?"

"Well, I don't know," replied Molly, after some consideration. "I suppose because Chattaway is."

"But surely Rupert Trevlyn inherited it on the death of his grandfather, Squire Trevlyn?"

"No, he didn't inherit it, sir. It was Chattaway."

So interested in the argument had the visitor become, that he neglected his plate, and was looking at Molly with astonished eyes. "Why did he not inherit it? He was the heir."

"It's what folks can't rightly make out," answered the woman. "Chattaway came in for it, that's certain. But folks have never called him the Squire, though he's as sick as a dog for it."

"Who is Mr. Chattaway? What is his connection with the Trevlyns? I forget."

"His wife was Miss Edith Trevlyn, the Squire's daughter. There was but three of 'em,—Mrs. Ryle, and her, and Miss Diana. Miss Diana was never married, and I suppose won't be now."

"Miss Diana?—Miss Diana? Yes, yes, I recollect," repeated the stranger. "It was Miss Diana whom Mrs. Trevlyn—Does Rupert Trevlyn live with Miss Diana?" he broke off again.

"Yes, sir; they all live at the Hold. The Chattaways, and Miss Diana, and young Mr. Rupert. Miss Diana has been out on a visit these two or three weeks past, but I heard this morning that she had come home."

"There was a pretty little girl—Maude—a year older than her brother," proceeded the questioner. "Where is she?"

"She's at the Hold, too, sir. They were brought to the Hold quite little babies, those two, and they have lived at it ever since, except when they've been at school. Miss Maude's governess to Chattaway's children."

Mr. Daw looked at Molly doubtingly. "Governess to Chattaway's children?" he mechanically repeated.

Molly nodded. She was growing quite at home with her guest. "Miss Maude has had the best of educations, they say: plays and sings wonderful; and so they made her the governess."

"But has she no fortune—no income?" reiterated the stranger, lost in wonder.

"Not a penny-piece," returned Molly, decisively. "Her and Mr. Rupert haven't a halfpenny between 'em of their own. He's clerk, or something of that sort, at Chattaway's coal mine, down yonder."

"But they were the heirs to the estate," the stranger persisted. "Their father was son and heir to Squire Trevlyn, and they are his children! How is it? How can it be?"

The words were spoken in the light of a remark. Mr. Daw was evidently debating the question with himself. Molly thought the question was put to her.

"I don't know the rights of it, sir," was all she could answer. "All I can tell you is, the Chattaways have come in for it, and the inheritance is theirs. But there's many a one round about here calls Mr. Rupert the heir to this day, and will call him so, in spite of Chattaway."

"He is the heir—he is the heir!" reiterated Mr. Daw. "I can prove—"

Again came that break in his discourse which had occurred before. Molly resumed.

"Master will be able to tell you better than me, sir, why the property should have went from Master Rupert to Chattaway. It was him that buried the old Squire, sir, and he was at the Hold after, and heard the Squire's will read. Nora told me once that he, the parson, cried shame upon it when he came away. But she was in a passion with Chattaway when she said it, so perhaps it wasn't true. I asked my missis about it one day that we was folding clothes together, but she said she knew nothing about it. She wasn't married then."

"Who is Nora?" inquired Mr. Daw.

"She's housekeeper and manager at Trevlyn Farm; a sort of relation. It was where I lived before I come here, sir; four year turned I was at that one place. I have always been one to keep my places a good while," added Molly, with pride.

Apparently the boast was lost upon him; he did not seem to hear it. "Not heir to Trevlyn!" he muttered; "not heir to Trevlyn! It puzzles me."

"I'm sorry master's out," repeated Molly, with sympathy. "But you can hear all about it to-night. They'll be home by seven o'clock. Twice a year, or thereabouts, they both go over to stop a day with missis's sister. Large millers they be, fourteen mile off, and live in a great big handsome house, and keep three or four indoor servants. The name's Whittaker, sir."

Mr. Daw did not show himself very much interested in the name, or in the worthy millers themselves. He was lost in a reverie. Molly made a movement about the plates and cheese and butter; insinuated the glass of milk under his very nose. All in vain.

"Not the heir!" he reiterated again; "not the heir! And I have been picturing him in my mind as the heir all through these long years!"

CHAPTER XXI
THE STRANGER

When Mrs. Chattaway and Cris drove off in the dog-cart, George Ryle did not follow them down the avenue, but turned to pursue his way round the house, which would take him to the fields: a shorter cut to his own land than the road. For a long time after his father's death, George could not bear to go through the field which had been so fatal to him; but he had lived down the feeling with the aid of that great reconciler—Time.

Happening to cast his eyes on the grounds as he skirted them, which lay on this side the Hold, he saw Rupert Trevlyn. Leaping a dwarf hedge of azaroles, he hastened to him.

"Well, old fellow! Taking a nap?"

Rupert opened his half-closed eyes, and looked round. "I thought it was Cris again!" he exclaimed. "He was here just now."

"Cris has gone out with his mother in the dog-cart. I don't like the horse he is driving, though."

"Is it that new horse he has been getting?"

"Yes; the one Allen had to sell."

"What's the matter with it?" asked Rupert. "I saw it carrying Allen one day, and thought it a beautiful animal!"

"It has a vicious temper, as I have been given to understand. And I believe it has never been properly broken in for driving. How do you feel to-day, Rupert?"

"No great shakes. I wish I was as strong as you, George."

George laughed pleasantly; and his voice, when he spoke, had a soothing sound in it. "So you may be, by the time you are as old as I am. Why, you have hardly done growing yet, Rupert. There's plenty of time for you to get strong."

"What brings you up here, George? Anything particular?"

"I saw Amelia to-day, and brought a message from her to her mother. Caroline is coming to us for the harvest-home, and Amelia wants to come too."

"Oh, they'll let her," cried Rupert. "The girls can do just as they like."

He, Rupert, leaned his chin on his hand, and began thinking of Amelia Chattaway. She was the oldest of the three younger children, and was at first under the tuition of Maude. But Maude could do nothing with her, the girl liking and taking; in fact she was too old both for Maude's control and instruction, and it was thought well to place her at a good school at Barmester, the school at which Caroline Ryle was being educated. Somehow Rupert's comforts were never added to by the presence of Amelia in the house, and he might have given way to a hope that she would not come home, had he been of a disposition to encourage such feelings.

Octave, who had discerned George Ryle from the windows of the Hold, came out to them, her pink parasol shading her face from the sun. A short time and Miss Trevlyn came home and joined them; next came Maude and her charges. It was quite a merry gathering. Miss Trevlyn unbent from her coldness, as she could do sometimes; Octave was all smiles and suavity, and every one, except Rupert, seemed at ease. Altogether, George Ryle was beguiled into doing what could not be often charged upon him—spending a good part of an afternoon in idleness.

But he went away at last. And as he was turning into the first field—never called anything but "the Bull field," by the country people, from the hour of Mr. Ryle's accident—he encountered Jim Sanders, eager and breathless.

"What's the matter?" asked George. "What do you want here?"

"I was speeding up to the Hold to tell 'em, sir. There's been an accident with Mr. Cris's dog-cart. I thought I'd warn the men up at his place."

"What accident?" hastily asked George, mentally beholding one sole object, and that was Mrs. Chattaway.

"I don't know yet, sir, what it is. I was in the road by the gate, when a horse came tearing along with broken shafts after it. It was that horse of Allen's which I saw Mr. Cris driving out an hour ago in his dog-cart, and Madam along of him. So I cut across the fields at once."

"You can go on," said George; "some of the men will be about. Should you see Miss Diana, or any of the young ladies, take care you say nothing to them. Do you hear?"

"I'll mind, sir."

Jim Sanders hastened out of the field on his way to the back premises of the Hold, and George flew onwards. When he gained the road, he looked up and down, but could see no traces of the accident. Nothing was in sight. Which way should he turn? Where had it occurred? He began reproaching himself for not asking Jim Sanders which way the horse had been coming from. As he halted in indecision some one suddenly came round the turning of the road lower down. It was Cris Chattaway, with a rueful expression and a gig-whip in his hand.

George made but few strides towards him. "What is the worst, Cris? Let me know it."

"I'll have him taken in charge and prosecuted, as sure as a gun," raved Cris. "I will. It's infamous that these things should be allowed in the public road."

"What—the horse?" exclaimed George.

"Horse be hanged!" politely returned Cris, whose irritation was excessive. "It wasn't the horse's fault. Nothing could go steadier and better than he went all the way and back again, as far as this—"

"Where's Mrs. Chattaway?" interrupted George.

"On the bank, down there. She's all right; only shaken a bit. The fellow's name was on the thing, and I have copied it down, and I've sent a man off for a constable. I'll teach him that he can't go about the country, plying his trade and frightening gentlemen's horses with impunity."

In spite of Cris's incoherence and passion, George contrived to gather an inkling of the facts. They had taken a short, easy drive down the lower road and through Barbrook, the horse going (according to Cris) beautifully. But on the road home, in that lonely part between the Hold and Trevlyn Farm, there stood a razor-grinder with his machine, grinding a knife. Whether the whirr of the wheel did not please the horse; whether it was the aspect of the machine; or whether it might be the razor-grinder himself, a somewhat tattered object in a fur cap, the animal no sooner came near, than he began to dance and backed towards the ditch. Cris did his best. He was a good whip and a fearless one; but he could not conquer. The horse turned Mrs. Chattaway into the ditch, relieved his mind by a few kicks, and started off with part of the shafts behind him.

"Are you much hurt, dear Mrs. Chattaway?" asked George, tenderly, as he bent over her.

She looked up with a smile, but her face was of a death-like whiteness. Fortunately, the ditch, a wide one, was dry; and she sat on the sloping bank, her feet resting in it. The dog-cart lay near, and several gazers, chiefly labouring men, stood around, helplessly staring. The razor-grinder was protesting *his* immunity from blame, and the hapless machine remained in its place untouched, drawn close to the pathway on the opposite side of the road.

"You need not look at me so anxiously, George," Mrs. Chattaway replied, the smile still on her face. "I don't believe I am hurt. One of my elbows is smarting, but I really feel no pain anywhere. I am shaken, of course; but that's not much. I wish I had taken your advice, not to sit behind that horse."

"Cris says he went beautifully, until he was frightened."

"Did Cris say so? It appeared to me that he had trouble with him all the way; but Cris knows, of course. He has gone to the Hold to bring the carriage for me, but I don't care to sit here to be stared at longer than I can help," she added, with a half-smile.

George leaped into the ditch, and partly helped and partly lifted her up the bank, and took her on his arm. She walked slowly, however, and leaned heavily upon him. When they reached the lodge, old Canham was gazing up and down the road, and Ann came out, full of consternation. They had seen the horse with the broken shafts gallop past.

"Then there's no bones broke, thank Heaven!" said Ann, with tears in her meek eyes.

She drew forward her father's armchair before the open door, and Mrs. Chattaway sat down in it, feeling she must have air, she said. "If I had but a drop o' brandy for Madam!" cried old Canham, as he stood near leaning all his weight on his stick.

George caught up the words. "I will go to the Hold and get some." And before Mrs. Chattaway could stop him, or say that she would prefer not to take the brandy he was away.

Almost at the same moment they heard the fast approach of a horse, and the master of Trevlyn Hold rode in at the gates. To describe his surprise when he saw his wife sitting, an apparent invalid, in old Canham's chair, and old Canham and Ann standing in evident consternation, almost as pale as she was, would be a difficult task. He reined in so quickly that his horse was flung back on its haunches.

"Is anything the matter? Has Madam been taken ill?"

"There has been an accident, sir," answered Ann Canham, with a meek curtsey. "Mr. Christopher was driving out Madam in the dog-cart, and they were thrown out."

Mr. Chattaway got off his horse. "How did it happen?" he asked his wife, an angry expression crossing his face. "Was it Cris's fault? I hate that random driving of his!"

"I am not hurt, James; only a little shaken," she replied, with gentleness. "Cris was not to blame. There was a razor-grinder in the road, grinding knives, and it frightened the horse."

"Which horse was he driving?" demanded Mr. Chattaway.

"A new one. One he bought from Allen."

The reply did not please Mr. Chattaway. "I told Cris he should not buy that horse," he angrily said. "Is the dog-cart injured?"

It was apparent from the question that Mr. Chattaway had not passed the *débris* on the road. He must have come the other way, or perhaps across the common. Mrs. Chattaway did not dare to say she believed the dog-cart was very much injured. "The shafts are broken," she said, "and something more."

"Where did it occur?" growled Mr. Chattaway.

"A little lower down the road. George Ryle came up soon after it happened, and I walked here with him. Cris went on to the Hold to send the carriage, but I shall get home without it."

"It might have been worse, Squire," interposed old Canham, who, as a dependant of Trevlyn Hold, felt compelled sometimes to give the "Squire" his title to his face, though he never would, or did, behind his back. "Nothing hardly happens to us, sir, in this world, but what's more eased to us than it might be."

Mr. Chattaway had stood with his horse's bridle over his arm. "Would you like to walk home with me now?" he asked his wife. "I can lead the horse."

"Thank you, James. I think I must rest here a little longer. I had only just got here when you came up."

"I'll send for you," said Mr. Chattaway. "Or come back myself when I have left the horse at home. Mr. Cris will hear more than he likes from me about this business."

"Such an untoward thing has never happened to Mr. Cris afore, sir," observed Mark Canham. "There's never a better driver than him for miles round. The young heir, now, he's different: a bit timid, I fancy, and—"

"Who?" burst forth Mr. Chattaway, taking his foot from the stirrup, for he was about to mount, and hurling daggers at Mark Canham. "The young heir! To whom do you dare apply that title!"

Had the old man purposely launched a sly shaft at the master of Trevlyn Hold, or had he spoken inadvertently? He hastened to repair the damage as he best could.

"Squire, I be growing old now—more by sickness, though, than by age—and things and people gets moithered together in my mind. In the bygone days, it was a Rupert Trevlyn that was the heir, and I can't at all times call to mind that this Rupert Trevlyn is not so: the name is the same, you see. What has set me to make such a stupid mistake this afternoon, I can't tell, unless it was the gentleman's words that was here but an hour ago. He kept calling Master Rupert the heir; and he wouldn't call him nothing else."

Mr. Chattaway's face grew darker. "What gentleman was that, pray?"

"I never see him before in my life, sir," returned old Canham. "He was a stranger to the place, and asked all manner of questions about it. He called Master Rupert the heir, and I stopped him, saying he made a mistake, for Master Rupert was not the heir. And he answered I was right so far, that Master Rupert, instead of being the heir of Trevlyn Hold, was its master and owner. I couldn't help staring at him when he said it."

Chattaway felt as if his blood were curdling. Was this the first act in the great drama he had so long dreaded? "Where did he come from? What sort of a man was he?" he mechanically asked, all symptoms of anger dying away in his sudden fear.

Old Canham shook his head. "I don't know nothing about where he's from, sir. He came strolling inside the gates, as folks strange to a place will do, looking about 'em just for curiosity's sake. He saw me sitting at the open window, and he asked what place this was, and I told him it was Trevlyn Hold. He said he thought so, that he had been walking about looking for Trevlyn Hold, and he leaned his arm upon the sill, and put nigh upon a hundred questions to me."

"What were the questions?" eagerly rejoined Mr. Chattaway.

"I should be puzzled to tell you half of 'em, sir, but they all bore upon Trevlyn Hold. About the Squire's death, and the will, and the succession; about everything in short. At last I told him that I didn't know the rightful particulars myself, and he'd better go to you or Miss Diana."

Mrs. Chattaway stole a glance at her husband. Her face was paler than the accident had made it; with a more alarmed pallor. The impression clinging to her mind, and of which she had spoken to her husband the previous night—that Rupert Trevlyn was on the eve of being restored to his rights—seemed terribly strong upon her now.

"He was a tall, thin, strange-looking man, with a foreign look about him, and a red umberella," continued old Canham. "A long white beard he had, sir, like a goat, and an odd hat made of cloth or crape, or some mourning stuff. His tongue wasn't quite like an English tongue, either. I shouldn't wonder but he was a lawyer, Squire: no one else wouldn't surely think of putting such a string of questions—"

"Did he—did he put the questions as an official person might put them?" rapidly interrupted Mr. Chattaway.

Old Canham hesitated; at a loss what precise reply to give. "He put 'em as though he wanted answers to 'em," returned he at length. "He said a word or two, sir, that made me think he'd been intimate once with the young Squire, Mr. Joe, and he asked whether his boy or his girl had growed up most like him. He wondered, he said, whether he should know either of 'em by the likeness, when he came to meet 'em, as he should do to-day or to-morrow."

"And what more?" gasped Mr. Chattaway.

"There was nothing more, Squire, in particular. He took his elbow off the window-sill, and went through the gates again down the road. It seemed to me as if he had come into the neighbourhood for some special purpose connected with the questions."

It seemed so to some one else also. When the master of Trevlyn Hold mounted his horse and rode him slowly through the avenue towards home, a lively fear, near and terrible, had replaced that vague dread which had so long lain latent in his heart.

CHAPTER XXII
COMMOTION

The beauty of the calm autumn afternoon was marred by the hubbub in the road. The rays of the sun came filtering through the foliage of the trees, the deep blue sky was without a cloud, the air was still and balmy: imparting an idea of peace. But in that dusty highway, so lonely at other times, a crowd of people had gathered, and they talked and swayed, and made much clatter and disturbance.

The affair had got wind. How these affairs do get wind who can tell? It had been exaggerated in the usual fashion. "Madam was killed; the dog-cart smashed to pieces; the horse lamed; and Mr. Cris wounded." Half the gaping people who came up believed it all: and the chief hubbub was caused, not so much by discussing the accident, as by endeavouring to explain that its effects were not very disastrous.

The news had travelled with its embellishments to Trevlyn Farm, amidst other places; and it brought out Nora. Without waiting to put anything on, she took her way to the spot. Mrs. Ryle was expecting company that afternoon, and Nora was at leisure and *en grande toilette*: a black silk gown, its flounces edged with velvet, and a cap of blonde lace trimmed with white flowers. The persons who were gathered on the spot made way for her. The wrecked dog-cart lay partly in the ditch, partly out of it. Opposite was the grinding-machine, its owner now silent and crestfallen, as he inwardly speculated upon what the law could do to him.

"Then it's not true that Madam's killed?" cried Nora, after listening to the various explanations.

A dozen voices answered. "Madam wasn't hurt to speak of, only a bit shook: she had told them so herself. She had walked off on Mr. George Ryle's arm, without waiting for the carriage that Mr. Cris had gone to fetch."

"I'll be about that Jim Sanders," retorted Nora, wrathfully. "How dare he come in with such tales? He said Madam was lying dead in the road."

She had barely spoken, when the throng standing over the dog-cart was invaded by a new-arrival, one who had been walking in a neighbouring field, and wondered what the collection could mean. The rustics fell back and stared at him: first, because he was a stranger; secondly, because his appearance was somewhat out of the common way; thirdly, because he carried a red umbrella. A tall man with a long white beard, a hat, the like of which had never been seen by country eyes, and a foreign look.

You will at once recognise him for the traveller who had introduced himself at the parsonage as the Reverend Mr. Daw, a friend of its owner. The crowd, having had no such introduction, could only stare, marvelling whether he had dropped from the clouds. He had been out all the afternoon, taking notes of the neighbourhood, and since his conversation with old Canham—which you heard related afterwards to Mr. Chattaway, to that gentleman's intense dread—he had plunged into the fields on the opposite side of the way. There he had remained, musing and wandering, until aroused by the commotion which he speedily joined.

"What has happened?" he exclaimed. "An accident?"

The assemblage fell back. Rustics are prone to be suspicious of strangers, if their appearance is peculiar, and not one of them found a ready answer. Nora, however, whose tongue had, perhaps, never been at fault in its whole career, stood her ground.

"There's not much damage done, as far as I can learn," she said, in her usual free manner. "The dog-cart's the worst of it. There it lies. It was Cris Chattaway's own; and I should think it will be a lesson to him not to be so fond of driving strange horses."

"Is it to the Chattaways the accident has occurred?" asked the stranger.

Nora nodded. She was stooping down to survey more critically the damages done to the dog-cart. "Cris Chattaway was driving his mother out," she said, rising. "He was trying a strange horse, and this was the result," touching the wheel with her foot. "Madam was thrown into the ditch here."

"And hurt?" laconically asked Mr. Daw.

"Only shaken—as they say. But a shaking may be dangerous for one so delicate as Madam Chattaway. A pity but it had been *him*."

Nora spoke the last word with emphasis so demonstrative that her hearer raised his eyes in wonderment. "Of whom do you speak?" he said.

"Of Chattaway: Madam's husband. A shaking might do him good."

"You don't like him, apparently," observed the stranger.

"I don't know who does," freely spoke Nora.

"Ah," said Mr. Daw, quietly. "Then I am not singular. *I* don't."

"Do you know him?" she rejoined.

But to this the stranger gave no reply; he had evidently no intention of giving any; and the silence whetted Nora's curiosity more than any answer could have done, however obscure or mysterious. Perhaps no living woman within a circuit of five miles possessed curiosity equal to that of Nora Dickson.

"Where have you known Chattaway?" she exclaimed.

"It does not matter," said the stranger. "He is in the enjoyment of Trevlyn Hold, I hear."

To say "I hear," as applied to the subject, imparted the idea that the stranger had only just gained the information. Nora threw her quick black eyes searchingly upon him.

"Have you lived in a wood not to know that James Chattaway was possessor of Trevlyn Hold?" she said, with her characteristic plainness of speech. "He has enjoyed it these twenty years to the exclusion of Rupert Trevlyn."

"Rupert Trevlyn is its rightful owner," said the stranger, almost as demonstratively as Nora herself could have spoken.

"Ah," said Nora, with a sort of indignant groan, "the whole parish knows that. But Chattaway has possession of it, you see."

"Why doesn't some one help Rupert Trevlyn to his rights?"

"Who's to do it?" crossly responded Nora. "Can you?"

"Possibly," returned the stranger.

Had the gentleman asserted that he might possibly cause the moon to shine by day instead of by night, Nora could not have shown more intense surprise. "Help—him—to—his—rights?" she slowly repeated. "Do you mean to say you could displace Chattaway?"

"Possibly," was the repeated answer.

"Why—who are you?" uttered the amazed Nora.

A smile flitted for a moment over Mr. Daw's countenance, the first symptom of a break to its composed sadness. But he gave no reply.

"Do you know Rupert Trevlyn?" she reiterated.

But even to that there was no direct answer. "I came to this place partly to see Rupert Trevlyn," were the words that issued from his lips. "I knew his father; he was my dear friend."

"Who can he be?" was the question reiterating itself in Nora's active brain. "Are you a lawyer?" she asked, the idea suddenly occurring to her: as it had, you may remember, to old Canham.

Mr. Daw coughed. "Lawyers are keen men," was his answering remark, and Nora could have beaten him for its vagueness. But before she could say more, an interruption occurred.

This conversation had been carried on aloud; neither the stranger nor Nora having deemed it necessary to speak in undertones. The consequence of which was, that those in the midst of whom they stood had listened with open ears, drawing their own deductions—and very remarkable deductions some of them were. The knife-grinder—though a stranger to the local politics, and totally uninterested in them—had listened with the rest. One conclusion *he* hastily came to, was, that the remarkable-looking gentleman with the white beard *was* a lawyer; and he pushed himself to the front.

"You be a lawyer, master," he broke in, with some excitement. "Would you mind telling of me whether they *can* harm me. If I ain't at liberty to ply my trade under a roadside hedge but I must be took up and punished for it, why, it's a fresh wrinkle I've got to learn. I've done it all my life; others in the same trade does it; can the law touch us?"

Mr. Daw had turned in wonderment. He had heard nothing of the grinding-machine in connection with the accident, and the man's address was unintelligible. A score of voices hastened to enlighten him, but before it was well done, the eager knife-grinder's voice rose above the rest.

"Can the laws touch me for it, master?"

"I cannot tell you," was the answer.

The man's low brow scowled fitfully: he was somewhat ill-looking to the eye of a physiognomist. "What'll it cost?" he roughly said, taking from his pocket a bag in which was a handful of copper money mixed with a sprinkling of small silver. "I might know. A lawyer wouldn't give nothing for nothing, but I'll pay. If the laws can be down upon me for grinding a knife in the highway open to the world, all I can say is, that the laws is infamous."

He stood looking at the stranger, with an air of demand, not of supplication—and rather insulting demand, too. Mr. Daw showed no signs of resenting the incipient insolence; on the contrary, his voice took a kind and sympathising tone.

"My good man, you may put up your money. I can give you no information about the law, simply because I am ignorant of its bearing on these cases. In the old days, when I was an inhabitant of England, I have seen many a machine such as yours plying its trade in the public roads, and the law, as I supposed, could not touch them, neither did it attempt to. But that may be altered now: there has been time enough for it; years and years have passed since I last set foot on English soil."

The razor-grinder thrust his bag into his pocket again, and began to push back to the spot whence he had come. The mob had listened with open ears, but had gained little further information. Whether he was a lawyer or whether he was not; where he had come from, and what his business was amongst them, unless it was the placing of young Rupert Trevlyn in possession of his "rights," they could not tell.

Nora could not tell—and the fact did not please her. If there was one thing provoked Nora Dickson more than all else, it was to have her curiosity unsatisfied. She felt that she had been thwarted now. Turning away in a temper, speaking not a syllable to the stranger by way of polite adieu, she began to retrace her steps to Trevlyn Farm, holding up the flounces of her black silk gown, that they might not come into contact with the dusty road.

But—somewhat to her surprise—she found the mysterious stranger had also extricated himself from the mob, and was following her. Nora was rather on the high ropes just then, and would not notice him. He, however, accosted her.

"By what I gathered from a word or two you let fall, I should assume that you are a friend of Rupert Trevlyn's, ma'am?"

"I hope I am," said Nora, mollified at the prospect of enlightenment. "Few folks about here but are friends to him, unless it's Chattaway and his lot at the Hold."

"Then perhaps you will have no objection to inform me—if you can inform me—how it was that Mr. Chattaway came into possession of the Hold, in place of young Rupert Trevlyn. I cannot understand how it could possibly have been. Until I came here to-day, I never supposed but the lad, Rupert, was Squire of Trevlyn Hold."

"Perhaps you'll first of all tell me what you want the information for?" returned Nora. "I don't know who you are, sir, remember."

"You heard me say I was a friend of his father's; I should like to be a friend to the boy. It appears to me to be a monstrous injustice that he should not have succeeded to the estate of his ancestors. Has he been *legally* deprived of it?"

"As legally as a properly-made will could deprive him," was the reply of Nora. "Legality and justice don't always go together in our parts: I don't know what they may do in yours."

"Joe Trevlyn—my friend—was the direct heir to Trevlyn Hold. Upon his death his son became the heir. Why did he not succeed?"

"There are folks that say he was cheated out of it," replied Nora, in very significant tones.

"Cheated out of it?"

"It is said the news of Rupert's birth was never suffered to reach the ears of Squire Trevlyn. That the Squire went to his grave, never knowing he had a grandson in the direct male line—went to it after willing the estate to Chattaway."

"Kept from it by whom?" eagerly cried Mr. Daw.

"By those who had an interest in keeping it from him—Chattaway and Miss Diana Trevlyn. It is so said, I say: *I* don't assert it. There may be danger in speaking too openly to a stranger," candidly added Nora.

"There is no danger in speaking to me," he frankly said. "I have told you the truth—that I am a friend of young Rupert Trevlyn's. Chattaway is not a friend of mine, and I never saw him in my life."

Nora, won over to forget caution and ill-temper, opened her heart to the stranger. She told him all she knew of the fraud; told him of Rupert's friendlessness, his undesirable position at the Hold. Nora's tongue, set going upon any grievance she felt strongly, could not be stopped. They walked on until the fold-yard gate of Trevlyn Farm was reached. There Nora came to a halt. And there she was in the midst of a concluding oration, delivered with forcible eloquence, and there the stranger was listening eagerly, when they were interrupted by George Ryle.

Nora ceased suddenly. The stranger looked round, and seeing a gentleman-like man who evidently belonged in some way to Nora, lifted his hat. George returned it.

"It's somebody strange to the place," unceremoniously pronounced Nora, by way of introducing him to George. "He was asking about Rupert Trevlyn."

CHAPTER XXIII
COMING VERY CLOSE

If they had possessed extraordinarily good eyes, any one of the three, they might have detected a head peering at them over a hedge about two fields off, in the direction of Trevlyn Hold. The head was Mr. Chattaway's. That gentleman rode home from the lodge, after hearing old Canham's account of the mysterious visit, in a state not to be described. Encountering Miss Diana, he despatched her with Octave to the lodge to see after his wife; he met George Ryle, and told him *his* services were no further needed—Madam wanted neither him nor the brandy; he sent his horse to the stable, and went indoors: all in a confused state of agitation, as if he scarcely knew what he was about.

Dinner was ready; the servants were perplexed at no one's coming in for it, and they asked if the Squire would sit down without Madam. *He* sit down to dinner—in that awful uncertainty? No; rather would he steal out and poke and pry about until he had learned something.

He left the house and plunged into the fields. He did not go back down the avenue, openly past the lodge into the road: cowards, with their fear upon them, prowl about stealthily—as Chattaway was doing now. Very grievously was the fear upon him.

He walked hither and thither: he stood for some minutes in the field which had once been so fatal to poor Mr. Ryle; his arms were folded, his head was bent, his newly-awakened imagination was in full play. He crept to the outer field, and walked under cover of its hedge until he came opposite all that hubbub and confusion. There he halted, found himself a peep-hole, and took in by degrees all that was to be seen: the razor-grinder and his machine, the dog-cart and its dilapidations, and the mob. Eagerly, anxiously did his restless eyes scan that mob; but he, upon whom they hoped to rest, was not amongst them. For you may be sure Mr. Chattaway was searching after none but the dreaded stranger. Miserly as he was, he would have given a ten-pound note out of his pocket to obtain only a moment's look at him. He had been telling over all the enemies he had ever made, as far as he could remember them. Was it one of those?—some one who owed him a grudge, and was taking this way of paying it? Or was it a danger coming from a totally unknown quarter? Ten pounds! Chattaway would have given fifty then for a good view of the stranger; and his eyes were unmindful of the unfriendly thorns, in their feverish anxiety to penetrate to the very last of that lazy throng, idling away the summer's afternoon.

The stranger was certainly not amongst them. Chattaway knew every chattering soul there. Some of his unconscious labourers made a part, and he only wished he dared appear and send them flying. But he did not care to do so. If ever there was a cautious man where he and his interests were concerned, it was Chattaway; and he would not run the risk of meeting this man face to face. No, no; rather let him get a bird's-eye view of him first, that he might be upon his guard.

The state of the dog-cart did not by any means tend to soothe his feelings; neither did the sight of George Ryle, who passed through the crowd in the direction of his own home. He could see what a pretty penny it would take to repair the one; he knew not how many pounds it might take to set right any mischief being hatched by the other. Mr. Chattaway turned away. He bore along noiselessly by the side of the hedge, and then over a stile into a lower field, and then into another. That brought Trevlyn Farm under his vision, and—and—what did his restless eyes catch sight of?

Leaning on the fold-yard gate, dressed in a style not often seen, stood Nora Dickson; on the other side was George Ryle, and with him one who might be recognised at the first glance—the strange-looking man, with his white hair, his red umbrella, and his queer hat, as described by old Canham. There could be no mistake about it; he it was: and the perspiration poured off the master of Trevlyn Hold in his mortal fear.

What were they hatching, those three? That it looked suspicious must be confessed, to one whose fears were awakened as were Chattaway's; for their heads were in close contact, and their attention was absorbed. Was he stopping at Trevlyn Farm, this man of treason? Undoubtedly: or why should Nora Dickson be decked out in company attire? Chattaway had always believed George Ryle to be a rogue, but now he knew him to be one.

It was a pity Chattaway could not be listening as well as peeping. He would only have heard the gentleman explain to George Ryle who he was; his name, his calling, and where he was visiting in Barbrook. So far, Chattaway's doubts would have been at rest; but he would have heard no worse. George was less impulsive than Nora, and would not be likely to enter on the discussion of the claims of Rupert Trevlyn *versus* Chattaway, with a new acquaintance.

A very few minutes, and they separated. The conversation had been general since George came up; not a word having been said that could have alarmed intruding ears. Nora hastened indoors; George turned off to his rick-yard; and the stranger stood in the road and gazed leisurely about him, as though considering the points for a sketch. Presently he disappeared from Chattaway's view.

That gentleman, taking a short time to recover himself, came to the conclusion that he might as well disappear also, in the direction of his home; where no doubt dinner was arrested, and its hungry candidates speculating upon what could have become of the master. It was of no use remaining where he was. He had ascertained one point—the dreaded enemy was an utter stranger to him. More than that he did not see that he could ascertain, in this early stage.

He wiped his damp face and set forth on his walk home, stepping out pretty briskly. It was as inadvisable to make known his fears abroad as to proclaim them at home. Were only an inkling to become known, it seemed to Chattaway that it would be half the business towards wresting Trevlyn Hold from him.

As he walked on, his courage partially came back to him, and the reaction once set in, his hopes went up, until he almost began to despise his recent terror. It was absurd to suppose this stranger could have anything to do with himself and Rupert Trevlyn. He was merely an inquisitive traveller looking about the place for his amusement, and in so doing had picked up bits of gossip, and was seeking further information about them—all to while away an idle hour. What a fool he had been to put himself into a fever for nothing.

These consoling thoughts drowning the mind's latent dread—or rather making pretence to do so, for that the dread was there still, Chattaway was miserably conscious—he went on increasing his speed. At last, in turning into another field, he nearly knocked down a man running in the same direction, who had come up at right angles with him: a labourer named Hatch, who worked on his farm.

It was a good opportunity to let off a little of his ill-humour, and he demanded where the man had been skulking, and why he was away from his work Hatch answered that, hearing of the accident to Madam and the young Squire, he and his fellow-labourers had been induced to run to the spot in the hope of affording help.

"Help!" said Mr. Chattaway. "You went off to see what there was to be seen, and for nothing else, leaving the rick half made. I have a great mind to dock you of a half-day's pay. Is there so much to look at in a broken dog-cart, that you and the rest of you must neglect my work?"

The man took off his hat and rubbed his head gently: his common resort in a quandary. They *had* hindered a great deal more time than was necessary; and had certainly not bargained for its coming to the knowledge of the Squire. Hatch, too simple or too honest to invent excuses, could only make the best of the facts as they stood.

"'Twasn't the dog-cart kept us, Squire. 'Twas listening to a strange-looking gentleman; a man with a white beard and a red umberellar. He were talking about Trevlyn Hold, saying it belonged to Master Rupert, and he were going to help him to it."

Chattaway turned away his face. Instinct taught him that even this stolid serf should not see the cold moisture that suddenly oozed from every pore. "*What* did he say?" he cried, in accents of scorn.

Hatch considered. And you must not too greatly blame the exaggerated reply. Hatch did not purposely deceive his master; but he did what a great many of us are apt to do—he answered according to the impression made on his imagination. He and the rest of the listeners had drawn their own conclusions, and in accordance with those conclusions he now spoke.

"He said for one thing, Squire, as he didn't like you—"

"How does he know me?" Mr. Chattaway interrupted.

"Nora Dickson asked him, but he wouldn't answer. He's a lawyer, and—"

"How do you know he's a lawyer?" again interrupted Mr. Chattaway.

"Because he said it," was the prompt reply. And the man had no idea that it was an incorrect one. He as much believed the white-bearded stranger to be a lawyer as that he himself was a day-labourer. "He said he had come to help Master Rupert to his rights, and displace you from 'em. Our hairs stood on end to hear him, Squire."

"Who is he?—where does he come from?" And to save his very life Chattaway could not have helped the words issuing forth in gasps.

"He never said where he come from—save he hadn't been in England for many a year. We was a wondering among ourselves where he come from, after he walked off with Nora Dickson."

"Does she know?"

"No, she don't, Squire. He come up while she were standing there, and she wondered who he were, as we did. 'Twere through her asking him questions that he said so much."

"But—what has he to do with my affairs?—what has he to do with Rupert Trevlyn?" passionately rejoined Mr. Chattaway.

It was a query Hatch was unable to answer. "He said he were a friend of the dead heir, Mr. Joe—I mind well he said that—and he had come to this here place partly to see Master Rupert. He didn't seem to know afore as

Master Rupert had not got the Hold, and Nora Dickson asked if he'd lived in a wood not to know that. So then he said he should help him to his rights, and Nora said, 'What! displace Chattaway?' and he said, 'Yes.' We was took aback, Squire, and stopped a bit longer maybe than we ought. It was that kep' us from the rick."

Every pulse beating, every drop of blood coursing in fiery heat, the master of Trevlyn Hold reached his home. He went in, and left his hat in the hall, and entered the dining-room, as a man in some awful dream. A friend of Joe Trevlyn's!—come to help Rupert to his rights!—to displace *him*! The words rang their changes on his brain.

They had not waited dinner. It had been Miss Diana's pleasure that it should be commenced, and Mr. Chattaway took a seat mechanically. Mechanically he heard that his wife had declined partaking of it—had been ill when she reached home; that Rupert, after a hasty meal, had gone upstairs to lie down, at the recommendation of Miss Diana; that Cris had now gone off to the damaged dog-cart. He was as a man stunned, and felt utterly unnerved. He sat down, but found he could not swallow a mouthful.

The cloth was removed and dessert placed upon the table. After taking a little fruit, the younger ones dispersed; Maude went upstairs to see how Mrs. Chattaway was; the rest to the drawing-room. The master of Trevlyn Hold paced the carpet, lost in thought. The silence was broken by Miss Diana.

"Squire, I am not satisfied with the appearance of Rupert Trevlyn. I fear he may be falling into worse health than usual. It must be looked to, and more care taken of him. I intend to buy him a pony to ride to and fro between here and Blackstone."

Had Miss Diana expressed her intention of purchasing ten ponies for Rupert, it would have made no impression then on Chattaway. In his terrible suspense and fear, a pony more or less was an insignificant thing, and he received the announcement in silence, to the intense surprise of Miss Diana, who had expected to see him turn round in a blaze of anger.

"Are you not well?" she asked.

"Well? Quite well. I—I over-heated myself riding, and—and feel quite chilly now. What should hinder my being well?" he continued, resentfully.

"I say I shall buy a pony for Rupert. Those walks to Blackstone are too much for him. I think it must be that which is making him feel so ill."

"I wish you'd not bother me!" peevishly rejoined Chattaway. "Buy it, if you like. What do I care?"

"I'll thank you to be civil to *me*, Mr. Chattaway," said Miss Diana, with emphasis. "It is of no use your being put out about this business of Cris and the accident; and that's what you are, I suppose. Fretting over it won't mend it."

Mr. Chattaway caught at the mistake. "It was such an idiotic trick, to put an untried horse into harness, and let it smash the dog-cart!" he cried. "Cris did it in direct disobedience, too. I had told him he should not buy that horse."

"Cris does many things in disobedience," calmly rejoined Miss Diana. "I hope it has not injured Edith."

"She must have been foolish—"

A ring at the hall-bell—a loud, long, imperative ring—and Mr. Chattaway's voice abruptly stopped. *He* stopped: stopped and stood stock still in the middle of the room, eyes and ears open, his whole senses on the alert. A prevision rushed over him that the messenger of evil had come.

"Are you expecting any one?" inquired Miss Diana.

"Be still, can't you?" almost shrieked Chattaway. Her voice hindered his listening.

They were opening the hall-door, and Chattaway's face was turning livid. James came into the room.

"A gentleman, sir, is asking to see Mr. Rupert."

"What gentleman?" interposed Miss Diana, before Chattaway could move or look.

"I don't know him, ma'am. He seems strange to the place; has a white beard, and looks foreign."

"He wants Mr. Rupert, did you say?"

"When I opened the door, first, ma'am, he asked if he could see young Squire Trevlyn; so I wanted to know who he meant, and said my master, Mr. Chattaway, was the Squire, and he replied that he meant Master Rupert, the son of Squire Trevlyn's heir, Mr. Joe, who had died abroad. He is waiting, ma'am."

Chattaway turned his white face upon the man. His trembling hands, his stealthy movements, showed his abject terror; even his very voice, which had dropped to a whisper.

"Mr. Rupert's in bed, and can't be seen, James. Go and say so."

Miss Diana had stood in amazement—first, at James's message; secondly, at Mr. Chattaway's strange demeanour. "Why, who is it?" she cried to the servant.

"He didn't give his name, ma'am."

"Will you go, James?" hoarsely cried Mr. Chattaway. "Go and get rid of the man."

"But he shall not get rid of him," interrupted Miss Diana. "I shall see the man. It is the strangest message I ever heard in my life. What are you thinking of, Squire?"

"Stop where you are!" returned Mr. Chattaway, arresting Miss Diana's progress. "Do you hear, James? Go and get rid of this man. Turn him out, at any cost."

Did Mr. Chattaway fear the visitor had come to take possession of the house in Rupert's name? Miss Diana could only look at him in astonishment. His face wore the hue of death; he was evidently almost beside himself with terror. For once in her life she did not assert her will, but suffered James to leave the room and "get rid" of the visitor in obedience to Mr. Chattaway.

He appeared to have no trouble in accomplishing it. A moment, and the hall-door was heard to close. Chattaway opened that of the dining-room.

"What did he say?"

"He said nothing, sir, except that he'd call again."

"James, does he—does he look like a madman?" cried Mr. Chattaway, his tone changing to what might almost be called entreaty. "Is he insane, do you think? I could not let a madman enter the house, you know."

"I don't know, sir, I'm sure. His words were odd, but he didn't seem mad."

Mr. Chattaway closed the door and turned to his sister-in-law, who was more puzzled than she had ever been in her life.

"I think it is you who are mad, Chattaway."

"Hush, Diana! I have heard of this man before. Sit down, and I will tell you about him."

He had come to a rapid conclusion that it would be better to confide to her the terrible news come to light. Not his own fears, or the dread which had lain deep in his heart: only this that he had heard.

We have seen how the words of the stranger had been exaggerated by Hatch to Mr. Chattaway, and perhaps he now unconsciously exaggerated Hatch's report. Miss Diana listened in consternation. A lawyer!—come down to depose them from Trevlyn Hold, and institute Rupert in it! "I never heard of such a thing!" she exclaimed. "He can't do it, you know, Chattaway."

Chattaway coughed ruefully. "Of course he can't. At least I don't see how he can, or how any one else can. My opinion is that the man must be mad."

Miss Diana was falling into thought. "A friend of Joe's?" she mused aloud. "Chattaway, could Joe have left a will?"

"Nonsense!" said Chattaway. "If Joe Trevlyn did leave a will, it would be null and void. He died in his father's lifetime, and the property was not his to leave."

"True. There can be no possibility of danger," she added, after a pause. "We may dismiss all fear as the idle wind."

"I wonder whether Rupert knows anything about this?"

"Rupert! What should he know about it?"

"I can't say," returned Mr. Chattaway, significantly. "I think I'll go up and ask him," he added, in a sort of feverish impulse.

Without a moment's pause he hastened upstairs to Rupert's room. But the room was empty!

Mr. Chattaway stood transfixed. He had fully believed Rupert to be in bed, and the silent bed, impressed, seemed to mock him. A wild fear came over him that Rupert's pretence of going to bed had been a *ruse*—he had gone out to meet that dangerous stranger.

He flew down the stairs as one possessed; shouting "Rupert! Rupert!" The household stole forth to look at him, and the walls echoed the name. But from Rupert himself there came no answer. He was not in the Hold.

CHAPTER XXIV
A MEETING AT MARK CANHAM'S

Rupert's leaving the Hold, however, had been a very innocent matter. The evening sun was setting gloriously, and he thought he would stroll out for a few minutes before going to his room. When he reached the lodge he went in and flung himself down on the settle, opposite old Canham and his pipe.

"How's Madam?" asked the old man. "What an accident it might have been!"

"So it might," assented Rupert, "Madam will be better after a night's rest. Cris might have killed her. I wonder how he'd have felt then?"

When Rupert came to an anchor, no matter where, he was somewhat unwilling to move from it. The settle was not a comfortable seat; rather the contrary; but Rupert kept to it, talking and laughing with old Canham. Ann was at the window, catching what remained of the fading light for her sewing.

"Here's that strange gentleman again, father!" she suddenly exclaimed in a whisper.

Old Canham turned his head, and Rupert turned his. The gentleman with the beard was going by in the direction of Trevlyn Hold as if about to make a call there.

"Ay, that's him," cried old Canham.

"What a queer-looking chap!" exclaimed Rupert. "Who is he?"

"I can't make out," was old Canham's reply. "Me and Ann have been talking about him. He came strolling inside the gates this afternoon with a red umberellar, looking here and looking there, and at last he see us, and come up and asked what place this was; and when I told him it was Trevlyn Hold, he said Trevlyn Hold was what he had been seeking for, and he stood there talking a matter o' twenty minutes, leaning his arms on the window-sill. He thought you was the Squire, Master Rupert. He had a red umberellar," repeated old Canham, as if the fact were remarkable.

Rupert glanced up in surprise. "Thought I was the Squire?"

"He came into this neighbourhood, he said, believing nothing less but that you were the rightful Squire, and couldn't make out why you were not: he had been away from England a many years, and had believed it all the while. He said you were the true Squire, and you should be helped to your right."

"Why! who can he be?" exclaimed Rupert, in excitement.

"Ah, that's it—who can he be?" returned old Canham. "Me and Ann have been marvelling. He said that he used to be a friend of the dead heir, Mr. Joe. Master Rupert, who knows but he may be somebody come to place you in the Hold?"

Rupert was leaning forward on the settle, his elbow on his knee, his eye fixed on old Canham.

"How could he do that?" he asked after a pause. "How could any one do it?"

"It's not for us to say how, Master Rupert. If anybody in these parts could have said, maybe you'd have been in it long before this. That there stranger is a cute 'un, I know. White beards always is a sign of wisdom."

Rupert laughed. "Look here, Mark. It is no good going over that ground again. I have heard about my 'rights' until I am tired. The subject vexes me; it makes me cross from its very hopelessness. I wish I had been born without rights."

"This stranger, when he called you the heir of Trevlyn Hold, and I told him you were not the heir, said I was right; you were not the heir, but the owner," persisted old Canham.

"Then he knew nothing about it," returned Rupert. "It's *impossible* that Chattaway can be put out of Trevlyn Hold."

"Master Rupert, there has always been a feeling upon me that he will be put out of it," resumed old Canham. "He came to it by wrong, and wrong never lasts to the end without being righted. Who knows that the same feeling ain't on Chattaway? He turned the colour o' my Sunday smock when I told him of this stranger's having been here and what he'd said."

"Did you tell him?" quickly cried Rupert.

"I did, sir. I didn't mean to, but it come out incautious-like. I called you the young heir to his face, and excused myself by saying the stranger had been calling you so, and I spoke out the same without thought. Then he wanted to know what stranger, and all about him. It was when Madam was resting here after the accident. Chattaway rode by and saw her, and got off his horse: it was the first he knew of the accident. If what I said didn't frighten him, I never had a day's rheumatiz in my life. His face went as white as Madam's."

"Chattaway go white!" scoffed Rupert. "What next? I tell you what it is, Mark; you fancy things. Aunt Edith may have been white; she often is; but not he. Chattaway knows that Trevlyn Hold is his, safe and sure. Nothing can take it from him—unless Squire Trevlyn came to life again, and made a fresh will. He's not likely to do that, Mark."

"No; he's not likely to do that," assented the old man. "Once we're out of this world, Master Rupert, we don't come back again. The injustice we have left behind us can't be repaired that way."

Rupert rose. He went to the window, opened it, and leaned out whistling. He was tired of the subject as touching himself; had long looked upon it as an unprofitable theme. As he stood there enjoying the calmness of the evening the tall man with the white beard came back again down the avenue.

Mr. Daw, for he it was, had the red umbrella in his hand. He turned his head to the window as he passed it, looked steadily at Rupert, paused, went close up, and put his hand on Rupert's arm.

"You are Rupert Trevlyn?"

"Yes," replied Rupert.

"I should have known you anywhere from your resemblance to your father; I should have known you had I met you in the crowded streets of London. You are wonderfully like him."

"Where did you know my father?" inquired Rupert.

Instead of answering, the stranger opened the house-door and stepped into the room. Ann curtseyed; old Canham rose and stood with his hat in his hand—that white beard seemed to demand respect. He—the stranger—took Rupert's hand in his.

"I have been up to the house to inquire for you: but they told me you were not well, and had gone to rest."

"Did they?" said Rupert. "I had intended to lie down, but the evening was so pleasant that I came out instead. You spoke of my father: did you know him?"

"I knew him very well," said the stranger, taking the seat Ann had been dusting before offering; a ceremony she apparently considered a mark of respect. "Though my acquaintance with him was short, it was close. Do you know who baptized you?"

"No," replied Rupert, rather astonished at the question.

"I did. I christened your sister Maude; I baptized you. You were to be christened in England, your mother said, but she wished you baptized ere the journey commenced, and I did it when you were only a day old. Ah, poor thing! she hoped to make the journey with you when she should be strong enough; but another journey claimed her—that of death! Before you were two days old she died. It was I who wrote to announce your birth to Squire Trevlyn; it was I who, by the next post, announced your mother's death. It was I—my young friend, it was I—who buried your father and your mother."

"You are a clergyman, then?" said Rupert, somewhat dubious about the beard, and the very unclerical cut of the stranger altogether.

It may be that Mr. Daw noticed the doubtful glances, and entered upon an explanation. How, when a working curate, he had married a young lady of fortune, but of delicate health, and had gone abroad with her, throwing up for the time his clerical preferment. The doctors had said that a warm climate was essential to her; as they had said, if you remember, in the case of Joe Trevlyn. It happened that both parties sought the same place—the curate and his wife, Joe and Mrs. Trevlyn—and a close friendship sprang up between them. A short time and Joe Trevlyn died; a shorter time still, and his wife died. There was no English clergyman near the spot, and Mr. Daw gave his services. He baptized the children; he buried the parents. His own fate was a happier one, for his wife lived. She lived, but did not grow strong. It may be said—you have heard of such cases—that she only existed from day to day. She had so existed all through those long years; from that time until within a few months of this. "If you attempt to take her back to England, she will not live a month," the local medical men had said; and perhaps they were right. He had gone to the place for a few months' sojourn, and never left it for over twenty years. It reads like a romance. His wife's fortune had enabled him to live comfortably, and in a pecuniary point of view there was no need to seek preferment or exercise his calling. He would never seek it now. Habit and use are second nature, and the Reverend William Daw had learnt to be an idle man; to love the country of his adoption, his home in the Pyrenees; to believe that its genial climate had become necessary to himself. His business in England concluded (it was connected with his late wife's will), he was hastening back to it. Had preferment been offered him, he would have doubted his ability to fulfil its duties after so many years of leisure. The money that was his wife's would be his for the remainder of his days; so on that score he was at rest. In short, the Reverend William Daw had degenerated into a useless man; one to whom all exertion had become a trouble. He honestly confessed to it now, as he sat before Rupert Trevlyn; told him he had been content to live wholly for the country of his adoption, almost completely ignoring his own; had kept up no correspondence with it. Of friends he could, as a young curate, boast but few, and he had been at no pains to keep them. At first he had believed that six or twelve months would be the limit of his absence from England, and he was content to let friendships await his return. But he did not return; and the lapsed correspondence was too pleasant to his indolent tastes to be reopened. He told all this quietly now to Rupert Trevlyn, and said that to it he owed his ignorance of the deposition of Rupert from Trevlyn Hold. Mr. Freeman was one of his few old college friends, and he might have heard all about it years ago had he only written to him.

"I cannot understand how Mr. Chattaway should have succeeded," he cried, bending his dark eyes upon Rupert. "I can scarcely believe the fact now; it has amazed me, as one may say. Had there been no direct male heir; had your father left only Maude, for instance, I could have understood its being left away from her, although it would have been unjust."

"The property is not entailed," said Rupert.

"I am aware of that. During the last few months of your father's life, we were like brothers, and I knew all particulars as well as he did. He had married in disobedience to his father's will, but he never for a moment glanced at the possibility of disinheritance. I cannot understand why Squire Trevlyn should have willed the estate from his son's children."

"He only knew of Maude—as they say."

"Still less can I understand how Mr. Chattaway can keep it. Were an estate willed to me, away from those who had a greater right to it, I should never retain it. I could not reconcile it to my conscience to do so. How can Mr. Chattaway?"

Rupert laughed—he believed that conscience and Mr. Chattaway had not a great deal to do with each other. "It is not much Mr. Chattaway would give up voluntarily," he observed. "Were my grandfather alive, Chattaway would not resign Trevlyn Hold to him, unless forced to it."

Old Canham could contain himself no longer. The conversation did not appear to be coming to the point. "Be you going to help young Master Rupert to regain his rights, sir?" he eagerly asked.

"I would—if I knew how to do it," said Mr. Daw. "I shall certainly represent to Mr. Chattaway the injustice—the wicked injustice—of the present state of things. When I wrote to the Squire on the occasion of your birth and Mrs. Trevlyn's death," looking at Rupert, "the answers to me were signed 'J. Chattaway,'—the writer being no doubt this same Mr. Chattaway. He wrote again, after Squire Trevlyn's death, requesting me to despatch the nurse and children to England."

"Oh, yes," said Rupert carelessly, "it was safe enough for us to come then. Squire Trevlyn dead, and the estate willed to Chattaway, there was no longer danger from me. If my grandfather had got to know that I was in existence, there would have been good-bye to Chattaway's ambition. At least people say so; *I* don't know."

The indifferent tone forcibly struck Mr. Daw. "Don't *you* feel the injustice?" he asked. "Don't you care that Trevlyn Hold should be yours?"

"I have grown up seeing the estate Chattaway's, and I suppose I don't feel it as I ought to. Of course, I should like it to be mine, but as it never can be mine, it is as well not to think about it. Have you heard of the Trevlyn temper?" he continued, a merry smile dancing in his eyes as he threw them on the stranger.

"I have."

"They tell me I have inherited it, as I suppose a true Trevlyn ought to do. Were I to think too much of the injustice, it might rouse the temper; and it would answer no end, you know."

"Yes, I have heard of the Trevlyn temper," repeated the stranger. "I have heard what it did for the first heir, Rupert Trevlyn."

"But it did not do it for him," passionately returned Rupert. "I never heard until the other day—not so many hours ago—of the slur that was cast upon his name. It was not he who shot the man; he had no hand in it: it was proved so later. Ask old Canham."

"Well, well," said the stranger, "it's all past and done with. Poor Joe reposed every confidence in me; treating me as a brother. It was a singular coincidence that the Squire's sons should both die abroad. I hope," he added, looking kindly at Rupert, "that yours will be a long life. Are you—are you strong?"

The question was put hesitatingly. He had heard from Nora that Rupert was not strong; and now that he saw him he was painfully struck with his delicate appearance. Rupert answered bravely.

"I should be very well if it were not for that confounded Blackstone walk night and morning. It's that knocks me up."

"Chattaway had no call to put him to it, sir," interrupted Mark Canham again. "It's not work for a Trevlyn."

"Not for the heir of Trevlyn Hold," acquiesced the stranger. "But I must be going. I have not seen my friend Freeman yet, and should like to be at the railway station when he arrives. What time shall I see you in the morning?" he added, to Rupert. "And what time can I see Mr. Chattaway?"

"You can see me at any time," replied Rupert. "But I can't answer for him. He breakfasts early, and generally goes out afterwards."

Had the Reverend William Daw been able to glance through a few trunks of trees, he might have seen Mr. Chattaway then. For there, hidden amidst the trees of the avenue, only a few paces from the lodge, was he.

Mr. Chattaway was pretty nearly beside himself that night. When he found that Rupert Trevlyn was not in the house, vague fears, to which he did not wait to give a more tangible name, rushed over his imagination. Had Rupert stolen from the house to meet this dangerous stranger clandestinely? He—Chattaway—scarcely knowing what he did, seized his hat and followed the stranger down the avenue, when he left the Hold after his fruitless visit.

Not to follow him openly and say, "What is your business with Rupert Trevlyn?" Cords would not have dragged Mr. Chattaway into that dreaded presence until he was sure of his ground.

He stole down with a fleet foot on the soft grass beside the avenue, and close upon the lodge he overtook the stranger. Mr. Chattaway glided into the trees.

Peeping from his hiding-place, he saw the stranger pause before the lodge window: heard him accost Rupert Trevlyn; watched him enter. And there he had been since,—altogether in an agony both of mind and body.

Do as he would, he could not hear their conversation. The sound of voices came upon him through the open window, but not the words spoken: and nearer he dared not go.

Hark! they were coming out. Chattaway's eyes glared and his teeth were set, as he cautiously looked round. The man's ugly red umbrella was in one hand; the other was laid on Rupert's shoulder. "Will you walk with me a little way?" he heard the stranger say.

"No, not this evening," was Rupert's reply. "I must go back to the Hold."

But he, Rupert, turned to walk with him to the gate, and Mr. Chattaway took the opportunity to hasten back toward the Hold. When Rupert, after shaking hands with the stranger and calling out a good evening to the inmates of the lodge as he passed, went up the avenue, he met the master of Trevlyn Hold pacing leisurely down it, as if he had come out for a stroll.

"Halloa!" he cried, with something of theatrical amazement. "I thought you were in bed!"

"I came out instead," replied Rupert. "The evening was so fine."

"Who was that queer-looking man just gone out at the gates?" asked Mr. Chattaway, with well-assumed indifference.

Rupert answered readily. His disposition was naturally open to a fault, and he saw no reason for concealing what he knew of the stranger. He was not aware that Chattaway had ever seen him until this moment.

"It is some one who has come on a visit to the parsonage: a clergyman. It's a curious name, though—Daw."

"Daw? Daw?" repeated Mr. Chattaway, biting his lips to get some colour into them. "Where have I heard that name—in connection with a clergyman?"

"He said he had some correspondence with you years ago: at the time my mother died, and I was born. He knew my father and mother well: has been telling me this at old Canham's."

All that past time, its events, its correspondence, flashed over Mr. Chattaway's memory—flashed over it with a strange dread. "What has he come here for?" he asked quickly.

"I don't know," replied Rupert. "He said—Whatever's this?"

A tremendous shouting from people who appeared, dragging something behind them. Both turned simultaneously—the master of Trevlyn Hold in awful fear. Could it be the stranger coming back with constables at his heels, to wrest the Hold from him? And if, my reader, you deem these fears exaggerated, you know very little of this kind of terror.

It was nothing but a procession of those idlers you saw in the road, dragging home the unlucky dog-cart: Mr. Cris at their head.

CHAPTER XXV
NEWS FOR MISS DIANA

In that pleasant room at the parsonage, with its sweet-scented mignonette boxes, and vases of freshly-cut flowers, sat the Reverend Mr. Freeman at breakfast, with his wife and visitor. It was a simple meal. All meals were simple at Barbrook Parsonage: as they generally are where means are limited. And you have not yet to learn, I dare say, that comfort and simplicity frequently go together: whilst comfort and grandeur are often separated. There was no lack of comfort and homely fare at Mr. Freeman's. Coffee and rich milk: home-made bread and the freshest of butter, new-laid eggs and autumn watercress. It was by no means starvation.

Mr. Daw, however, paid less attention to the meal than he might have done had his mind been less preoccupied. The previous evening, when he and Mr. Freeman had first met, after an absence of more than twenty years, their conversation had naturally run on their own personal interests: past events had to be related. But this morning they could go to other subjects, and Mr. Daw was not slow to do so. They were talking—you may have guessed it—of the Trevlyns.

Mr. Daw grew warm upon the subject. As on the previous day, when Molly placed the meal before him, he almost forgot to eat. And yet Mr. Daw, in spite of his assurance that he was contented with a crust of bread and a cup of milk knew how to appreciate good things. In plainer words, he liked them. Men who have no occupation for their days and years sometimes grow into epicureans.

"You are sparing the eggs," said Mrs. Freeman, a good-natured woman with a large nose, thin cheeks, and prominent teeth. Mr. Daw replied by taking another egg from the stand and chopping off its top. But there it remained. He was enlarging on the injustice dealt out to Rupert Trevlyn.

"It ought to be remedied, you know, Freeman. It must be remedied. It is a wrong in the sight of God and man."

The curate—Mr. Freeman was nothing more, for all his many years' services—smiled good-humouredly. He never used hard words: preferring to let wrongs, which were no business of his, right themselves, or remain wrongs, and taking life as it came, easily and pleasantly.

"We can't alter it," he said. "We have no power to interfere with Chattaway. He has enjoyed Trevlyn Hold these twenty years, and must enjoy it still."

"I don't know about that," returned Mr. Daw. "I don't know that he must enjoy it still. At any rate, he ought not to do so. Had I lived in this neighbourhood as you have, Freeman, I should have tried to get him out of it before this."

The parson opened his eyes in surprise.

"There's such a thing as shaming people out of injustice," continued Mr. Daw. "Has any one represented to Chattaway the fearful wrong he is guilty of in his conduct towards Rupert Trevlyn?"

"I can't say," equably answered the parson. "I have not."

"Will you go with me and do it to-day?"

"Well—no; I think I'd rather not, Daw. If any good could come of it, perhaps I might do so; but nothing could come of it. And I find it answers best not to meddle with the affairs of other folk."

"The wrongs dealt out to him are so great," persisted Mr. Daw. "Not content with having wrested Trevlyn Hold from the boy, Chattaway converts him into a common labourer in some coal office of his, making him walk to and fro night and morning. You know him?"

"Know him?" repeated Mr. Freeman. "I have known him since he first came here, a child in arms." In truth, it was a superfluous question.

"Did you know his father?"

"No; I came to Barbrook after his father went abroad."

"I was going to ask, if you had known him, whether you did not remark the extraordinary resemblance the young man bears to his father. The likeness is great; and he has the same suspiciously delicate complexion. I should fear that the boy will go off as his father did, and—"

"I have long said he ought to take cod-liver oil," interposed Mrs. Freeman, who was doctor in ordinary to her husband's parish, and very decided in her opinions.

"Well, ma'am, that boy must die—if he is to die—Squire of Trevlyn Hold. I shall use all my means while I am here to induce this Chattaway to resign his possessions to the rightful owner. The boy seems to have had no friend in the world to take up his cause. What this Miss Diana can have been about, to stand tamely by and not interfere, I cannot conceive. She is the sister of his father."

"Better let it alone, Daw," said the parson. "Rely upon it, you will make no impression on Chattaway. You must excuse me for saying it, but it's quite foolish to think that you will; quixotic and absurd. Chattaway possesses Trevlyn Hold—is not likely to resign it."

"I could not let it alone now," impulsively answered Mr. Daw. "The boy seems to have no friend, I say; and I have a right to constitute myself his friend. I should not be worthy the name of man were I not to do it. I intended to stay with you only two nights; you'll give me house-room a little longer, won't you?"

"We'll give it you for two months, and gladly, if you can put up with our primitive mode of living," was the hospitable answer.

Mr. Daw shook his head. "Two months I could not remain; two weeks I might. I cannot go away leaving things in this unsatisfactory state. The first thing I shall do this morning will be to call at the Hold, and seek an interview with Chattaway."

But Mr. Daw did not succeed in obtaining the interview with Chattaway. When he arrived at Trevlyn Hold, he was told the Squire was out. It was correct; Chattaway had ridden out immediately after breakfast. The stranger next asked for Miss Diana, and was admitted.

Chattaway had said to Miss Diana in private, before starting, "Don't receive him should he come here; don't let his foot pass over the door-sill." Very unwise advice, as Miss Diana judged; and she did not take it. Miss Diana had the sense to remember that an unknown evil is more to be feared than an open one. No one can fight in the dark. The stranger was ushered into the drawing-room by order of Miss Diana, and she came to him.

It was not a satisfactory interview, since nothing came of it; but it was a decently civil one. Miss Diana was cold, reserved, somewhat haughty, but courteous; Mr. Daw was pressing, urgent, but respectful and gentlemanly. Rupert Trevlyn was by right the owner of Trevlyn Hold, was the substance of the points urged by the one; Squire Trevlyn was his own master, made his own will, and it was not for his children and dependants to raise useless questions, still less for a stranger, was the answer of the other.

"Madam," said Mr. Daw, "did the enormity of the injustice never strike you?"

"Will you be so good as to tell me by what right you interfere?" returned Miss Diana. "I cannot conceive what business it can be of yours."

"I think the redressing of the injustice should be made the business of everyone."

"What a great deal everyone would have to do!" exclaimed Miss Diana.

"With regard to my right of interference, Miss Trevlyn, the law might not give me any; but I assume it by the bond of friendship. I was with his father when he died; I was with his mother. Poor thing! it was only within the last six or seven hours of her life that danger was apprehended. They both died in the belief that their children would inherit Trevlyn Hold. Madam," quite a blaze of light flushing from his dark eyes, "I have lived all the years since, believing they were in the enjoyment of it."

"You believed rightly," equably rejoined Miss Diana. "They have been in the enjoyment of it. It has been their home."

"As it may be the home of any of your servants," returned Mr. Daw; and Miss Diana did not like the comparison.

"May I ask," she continued, "if you came into this neighbourhood for the express purpose of putting this 'injustice' to rights?"

"No, madam, I did not. But it is unnecessary for you to be sarcastic with me. I wish to urge the matter upon you in a friendly rather than an adverse spirit. Business connected with my own affairs brought me to London some ten days ago, from the place where I had lived so long. As I was so near, I thought I would come down and see my former friend Freeman, before starting homewards; for I dare say I shall never again return to England. I knew Barbrook Parsonage and Trevlyn Hold were not very far apart, and I anticipated the pleasure of meeting Joe Trevlyn's children, whom I had known as infants. I never supposed but that Rupert was in possession of Trevlyn Hold. You may judge of my surprise when I arrived yesterday and heard the true state of the case."

"You have a covert motive in this," suddenly exclaimed Miss Diana, in a voice that had turned to sharpness.

"Covert motive?" he repeated, looking at her.

"Yes. Had you been, as you state, so interested in the welfare of Rupert Trevlyn and his sister, does it stand to reason that you would never have inquired after them through all these long years?"

"I beg your pardon, Miss Trevlyn: the facts are precisely as I have stated them. Strange as it may seem, I never once wrote to inquire after them, and the neglect strikes me forcibly now. But I am naturally inert, and all correspondence with my own country had gradually ceased. I did often think of the little Trevlyns, but it was always to suppose them as being at Trevlyn Hold, sheltered by their appointed guardian."

"What appointed guardian?" cried Miss Diana.

"Yourself."

"I! I was not the appointed guardian of the Trevlyns."

"Indeed you were. You were appointed by their mother. The letter—the deed, I may say, for I believe it to have been legally worded—was written when she was dying."

Miss Trevlyn had never heard of any deed. "Who wrote it?" she asked, after a pause.

"I did. When dangerous symptoms set in, and she was told she might not live, Mrs. Trevlyn sent for me. She had her little baby baptized Rupert, for it had been her husband's wish that the child, if a boy, should be so named, and then I sat down by her bedside at her request, and wrote the document. She entreated Miss Diana Trevlyn—you, madam—to reside at Trevlyn Hold as its mistress, when it should lapse to Rupert, and be the guardian and protector of her children, until Rupert came of age. She besought you to love them, and be kind to them for their father's sake; for her sake; for the sake, also, of the friendship which had once existed between you and her. This will prove to you," he added in a different tone, "that poor Mrs. Trevlyn, at least, never supposed there was a likelihood of any other successor to the estate."

"I never heard of it," exclaimed Miss Diana, waking up as from a reverie. "Was the document sent to me?"

"It was enclosed in the despatch which acquainted Squire Trevlyn with Mrs. Trevlyn's death. I wrote them both, and I enclosed them together, and sent them."

"Directed to whom?"

"To Squire Trevlyn."

Miss Diana sent her thoughts into the past. It was Chattaway who had received that despatch. Could he have dared to suppress any communication intended for her? Her haughty brow grew crimson at the thought; but she suppressed all signs of annoyance.

"Will you allow me to renew my acquaintance with little Maude?" resumed Mr. Daw. "Little Maude then, and a lovely child; a beautiful girl, as I hear, now."

Miss Diana hesitated—a very uncommon thing for her to do. It is strange what trifles turn the current of feelings: and this last item of intelligence had wonderfully softened her towards this stranger. But she remembered the interests at stake, and thought it best to be prudent.

"You must pardon the refusal," she said. "I quite appreciate your wish to serve Rupert Trevlyn, but it can only fail, and further intercourse will not be agreeable to either party. You will allow me to wish you good morning, and to thank you."

She rang the bell, and bowed him out, with all the grand courtesy belonging to the Trevlyns. As he passed through the hall, he caught a glimpse of a lovely girl with a delicate bloom on her cheeks and large blue eyes. Instinct told him it was Maude; and he likewise thought he traced some resemblance to her mother. He took a step forward involuntarily, to accost her, but recollecting himself, drew back again.

It was scarcely the thing to do: in defiance of Miss Diana Trevlyn's recent refusal.

CHAPTER XXVI
AN IMPROMPTU JOURNEY

The dew was lying upon the grass in the autumn morning as the Squire of Trevlyn Hold rode from his door. He had hurried over his breakfast, his horse waiting for him, and he spurred him impatiently along the avenue. Ann Canham had not yet opened the gate. Upon hearing a horse's hoofs, she ran out to do so; and stood holding it back, dropping her humble curtsey as Mr. Chattaway rode past. He vouchsafed not the slightest notice: neither by glance nor nod did he appear conscious of her presence. It was his usual way.

"He's off to Blackstone early," thought Ann, as she fastened back the gate.

But Mr. Chattaway did not turn towards Blackstone. He turned in the opposite direction and urged his horse to a gallop. Ann Canham looked after him.

"He has business at Barmester, maybe," was the conclusion to which she came.

Nothing more sure. He rode briskly to the town, and pulled up his horse almost at the same spot where you once saw him pull it up before—the house of Messrs. Wall and Barnes.

Not that he was about to visit that flourishing establishment this morning. Next to it was a private house, on the door-plate of which might be read, "Mr. Flood, Solicitor": and he was the gentleman Mr. Chattaway had come to see.

Attracted probably by the clatter of the horse—for Chattaway had pulled up suddenly, and with more noise than he need have done, there came one to the shop-door and looked out. It was Mr. Wall, and he stepped forth to shake hands with Chattaway.

"Good morning, Chattaway. You are in Barmester betimes. What lovely weather we are having for the conclusion of the harvest!"

"Very; it has been a fine harvest altogether," replied Chattaway; and from his composure no one could have dreamt of the terrible care and perplexity running riot in his heart. "I want to say a word to Flood about a lease that is falling in, so I thought I'd start early and make a round of it on my way to Blackstone."

"An accident occurred yesterday to your son and Madam Chattaway, did it not?" asked Mr. Wall. "News of it was flying about last night. I hope they are not much hurt."

"Not at all. Cris was so stupid as to attempt to drive a horse unbroken for driving—a vicious temper, too. The dog-cart is half smashed. Here, you! come here."

The last words were addressed to a boy in a tattered jacket, who was racing after a passing carriage. Mr. Chattaway wanted him to hold his horse; and the boy quickly changed his course, believing the office would be good for sixpence at least.

The lawyer's outer door was open. There was a second door in the passage, furnished with a knocker: the office opened on the left. Mr. Chattaway tried the office-door; more as a matter of form than anything else. It was locked, as he expected, and would be until nine o'clock. So he gave an imposing knock at the other.

"I shall just catch him after breakfast," soliloquised he, "and can have a quiet quarter-of-an-hour with him, undisturbed by—Is Mr. Flood at home?"

He had tried the door as a matter of form, and in like manner put the question, passing in without ceremony: the servant arrested him.

"Mr. Flood's out, sir. He is gone to London."

"Gone to London!" ejaculated Chattaway.

"Yes, sir, not an hour ago. Went by the eight o'clock train."

It was so complete a check to all his imaginings, that for a minute the master of Trevlyn Hold found speech desert him. Many a bad man on the first threat of evil flies to a lawyer, in the belief that he can, by the exercise of his craft, bring him out of it. Chattaway, after a night of intolerable restlessness, had come straight off to his lawyer, Flood, with the intention of confiding the whole affair to him, and asking what was to be done in it; never so much as glancing at the possibility of that legal gentleman's absence.

"Went up by the eight o'clock train?" he repeated when he found his voice.

"Yes, sir."

"And when's he coming home?"

"He expects to be away about a week, sir."

A worse check still. Chattaway's terrible fear might have waited a day; but a week!—he thought suspense would drive him mad. He was a great deal too miserly to spend money upon an unnecessary journey, yet there appeared nothing for it but to follow Mr. Flood to London. That gentleman had heard perplexing secrets of Chattaway's before, had always given him the best advice, and remained faithful to the trust; and Chattaway believed he might safely confide this new danger to him. Not to any other would he have breathed a word. In short, Flood was the only confidential adviser he possessed in the world.

"Where will Mr. Flood put up in London?"

"I can't say, sir. I don't know anything about where he stays. He goes up pretty often."

"At the old place, I daresay," muttered Chattaway to himself. "If not, I shall learn where, through his agents in Essex Street."

He stood a moment on the pavement before mounting. A slow and cheap train would leave Barmester in half-an-hour for London. Should he go by that train?—go from Barmester, instead of returning home and taking the train at the little station near his own home? Was there need of so much haste? In Chattaway's present frame of mind the utmost haste he could make was almost a necessary relief: but, on the other hand, would his sudden departure excite suspicion at home, or draw unwelcome attention to his movements abroad? Deep in thought was he, when a hand was laid upon his shoulder. Turning sharply, he saw the honest face of the linen-draper close to his.

"The queerest thing was said to me last night, Chattaway. I stepped into Robbins, the barber's, to have my hair and whiskers trimmed, and he told me a great barrister was down here, a leading man from the Chancery court, come upon some business connected with you and the late Squire Trevlyn. With the property, I mean."

Chattaway's heart leaped into his mouth.

"I thought it a queer tale," continued Mr. Wall. "His mission here being to restore Rupert Trevlyn to the estates of his grandfather, Robbins said. Is there anything in it?"

Had the public already got hold of it, then? Was the awful thing no longer a fear but a reality? Chattaway turned his face away, and tried to be equal to the emergency.

"You are talking great absurdity, Wall. Who's Robbins? Were I you, I should be ashamed to repeat the lies propagated by that chattering old woman."

Mr. Wall laughed. "He certainly deals in news, does Robbins; it's part of his trade. Of course one only takes his marvels for what they are worth. He got *this* from Barcome, the tax-collector. The man had arrived at the scene of the dog-cart accident shortly after its occurrence, and heard this barrister—who, as it seems, was also there—speaking publicly of the object of his mission."

Chattaway snatched the reins from the ragged boy's hands and mounted; his air expressing all the scorn he could command. "When they impound Squire Trevlyn's will, then they may talk about altering the succession. Good morning, Wall."

A torrent of howls, accompanied by words a magistrate on the bench must have treated severely, saluted his ears as he rode off. They came from the aggrieved steed-holder. Instead of the sixpence he fondly reckoned on, Chattaway had flung him a halfpenny.

He rode to an inn near the railway station, went in and called for pen and ink. The few words he wrote were to Miss Diana. He found himself obliged to go up unexpectedly to London on the business *which she knew of*, and requested her to make any plausible excuse for his absence that would divert suspicion from the real facts. He should be home on the morrow. Such was the substance of the note.

He addressed it to Miss Trevlyn of Trevlyn Hold, sealed it with his own seal, and marked it "private." A most unnecessary additional security, the last. No inmate of Trevlyn Hold would dare to open the most simple missive, bearing the address of Miss Trevlyn. Then he called one of the stable-men.

"I want this letter taken to my house," he said. "It is in a hurry. Can you go at once?"

The man replied that he could.

"Stay—you may ride my horse," added Mr. Chattaway, as if the thought that moment struck him. "You will get there in half the time that you would if you walked."

"Very well, sir. Shall I bring him back for you?"

"Um—m—m, no, I'll walk," decided Mr. Chattaway, stroking his chin as if to help his decision. "Leave the horse at the Hold."

The man mounted the horse and rode away, never supposing Mr. Chattaway had been playing off a little *ruse* upon him, and had no intention of going to Trevlyn Hold that day, but was bound for a place rather farther off. In this innocent state he reached the Hold, while Mr. Chattaway made a *détour* and gained the station by a cross route, where he took train for London.

Cris Chattaway's groom, Sam Atkins, was standing with his young master's horse before the house, in waiting for that gentleman, when the messenger arrived. Not the new horse of the previous day's notoriety, nor the one lamed at Blackstone, but a despised and steady old animal sometimes used in the plough.

"There haven't been another accident surely!" exclaimed Sam Atkins, in his astonishment at seeing Mr. Chattaway's steed brought home. "Where's the Squire?"

"He's all right; and has sent me up here with this," was the man's reply, producing the note. And at that moment Miss Diana Trevlyn appeared at the hall-door. Miss Diana was looking out for Mr. Chattaway. After the communication made to her that morning by Mr. Daw, she could only come to the conclusion that the paper had been suppressed by Chattaway, and was waiting in much wrath to demand his explanation of it.

"What brings the Squire's horse back?" she imperiously demanded.

Sam Atkins handed her the note, which she opened and read. Read it twice attentively, and then turned indoors. "Chattaway's a fool!" she angrily decided, "and is allowing this mare's nest to prey on his fears. He ought to know that while my father's will is in existence no earthly power can deprive him of Trevlyn Hold."

She went upstairs to Mrs. Chattaway's sitting-room. That lady, considerably recovered from the shock of the fall, was writing an affectionate letter to her daughter Amelia, telling her she might come home with Caroline Ryle. Miss Diana went straight up to the table, took a seat, and without the least apology closed Mrs. Chattaway's desk.

"I want your attention for a moment, Edith. You can write afterwards. Carry your memory back to the morning, so many years ago, when we received the news of Rupert's birth?"

"No effort is need to do that, Diana. I think of it all too often."

"Very good. Then perhaps, without effort, you can recall the day following, when the letter came announcing Mrs. Trevlyn's death?"

"Yes, I remember it also."

"The minute details? Could you, for instance, relate any of the circumstances attending the arrival of that letter, if required to do so in a court of law? What time of the day it came, who opened it, where it was opened, and so forth?"

"Why do you ask me?" returned Mrs. Chattaway, surprised at the questions.

"I ask you to be answered. I have a reason for wishing to recall these past things. Think it over."

"Both letters, so far as I can recollect, were given to Mr. Chattaway, and he opened them. He was in the habit then of opening papa's business letters. I have no doubt they were opened in the steward's room; James used to be there a great deal with the accounts and other matters connected with the estate."

"I have always known that James Chattaway did open those letters," said Miss Diana; "but I thought you might have been present when he did so. Were you?"

"No. I remember his coming into my chamber later, and telling me Mrs. Trevlyn was dead. I never shall forget the shock I felt."

"Attend to me, Edith. I have reason to believe that the last of those letters contained an inclosure for me. It never reached me. Do you know what became of it?"

The blank surprise on Mrs. Chattaway's countenance, her open questioning gaze, was a sufficient denial.

"I see you do not. And now I am going to ask you something else. Did you ever hear that Emily Trevlyn, when she was dying, left a request that I should be guardian to her children?"

"Never. Have you been dreaming these things, Diana? Why should you ask about them now?"

"I leave dreams to you," was Miss Diana's reply. "My health is too sound to admit of sleeping dreams; my mind too practical to indulge in waking ones. Never mind why I asked: it was only as a personal matter of my own. By the way, I have had a line from your husband, written from Barmester. A little business has taken him out, and he may not be home until to-morrow. We are not to sit up for him."

"Has he gone to Nettleby hop-fair?" hastily rejoined Mrs. Chattaway.

"Perhaps so," said Miss Diana, carelessly. "At any rate, say nothing about his absence to any one. The children are unruly if they know he is away. I suppose he will be home to-morrow."

But Mr. Chattaway was not home on the morrow. Miss Diana was burning with impatience for his return; that explanation was being waited for, and she was one who brooked not delay: but she was obliged to submit to it now. Day after day passed on, and Mr. Chattaway was still absent from Trevlyn Hold.

CHAPTER XXVII
A WALK BY STARLIGHT

A harvest-home used to be a great *fête* in farmhouses; chiefly so, as you are aware, for its servants and labourers. It is so in some houses still. A rustic, homely gathering; with plenty of good fare in a plain way, and where the masters and mistresses and their guests enjoy themselves as freely as their dependants.

Trevlyn Farm was lighted up to-night. The best kitchen, where you have seen Nora sitting sometimes, and never used for kitchen purposes, was set out with a long table. Cold beef and ham, substantial and savoury meat pies, fruit pies, cakes, cheese, ale and cider, were being placed on it. Benches lined the walls, and the rustic labourers were coming sheepishly in. Some of them had the privilege of bringing their wives, who came in a great deal less sheepishly than the men.

Nanny was in full attire, a new green stuff gown and white apron; Molly from the parsonage was flaunting in a round cap, patronised by the fashionable servants in Barmester, with red streamers; Ann Canham had a new Scotch plaid kerchief, white and purple, crossed on her shoulders; and Jim Sanders's mother, being rather poorly off for smart caps, wore a bonnet. These four were to do the waiting; and Nora was casting over them all the superintending eye of a mistress. George Ryle liked to make his harvest-homes liberal and comfortable, and Mrs. Ryle seconded it with the open-handed nature of the Trevlyns.

What Mrs. Ryle would have done but for Nora Dickson it was impossible to say. She really took little more management in the house than a visitor would take. Her will, it is true, was law: she gave orders, but left their execution to others. Though she had married Thomas Ryle, of Trevlyn Farm, she never forgot that she was the daughter of Trevlyn Hold.

She sat in the small room opening from the supper-room—small in comparison with the drawing-room, but still comfortable. On harvest-home night, Mrs. Ryle's visitors were received in that ordinary room and sat there, forming as it were part of the supper-room company, for the door was kept wide, and the great people went in and out, mixing with the small. George Ryle and Mr. Freeman would be more in the supper-room than in the other;

they were two who liked to see the hard-working people happy now and then.

Mrs. Ryle had taken up her place in the sitting-room; her rich black silk gown and real lace cap contrasting with the more showy attire of Mrs. Apperley, who sat next her. Mrs. Apperley was in a stiff brocade, yellow satin stripes flanking wavy lines of flowers. It had been her gala robe for years and years, and looked new yet. Mrs. Apperley's two daughters, in cherry-coloured ribbons and cherry-coloured nets, were as gay as she was; they were whispering to Caroline Ryle, a graceful girl in dark-blue silk, with the blue eyes and the fair hair of her deceased father. Farmer Apperley, in top-boots, was holding an argument on the state of the country with a young man of middle height and dark hair, who sat carelessly on the arm of the old-fashioned sofa. It was Trevlyn Ryle. George had set his back against the wall, and was laughingly quizzing the Miss Apperleys, of which they were blushingly conscious. Were you to believe Nora, there was scarcely a young lady within the circuit of a couple of leagues but was privately setting her cap at handsome George.

A bustle in the outer room, and Nanny appeared with an announcement: "Parson and Mrs. Freeman." I am not responsible for the style of the introduction: you may hear it for yourselves if you choose to visit some of our rural districts.

Parson and Mrs. Freeman came in without ceremony; the parson with his hat and walking stick, Mrs. Freeman in a green calico hood and an old cloak. George, with laughing gallantry, helped her to take them off, and handed them to Nanny, and Mrs. Freeman went up to the pier-glass and settled the white bows in her cap to greater effect.

"But I thought you were to have brought your friend," said Mrs. Ryle.

"He will come in presently," replied the parson. "A letter arrived by this evening's post, and he wished to answer it."

Farmer Apperley turned from his debate with Trevlyn. "D'ye mean that droll-looking man who walks about with a red umbrella and a beard, parson?"

"The same," said Mr. Freeman, settling his double chin more comfortably in his white cravat. "He has been staying with us for a week past."

"Ay. Some foreign folk, isn't he, named Daw? There's all sorts of tales abroad in the neighbourhood as to what he is doing down here. I don't know whether they be correct."

"I don't know much about it myself either," said Mr. Freeman. "I am glad to entertain him as an old friend, but as for any private affairs or views of his, I don't meddle with them."

"Best plan," nodded the farmer. And the subject, thus indistinctly hinted at, was allowed to drop, owing probably to the presence of Mrs. Ryle.

"The Chattaways are coming here to-night," suddenly exclaimed Caroline Ryle. She spoke only to Mary Apperley, but there was a pause in the general conversation just then, and Mr. Apperley took it up.

"Who's coming? The Chattaways! Which of the Chattaways?" he said in some surprise, knowing they had never been in the habit of paying evening visits to Trevlyn Farm.

"All the girls, and Maude. I don't know whether Rupert will come; and I don't think Cris was asked."

"Eh, but that's a new move," cried Farmer Apperley, his long intimacy with the Farm justifying the freedom. "Did you invite them?"

"In point of fact, they invited themselves," interposed Mrs. Ryle, before George, to whom the question had been addressed, could speak. "At least, Octave did so: and then George, I believe, asked the rest of the girls."

"They won't come," said Farmer Apperley.

"Not come!" interrupted Nora, sharply, who kept going in and out between the two rooms. "That's all you know about it, Mr. Apperley. Octave Chattaway is sure to be here to-night—"

"Nora!"

The interruption came from George. Was he afraid of what she might say impulsively? Or did he see, coming in at the outer door, Octave herself, as though to refute the opinion of Mr. Apperley?

But only Amelia was with her. A tall girl with a large mouth and very light hair, always on the giggle. "Where are the rest?" impulsively asked George, his accent too unguarded to conceal its disappointment.

Octave detected it. She had thrown off her cloak and stood in attire scarcely suited to the occasion—a pale blue evening dress of damask, a silver necklace, silver bracelets, and a wreath of silver flowers in her hair. "What 'rest'?" asked Octave.

"Your sisters and Maude. They promised to come."

Octave tossed her head good-humouredly. "*Do* you think we could inflict the whole string on Mrs. Ryle? Two of us are sufficient to represent the family."

"Inflict! On a harvest-home night!" called out Trevlyn. "You know, Octave, the more the merrier on these occasions."

"Why, I really believe that's Treve!" exclaimed Octave. "When did you arrive?"

"This morning. You have grown thinner, Octave."

"It is nothing to you if I have," retorted Octave, offended at the remark. The point was a sore one; Octave being unpleasantly conscious that she was thin to plainness. "*You* have grown plump enough, at any rate."

"To be sure," said Treve. "I'm always jolly. It was too bad of you, Octave, not to bring the rest."

"So it was," said Amelia. "They had dressed for it, and at the last moment Octave made them stay at home."

But George was not going to take this quietly. Saying nothing, he left the room and made the best of his way to Trevlyn Hold. The rooms seemed deserted. At length he found Maude in the schoolroom, correcting exercises, and shedding a few quiet tears. After they had dressed for the visit, Octavia had placed her veto upon it, and Emily and Edith had retired to bed in vexation. Miss Diana was spending the evening out with Mrs. Chattaway, and Octave had had it all her own way.

"I have come for you, Maude," said George.

Maude's heart beat with anticipation. "I don't know whether I may dare to go," she said, glancing shyly at him.

"Has anyone except Octave forbidden you?"

"Only Octave."

Lying on a chair, George saw a bonnet and a cloak which he recognised as Maude's. In point of fact, she had thrown them off when forbidden the visit by Miss Chattaway. His only answer was to fold the cloak around her. And she put on the bonnet, and went out with him, shocked at her own temerity, but unable to resist the temptation.

"You are trembling," he cried, drawing her closer to him as he bent his head.

"I am afraid of Octave. I know she will be so angry. What if she should meet me with angry words?"

"Then—Maude—you will give me leave to answer her?"

"Yes. Oh yes."

"It will involve more than you think," said George, laughing at her eager tones. "I must tell her, if necessary, that I have a right to defend you."

Maude stopped in her surprise, and half drew her arm from his as she looked up at him in the starlight. His pointed tone stirred all the pulses of her heart.

"You cannot have mistaken me, Maude, this long time past," he quietly said. "If I have not spoken to you more openly; if I do not yet speak out to the world, it is that I see at present little prospect before us. I would prefer not to speak to others until that is more assured."

Maude, in spite of the intense happiness which was rising within her, felt half sick with fear. What of the powers at Trevlyn Hold?

"Yes, there might be opposition," said George, divining her thoughts, "and the result—great unpleasantness altogether. I am independent enough to defy them, but you are not, Maude. For that reason I will not speak if I can help it. I hope Octave will not provoke me to excess."

Maude started as a thought flashed over her, and she looked up at George, a terrified expression in her face. "You *must not* speak, George; you must not, for my sake. Were Octave only to suspect this, she—"

"Might treat you to a bowl of poison—after the stage fashion of the good old days," he laughed. "Maude, do you think I have been blind? I understand."

"You will be silent, then?"

"Yes," he answered, after a pause. "For the present."

They had taken the way through the fields—it was the nearest way—and George spoke of his affairs as he walked; more confidentially than he had ever in his life entered upon them to any one. That he had been in a manner sacrificed to the interests of Treve, there was no denying, and though he did not allude to it in so many words, it was impossible to ignore the fact entirely to Maude. One more term at Oxford, and Treve was to enter officially upon his occupation of Trevlyn Farm. The lease would be transferred to his name; he would be its sole master; and George must look out for another home: but until then he was bound to the farm—and bound most unprofitably. To the young, however, all things wear a hopeful *couleur-de-rose*. What would some of us give for it in after-life!

"By the spring I may be settled in a farm of my own, Maude. I have been giving a longing eye to the Upland. Its lease will be out at Lady-day, and Carteret leaves it. An unwise man in my opinion to leave a certain competency here for uncertain riches in the New World. But that is his business; not mine. I should like the Upland Farm."

Maude's breath was nearly taken away. It was the largest farm on the Trevlyn estate. "You surely would not risk that, George! What an undertaking!"

"Especially with Chattaway for a landlord, you would say. I shall take it if I can get it. The worst is, I should have to borrow money, and borrowed money weighs one down like an incubus. Witness what it did for my father. But I daresay we should manage to get along."

Maude opened her lips, wishing to say something she did not quite well know how to say. "I—I fear—" and there she stopped timidly.

"What do you fear, Maude?"

"I don't know how I should ever manage in a farm," she said, feeling she ought to speak out her doubts, but blushing vividly under cover of the dark night at having to do it. "I have been brought up so—so—uselessly—as regards domestic duties."

"Maude, if I thought I should marry a wife only to make her work, I should not marry at all. We will manage better than that. You have been brought up a lady; and, in truth, I should not care for my wife to be anything else. Mrs. Ryle has never done anything of the sort, you know, thanks to good Nora. And there are more Noras in the world. Shall I tell you a favourite scheme of mine, one that has been in my mind for some time now?"

She turned—waiting to hear it.

"To give a home to Rupert. You and I. We could contrive to make him happier than he is now."

Maude's heart leaped at the vision. "Oh, George! if it could only be! How good you are! Rupert—"

"Hush, Maude!" For he had become conscious of the proximity of others walking and talking like themselves. Two voices were contending with each other; or, if not contending, speaking as if their opinions did not precisely coincide. To George's intense astonishment he recognised one of the voices as Mr. Chattaway's, and uttered a suppressed exclamation.

"It cannot be," Maude whispered. "He is miles and miles away. Even allowing that he had returned, what should bring him here?—he would have gone direct to the Hold."

But George was positive that it was Chattaway. The voices were advancing down the path on the other side the hedge, and would probably come through the gate, right in front of George and Maude. To meet Chattaway was not particularly coveted by either of them, even at the most convenient times, and just now it was not convenient at all. George drew Maude under one of the great elm trees, which overshadowed the hedge on this side.

"Just for a moment, Maude, until they have passed. I am certain it is Chattaway!"

The gate swung open and someone came through it. Only one. Sure enough it was Chattaway. He strode onwards, muttering to himself, a brown paper parcel in his hand. But ere he had gone many steps, he halted, turned, came creeping back and stood peering over the gate at the man who was walking away. A little movement to the right, and Mr. Chattaway might have seen George and Maude standing there.

But he did not. He was grinding his teeth and working his disengaged hand, altogether too much occupied with the receding man, to pay attention to what might be around himself. Finally, his display of anger somewhat cooling down, he turned again and continued his way towards Trevlyn Hold.

"Who can it be that he is so angry with?" whispered Maude.

"Hush!" cautioned George. "His ears are sharp."

Very still they remained until he was at a safe distance, and then they went through the gate. Almost beyond their view a tall man was pacing slowly along in the direction of Trevlyn Farm, whirling an umbrella round and round in his hand.

"Just as I thought," was George's comment to himself.

"Who is it, George?"

"That stranger who is visiting at the parsonage."

"He seemed to be quarrelling with Mr. Chattaway."

"I don't know. Their voices were loud. I wonder if Rupert has found his way to the Farm?"

"Octave forbade him to go."

"Were I Ru I should break through *her* trammels at any rate, and show myself a man," remarked George. "He may have done so to-night."

They turned in at the garden-gate, and reached the porch. All signs of the stranger had disappeared, and sounds of merriment came from within.

George turned Maude's face to his. "You will not forget, Maude?"

"Forget what?" she shyly answered.

"That from this night we begin a new life. Henceforth we belong to each other. Maude! you will not forget!" he feverishly continued.

"I shall not forget," she softly whispered.

And, possibly by way of reminder, Mr. George, under cover of the silent porch, took his first lover's kiss from her lips.

CHAPTER XXVIII
AT DOCTORS' COMMONS

But where had Mr. Chattaway been all that time? And how came he to be seen by George Ryle and Maude hovering about his own ground at night, when he was supposed to be miles away? The explanation can be given.

Mr. Chattaway found, as many of us do, that lets and hindrances intrude themselves into the most simple plans. When he took the sudden resolution that morning to run up to London from Barmester after Flood the lawyer, he never supposed that his journey would be prolonged. Nothing more easy, as it appeared, than to catch Flood at his hotel, get a quarter-of-an-hour's conversation with him, take his advice, and return home again. But a check intervened.

Upon arriving at the London terminus, Mr. Chattaway got into a cab, and drove to the hotel ordinarily used by Mr. Flood. After a dispute with the cab-driver he entered the hotel, and asked to see Mr. Flood.

"Mr. Flood?" repeated the waiter. "There's no gentleman of that name staying here, sir."

"I mean Mr. Flood of Barmester," irritably rejoined the master of Trevlyn Hold. "Perhaps you don't know him personally. He came up an hour or two ago."

The waiter, a fresh one, was not acquainted with Mr. Flood. He went to another waiter, and the latter came forward. But the man's information was correct; Mr. Flood of Barmester had not arrived.

"He travelled by the eight-o'clock train," persisted Mr. Chattaway, as if he found the denial difficult to reconcile with that fact. "He must be in London."

"All I can say, sir, is that he has not come here," returned the head-waiter.

Mr. Chattaway was considerably put out. In his impatience, the delay seemed most irritating. He left the hotel, and bent his steps towards Essex Street, where Mr. Flood's agents had their offices. Chattaway went in hoping that the first object his eyes rested upon would be his confidential adviser.

His eyes did not receive that satisfaction. Some clerks were in the room, also one or two persons who seemed to be clients; but there was no Mr. Flood, and the clerks could give no information concerning him. One of the firm, a Mr. Newby, appeared and shook hands with Mr. Chattaway, whom he had once or twice seen.

"Flood? Yes. We had a note from Flood yesterday morning, telling us to get some accounts prepared, as he should be in town in the course of a day or two. He has not come yet; up to-morrow perhaps."

"But he has come," reiterated Chattaway. "I have followed him up to town, and want to see him upon a matter of importance."

"Oh, has he?" carelessly replied Mr. Newby, the indifferent manner appearing almost like an insult to Chattaway's impatient frame of mind. "He'll be in later, then."

"He is sure to come here?" inquired Mr. Chattaway.

"Quite sure. We shall have a good bit of business to transact with him this time."

"Then, if you'll allow me, I'll wait here. I must see him, and I want to get back to Barbrook as soon as possible."

Mr. Chattaway was told that he was welcome to wait, if it pleased him to do so. A chair was handed him in the entrance room, where the clerks were writing, and he took his seat in it: sat there until he was nearly driven wild. The room was in a continual bustle; persons constantly coming in and going out. For the first hour or so, to watch the swaying door afforded Chattaway a sort of relief, for in every fresh visitor he expected to see Mr. Flood. But this grew tedious at last, and the ever-recurring disappointment told upon his temper.

Evening came, the hour for closing the office, and the country lawyer had not made his appearance. "It is most extraordinary," remarked Chattaway to Mr. Newby.

"He has been about some other business, and couldn't get to us to-day, I suppose," rejoined Mr. Newby, in the most provokingly matter-of-fact tone. "If he has come up for a week, as you say, he must have some important affair on hand; in which case it may be a day or two before he finds his way here."

A most unsatisfactory conclusion for Mr. Chattaway; but that gentleman was obliged to put up with it, in the absence of any more tangible hope. He went back to the hotel, and there found that Mr. Flood was still amongst the non-arrivals.

It was bad enough, that day and night's disappointment and suspense; but when it came to be extended over more days and nights, you may judge how it was increased. Mr. Flood did not make his appearance. Chattaway, in a state of fume, divided his time between the hotel, Essex Street, and Euston Square station, in the wild hope of coming upon the lawyer. All to no purpose. He telegraphed to Barmester, and received for reply that Mr. Flood was in London, and so he redoubled his hauntings, and worked himself into a fever.

It appeared absolutely necessary that he should consult Flood before venturing back to home quarters, where he should inevitably meet that dangerous enemy. But how see Flood?—where look for him? Barmester telegraphed up that Mr. Flood was in London; the agents persisted in asserting that they expected him hourly, at their office, and yet Chattaway could not come upon him. He visited all the courts open in the long vacation; prowled about the Temple, Lincoln's Inn, and other places where lawyers congregated, in the delusive hope that he might by good luck meet with him. All in vain; and Chattaway had been very nearly a week from home, when his hopes were at length realised. There were other lawyers whom he might have consulted—Mr. Newby himself, for instance—but he shrank from laying bare his dread to a stranger.

He was walking slowly up Ludgate Hill, his hands in his pockets, his brow knit, altogether in a disconsolate manner, some vague intention in his mind of taking a peep inside Doctors' Commons, when, by the merest accident, he happened to turn his eyes on the string of vehicles passing up and down. In that same moment a cab, extricating itself from the long line, whirled past him in the direction of Fleet Street; and its occupant was Flood the lawyer.

All his listlessness was gone. Chattaway threw himself into the midst of the traffic, and tore after the cab. Sober pedestrians thought he had gone mad: but bent on their own business, had only time for a wondering glance. Chattaway bore on his way, and succeeded in keeping the cab in view. It soon stopped at an hotel, and by the time the lawyer had alighted, a portmanteau in hand, and was paying the driver, Chattaway was up with him, breathless, excited, grasping his arm as one demented.

"What on earth's the matter?" exclaimed Mr. Flood, in astonishment. "You here, Chattaway? Do you want me?"

"I followed you to town by the next train a week ago; I have been looking for you ever since," gasped Chattaway, unable to regain his breath between racing and excitement. "Where have you been hiding yourself? Your agents have been expecting you all this time."

CHAPTER XXIX
A WELCOME HOME

Was there a fatality upon the master of Trevlyn Hold?—was he never to be at rest?—could not even one little respite be allowed him in this, the first hour of his return home? It seemed not. He was turning into the first of those fields you have so often heard of, next to the one which had been the scene of poor Mr. Ryle's unhappy ending, when a tall man suddenly pounced upon him, came to a standstill, and spoke.

"I believe I am not mistaken in supposing that I address Mr. Chattaway?"

In his panic Mr. Chattaway nearly dropped a small parcel he held. An utter fear had taken possession of him: for in the speaker he recognised his dreaded enemy; the man who had proclaimed that he was about to work evil against him. It seemed like a terrible omen, meeting him the first moment of his arrival.

"I have been wishing to see you for some days past," continued the stranger, "and have been to the Hold three or four times to ask if you had come home. I was a friend of the late Joe Trevlyn's. I am a friend now of his son."

"Yes," stammered Chattaway—for in his fear he did not follow his first impulse, to meet the words with a torrent of anger. "May I ask what you want with me?"

"I wish to converse upon the subject of Rupert Trevlyn. I would endeavour to impress upon you the grievous wrong inflicted upon him in keeping him out of the property of his forefathers. I do not think you can ever have reflected upon the matter, Mr. Chattaway, or have seen it in its true light—otherwise you would surely never deprive him of what is so indisputably his."

Mr. Chattaway, his fears taking deeper and deeper possession of him, had turned into the field, in the hope of getting rid of the stranger. In any direction, no matter what, so that he could shake him off—for what to answer he did not know. It must be conciliation or defiance; but in that hurried moment he could not decide which would be the better policy. The stranger also turned and kept up with him.

"My name is Daw, Mr. Chattaway. You may possibly remember it, for I had the honour of a little correspondence with you about the time of Mrs. Trevlyn's death. It was I who transmitted to you the account of the birth of the boy Rupert. I am now informed that that fact was not suffered to reach the ears of Squire Trevlyn."

"I wish to hear nothing about it, sir; I desire to hold no communication with you at all," cried Mr. Chattaway, bearing on his way.

"But it may be better for you that you should do so, and I ask it in courtesy," persisted Mr. Daw, striding beside him. "Appoint your own time and place, and I will wait upon you. These things are always better settled amicably than the reverse: litigation generally brings a host of evil in its train; and Rupert Trevlyn has no money to risk. Not but that his costs could come out of the estate," equably concluded Mr. Daw.

The master of Trevlyn Hold turned passionately, arresting his course for an instant. "Litigation! what do you mean? How dare you speak to me in this manner? Who but a footpad would accost a gentleman by night, as you are accosting me?"

The discourteous thrust did not seem to put out Mr. Daw. "I only wish you to appoint a time to see me—at your own home, or anywhere else you may please," he reiterated, not losing his manners. "But I am not to be balked in this, Mr. Chattaway. I have taken up the cause of Rupert Trevlyn, and shall try to carry it through."

A blaze of anger burst from Mr. Chattaway, words and tones alike fierce, and Mr. Daw turned away. "I will see you when you are in a reasonable mood," he said. "To-morrow I will call at the Hold, and I hope you will meet me more amicably than you have done to-night."

"I will never meet you; I will never see or listen to you," retorted Chattaway, his anger mastering him and causing him to forget prudence. "If you want to know by what right I retain the Hold over the boy, Rupert Trevlyn, go and consult Squire Trevlyn's will. That is the only answer you will get from me."

Panting with the anger he could not restrain, Mr. Chattaway stood and watched the calm, retreating steps of the stranger, and then turned his own in the direction of home; unconscious that he in his turn was also watched, and by two who were very close to him—George Ryle and Maude Trevlyn.

They—as you remember—proceeded immediately to Trevlyn Farm; and words were spoken between them which no time could efface. Impulsive words, telling of the love that had long lain in the heart of each, almost as suppressed, quite as deep, as the great dread which had made the skeleton in Mr. Chattaway's.

The hilarity of the evening had progressed, as they found on entering. The company were seated round the table eating the good things, and evidently enjoying themselves heartily. The parlour-door was crowded with merry faces. Mrs. Ryle and others were at one end of the large room; George steered Maude direct to the parlour; the group made way for her, and welcomed her noisily.

But there came no smile to the face of Octave Chattaway. With a severe eye and stern tones, she confronted Maude, her lips drawn with anger.

"Maude, what do you do here? How dare you come?"

"Is there any harm in it, Octave?"

"Yes, there is," said Miss Chattaway, with flashing eyes. "There is harm because I desired you not to come. A pretty thing for Mrs. Ryle to be invaded by half-a-dozen of us! Have you no sense of propriety?"

"Not a bit of it," gaily interrupted George. "No one understands that in connection with a harvest-home. I have been to the Hold for Maude, Octave; and should have brought Edith and Emily, but they were in bed."

"In bed!" exclaimed Caroline Ryle, in surprise.

"Having retired in mortification and tears at being excluded from the delights of a harvest-home," continued George, with mock gravity. "Miss Chattaway had preached propriety to them, and they could only bow to it. We must manage things better another time."

Octave's cheeks burnt. Was George Ryle speaking in ridicule? To stand well with him, she would have risked much.

"They are better at home," she quietly said: "and I have no doubt Mrs. Ryle thinks so. Two of us are sufficient to come. Quite sufficient, in my opinion," she pointedly added, turning a reproving look on Maude. "I am surprised you should have intruded—"

"Blame me, if you please, Miss Chattaway—if you deem blame due anywhere," interrupted George. "I have a will of my own, you know, and I took possession of Maude and brought her, whether she would or no."

Octave pushed her hair back with an impatient movement. Her eyes fell before his; her voice, as she addressed him, turned to softness. George was not a vain man; but it was next to impossible to mistake these signs; though neither by word nor look would he give the faintest colouring of hope to them. If Octave could only have read the indifference at his heart! nay, more—his positive dislike!

"Did you see anything of Rupert?" she asked, recalling his attention to herself.

"I saw nothing of any one but Maude. I might have laid hands on all I found; but there was no one to meet, Maude excepted. What makes you so cross about it, Octave?"

She laughed pleasantly. "I am not cross, George," lowering her tones, "sometimes I think you do not understand me. You seem to—"

Octave's words died away. Coming in at the door was the tall, conspicuous form of the parsonage guest, Mr. Daw. Maude was just then standing apart, and he went deliberately up to her and kissed her forehead.

Startled and resentful, a half-cry escaped her lips; but Mr. Daw laid his hand gently on her arm.

"My dear young lady, I may almost claim that as a right. I believe I was the first person, except your mother, who ever pressed a kiss upon your little face. Do you know me?"

Maude faltered in her answer. His appearance and salutation had altogether been so sudden, that she was taken by surprise; but she did not fail to recognise him now. Yet she hesitated to acknowledge that she knew him, on account of Octave Chattaway. Rupert had told her all about the stranger; but it might be inconvenient to say so much to an inmate of Trevlyn Hold.

"It was I who christened you," he resumed. "It was I who promised your father to—to sometimes watch over you. But I could not keep my promise; circumstances worked against it. And now that I am brought for a short time into the same neighbourhood, I may not call to see you."

"Why not?" exclaimed Maude, wondering much.

"Because those who are your guardians forbid me. I went to the Hold and asked for you, and then became aware that in doing so I had committed something like a crime, or what was looked upon as one. Should Rupert, your brother, regain possession of his father's inheritance and his father's home, then, perhaps, I may be a more welcome visitor."

The room stood in consternation. To some of them, at any rate, these words were new; to the ears of Octave Chattaway they were tainted with darkest treason. Octave had never heard anything of this bold stranger's business at Barbrook, and she gazed at him with defiant eyes and parted lips.

"Were you alluding to the Hold, sir?" she asked in a cold, hard voice, which might have been taken for Chattaway's own.

"I was. The Hold was the inheritance of Rupert Trevlyn's father: it ought to be that of Rupert."

"The Hold is the inheritance of my father," haughtily spoke Octave. "Is he mad?" she added in a half-whisper, turning to George.

"Hush, Octave. No."

It was not a pleasant or even an appropriate theme to be spoken of in the presence of Mr. Chattaway's daughters. George Ryle, at any rate, thought so, and was glad that a burst of rustic merriment came overpoweringly at that moment from the feasting in the other room.

Under cover of the noise, Octave approached Nora. Nora immediately drew an apple-pie before her, and began to cut unlimited helpings, pretending to be absorbed in her work. She had not the least inclination for a private interview with Miss Chattaway. Miss Chattaway was one, however, not easily repulsed.

"Nora, tell me—who is that man, and what brings him here?"

"What man, Miss Chattaway?" asked Nora, indifferently, unable to quite help herself. "Ann Canham, how many are there to be served with pie still?"

"*That* man. That bold, bad man who has been speaking so strangely."

"Does he speak strangely?" retorted Nora.

"His voice is gruff certainly. And what a lot of plum-pudding he is eating! He is our young master's new waggoner, Miss Chattaway."

"Not *he*!" shrieked Octave, in her anger. "Do you suppose I concern myself with those stuffing clodhoppers? I speak of that tall, strange man amongst the guests."

"Oh, he!" said Nora, carelessly glancing over her shoulder. "Nanny, here's unlimited pie, if it's wanted. What about him, Miss Chattaway?"

"I asked you who he was, and what brought him here."

"Then you had better ask himself, Miss Chattaway. He goes about with a red umbrella; and that's about all I know of him."

"Why does Mrs. Ryle invite suspicious characters to her house?"

"Suspicious characters! Is he one? Madge Sanders, if you let Jim cram himself with pie in that style, you'll have something to do to get him home. He is staying at the parsonage, Miss Chattaway; an acquaintance of Mr. Freeman's. I suppose they brought him here to-night out of politeness; it wouldn't have been good manners to leave him at home. He is an old friend of the Trevlyns, I hear; has always believed, until now, that Master Rupert enjoyed the Hold—can't be brought to believe he doesn't. It is a state of things that does sound odd to a stranger, you know."

Octave might rest assured she would not get the best of it with Nora. She turned away with a displeased gesture, and regained the sitting-room, where refreshments for Mrs. Ryle's friends were being laid. But somehow the sunshine of the evening had gone out for her. What had run away with it? The stranger's ominous words? No; for those she had nothing but contempt. It was George Ryle's unsatisfactory manner, so intensely calm and equable. And those calm, matter-of-fact manners, in one beloved, tell sorely upon the heart.

The evening passed, and it grew time to leave. Cris Chattaway and Rupert had come in, and they all set off in a body to Trevlyn Hold—those who had to go there. George went out with them.

"Are you coming?" asked Octave.

"Yes, part of the way."

So Octave stood, ready to take his arm, never supposing that he would not offer it; and her pulses began to beat. But he turned round as if waiting for something, and Octave could only walk on a few steps. Soon she heard him coming up and turned to him. And then her heart seemed to stand still and bound on again with fiery speed, and a flush of anger dyed her brow. He was escorting Maude on his arm!

"Oh, George, do not let Maude trouble you," she exclaimed. "Cris will take care of her. Cris, come and relieve George of Maude Trevlyn."

"Thank you, Octave; it's no trouble," replied George, his tone one of indifference. "As I brought Maude out, it is only fair that I should take her home—the task naturally falls to me, you see."

Octave did not see it at all, and resentfully pursued her way; something very like hatred for Maude taking possession of her breast. It is not pleasant to write of these things; but I know of few histories in which they can be quite avoided, if the whole truth is adhered to, for many and evil are the passions assailing the undisciplined human heart.

"Good-bye!" George whispered to Maude as he left her. "This night begins a new era in our lives."

The Hold was busy when they entered. Mrs. Chattaway and her sister had just returned from Barmester, and were greeted by Mr. Chattaway. They had expected him for so many days past, and been disappointed, that his appearance now brought surprise with it. He answered the questions evasively put to him by Mrs. Chattaway and Diana, as to where he had been. Business had kept him, was all they could obtain from him.

"I cannot think what you have done for clothes, James," said Mrs. Chattaway.

"I have done very well," he retorted. "Bought what I wanted."

But it was not upon the score of his wardrobe, or what had kept him so long, that Miss Diana Trevlyn required Chattaway. She had been waiting since the first morning of his absence, for information on a certain point, and now demanded it in a peremptory manner.

"Chattaway," she began, when the rest had dispersed, and she waited with him, "I have had a strange communication made to me. In that past time—carry your thoughts back to it, if you please—when there came to this house the news of Rupert Trevlyn's birth and his mother's death—do you remember it?"

"Yes, I do," said Mr. Chattaway. "What should hinder me?"

"The tidings were conveyed by letter. Two letters came, the second a day after the first."

"Well?" returned Chattaway, believing the theme, in some shape or other, was to haunt him for ever. "What of the letters?"

"In that last letter, which must have been a heavy one, there was a communication enclosed for me."

"I don't remember it," said Mr. Chattaway.

"It was no doubt there. A document written at the request of Mrs. Trevlyn; appointing me guardian to the two children. What did you do with it?"

"I?" returned Chattaway, speaking with apparent surprise, and looking full at Miss Diana with an unmoved face. "I did nothing with it. I don't know anything about it."

"You must have taken it out and suppressed it," observed Miss Diana.

"I never saw it or heard of it," obstinately persisted Chattaway. "Why should I? You might have been their appointed guardian, and welcome, for me: you have chiefly acted as guardian. I tell you, Diana, I neither saw nor heard of it: you need not look so suspiciously at me."

"Is he telling the truth?" thought Miss Diana, and her keen eyes were not lifted from Mr. Chattaway's face. But that gentleman was remarkably inscrutable, and never appeared more so than at this moment.

"If he did *not* do anything with it," continued Miss Diana in her train of thought, "what could have become of the thing? Where can it be?"

CHAPTER XXX
MR. CHATTAWAY COMES TO GRIEF

A few days passed on, and strange rumours began to be rife in the neighbourhood. Various rumours, vague at the best; but all tending to one point—the true heir was coming to his own again. They penetrated even to the ears of Mr. Chattaway, throwing that gentleman into a state not to be described. Some said a later will of the Squire's had been found; some said a will of Joe Trevlyn's; some that it was now discovered the estate could only descend in the direct male line, and consequently it had been Rupert's all along. Chattaway was in a raging fever; it preyed upon him, and turned his days to darkness. He seemed to look upon Rupert with the most intense suspicion, as if it were from him alone—his plotting and working—that the evil would come. He feared to trust him out of his sight; to leave him alone for a single instant. When he went to Blackstone he took Rupert with him; he hovered about all day, keeping Rupert in view, and brought him back in the evening.

Miss Diana had not yet bought the pony she spoke of, and Chattaway either mounted him on an old horse that was good for little now, and rode by his side, or drove him over. Rupert was intensely puzzled at this new consideration, and could not make it out.

One morning Mr. Chattaway so far sacrificed his own ease as to contemplate walking over: the horses were wanted that day. "Very well," Rupert answered, in his half-careless, half-obedient fashion, "it was all the same to him." And so they started. But as they were going down the avenue a gentleman was discerned coming up it. Mr. Chattaway knit his brows and peered at him; his sight for distance was not quite as good as it had been.

"Who's this?" asked he of Rupert.

"It is Mr. Peterby," replied Rupert.

"Peterby!" ejaculated Chattaway. "What Peterby?"

"Peterby of Barmester, the lawyer," explained Rupert, wondering that there was any need to ask.

For only one gentleman of the name of Peterby was known to Trevlyn Hold, and Mr. Chattaway was, so to say, familiar with him. He had been solicitor to Squire Trevlyn, and though Mr. Chattaway had not continued him in that post when he succeeded to the estate, preferring to employ Mr. Flood, he yet knew him well. The ejaculation had not escaped him so much in doubt as to the man, as to what he could want with him. But Mr. Peterby was solicitor for some of his tenants, and he supposed it was business touching the renewal of leases.

They met. Mr. Peterby was an active little man of more than sixty years, with a healthy colour and the remains of auburn hair. He had walked all the way from Barmester, and enjoyed the walk as much as a schoolboy. "Good morning, Mr. Chattaway," he said, holding out his hand, "I am fortunate in meeting you. I came early, to catch you before you went to Blackstone. Can you give me half-an-hour's interview?"

Mr. Chattaway thought he should not like to give the interview. He was in a bad temper, in no mood for business, and he really wanted to be at Blackstone. Besides all that he had no love for Mr. Peterby. "I am pressed for time this morning," he replied, "am much later than I ought to have been. Is it anything particular you want me for?"

"Yes, very particular," was the answer, delivered in uncompromising tones. "I must request you to accord me the interview, Mr. Chattaway."

Mr. Chattaway turned back to the house with his visitor, and marshalled him into the drawing-room. Rupert remained at the hall-door.

"I have come upon a curious errand, Mr. Chattaway, and no doubt an unwelcome one; though, from what I hear, it may not be altogether unexpected," began the lawyer, as they took seats opposite each other. "A question has been arising of late, whether Rupert Trevlyn may not possess some right to the Hold. I am here to demand if you will give it up to him."

Was the world coming to an end? Chattaway thought it must be. He sat and stared at the speaker as if he were in a dream. Was *every one* turning against him? He rubbed his handkerchief over his hot face, and imperiously demanded of Mr. Peterby what on earth he meant, and where he could have picked up his insolence.

"I am not about to wrest the estate from you, Mr. Chattaway, or to threaten to do so," was the answer. "You need not fear that. But—you must be aware that you have for the last twenty years enjoyed a position that ought in strict justice to belong to the grandson of Squire Trevlyn."

"I am not aware of anything of the sort," groaned Chattaway. "What do you mean by 'wresting the estate'?"

"Softly, my good sir; there's no need to put yourself out with me. I am come on a straightforward, peaceable errand; not one of war. A friendly errand, if you will allow me so to express myself."

The master of the Hold could only marvel at the words. A friendly errand! requiring him to give up his possessions!

Mr. Peterby proceeded to explain; and as there is no time to give the interview in detail, it shall be condensed. It appeared that the Reverend Mr. Daw had in his zeal sought out the solicitors of the late Squire Trevlyn. He had succeeded in impressing upon them a sense of the great injustice dealt out to Rupert; had avowed his intention of endeavouring, by any means in his power, to remedy this injustice; but at this point he had been somewhat obscure, and had, in fact, caused the lawyers to imagine that this power was real and tangible. Could there be, they asked themselves afterwards, any late will of Squire Trevlyn's which would supersede the old one? It was the only hinge on which the matter could turn; and Mr. Daw's mysterious hints certainly encouraged the thought. But Mr. Daw had said, "Perhaps Chattaway will give up amicably, if you urge it upon him," and Mr. Peterby had now come for that purpose.

"What you say is utterly absurd," urged Chattaway; the long explanation, which Mr. Peterby had given openly and candidly, having afforded him time to recover somewhat of his fears and his temper. "I can take upon myself most positively to assert that no will or codicil was made, or attempted to be made, by Squire Trevlyn, subsequently to the one on which I inherit. Your firm drew that up."

"I know we did," replied the lawyer. "But that does not prove that none was drawn up after it."

"But I tell you there was not any. I am certain upon the point."

"Well, it was the only conclusion we could come to," rejoined Mr. Peterby. "This Mr. Daw must have some grounds for urging the thing on; he wouldn't be so stupid as to do so if he had none."

"He has none," said Chattaway.

"Ah, but I am sure he has. But for being convinced of this, do you suppose I should have come to you now, asking you to give up an estate which you have so long enjoyed? I assure you I came as much in your interests as in his. If there is anything in existence by which you can be disturbed, it is only fair you should know of it."

Fair! In Mr. Chattaway's frame of mind, he could scarcely tell what was fair and what was not fair. The interview was prolonged, but it brought forth no satisfactory conclusion. Perhaps none could be expected. Mr. Peterby took his departure, impressed with the conviction that the present owner of Trevlyn Hold would retain possession to the end, contesting it inch by inch; and as he walked down the avenue he asked himself whether he had not been induced to enter upon a foolish errand, in coming to suggest that it should be voluntarily resigned.

The master of Trevlyn Hold watched him away, and then opened the breakfast-room door. "Where's Rupert?" he inquired, not seeing Rupert there.

"Rupert?" answered Mrs. Chattaway, looking up. "I think he has gone to Blackstone. He wished me good morning; and I saw him walk down the avenue."

All things seemed to be against Mr. Chattaway. Here was Rupert out of sight now; it was hard to say where he might have gone, or what mischief he might be up to. As he turned from the door, Cris Chattaway's horse—the unlucky new one which had damaged the dog-cart—was brought up, and Cris appeared, prepared to mount him.

"Where are you going, Cris?"

"Nowhere in particular this morning," answered Cris. "I have a nasty headache, and a canter may take it away."

"Then I'll ride your horse to Blackstone," returned Mr. Chattaway. "Alter the stirrups, Sam."

"Why, where's your own horse?" cried Cris, with a blank look.

"In the stable," shortly returned Chattaway.

He mounted the horse and rode away, his many cares perplexing him. A hideous wall separating him from all good fortune seemed to be rising up round about him; and the catastrophe he so dreaded—a contest between himself and Rupert Trevlyn for possession of the Hold—appeared to be drawing within the range of probability. In the gloomy prospect before him, only one loophole of escape presented itself to his imagination—the death of Rupert.

But you must not think worse of Mr. Chattaway than he deserves. He did not deliberately contemplate such a calamity; or set himself to hope for it. The imagination is rebelliously evil, often uncontrollable; and the thought rose up unbidden and unwished for. Mr. Chattaway could not help it; could not at first drive it away again; the somewhat dangerous argument, "Were Rupert dead I should be safe, and it is the only means by which I can feel assured of safety," did linger with him longer than was expedient; but he never for one moment contemplated the possibility as likely to take place; most certainly it never occurred to him that he could be accessory to it. Though not a good man, especially in the way of temper and covetousness, Chattaway would have started with horror had he supposed he could ever be so bad as that.

He rode swiftly along in the autumn morning, urging his horse to a hard gallop. Was his haste merely caused by his anxiety to be at Blackstone, or that he would escape from his own thoughts? He rode directly to the coal mine, up to the mouth of the pit. Two or three men, looking like blackamoors, were standing about.

"Why are you not down at work?" angrily demanded Mr. Chattaway. "What do you do idling here!"

They had been waiting for Pennet, the men replied. But word had just been brought that Pennet was not coming.

"Where is he?" asked Mr. Chattaway. "Skulking again?"

"I dunna think he be skulking, sir," was the reply of one. "He's bad a-bed."

An angry frown darkened Mr. Chattaway's countenance. Truth to say, this man, Pennet, though a valuable workman from his great strength, his perseverance when in the pit, did occasionally absent himself from it, to the wrath of his overseers; and Mr. Chattaway knew that illness might be only an excuse for taking a holiday in the drinking shop.

"I'll soon see that," he cried. "Bring that horse back. If Pennet is skulking, I'll discharge him this very day."

He had despatched his horse round to the stable; but now mounted him again, and was riding away, after ordering the men down to their work, when he stopped to ask a question respecting one of his overseers.

"Is Bean down the shaft?"

No; the men thought not. They believed he was round at the office.

Mr. Chattaway turned his horse's head towards the office, and galloped off, reining in at the door. The clerk Ford and Rupert Trevlyn both came out.

"Oh, so you have got here!" ungraciously grunted Mr. Chattaway to Rupert. "I want Bean."

"Bean's in the pit, sir," replied Ford.

"The man told me he was not in the pit," returned Mr. Chattaway. "They said he was here."

"Then they knew nothing about it," observed Ford. "Bean has been down the pit all the morning."

Mr. Chattaway turned to Rupert. "Go down the shaft and tell Bean to come up. I want him."

He rode off as he spoke, and Rupert departed for the pit. The man Pennet lived in a hovel, one of many, about a mile and a half away. Chattaway between haste and temper, was in a heat when he arrived. A masculine-looking woman with tangled hair came out to salute him.

"Where's Pennet?"

"He's right bad, master."

Mr. Chattaway's lip curled. "Bad from drink?"

"No," replied the woman, defiantly; for the owner of the mine was held in no favour, and this woman was of too independent a nature to conceal her sentiments when provoked. "Bad from rheumatiz."

He got off his horse, rudely pushed her aside, and went in. Pennet was dressed, but was lying on a wooden settle, as the benches were called in that district.

"I be too bad for the pit to-day, sir; I be, indeed. This, rheumatiz have been a-flying about me for weeks; and now it's settled in my loins, and I can't stir."

"Let's see you walk," responded Chattaway.

Pennet got off the bench with difficulty, and walked across the brick floor slowly, his arms behind him.

"I thought so," said Chattaway. "I knew you were skulking. You are as well able to walk as I am. Be off to the pit."

The man lifted his face. "If you was in the pain I be, master, you wouldn't say so. I mote drag myself down to 'im, but I couldn't work."

"We will see about that," said Mr. Chattaway, in his determined manner. "You work to-day, my man, or you never work again for me: so take your choice."

There was a pause. Pennet looked irresolute, the woman bitter. Perhaps what these people hated most of all in Chattaway was his personal interference and petty tyranny. What he was doing now—looking up the hands—was the work of an overseer; not of the owner.

"Come," he authoritatively repeated. "I shall see you start before me. We are too busy for half of you to be basking in idleness. Are you going? Work to-day, or leave the pit, just which you please."

The man glanced at his children—a ragged little group, cowering in silence in a corner, awed by the presence of the master; took his cap without a word, and limped slowly away, though apparently scarcely able to drag one foot before the other.

"Where be your bowels of compassion?" cried the woman, in her audacity, placing herself before Mr. Chattaway.

"I know where my whip will be if you don't get out of my way and change your tone," was his answer. "What do you mean, woman, by speaking so to me?"

"Them as have no compassion for their men, but treads 'em down like beasts o' burden, may come, perhaps, to be treaded down themselves," was the woman's retort, as she withdrew out of Mr. Chattaway's vicinity.

He made no answer, except that he lifted his whip significantly. As he rode off, he saw Pennet pursuing his way to the mine by the nearest path—one inaccessible to horses. When he was near the man, he lifted his whip as significantly at him as he had done at the wife, and then urged his horse to a gallop. It was a busy day, both in the office and in the mine; and Chattaway, taking as you perceive a somewhat practical part in his affairs, had wished to be present some two hours before. Consequently, these delays had not improved his temper.

About midway between the Pennets' hut and the mine were the decaying walls of what had once been a shed. Part of the wall was still standing, about four feet high. It lay right in Mr. Chattaway's way: one single minute given to turning either to the right or left, and he would have avoided it. But he saw no reason for avoiding it: he had leaped it often: it was not likely that he would in his hurry turn from it now.

He urged his horse to it, and the animal was in the very act of taking the leap, when a sudden obstacle interposed. A beggar, who had been quietly ensconced on the other side, basking in the sun and eating his dinner, heard the movement, and not wishing to be run over started up to escape the danger. The movement frightened the horse, causing him to strike the wall instead of clearing it: he fell, and his master with him.

The horse was not hurt, and soon found its legs. If the animal had misbehaved himself a few days previously, under the hands of Mr. Cris, he appeared determined to redeem his character now. He stood patient and silent, turning his head to Mr. Chattaway, as if waiting for him to get up.

Which that gentleman strove to do. But he found he could not. Something was the matter with one of his ankles, and he was in a towering passion. The offending beggar scampered off, frightened at his unbounded rage and threats of vengeance.

The intemperate words did him no good; you may be very sure of that they never do any one good. For more than an hour Mr. Chattaway lay there, his horse patiently standing by him, and no one coming to his aid. It would have seemed that he lay three times as long, but that he had his watch, and could consult it as often as he pleased. It was an unfrequented by-road, leading nowhere in particular, except to the hovels; and Chattaway had therefore full benefit of the solitude.

The first person to come up was no other than Mrs. Pennet—Meg Pennet, as she was familiarly called. Her tall, gaunt form came striding along, and her large eyes grew larger as she saw who was lying there.

"Ah, master! what's it your turn a'ready! Have you been there ever sin'? Can't you get up?"

"Find assistance," he cried in curt tones of authority. "Mount my horse and you'll go the quicker."

"Na, na; I mount na horse. The brute might be flinging me, as it seems he ha' flinged you. Women and horses be best apart. Shall I help you up?"

His haughty, ill-conditioned spirit would have prompted him to say "No"; his helplessness and impatience obliged him to say "Yes." The powerful woman took him by the shoulders and raised him. So far, so good. But his ankle gave him intense pain; was, in short, almost useless; and a cry escaped him. In his agony, he flung her rudely from him with his elbow. "Go and get assistance, woman."

"Be that'n the thanks I get? Ah! it be coming home to ye, be it! Ye sent my man off to work in pain; he couldn't hardly crawl: how d'you like pain yerself? If the leg's broke, Squire, you'll ha' time to lie and think on't."

She strode on, Chattaway sending an ugly word after her, and soon came in sight of the mine—which appeared to be in an unusual bustle. A crowd had collected round the mouth of the pit, and people were running to it from all quarters. Loud talking, gesticulating, confusion prevailed: what could be causing it?

"Happen they be looking for him as is lying yonder!" quoth she. But scarcely were the words out of her mouth when a group of women running, filling the air with cries and lamentations, came in sight. Her coarse face grew white and her heart turned sick as the fatal truth burst upon her conviction. There had been an accident in the mine!

CHAPTER XXXI
DOWN THE SHAFT

It was only too true. Whether from fire-damp, the rushing in of water, or some other mischief to which coal-pits are liable, was as yet scarcely known: nothing was certain except the terrible calamity itself. Of the men who had gone down the mine that morning, some were dead, others dying. Meg Pennet echoed the shrieks of the women as she flew forward and pushed through the crowd collected round the mouth of the pit. The same confusion prevailed there that prevails in similar scenes of distress and disaster elsewhere.

"And Mr. Chattaway himself was down the shaft, you say? He went down this morning? My friends, it is altogether an awful calamity."

The woman pushed in yet further and confronted the speaker, her white face drawn with anguish. He was the minister of a dissenting chapel, a Mr. Lloyd, and well known to the miners, some of whom went regularly to hear him preach.

"No, sir; Chattaway was na down the shaft; he is na one of the dead, more luck to him," she said, her words brought out brokenly, her bosom heaving. "Chattaway have this morning made me a widda and my young children fatherless. My man was stiff with rheumatiz, he was—no more fit to go to work nor I be to go down that shaft and carry up his poor murdered body. I knowed his errand as soon as I heerd his horse's feet. He made him get off the settle, and druv him out to work as he'd drive a dog; and when I told him of his hardness, he lifted up his whip agin me. Yes! Pennet's down with the rest of 'em; sent by him: and I be a lone widda."

"Her says right," interposed a voice. "It wasn't the master as went down the shaft; it were young Rupert Trevlyn."

"Rupert Trevlyn," uttered the minister in startled tones. "I hope he is not down."

"Yes, he's down, sir."

"But where can Mr. Chattaway be?" exclaimed Ford, the clerk, who made one of the throng. "Do you know, Meg Pennet?"

"He's where ill-luck have overtook him for his cruelty to us," answered Meg Pennet, flinging her hair from her sorrowful face. "I telled him the ill he forced on others might happen come home to him—that he might soon be lying in his pain, for aught he knew. And he went right off to the ill then and there—and he's a-lying in it."

The sympathies of the hearers were certainly not given to Mr. Chattaway. He was no favourite with his dependants at Blackstone, any more than with his neighbours around the Hold. But the woman's words were strange, and they pressed for an explanation.

"He be lying under the wall o' the old ruin," was her reply. "I come upon him there, and I guess his brave horse had flung him. When I'd ha' lifted him, he cried out with pain—as my poor man was a-crying in the night with his back—and I saw him lay hisself down again after I'd left him. And Chattaway he swore at me for my help—and you can go to him and be swore at too. Happen his leg be broke."

The minister turned away to seek Mr. Chattaway. Unless completely disabled, it was necessary that he should be at the scene; no one of any particular authority was there to give orders; and the inevitable confusion attendant on such a calamity was thereby increased. Ford, the clerk, sped after Mr. Lloyd, and one or two stragglers followed him; but the rest were chained to the more exciting scene of the disaster.

Mr. Chattaway had raised himself when they reached him, and was holding on by the wall. He broke into a storm of grumbling, especially at Ford, and asked why he could not have found him out sooner. As if Ford could divine what had befallen him! Mr. Lloyd stooped and touched the ankle, which was a good deal swollen. It was sprained, Chattaway said; but he thought he could manage to get on his horse with their assistance. He abused the beggar unmercifully, and expressed his intention of calling a meeting of his brother-magistrates, that measures might be taken to rid the country of tramps and razor-grinders; and he finished up in the heat of argument by calling the accident which had befallen him a cursed misfortune.

"Hush!" quietly interrupted Mr. Lloyd. "I should call it a blessing."

Chattaway stared at him and deemed that he was carrying religion rather too far. As he looked, it struck him that both his rescuers wore very sad countenances; Ford in particular was excessively crestfallen. A sarcastic smile crossed his face.

"A blessing! to have my ankle sprained, and waste my morning in this fashion? Thank you, Mr. Lloyd! You gentlemen who have nothing better to do with your time than preach it away may think little of such an interruption, but to men of business it is not agreeable. A blessing!"

"Yes, I believe it to have come to you as such—sent direct from God. Were you not going into the pit this morning?"

"Yes, I was," impatiently answered Mr. Chattaway. "I should be there now, but for this—blessing! I wish you would not—"

"Just so," interrupted Mr. Lloyd, calmly. "And this fall has no doubt saved your life. There has been an accident in the pit, and the poor fellows who went down a few hours ago full of health and life, are about to be carried up dead."

The words brought Mr. Chattaway to his senses. "An accident!" he repeated. "What accident?—of what nature?" turning hastily to Ford.

"Fire-damp, I believe, sir."

"Who was down?" was the next eager question.

"The usual men, sir. And—and—Mr. Rupert Trevlyn."

Chattaway with some difficulty repressed a shout. Idea after idea crowded upon his brain, one chasing another. Foremost amongst them rose distinctly the one thought of the morning from which he had striven to escape and could not: "Nothing can bring me security save the death of Rupert." Had the half-encouraged wish brought its realisation.

"Rupert Trevlyn down the shaft!" he repeated, the moisture breaking over his face. "I know he went down; I sent him; but—but—did he not come up again?"

"No," gloomily replied Ford, who really liked Rupert; "he is down now. There's no hope that he'll come up alive."

Whether consternation deadened his physical suffering, or his ankle, from the rest it had had, was really less painful, Mr. Chattaway contrived to get pretty comfortably to the scene of action. The crowd had increased; people were coming up from far and near. Medical men had arrived, ready to give their services in case any sufferers were brought up alive. One of them examined Mr. Chattaway's ankle, and bound it up; the hurt, he said, was only a temporary one.

He, the owner of that pit, sat down on the side of a hand-barrow, for he could not stand, and issued his orders in sharp, concise tones; and the bodies began to be brought to the surface. One of the first to appear was that of the unfortunate man, Bean, to whom he had sent the message by Rupert. Chattaway looked on, half-dazed. Would Rupert's body be the next? He could not realise the fact that he, from whom he had dreaded he knew not what, should soon be laid at his feet, cold and lifeless. Was he glad or sorry? Did grief for Rupert predominate? Or did the intense relief the death must bring overpower any warmer feeling? Perhaps Mr. Chattaway could not yet tell.

They were being brought up pretty quickly now, and were laid on the ground beside him, to be recognised by the unhappy relatives. The men to whom Chattaway had spoken that morning were amongst them: he had ordered them down as he rode off, and one and all had obeyed the mandate. Did he regret their fate? Did he compassionate the weeping wives and children? In a degree, perhaps, yes; but not as most men would have done.

A tall form interposed between him and the mouth of the pit—that of Meg Pennet. She had been watching for a body which had not yet been brought up. Suddenly she turned to Mr. Chattaway.

"You have killed him, master; you have made my children orphans. But for your coming in your hardness to drive him out when he warn't fit to go, we should ha' had somebody still to work for us. Happen you may have heered of a curse? I'd like to give ye one now."

"Somebody take this woman away," cried Chattaway. "She'll be better at home."

"Ay, take her away," retorted Meg; "don't let her plaints be heered, lest folk might say they be just. Send her home to her fatherless children, and send her dead man after her to lie among 'em till his burial. Happen, when you come to your death, Mr. Chattaway, you'll have us all afore your mind, to comfort you!"

She stopped. Another ill-fated man was being drawn up, and she turned to wait for it, her hands clenched, her face white and haggard in its intensity. The burden came, and was laid near the rest; but it was not the one for which she waited. Another woman darted forward; *she* knew it too well; and she clasped her hands round it, and sobbed in agony. Meg Pennet turned resolutely to the mouth of the pit again, watching still.

"Be they all dead? How many was down?"

The voice came from behind Meg Pennet, and she screamed and started. There stood her husband. How had he escaped from the pit?

"I haven't been a-nigh it," he answered. "I couldn't get down to the pit, try as I would, without a rest, and I halted at Green's. Who's dead among 'em, and who's alive?"

"God be thanked!" exclaimed Meg Pennet, with a sob of emotion.

All Mr. Chattaway's faculties were strained on the mouth of that yawning pit, and what it might yield up. As body after body was brought to the surface—seven of them were up now—he cast his anxious looks upon it, expecting to recognise the fair face of Rupert Trevlyn. Expecting and yet dreading—don't think him worse than he was; with the frightened, half-shrinking dread ordinarily experienced by women, or by men of nervous and timid temperament. So utterly did this suspense absorb him as to make him almost oblivious to the painful features of the scene, the wails of woe and bursts of lamentation.

Happening for a minute to turn his eyes from the pit, he saw in the distance a pony-carriage approaching, which looked uncommonly like that of Miss Diana Trevlyn. Instinct told him that the two figures seated in it were his wife and Miss Diana, although as yet he could not see whether they were women or men. It was slowly winding down a distant hill, and would have to ascend another and come over the flat stretch of country ere it could reach them. He beckoned his clerk Ford to him in a sort of terror.

"Run, Ford! Make all speed. I think I see Miss Trevlyn's pony-carriage yonder with the ladies in it. Don't let them approach. Tell them to turn aside, to the office, and I'll come to them. Anywhere; anywhere but here."

Ford ran with all his might. He met the carriage just at the top of the nearest hill, and unceremoniously laid his hand upon the pony, giving Mr. Chattaway's message as well as his breathless state would allow—begging they would turn aside and not approach the pit.

It was evident that they were strangers as yet to the news, but the crowd and excitement round the pit had been causing them apprehension and a foreshadowing of the truth. Miss Diana, paying, as it appeared, little heed to the message, extended her whip in the direction of the scene.

"I see what it is, Ford. Don't beat about the bush. How many were down the shaft?"

"A great many, ma'am," was Ford's reply. "The pit was in full work to-day."

"Was it fire-damp?"

"I believe so."

"Mr. Chattaway's safe, you say? He was not down? I suppose he was not likely to be down?"

"No," answered Ford. But the thought of Mr. Chattaway's accident from another source, which he did not know whether to disclose or not, and the consciousness of a worse calamity, caused him to speak hesitatingly. Miss Diana was quick of apprehension, and awoke it.

"Was any one down the shaft besides the men? Was—where's Rupert Trevlyn?"

Ford looked as if he dared not answer.

Mrs. Chattaway caught the alarm. She half rose in the low carriage, and stretched out her hands in a pleading attitude; as though Ford held the issues of life and death.

"Oh, speak, speak! He was not down the shaft! Surely Rupert was not down the shaft!"

"He had gone down but a short time before," said the young man in a whisper—for where was the use of denying the fact, now that they had guessed it? "We shall all mourn him, ma'am. I had almost as soon it had been me."

"Gone down the shaft but a short time before!" mechanically repeated Miss Diana in her horror. But she was interrupted by a cry from Ford. Mrs. Chattaway had fallen back on her seat in a fainting-fit.

CHAPTER XXXII
A SHOCK FOR MR. CHATTAWAY

The brightness of the day was turning to gloom, as if the heavens sympathised with the melancholy scene upon earth. Quietly pushing his way through the confusion, moans and lamentations, the mass of human beings surrounding the mouth of the pit, was a tall individual whose acquaintance you have made before. It was Mr. Daw with his red umbrella: the latter an unvarying appendage, whether the sun was shining or the clouds dropped rain. He went straight up to certain pale faces lying there in a row, and glanced at them one by one.

"They are saying that Rupert Trevlyn is amongst the sufferers," he observed to those nearest to him.

"So he is, master."

"I do not see him here."

"No; he ain't up yet."

"Is there no hope that he may be brought to the surface alive?"

They shook their heads. "Not now. He have been down too long. There's not a chance for him."

Something like emotion passed over Mr. Daw's features.

"How came *he* to be down the pit?" he asked. "Was it his business to go down?"

"Not in ord'nary. No: 'tworn't once in six months as there was aught to take him there."

"Then what took him there to-day?" was Mr. Daw's next question.

"The master sent him," replied the man, pointing towards Chattaway.

Apparently Mr. Daw had not observed Chattaway before, and he turned and walked towards him. Vexation at the loss of Rupert—it may surely be called vexation rather than grief, since he had not known Rupert sufficiently long to *love* him—a loss so sudden and terrible, was rendering Mr. Daw unjust. Chattaway's worst enemy could not fairly blame him with reference to the fate of Rupert: but Mr. Daw was in a hasty mood.

"Is it true that you sent Rupert Trevlyn down the shaft only a few minutes before this calamity occurred?"

The address and the speaker equally took Mr. Chattaway by surprise. His attention was riveted on something then being raised from the shaft, and he had not noticed the stranger. Hastily turning his head, he saw, first the conspicuous red umbrella, next its obnoxious and dangerous owner.

Ah, but no longer dangerous now. That terrible fear was over for ever. With the first glimpse, Mr. Chattaway's face had turned to a white heat, from the force of habit; but the next moment's reflection reassured him, and he retained his equanimity.

"What did you say, sir?"

"Was there no one else, Mr. Chattaway, to serve your turn, but you must send down your wronged and unhappy nephew?" reiterated Mr. Daw, in tones that penetrated to every ear. "I have heard it said, since I came into this neighbourhood, that Mr. Chattaway would be glad, if by some lucky chance Squire Trevlyn's grandson and legal heir could be put out of his path. It seems he has succeeded in accomplishing it."

Mr. Chattaway's face grew dark and frowning. "Take care what you say, sir, or you shall answer for your words. I ask you what you mean."

"And I ask you—Was there no one you could despatch this morning into that dangerous mine, then on the very eve of exploding, but that helpless boy, Rupert, who might not resist your authority, and so went to his death? Was there no one, I ask?"

Mr. Daw's zeal was decidedly outrunning his discretion. It is the province of exaggeration to destroy its cause, and the unfounded charge—which, temperately put, might have inflicted its sting—fell comparatively harmless on the ear of Mr. Chattaway. He could only stare and wonder—as if a proposition had been put to him in some foreign language.

"Why—bless my heart!—are you mad?" he presently exclaimed. His tone was sufficiently equable. "Could *I* tell the mine was going to explode? Had but the faintest warning reached me, do you suppose I should not have emptied the pit of all human souls? I am as sorry for Rupert as you can be: but the blame is not mine. It is not any one's—unless it be his own. There was plenty of time to leave the pit after he had delivered the message I sent him down with, had he chosen to do so. But I suppose he stopped gossiping with the men. This land belongs to me, sir. Unless you have any business here, I must request you to leave it."

There was so much truth in what Mr. Chattaway urged that the stranger began to be a little ashamed of his heat. "Nevertheless, it is a thorn removed from your path," he cried aloud. "And you would have removed him from it yourself long ago, could you have done it without sin."

A half murmur of assent arose from the crowd. The stranger had hit the exact facts. Could the master of Trevlyn Hold have removed Rupert Trevlyn from his path without "sin," without danger or trouble, it had been done long ago. In short, were it as easy to put some obnoxious individual out of life, as it is to stow away an offending piece of furniture, Mr. Chattaway had most assuredly not waited until now to rid himself of Rupert: and those listeners knew it.

Mr. Chattaway turned his frowning face on the murmurers; but before more could be said by any one, the circle was penetrated by some new-comers, one of them in distress of mind that could not be hidden or controlled. Mrs. Chattaway having recovered from her apparent fainting-fit—though in reality she had not lost consciousness, and her closed eyes and intense pallor had led to the mistake—the pony-carriage had been urged with all speed to the scene of action. In vain the clerk Ford reiterated Mr. Chattaway's protest against their approach. Miss Diana Trevlyn was not one to attend against her will to the protests of Mr. Chattaway.

"I would have saved his life with my own; I would have gone down in his place had it been possible," wailed poor Mrs. Chattaway, wringing her hands, and wholly forgetting the reticence usually imparted by the presence of her husband.

Her grief was genuine; and the crowd sympathised with her almost as it did with those despairing women, weeping in their new widowhood. But the neighbours had not now to learn that Madame Chattaway loved her dead brother's children, if her husband did not.

"For Heaven's sake don't make a scene here!" growled Mr. Chattaway, in impotent anger. "Have you no sense of the fitness of things?"

But his wife, however meekly submissive at other times, was not in a state for submission then. Unable to define the sensations that oppressed her, she only felt that all was over; the unhappy boy had gone from them for ever; the cruel wrongs inflicted on him throughout life were now irreparable.

"He has gone with all our unkindness on his head," she wailed, partially unconscious, no doubt, of what she said; "gone to meet his father, my poor lost brother, bearing to him the tale of his wrongs! Oh, if—"

"Be silent, will you?" shrieked Chattaway. "Are you going mad?"

Mrs. Chattaway covered her face with her hands, and leaned against the barrow on which her husband was sitting. Miss Diana Trevlyn, who had been gathering various particulars from the crowd, who had said a word of comfort—though it was little comfort they could listen to yet—to the miserable women, came up at this moment to Chattaway.

"It was a very unhappy thing that you should have sent Rupert into the pit this morning," she said, her face wearing its most haughty expression.

"Yes," he answered. "But I could not foresee what was about to happen. It—it might have been Cris. Had Cris been in the way at the time, and not Rupert, I should have despatched him."

"Chattaway, I would give all my fortune to have him back again. I—"

A strange commotion on the outskirts of the crowd attracted their attention, and Miss Diana brought her sentence to an abrupt conclusion, and turned sharply towards it, for the shouts bore the sound of triumph; and a few voices were half breaking into hurrahs. Strange sounds, in that awful death-scene!

Who was this advancing towards them? The crowd had parted to give him place, and he came leaping to the centre, all haste and excitement—a fair, gentlemanly young man, his silken hair uncovered, his cheeks hectic with excitement. Mrs. Chattaway cried aloud with a joyful cry, and her husband's eyes and mouth slowly opened as though he saw a spectre.

It was Rupert Trevlyn. Rupert, it appeared, had not been down the pit at all. Sufficiently obedient to Mr. Chattaway, but not obedient to the letter, Rupert, when he reached the pit's mouth, had seen the last of those men descending whom Chattaway had imperiously ordered down, and sent the message to Bean by him. His chief inducement was that he had just met an acquaintance who had come to tell him of a pony for sale—for Rupert, commissioned by Miss Trevlyn, had been making inquiries for one. It required little pressing to induce Rupert to abandon the office and Blackstone for some hours, and start off to see this pony. And that was where he had been. Mrs. Chattaway clasped her arms around his neck, in utter defiance of her husband's prejudices, unremembered then, and sobbed forth her emotion.

"Why, Aunt Edith, you never thought I was one of them, did you? Bless you! I am never down the pit. I should not be likely to fall into such a calamity as that. Poor fellows! I must go and ascertain who was there."

The crowd, finding Rupert safe, broke into a cheer, and a voice shouted—could it have been Mr. Daw's?—"Long live the heir! long live young Squire Trevlyn!" and the words were taken up and echoed in the air.

And Mr. Chattaway? If you want me to describe his emotions to you, I cannot do it. They were of a mixed nature. We must not go so far as to say he *regretted* to see Rupert back in life; felt no satisfaction at his escape; but with his reappearance all the old fears returned. They returned tenfold from the very fact of his short immunity from them, and the audacious words of the crowd turned his face livid. In conjunction with the yet more audacious words previously spoken by the stranger and the demonstrative behaviour of his wife, they were as a sudden blow to Mr. Chattaway.

Those shouters saw his falling countenance, his changed look, and drew their own conclusions. "Ah! he'd put away the young heir if he could," they whispered one to another. "But he haven't got shut of him this time."

No; Mr. Chattaway certainly had not.

"God has been merciful to your nephew," interposed the peaceful voice of Mr. Lloyd, drawing near. "He has been pleased to save him, though He has seen fit to take others. We know not why it should be—some struck down, others spared. His ways are not as our ways."

They lay there, a long line of them, and the minister pointed with his finger as he spoke. Most of the faces looked calm and peaceful. Oh! were they ready? Had they lived to make God their friend? Trusting in Christ their Saviour? My friends, this sudden call comes to others as well as to miners: it behoves us all to be ready for it.

As the day drew on, the excitement did not lessen; and Mr. Chattaway almost forgot the hurt, which he would have made a great deal of at another time. But the ankle was considerably swollen and inflamed, giving him pain still, and it caused him to quit the scene for home earlier than he might otherwise have done.

He left Cris to superintend. Cris was not incompetent for the task; but he might have displayed a little more sympathy with the sufferers without compromising his dignity. Cris had arrived in much bustle and excitement at the scene of action: putting eager questions about Rupert, as to how he came to be down the shaft, and whether he was really dead. The report that he was dead had reached Cris Chattaway's ears at some miles' distance, as it had reached those of many others.

It reached Maude Trevlyn's. The servants at the Hold heard it, and foolishly went to her. "There had been an explosion in the pit, and Master Rupert was amongst the killed." Maude was as one stricken with horror. She did not faint or cry; putting on a shawl and bonnet mechanically, as she would for any ordinary walk, she left the house on her way to Blackstone. "Don't go, Maude; it will only be more painful to you," Octave had said in kindly tones, as she saw her departing; but Maude, as though she heard not, bore swiftly on with a dry eye and burning brow. Turning from the fields into the road, she met George Ryle.

"Where are you going, Maude?"

"Oh, George, don't stop me! I had no one but him."

But George did stop her. He saw her countenance of despair, and suspected what was wrong. Putting his arm gently round her, he held her to him. Maude supposed he had heard the tidings, and was unwilling that she should approach the terrible scene.

"My darling, be comforted. You have been hearing that Rupert shared the calamity, but the report was a false one. Rupert is alive and well. It is the happy truth, Maude."

Overcome by emotion, Maude leaned upon him and sobbed out more blissful tears than perhaps she had ever shed. Mr. George would have had no objection to apply himself to the task of soothing her until the shades of night fell; but scarcely a minute had they so stood when an interruption, in the shape of some advancing vehicle, was heard. These envious interruptions will occur at the most unwelcome moments, as perhaps your own experience may bear witness to.

It proved to be the pony-carriage of Miss Diana Trevlyn. Mr. Chattaway with his lame foot sat beside her, and Mrs. Chattaway occupied the groom's place behind. Miss Diana, who chose to drive her own pony, although she had a gentleman at hand, drew up in surprise at the sight of Maude.

"I had heard that Rupert was killed," she explained, advancing to the carriage, her face still wet with tears. "But George Ryle has told me the truth."

"And so you were starting for Blackstone!" returned Miss Diana. "Would it have done any good, child? But that is just like you, Maude. You will act upon impulse to the end of life."

Mrs. Chattaway bent forward with her sweet smile. "Rupert is on his way home, Maude, alive and well. I am sorry you should have heard what you did."

"It seems to me the whole parish has heard it," ejaculated Mr. Chattaway.

Room was made for Maude beside Mrs. Chattaway, and the pony-carriage went on. It had gone only a few paces when the Reverend Mr. Daw came in sight. Was the man gifted with ubiquity! But an hour or two, as it seemed, and he had been bearding Mr. Chattaway at the mine. He lifted his hat as he passed, and Miss Diana and Maude bowed in return. He did not approach the carriage, or attempt to stop it; but went on with long strides, as one in a hurry.

Mr. Chattaway, who had never looked towards the man, never moved a muscle of his face, turned his head to steal a glance when he deemed him at a safe distance. There stood Mr. Daw, talking to George Ryle, one hand stretched out in the heat of argument, the other grasping the red umbrella, which was turned over his shoulder.

"Treason, treason!" mentally ejaculated the master of Trevlyn Hold, as he raised his handkerchief to his heated face. "How I might have laughed at them now, if—if—if that had turned out to be true about Rupert!"

CHAPTER XXXIII
THE OLD TROUBLE AGAIN

From ten days to a fortnight went by, and affairs were resuming their ordinary routine. All outward indications of the accident were over; the bodies of the poor sufferers were buried; the widows, mothers, orphans, had begun to realise their destitution. It was not all quite done with, however. The inquest, adjourned from time to time, was not yet concluded; and popular feeling ran high against Mr. Chattaway. Certain precautions, having reference to the miners' safety, which ought to have been observed in the pit, had not been observed; hence the calamity. Other mine owners in the vicinity had taken these precautions long ago; but Mr. Chattaway, whether from inertness, or regard to expense, had not done so. People spoke out freely now, not only in asserting that these safeguards must no longer be delayed—and of that Mr. Chattaway was himself sensible, in a sullen sort of way—but also that it was incumbent on him to do something for the widows and orphans. A most distasteful hint to a man of so near a disposition. Miss Diana Trevlyn had gone down to the desolate homes and rendered them glad with her bounty; but to make anything like a permanent provision for them was Mr. Chattaway's business, and not hers. The sufferers believed Mr. Chattaway was not likely to make even the smallest for them; and they were not far wrong. His own hurt, the sprained ankle, had speedily recovered, and he was now well again.

And the officious stranger, and his interference for the welfare of Rupert? That also was falling to the ground, and he, Mr. Daw, was now on the eve of departure. However well meant these efforts had been, they could only be impotent in the face of Squire Trevlyn's will. Mr. Daw himself was at length convinced of the fact, and began to doubt whether his zeal had not outrun his discretion. Messrs. Peterby and Jones angrily told him that it had, when he acknowledged, in answer to their imperative question, that he had had no grounds whatever to go upon, save goodwill to Rupert. Somewhat of this changed feeling may have prompted him to call at Trevlyn Hold to pay a farewell visit of civility; which he did, and got into hot water.

He asked for Miss Diana Trevlyn. But Miss Diana happened to be out, and Octave, who was seated at the piano when he was shown in, whirled round upon the stool in anger. She had taken the most intense dislike to this officious man: possibly a shadow of the same dread which filled her father's heart had penetrated to hers.

"Miss Trevlyn! If Miss Trevlyn were at home, she would not receive you," was her haughty salutation, as she rose from her stool. "It is impossible that you can be received at the Hold. Unless I am mistaken, sir, you had an intimation of this from Squire Chattaway."

"My visit, young lady, was not to Mr. Chattaway, but to Miss Trevlyn. So long as the Hold is Miss Trevlyn's residence, her friends must call there—although it may happen to be also that of Mr. Chattaway. I am sorry she is out: I wish to say a word to her before my departure. I leave to-night for good."

"And a good thing too," said angry Octave, forgetting her manners. But this answer had not conciliated her, especially the very pointed tone with which he had called her father *Mr.* Chattaway.

She rang the bell loudly to recall the servant. She did not ask him to sit down, but stood pointing to the door; and Mr. Daw had no resource but to obey the movement and go out—somewhat ignominously it must be confessed.

In the avenue he met Miss Trevlyn, and she was more civil than Octave had been. "I leave to-night," he said to her. "I go back to my residence abroad, never in all probability to quit it again. I should have been glad to serve poor Rupert by helping him to his rights—Miss Trevlyn, I cannot avoid calling them so—but I find the law and Mr. Chattaway stronger than my wishes. It was, perhaps, foolish ever to take up the notion, and I feel half inclined to apologise to Mr. Chattaway."

"Of all visionary notions, that was about the wildest I ever heard of," said Miss Diana.

"Yes, utterly vain and useless. I see it now. I do not the less feel Rupert Trevlyn's position, you must understand; the injustice dealt out to him lies on my mind with as keen a sense as ever: but I do see how hopeless, and on my part how foolish, was any attempt at remedy. I should be willing to say this to Mr. Chattaway if I saw him, and to tell him I had done with it. Mr. Freeman hints that I was not justified in thus attempting to disturb the peace of a family, and he may be right. But, Miss Trevlyn, may I ask you to be kind to Rupert?"

Miss Trevlyn threw back her head. "I have yet to learn that I am not kind to him, sir."

"I mean with a tender kindness. I fancy I see in him indications of the disease that was so fatal to his father. It has been on my mind to invite him to go back home with me, and try what the warmer climate may do for him;

but the feeling (amounting almost to a prevision) that the result in his case would be the same as his father's, withholds me. I should not like to take him out to die: neither would I charge myself with the task of nursing one in a fatal malady."

"You are very good," said Miss Diana, somewhat stiffly. "Rupert will do well where he is, I have no doubt: and for myself, I do not anticipate any such illness for him. I wish you a pleasant journey, Mr. Daw."

"Thank you, madam. I leave him to your kindness. It seems to me only a duty I owe to his dead father to mention to you that he *may* need extra care and kindness; and none so fitting to bestow it upon him as you—the guardian appointed by his mother."

"By the way, I cannot learn anything about that document," resumed Miss Diana. "Mr. Chattaway says that it never came to hand."

"Madam, it must have come to hand. If the letter in which it was enclosed reached Trevlyn Hold, it is a pretty good proof that the document also reached it. Mr. Chattaway must be mistaken."

Miss Diana did not see how, unless he was wilfully, falsely denying the fact. "A thought struck me the other day, which I wish to mention to you," she said aloud, quitting the subject for a different one. "The graves of my brother and his wife—are they kept in order?"

"Quite so," he answered. "I see to that."

"Then you must allow me to repay to you any expense you may have been put to. I—"

"Not so," he interrupted. "There is no expense—or none to speak of. The ground was purchased for ever, *à perpétuité*, as we call it over there, and the shrubs planted on the site require little or no care in the keeping. Now and then I do a half-day's work there myself, for the love of my lost friends. Should you ever travel so far and I should be happy to welcome you—you will find their last resting-place well attended to, Miss Trevlyn."

"I thank you much," she said in heartier tones, as she held out her hand. "And I regret now that circumstances have prevented my extending hospitality to you."

And so they parted amicably. And the great ogre Mr. Chattaway had feared would eat him up, had subsided into a very harmless man indeed. Miss Diana went on to the Hold, deciding that her respected brother-in-law was a booby for having been so easily frightened into terror.

As Mr. Daw passed the lodge, old Canham was airing himself at the door, Ann being out at work. The gentleman stopped.

"You were not here when I passed just now," he said. "I looked in at the window, and opened the door, but could see no one."

"I was in the back part, maybe, sir. When Ann's absent, I has to get my own meals, and wash up my cups and things."

"I must say farewell to you. I leave to-night."

"Leave the place! What, for good, sir?"

"Yes," replied Mr. Daw. "In a week's time from this, I hope to be comfortably settled in my own home, some hundreds of miles away."

"And Master Rupert? and the Hold?" returned old Canham, the corners of his mouth considerably drawn down. "Is he to be rei'stated in it?"

Mr. Daw shook his head. "I did all I could, and it did not succeed: I can do no more. My will is good enough—as I think I have proved; but I have no power."

"Then it's all over again, sir—dropped through, as may be said?"

"It has."

Old Canham leaned heavily on his crutch, lost in thought. "It won't drop for ever, sir," he presently raised his head to say. "There have been something within me a long, long while, whispering that Master Rupert's as safe to come to his own before he dies, as that I be to go into my grave. When this stir took place, following on your arrival here, I thought the time had come then. It seems it hadn't; but come it *will*, as sure as I be saying it—as sure as he's the true heir of Squire Trevlyn."

"I hope it will," was the warm answer. "You will none of you rejoice more truly than I. My friend Freeman has promised to write occasionally to me, and—"

Mr. Daw was interrupted. Riding his shaggy pony in at the lodge gate—a strong, brisk little Welsh animal bought a week ago by Miss Diana, was Rupert himself. Upon how slender a thread do the great events of life turn! The reflection is so trite that it seems the most unnecessary reiteration to record it; but there are times when it is brought to the mind with an intensity that is positively startling.

Mr. Chattaway, by the merest accident—as it appeared to him—had forgotten a letter that morning when he went to Blackstone. He had written it before leaving home, intending to post it on his road, but left it on his desk. It was drawing towards the close of the afternoon before he remembered it. He then ordered Rupert to ride home as fast as possible and post it, so that it might be in time for the evening mail. And this Rupert had now come to do. All very simple, you will say: but I can tell you that but for the return of

Rupert Trevlyn at that hour, the most tragical part of this history would in all probability never have taken place.

"The very man I was wishing to see!" exclaimed Mr. Daw, arresting Rupert and his pony in their career. "I feared I should have to leave without wishing you good-bye."

"Are you going to-day?" asked Rupert.

"To-night. You seem in a hurry."

"I am in a hurry," replied Rupert, as he explained about the letter. "If I don't make haste, I shall lose the post."

"But I want to talk to you a bit. Do you go back to Blackstone?"

"Oh no; not to-day."

"Suppose you come in to the parsonage for an hour or two this evening?" suggested Mr. Daw. "Come to tea. I am sure they'll be glad to see you."

"All right; I'll come," cried Rupert, cantering off.

But a few minutes, and he cantered down again, letter in hand. Old Canham was alone then. Rupert looked towards him, and nodded as he went past. There was a receiving-house for letters at a solitary general shop, not far beyond Trevlyn Farm, and to this Rupert went, posted the letter, and returned to Trevlyn Hold. Sending his pony to the stable, he began to get ready for his visit to Mr. Freeman's—a most ill-fated visit, as it was to turn out.

They took tea at the parsonage at six, and he had to hasten to be in time. He had made his scanty dinner, as usual, at Blackstone. In descending the stairs from his room he encountered Mrs. Chattaway in the lower corridor.

"Are you going out, Rupert?"

"I am going to the parsonage, Aunt Edith. Mr. Daw leaves this evening, and he asked me to go in for an hour or two."

"Very well. Remember me kindly to Mrs. Freeman. And, Rupert—my dear—"

"What?" he asked, arresting his hasty footsteps and turning to speak.

"You will not be late?"

"No, no," he answered, his careless tone a contrast to her almost solemn one. "It's all right, Aunt Edith."

But for that encounter with Mrs. Chattaway, the Hold would have been in ignorance of Rupert's movements that evening. He spent a very pleasant one. It happened that George Ryle called in also at the parsonage on Mr.

Freeman, and was induced to remain. Mrs. Freeman was hospitable, and they sat down to a good supper, to which Rupert at least did justice.

The up-train was due at Barbrook at ten o'clock, and George Ryle and Rupert accompanied Mr. Daw to it. The parson remained at home not caring to go out at night, unless called forth by duty. They reached the station five minutes before the hour, and Mr. Daw took his ticket and waited for the train.

Waited a long time. Ten o'clock struck, and the minutes went on and on. George, who was pacing the narrow platform with him, drew Rupert aside and spoke.

"Should you not get back to the Hold? Chattaway may lock you out again."

"Let him," carelessly answered Rupert. "I shall get in somehow, I dare say."

It was not George's place to control Rupert Trevlyn, and they paced the platform as before, talking with Mr. Daw. Half-past ten, and no train! The porters stood about, looking and wondering; the station-master was fidgety, wanting to get home to bed.

"Will it come at all?" asked Mr. Daw, whose patience appeared exemplary.

"Oh, it'll come, safe enough," replied one of the two porters. "It never keeps its time, this train don't: but it's not often as late as this."

"Why does it not keep its time?"

"It has got to wait at Layton's Heath for a cross-train; and if that don't keep its time—and it never do—this one can't."

With which satisfactory explanation, the porter made a dash into a shed, and appeared to be busy with what looked like a collection of dark lanthorns.

"I shall begin to wish I had taken my departure this afternoon, as I intended, if this delay is to be much prolonged," remarked Mr. Daw.

Even as he spoke, there were indications of the arrival of the train. At twenty minutes to eleven it came up, and the station-master gave some sharp words to the guard. The guard returned them in kind; its want of punctuality was not his fault. Mr. Daw took his seat, and George and Rupert hastened away to their respective homes. But it was nearly eleven o'clock and Rupert, in spite of his boasted bravery, did fear the wrath of Mr. Chattaway.

The household had retired to their rooms, but that gentleman was sitting up, looking over some accounts. The fact of Rupert's absence was known to him, and he experienced a grim satisfaction in reflecting that he was locked out for the night. It is impossible for me to explain to you why this should have gratified the mind of Mr. Chattaway; there are things in this world not easily accounted for, and you must be contented with the simple fact that it was so.

But Mrs. Chattaway? She had gone to her chamber sick and trembling, feeling that the old trouble was about to be renewed to-night. If the lad was not allowed to come in, where could he go? where find a shelter? Could *she* let him in, was the thought that hovered in her mind. She would, if she could accomplish it without the knowledge of her husband. And that might be practicable to-night, for he was shut up and absorbed by those accounts of his.

Gently opening her dressing-room window, she watched for Rupert: watched until her heart failed her. You know how long the time seems in this sort of waiting. It appeared to her that he was never coming—as it had recently appeared to Mr. Daw, with regard to the train. The distant clocks were beginning to chime eleven when he arrived. He saw his aunt; saw the signs she made to him, and contrived to hear and understand her whispered words.

"Creep round to the back-door, and I will let you in."

So Rupert crept softly round; walking on the grass: and Mrs. Chattaway crept softly down the stairs without a light, undid the bolt silently, and admitted Rupert.

"Thank you, dear Aunt Edith. I could not well help being late. The train—"

"Not a word, not a breath!" she interrupted, in a terrified whisper. "Take off your boots, and go up to bed without noise."

Rupert obeyed in silence. They stole upstairs, one after the other. Mrs. Chattaway turned into her room, and Rupert went on to his.

And the master of Trevlyn Hold, bending over his account-books, knew nothing of the disobedience enacted towards him, but sat expecting and expecting to hear Rupert's ring echoing through the house. Better, far better that he had heard it!

CHAPTER XXXIV
THE NEXT MORNING

The full light of day had not come, and the autumn night's gentle frost lingered yet upon the grass, when the master of Trevlyn Hold rose from his uneasy couch. Things were troubling him; and when the mind is uneasy, the night's rest is apt to be disturbed.

That business of the mine explosion was not over, neither were its consequences to Mr. Chattaway's pocket. The old far regarding the succession, which for some days had been comparatively quiet, had broken out again in his mind, he could not tell why or wherefore; and the disobedience of Rupert, not only in remaining out too late the previous night, but in not coming in at all, angered him beyond measure. Altogether, his bed had not been an easy one, and he arose with the dawn unrefreshed.

It was not the fact of having slept little which got him up at that unusually early hour; but necessity has no law, and he was obliged to rise. A famous autumn fair, held at some fifteen miles' distance, and which he never failed to attend, was the moving power. His horse was to be ready for him, and he would ride there to breakfast; according to his annual custom. Down he went; sleepy, cross, gaping; and the first thing he did was to stumble over a pair of boots at the back-door.

The slightest thing would put Mr. Chattaway out when in his present temper. For the matter of that, a slight thing would put him out at any time. What business had the servants to leave boots about in *his* way? They knew he would be going out by the back-door the first thing in the morning, on his way to the stables. Mr. Chattaway gave the things a kick, unbolted the door, and drew it open. Whose were they?

Now that the light was admitted, he saw at a glance that they were a gentleman's boots, not a servant's. Had Cris stolen in by the back-door last night and left his there? No; Cris came in openly at the front, came in early, before Mr. Chattaway went to bed. And—now that he looked more closely—those boots were too small for Cris.

They were Rupert's! Yes, undoubtedly they were Rupert's boots. What brought them there? Rupert could not pass through thick walls and barred up doors. Mr. Chattaway, completely taken back, stooped and stared at the boots as if they had been two curious animals.

A faint sound interrupted him. It was the approach of the first servant coming down to her day's work; a brisk young girl called Bridget, who acted as kitchenmaid.

"What brings these boots here?" demanded Mr. Chattaway, in the repelling tone he generally used to his servants.

Bridget advanced and looked at them. "They are Mr. Rupert's, sir," answered she.

"I did not ask you whose they were: I asked what brought them here. These boots must have been worn yesterday."

"I suppose he left them here last night; perhaps came in at this door," returned the girl, wondering what business of her master's the boots could be.

"Perhaps he did not," retorted Mr. Chattaway. "He did not come in at all last night."

"Oh yes, he did, sir. He's in his room now."

"Who's in his room?" rejoined Mr. Chattaway, believing the girl was either mistaken or telling a wilful untruth.

"Mr. Rupert, sir. Wasn't it him you were asking about?"

"Mr. Rupert is not in his room. How dare you say so to my face?"

"But he is," said the girl. "Leastways, unless he has gone out of it this morning."

"Have you been in his room to see?" demanded Mr. Chattaway, in his ill-humour.

"No, sir, I have not; it's not likely I should presume to do such a thing. But I saw Mr. Rupert go into his room last night; so it's only natural to suppose he is there this morning."

The words confounded Mr. Chattaway. "You must have been dreaming, girl."

"No, sir, I wasn't; I'm sure I saw him. I stepped on my gown and tore it as I was going up to bed last night, and I went to the housemaid's room to borrow a needle and cotton to mend it. I was going back across the passage when I saw Mr. Rupert at the end of the corridor turn into his chamber." So far, true. Bridget did not think it necessary to add that she had remained a good half-hour gossiping with the housemaid. Mr. Chattaway, however, might have guessed that, for he demanded the time, and Bridget confessed it was past eleven.

Past eleven! The whole house, himself excepted, had gone upstairs at half-past ten, and Rupert was then not in. Who had admitted him?

"Which of you servants opened the door to him?" thundered Mr. Chattaway.

"I shouldn't think any of us did, sir. I can answer for me and cook and Mary. We never heard Mr. Rupert ring at all last night: and if we had, we shouldn't have dared let him in after your forbidding it."

The girl was evidently speaking the truth, and Mr. Chattaway was thrown into perplexity. Who *had* admitted him? Could it have been Miss Diana Trevlyn? Scarcely. Miss Diana, had she taken it into her head, would have admitted him without the least reference to Mr. Chattaway; but she would not have done it in secret. Had it pleased Miss Diana to come down and admit Rupert, she would have done it openly; and what puzzled Mr. Chattaway more than anything, was the silence with which the admission had been accomplished. He had sat with his ears open, and not the faintest sound had reached them. Was it Maude? No: he felt sure Maude would be even more chary of disobeying him than the servants. Then who was it? A half-suspicion of his wife suggested itself to him, only to be flung away the next moment. His submissive, timorous wife! She would be the last to array herself against him.

But the minutes were passing, and Mr. Chattaway had no time to waste. The fair commenced early, its business being generally over before mid-day. He went round to the stables, found his horse ready, and rode away, the disobedience he had just discovered filling his mind to the exclusion of every other annoyance.

He soon came up with company. Riding out of the fold-yard of Trevlyn Farm as he passed it, came George Ryle and his brother Treve. They were bound for the same place, and the three horses fell in together.

"Are you going?" exclaimed Mr. Chattaway to Trevlyn, surprise in his tone.

"Of course I am," answered Treve. "There's always some fun at Whitterbey fair. George is going to initiate me to-day into the mysteries of buying and selling cattle."

"Against you set up for yourself?" remarked Mr. Chattaway, cynically.

"Just so," said Treve. "I hope you'll find me as good a tenant as you have found George."

George was smiling. "He is about to settle down into a steady-going farmer, Mr. Chattaway."

"When?" asked Chattaway.

George hesitated, and glanced at Trevlyn, as if waiting for the answer to come from him.

"At once," said Treve, readily. "There's no reason why it should not be known. I am home for good, Mr. Chattaway, and don't intend to leave it again."

"And Oxford?" returned Chattaway, surprised at the news. "You had another term to keep."

"Ay, but I shall not keep it. I have had enough of Oxford. One can't keep straight there, you know: there's no end of expense to be gone into; and my mother is tired of it."

"Tired of the bills?"

"Yes. Not but that paying them has been George's concern more than hers. No one can deny that; but George is a good fellow, and *he* has not complained."

"Are there to be two masters on Trevlyn Farm?"

"No," cried Treve. "I know my place better, I hope, than to put my incompetent self above George—whatever my mother may wish. So long as George is on Trevlyn Farm, he is sole master. But he is going to leave us, he says."

Mr. Chattaway turned to George, as if for confirmation. "Yes," answered George, quietly; "I shall try to take a farm on my own account. You have one soon to be vacant that I should like, Mr. Chattaway."

"I have?" exclaimed Mr. Chattaway. "There's no farm of mine likely to be vacant that would suit your pocket. You *can't* mean you are turning your ambitious eyes to the Upland?" he added, after a moment's pause.

"Yes, I am," replied George. "And I must have a talk with you about it. I should like the Upland Farm."

"Why, it would take—"

George did not wait to hear the conclusion of the sentence.

They were at that moment passing the parsonage, and Mr. Freeman, in a velvet skull-cap and slippers, was leaning over the gate. George checked his horse.

"Well, did he get safe off last night?" asked Mr. Freeman.

"Yes, at last. The train was forty minutes behind time."

"Ah! it's a shame they don't arrange matters so as to make that ten-o'clock train more punctual. Passengers are often kept waiting half-an-hour. Did you and Rupert remain to see him off?"

"Yes," replied George.

"Then Rupert would be late home," observed the clergyman, turning to Chattaway, who had also reined in. "I hope you excused him, Mr. Chattaway, under the circumstances."

Chattaway answered something very indistinctly, and the clergyman took it to imply that he *had* excused Rupert. George said good morning, and turned his horse onwards; they must make good speed, unless they would be "a day too late for the fair."

Not a syllable of the above conversation had Mr. Chattaway understood; it had been as Hebrew to him. He did not like Mr. Freeman's allusion to his "excusing the lateness of Rupert's return," for it proved that his harsh rule had become public property.

"I did not quite take Mr. Freeman," he said, turning equably to George, and speaking in careless accents. "Were you out last night with Rupert?"

"Yes. We spent the evening at the parsonage with Mr. Daw, and then went to see him off by the ten-o'clock train. It is a shame, as Mr. Freeman says, that the train is not made to keep better time. It was Mr. Daw's last night here."

"And therefore you and Rupert must spend it with him! It is a sudden friendship."

"I don't know that there's much friendship in the matter," replied George. "Rupert, I believe, was at the parsonage by appointment, but I called in accidentally. I did not know that Mr. Daw was leaving."

"Is he returning to France?"

"Yes. He crosses the Channel to-night. We shall never see him again, I expect; he said he should never more quit his home, so far as he believed."

"Is he a madman?"

"A madman! Certainly not."

"He talked enough folly and treason for one."

"Run away with by his zeal, I suppose," remarked George. "No one paid any attention to him. Mr. Chattaway, do you think we Barbrook people could not raise a commotion about the irregularity of that ten-o'clock train and so get it rectified?"

"Its irregularity does not concern me," returned Mr. Chattaway.

"It would if you had to travel by it; or to see friends off by it as Rupert and I had last night. Nearly forty-five minutes were we cooling our heels on the platform. It must have been eleven o'clock when Rupert reached the Hold. I suppose he was let in."

"It appears he did get in," replied Mr. Chattaway, in by no means a genial tone. "I don't know by whom yet; but I will know before to-night."

"If any one locked me out of my home, I should break the first window handy," cried bold Treve, who had been brought up by his mother in defiance of Mr. Chattaway, and would a great deal rather treat him with contempt than civility. "Rupert's a muff not to do it."

George urged on his horse. Words between Treve and Mr. Chattaway would not be agreeable, and the latter gentleman's face was turning fiery. "I am sure we shall be late," he cried. "Let us see what mettle our steeds are made of."

It diverted the anticipated dispute. Treve, who was impulsive at times, dashed on with a spring, and Mr. Chattaway and George followed. Before they reached Whitterbey, they fell in with other horsemen, farmers and gentlemen, bound on the same errand, and got separated.

Beyond a casual view of them now and then in the crowded fair, Mr. Chattaway did not again see George and Treve until they all met at what was called the ordinary—the one-o'clock dinner. Of these ordinaries there were several held in the town on the great fair day, but Mr. Chattaway and George Ryle had been in the habit of attending the same. Immediately after the meal was over, Mr. Chattaway ordered his horse, and set off home.

It was earlier than he usually left, for the men liked to sit an hour or two after dinner at these annual meetings, and discuss the state of affairs in general, especially those relating to farming; but Mr. Chattaway intended to take Blackstone on his road home, and that would carry him some miles out of his way.

He did not arrive at Blackstone until five o'clock. Rupert had gone home; Cris, who had been playing at master all day in the absence of Mr. Chattaway, had also gone home, and only Ford was there. That Cris should have left, Mr. Chattaway thought nothing of; but his spirit angrily resented the departure of Rupert.

"It's coming to a pretty pass," he exclaimed, "if he thinks he can go and come at any hour he pleases. What has he been about to-day?"

"We have none of us done much to-day, sir," replied Ford. "There have been so many interruptions. They had Mr. Rupert before them at the inquest, and examined him—"

"Examined *him*!" interrupted Chattaway. "What about?"

"About the precautions taken for safety, and all that," rejoined Ford, who liked to launch a shaft or two at his master when he might do it with discretion. "Mr. Rupert could not tell them much, though, as he was not in the habit of being down in the pit; and then they called some of the miners again."

"To what time is it adjourned?" growled Mr. Chattaway, after a pause.

"It's not adjourned, sir; it's over."

"Oh," said Mr. Chattaway, feeling a sort of relief. "What was the verdict?"

"The verdict, sir? Mr. Cris wrote it down, and took it up to the Hold for you."

"What was it? You can tell me its substance, I suppose."

"Well, it was 'Accidental death.' But there was something also about the absence of necessary precautions in the mine; and a strong recommendation was added that you should do something for the widows."

The very verdict Chattaway had so dreaded! As with many cowards, he *could not* feel independent of his neighbours' opinion, and knew the verdict would not add to his popularity. And the suggestion that he should do something for the widows positively appalled him. Finding no reply, Ford continued.

"We had some gentlemen in here afterwards, sir. I don't know who they were; strangers: they said they must see you, and are coming to-morrow. We wondered whether they were Government inspectors, or anything of that sort. They asked when the second shaft to the pit was going to be begun."

"The second shaft to the pit!" repeated Mr. Chattaway.

"It's what they said," answered Ford. "But it will be a fine expense, if that has to be made."

An expense the very suggestion of which turned that miserly heart cold. Mr. Chattaway thought the world was terribly against him. Certainly, what with one source of annoyance and another, the day had not been one of pleasure. In point of fact, Mr. Chattaway was of too suspicious a nature ever to enjoy much ease. It may be thought that with the departure of the dreaded stranger, he would have experienced complete immunity from the fears which had latterly so shaken him. Not so; the departure had only served to augment them. He had been informed by Miss Diana on the previous night of Mr. Daw's proposed return to his distant home, of his having relinquished Rupert's cause, of his half apology for having ever taken it up; he had heard again from George Ryle this morning that the gentleman had actually gone. Most men would have accepted this as a termination to the unpleasantness, and been thankful for it; but Mr. Chattaway, in his suspicious nature, doubted whether it did not mean treachery; whether it was not, in short, a *ruse* of the enemy. Terribly awakened were his fears that day. He suspected an ambush in every turn, a thief behind every tree; and he felt that he hated Rupert with a bitter hatred.

Poor Rupert at that moment did not look like one to be either hated or dreaded, could Mr. Chattaway have seen him through some telescope. When Chattaway was sitting in his office, Ford meekly standing to be questioned, Rupert was toiling on foot towards Trevlyn Hold. In his good nature he had left his pony at home for the benefit of Edith and Emily Chattaway. Since its purchase, they had never ceased teasing him to let them try it, and he had this day complied, and walked to Blackstone. He looked pale, worn, weary; his few days' riding to and fro had unfitted him for the walk, at least in inclination, and Rupert seemed to feel the fatigue this evening more than ever.

That day had not brought happiness to Rupert, any more than to Mr. Chattaway. It was impossible but his hopes should have been excited by the movement made by Mr. Daw. And now all was over. That gentleman had taken his departure for good, and the hopes had faded, and there was an end to it altogether. Rupert had felt it keenly that morning as he walked to Blackstone; felt that he and hope had bid adieu to each other for ever. Was his life to be passed at that dreary mine? It seemed so. The day, too, was spent even more unpleasantly than usual, for Cris was in one of his overbearing moods, and goaded Rupert's spirit almost to explosion. Had Rupert been the servant of Cris Chattaway, the latter could not have treated him with more complete contempt and unkindness than he did this day. Cris asked him who let him in to the Hold the previous night, and Rupert answered that it was no business of his. Cris then insisted upon knowing, but Rupert only laughed at him; and so Cris, in his petty spite, paid him out for it, and made the day one long humiliation to Rupert. Rupert reached home at last, and took tea with the family. He kissed Mrs. Chattaway ten times, and whispered to her that he had kept counsel, and would never, never, for her sake, be late again.

CHAPTER XXXV
AN ILL-STARRED CHASTISEMENT

It was growing dark on this same night, and Rupert Trevlyn stood in the rick-yard, talking to Jim Sanders. Rupert had been paying a visit to his pony in the stable, to see that it was alive after the exercise the girls had given it,—not a little, by all accounts. The nearest way from the stables to the front of the house was through the rick-yard, and Rupert was returning from his visit of inspection when he came upon Jim Sanders, leaning against a hay-rick. Mr. Jim had stolen up to the Hold on a little private matter of his own. In his arms was a little black puppy, very, very young, as might be known by the faint squeaks it made.

"Jim! Is that you?" exclaimed Rupert, having some trouble to discern who it was in the fading light. "What have you got squeaking there?"

Jim displayed the little animal. "He's only a few days old, sir," said he, "but he's a fine fellow. Just look at his ears!"

"How am I to see?" rejoined Rupert. "It's almost pitch dark."

"Stop a bit," said Jim, producing a sort of torch from under his smock-frock, and by some contrivance setting it alight. The wood blazed away, sending up its flame in the yard, but they advanced into the open space, away from the ricks and danger. These torches, cut from a peculiar wood, were common enough in the neighbourhood, and were found very useful on a dark night by those who had to go about any outdoor work. They gave the light of a dozen candles, and were not extinguished with every breath of wind. Dangerous things for a rick-yard, you will say: and so they were, in incautious hands.

They moved to a safe spot at some distance from the ricks. The puppy lay in Rupert's arms now, and he took the torch in his hand, whilst he examined it. But not a minute had they thus stood, when some one came upon them with hasty steps. It was Mr. Chattaway. He had, no doubt, just returned from Blackstone, and was going in after leaving his horse in the stable. Jim Sanders disappeared, but Rupert stood his ground, the lighted torch still in his one hand, the puppy lying in the other.

"What are you doing here?" angrily demanded Mr. Chattaway.

"Not much," said Rupert. "I was only looking at this little puppy," showing it to Mr. Chattaway.

The puppy did not concern Mr. Chattaway. It could not work him treason, and Rupert was at liberty to look at it if he chose; but Mr. Chattaway would not let the opportunity slip of questioning him on another matter. It was the first time they had met, remember, since that little episode which had so disturbed Mr. Chattaway in the morning—the finding of Rupert's boots.

"Pray where did you spend last evening?" he began.

"At the parsonage," freely answered Rupert; and Mr. Chattaway detected, or fancied he detected, defiance in the voice, which, to his ears, could only mean treason. "It was Mr. Daw's last evening there, and he asked me to spend it with him."

Mr. Chattaway saw no way of entering opposition to this; he could not abuse him for taking tea at the parsonage; could not well forbid it in the future. "What time did you come home?" he continued.

"It was eleven o'clock," avowed Rupert. "I went with Mr. Daw to the station to see him off, and the train was behind time. I thought it was coming up every minute, or I would not have stayed."

Mr. Chattaway had known as much before. "How did you get in?" he asked.

Rupert hesitated for a moment before speaking. "I was let in."

"I conclude you were. By whom?"

"I would rather not tell."

"But I choose that you shall tell."

"No," said Rupert. "I can't tell, Mr. Chattaway."

"But I insist on your telling," thundered Chattaway. "I order you to tell."

He lifted his riding-whip menacingly as he spoke. Rupert stood his ground fearlessly, the expression of his face showing out calm and firm, as the torchlight fell upon it.

"Do you defy me, Rupert Trevlyn?"

"I don't wish to defy you, sir, but it is quite impossible that I can tell you who let me in last night. It would not be fair, or honourable."

His refusal may have looked like defiance to Mr. Chattaway, but in point of fact it was dictated by a far different feeling—regard for his aunt Edith. Had any one else in the Hold admitted him, he might have confessed it, under Mr. Chattaway's stern command; but he would have died rather than bring *her*, whom he so loved, into trouble with her husband.

"Once more, sir, I ask you—will you tell me?"

"No, I will not," answered Rupert, with that quiet determination which creates its own firmness more surely than any bravado. Better for him that he had told! better even for Mrs. Chattaway.

Mr. Chattaway caught Rupert by the shoulder, lifted his whip, and struck him—struck him not once, but several times. The last stroke caught his face, raising a thick weal across it; and then Mr. Chattaway, his work done, walked quickly away towards his house, never speaking, the whip resting quietly in his hand.

Alas, for the Trevlyn temper! Maddened by the outrage, smarting under the pain, the unhappy Rupert lost all self-command. Passion had never overcome him as it overcame him now. He knew not what he did; he was as one insane; in fact, he was insane for the time being—irresponsible (may it not be said?) for his actions. With a yell of rage he picked up the torch, then blazing on the ground, dashed into the rick-yard as one possessed, and thrust the torch into the nearest rick. Then leaping the opposite palings, he tore away across the fields.

Jim Sanders had been a witness to this: and to describe Jim's consternation would be beyond the power of any pen. Standing in the darkness, out of reach of Mr. Chattaway's eyes, he had heard and seen all. Snatching the torch out of the rick—for the force with which Rupert had driven it in kept it there—Jim pulled out with his hands the few bits of hay already ignited, stamped on them, and believed the danger to be over. Next, he began to look for his puppy.

"Mr. Rupert can't have taken it off with him," soliloquised he, pacing the rick-yard dubiously with his torch, eyes and ears on the alert. "He couldn't jump over them palings with that there puppy in his arms. It's a wonder that a delicate one like him could jump 'em at all, and come clean over 'em."

Mr. Jim Sanders was right: it was a wonder, for the palings were high. But it is known how strong madmen are, and I have told you that Rupert was mad at that moment.

Jim's search was interrupted by fresh footsteps, and Bridget, the maid you saw in the morning talking to Mr. Chattaway, accosted him. She was a cousin of Jim's, three or four years older than he; but Jim was very fond of her, in a rustic fashion, deeming the difference of age nothing, and was always finding his way to the Hold with some mark of good will.

"Now, then! What do you want to-night?" cried she, for it was the pleasure of her life to snub him. "Hatch comes in just now, and says, 'Jim Sanders is in the rick-yard, Bridget, a-waiting for you.' I'll make you know better, young Jim, than send me in messages before a kitchen-ful."

"I've brought you a little present, Bridget," answered Jim, deprecatingly; and it was this offering which had taken Jim to the Hold. "The beautifullest puppy you ever see—if you'll accept him; black and shiny as a lump of coal. Leastways, I had brought him," he added, ruefully. "But he's gone, and I can't find him."

Bridget had a weakness for puppies—as Jim knew; consequently, the concluding part of his information was not agreeable to her.

"You have brought me the beautifullest puppy—and have lost him and can't find him! What d'ye mean by that, Jim? Can't you speak sense, so as a body may understand?"

Jim supposed he had worded his communication imperfectly. "There's been a row here," he explained, "and it frighted me so that I dun know what I be saying. The master took his riding-whip to Mr. Rupert and horsewhipped him."

"The master!" uttered the girl. "What! Mr. Chattaway?"

"He come through the yard when I was with Mr. Rupert a-showing him the puppy, and they had words, and the master horsewhipped him. I stood round the corner frighted to death for fear Chattaway should see me. And Mr. Rupert must have dropped the puppy somewhere, but I can't find him."

"Where is Mr. Rupert? How did it end?"

"He dashed into the yard across to them palings, and leaped 'em clean," responded Jim. "And he'd not have cleared 'em with the puppy in his arms, so I know it must be somewhere about. And he a'most set that there rick a-fire first," the boy added, in a whisper, pointing in the direction of the particular rick, from which they had strayed in Jim's search. "I pretty nigh dropped when I saw it catch alight."

Bridget felt awed, yet uncertain. "How could he set a rick a-fire, stupid?" she cried.

"With the torch. I had lighted it to show him the puppy, and he had it in his hand; had it in his hand when Chattaway began to horsewhip him, but he dropped it then; and when Chattaway went away, Mr. Rupert picked it up and pushed it into the rick."

"I don't like to hear this," said the girl, shivering. "Suppose the rick-yard had been set a-fire! Which rick was it? It mayn't "

"Just hush a minute, Bridget!" suddenly interrupted Jim. "There he is!"

"There's who?" asked she, peering around in the darkness. "Not master!"

"Law, Bridget! I meant the puppy. Can't you hear him? Them squeaks is his."

Guided towards the sound, Jim at length found the poor little animal. It was lying close to the spot where Rupert had leaped the palings. The boy took it up, fondling it almost as a mother would fondle a child.

"See his glossy skin, Bridget! feel how sleek it is! He'll lap milk out of a saucer now! I tried him—"

A scream from Bridget. Jim seemed to come in for nothing but shocks to his nerves this evening, and almost dropped the puppy again. For it was a loud, shrill, prolonged scream, carrying a strange amount of terror as it went forth in the still night air.

Meanwhile Mr. Chattaway had entered his house. Some of the children who were in the drawing-room heard him and went into the hall to welcome him after his long day's absence. But they were startled by the pallor of his countenance; it looked perfectly livid as the light of the hall-lamp fell upon it. Mr. Chattaway could not inflict such chastisement on Rupert without its emotional effects telling upon himself. He took off his hat, and laid his whip upon the table.

"We thought you would be home before this, papa."

"Where's your mother?" he rejoined, paying no attention to their remark.

"She is upstairs in her sitting-room."

Mr. Chattaway turned to the staircase and ascended. Mrs. Chattaway was not in her room; but the sound of voices in Miss Diana's guided him to where he should find her. This sitting-room, devoted exclusively to Miss Diana Trevlyn, was on the side of the house next the rick-yard and farm-buildings, which it overlooked.

The apartment was almost in darkness; the fire had dimmed, and neither lamp nor candles had been lighted. Mrs. Chattaway and Miss Diana sat there conversing together.

"Who is this?" cried the former, looking round. "Oh, is it you, James? I did not know you were home again. What a fine day you have had for Whitterbey!"

Mr. Chattaway growled something about the day not having been particularly fine.

"Did you buy the stock you thought of buying?" asked Miss Diana.

"I bought some," he said, rather sulkily. "Prices ran high to-day."

"You are home late," she resumed.

"I came round by Blackstone."

It was evident by his tone and manner that he was in one of his least genial humours. Both ladies knew from experience that the wisest plan at those times was to leave him to himself, and they resumed their own converse. Mr. Chattaway stood with his back to them, his hands in his pockets, his eyes peering into the dark night. Not in reality looking at anything, or attempting to look; he was far too deeply engaged with his thoughts to attend to outward things.

He was beginning very slightly to repent of the horsewhipping, to doubt whether it might not have been more prudent had he abstained from inflicting it. As many more of us do, when we awake to reflection after some act committed in anger. If Rupert *was* to be dreaded; if he, in connection with others, was hatching treason, this outrage would only make him a more bitter enemy. Better, perhaps, not to have gone to the extremity.

But it was done; it could not be undone; and to regret it were worse than useless. Mr. Chattaway began thinking of the point which had led to it—the refusal of Rupert to say who had admitted him. This at least Mr. Chattaway determined to ascertain.

"Did either of you let in Rupert last night?" he suddenly inquired, looking round.

"No, we did not," promptly replied Miss Diana, answering for Mrs. Chattaway as well as for herself, which she believed she was perfectly safe in doing. "He was not in until eleven, I hear; we went up to bed long before that."

"Then who did let him in?" exclaimed Mr. Chattaway.

"One of the servants, of course," rejoined Miss Diana.

"But they say they did not," he answered.

"Have you asked them all?"

No. Mr. Chattaway remembered that he had not asked them all, and he came to the conclusion that one of them must have been the culprit. He turned to the window again, standing sulkily as before, and vowing in his own mind that the offender, whether man or woman, should be summarily turned out of the Hold.

"If you have been to Blackstone, you have heard that the inquest is over, James," observed Mrs. Chattaway, anxious to turn the conversation from the subject of last night. "Did you hear the verdict?"

"I heard it," he growled.

"It is not an agreeable verdict," remarked Miss Diana. "Better you had made these improvements in the mine—as I urged upon you long ago—than wait to be forced to do them."

"I am not forced yet," retorted Chattaway. "They must—Halloa! What's that?"

His sudden exclamation called them both to the window. A bright light, a blaze, was shooting up into the sky. At the same moment a shrill scream of terror—the scream from Bridget—arose with it.

"The rick-yard!" exclaimed Miss Diana. "It is on fire!"

Mr. Chattaway stood for an instant as one paralysed. The next he was leaping down the stairs, something like a yell bursting from him.

CHAPTER XXXVI
THE FIRE

There is a terror which shakes man's equanimity to its foundation—and that terror fell upon Trevlyn Hold. At the evening hour its inmates were sitting in idleness; the servants gossiping quietly in the kitchen, the girls lingering over the fire in the drawing-room; when those terrible sounds disturbed them. With a simultaneous movement, all flew to the hall, only to see Mr. Chattaway leaping down the stairs, followed by his wife and Miss Diana Trevlyn.

"What is it? What is the matter?"

"The rick-yard is on fire!"

None knew who answered. It was not Mr. Chattaway's voice; it was not their mother's; it did not sound like Miss Diana's. A startled pause, and they ran out to the rick-yard, a terrified group. Little Edith Chattaway, a most excitable girl, fell into hysterics, and added to the confusion of the scene.

The blaze was shooting upwards, and men were coming from the out-buildings, giving vent to their dismay in various exclamations. One voice was heard distinctly above all the rest—that of Miss Diana Trevlyn.

"Who has done this? It must have been purposely set on fire."

She turned sharply on the group of servants as she spoke, as if suspecting one of them. The blaze fell on their alarmed faces, and they visibly recoiled; not from any consciousness of guilt, but from the general sense of fear which lay upon all. One of the grooms spoke impulsively.

"I heard voices not a minute ago in the rick-yard," he cried. "I was going across the top there to fetch a bucket of water from the pump, and heard 'em talking. One was a woman's. I saw a light, too."

The women-servants were grouped together, staring helplessly at the blaze. Miss Diana directed her attention particularly to them: she possessed a ready perception, and detected such unmistakable signs of terror in the face of one of them, that she drew a rapid conclusion. It was not the expression of general alarm, seen on the countenance of the rest; but a lively, conscious terror. The girl endeavoured to draw behind, out of sight of Miss Diana.

Miss Diana laid her hand upon her. It was Bridget, the kitchenmaid. "You know something of this!"

Bridget burst into tears. A more complete picture of helpless fear than she presented at that moment could not well be drawn. In her apron was something hidden.

"What have you got there?" sharply continued Miss Diana, whose thoughts may have flown to incendiary adjuncts.

Bridget, unable to speak, turned down the apron and disclosed a little black puppy, which began to whine. There was nothing very guilty about that.

"Were you in the rick-yard?" questioned Miss Diana; "was it your voice Sam heard?" And Bridget was too frightened to deny it.

"Then, what were you doing? What brought you in the rick-yard at all?"

Mrs. Chattaway, timid Mrs. Chattaway, trembling almost as much as Bridget, but who had compassion for every one in distress, came to the rescue. "Don't, Diana," she said. "I am sure Bridget is too honest a girl to have taken part in anything so dreadful as this. The rick may have got heated and taken fire spontaneously."

"No, Madam, I'd die before I'd do such a thing," sobbed Bridget, responding to the kindness. "If I was in the rick-yard, I wasn't doing no harm—and I'm sure I'd rather have went a hundred miles the other way if I'd thought what was going to happen. I turned sick with fright when I saw the flame burst out."

"Was it you who screamed?" inquired Miss Diana.

"I did scream, ma'am. I couldn't help it."

"Diana," whispered Mrs. Chattaway, "you may see she's innocent."

"Yes, most likely; but there's something behind for all that," replied Miss Diana, decisively. "Bridget, I mean to come to the bottom of this business, and the sooner you explain it, the less trouble you'll get into. I ask what took you to the rick-yard?"

"It wasn't no harm, ma'am, as Madam says," sobbed Bridget, evidently very unwilling to enter on the explanation. "I never did no harm in going there, nor thought none."

"Then it is the more easily told," responded Miss Diana. "Do you hear me? What business took you to the rick-yard, and who were you talking to?"

There appeared to be no help for it; Bridget had felt this from the first; she should have to confess to her rustic admirer's stolen visit. And Bridget, whilst liking him in her heart, was intensely ashamed of him, from his being so much younger than herself.

"Ma'am, I only came into it for a minute to speak to a young boy; my cousin, Jim Sanders. Hatch came into the kitchen and said Jim wanted to see me, and I came out. That's all—if it was the last word I had to speak," she added, with a burst of grief.

"And what did Jim Sanders want with you?" pursued Miss Diana, sternly.

"It was to show me this puppy," returned Bridget, not choosing to confess that the small animal was brought as a present. "Jim seemed proud of it, ma'am, and brought it up for me to see."

A very innocent confession; plausible also; and Miss Diana saw no reason for disbelieving it. But she was one who liked to be on the sure side, and when corroborative testimony was to be had, did not allow it to escape her. "One of you find Hatch," she said, addressing the maids.

Hatch was found with the men-servants and labourers, who were tumbling over each other in their endeavours to carry water to the rick under the frantic directions of their master. He came up to Miss Diana.

"Did you go into the kitchen, and tell Bridget Jim Sanders wanted her in the rick-yard?" she questioned.

I think it has been mentioned once before that this man, Hatch, was too simple to answer anything but the straightforward truth. He replied that he did so; had been called to by Jim Sanders as he was passing along the rick-yard near the stables, who asked him to go to the house and send out Bridget.

"Did he say what he wanted with her?" continued Miss Diana.

"Not to me," replied Hatch. "It ain't nothing new for that there boy to come up and ask for Bridget, ma'am. He's always coming up for her, Jim is. They be cousins."

A well-meant speech, no doubt, on Hatch's part; but Bridget would have liked to box his ears for it there and then. Miss Diana, sufficiently large-hearted, saw no reason to object to Mr. Jim's visits, provided they were paid at proper times and seasons, when the girl was not at her work. "Was any one with Jim Sanders?" she asked.

"Not as I saw, ma'am. As I was coming back after telling Bridget, I see Jim a-waiting there, alone. He—"

"How could you see him? Was it not too dark?" interrupted Miss Diana.

"Not then. Bridget kep' him waiting ever so long afore she came out. Jim must a' been a good half-hour altogether in the yard; 'twas that, I know, from the time he called me till the blaze burst out. But Jim might have went away afore that," added Hatch, reflectively.

"That's all, Hatch; make haste back again," said Miss Diana. "Now, Bridget, was Jim Sanders in the yard when the flames broke out, or was he not?"

"Yes, ma'am, he was there."

"Then if any suspicious characters got into the rick-yard, he would no doubt have seen them," thought Miss Diana, to herself. "Do you know who did set it on fire?" she impatiently asked.

Bridget's face, which had regained some of its colour, grew white again. Should she dare to tell what she had heard about Rupert? "I did not see it done," she gasped.

"Come, Bridget, this will not do," cried Miss Diana, noting the signs. "There's more behind, I see. Where's Jim Sanders?"

She looked around as she spoke but Jim was certainly not in sight. "Do you know where he is?" she sharply resumed.

Instead of answering, Bridget was taken with a fresh fit of shivering. It amazed Miss Diana considerably.

"Did Jim do it?" she sharply asked.

"No, no," answered Bridget. "When I got to Jim he had somehow lost the puppy"—glancing down at her apron—"and we had to look about for it. It was just in the minute he found it that the flames broke forth. Jim was showing of it to me, ma'am, and started like anything when I shrieked out."

"And what has become of Jim?"

"I don't know," sobbed Bridget. "Jim seemed like one dazed when he turned and saw the blaze. He stood a minute looking at it, and I could see his face turn all of a fright; and then he flung the puppy into my arms and scrambled off over the palings, never speaking a word."

Miss Diana paused. There was something suspicious in Jim's making off in the manner described; it struck her so at once. On the other hand she had known Jim from his infancy—known him to be harmless and inoffensive.

"An honest lad would have remained to see what assistance he could render towards putting it out, not have run off in that cowardly way," spoke Miss Diana. "I don't like the look of this."

Bridget made no reply. She was beginning to wish the ground would open and swallow her up for a convenient half-hour; wished Jim Sanders had been buried also before he had brought this trouble upon her. Miss Diana, Madam, and the young ladies were surrounding her; the maid-servants began to edge away suspiciously; even Edith had dismissed her hysterics to stare at Bridget.

Cris Chattaway came leaping past them. Cris, who had been leisurely making his way to the Hold when the flames broke out, had just come up, and after a short conference with his father, was now running to the stables. "You are a fleet horseman, Cris," Mr. Chattaway had said to him: "get the engines here from Barmester." And Cris was hastening to mount a horse, and ride away on the errand.

Mrs. Chattaway caught his arm as he passed. "Oh, Cris, this is dreadful! What can have caused it?"

"What?" returned Cris, in savage tones—not, however, meant for his mother, but induced by the subject. "Don't you know what has caused it? He ought to swing for it, the felon!"

Mrs. Chattaway in her surprise connected his words with what she had just been listening to. "Cris!—do you mean—It never could have been Jim Sanders!"

"Jim Sanders!" slightingly spoke Cris. "What should have put Jim Sanders into your head, mother? No; it was your favoured nephew, Rupert Trevlyn!"

Mrs. Chattaway broke into a cry as the words came from his lips. Maude started a step forward, her face full of indignant protestation; and Miss Diana imperiously demanded what he meant.

"Don't stop me," said Cris. "Rupert Trevlyn was in the yard with a torch just before it broke out, and he must have set it on fire."

"It can't be, Cris!" exclaimed Mrs. Chattaway, in accents of intense pain, arresting her son as he was speeding away. "Who says this?"

Cris twisted himself from her. "I can't stop, mother, I say. I am going for the engines. You had better ask my father; it was he told me. It's true enough. Who *would* do it, except Rupert?"

The shaft lanced at Rupert struck to the heart of Mrs. Chattaway; unpleasantly on the ear of Miss Diana Trevlyn: was anything but agreeable to the women-servants. Rupert was liked in the household, Cris hated. One of the latter spoke up in her zeal.

"It's well to try to throw it off the shoulders of Jim Sanders on to Mr. Rupert! Jim Sanders—"

"And what have you to say agin' Jim Sanders?" interrupted Bridget, fearing, it may be, that the crime should be fastened on him. "Perhaps if I had spoken my mind, I could have told it was Mr. Rupert as well as others could; perhaps Jim Sanders could have told it, too. At any rate, it wasn't—"

"What is that, Bridget?"

The quiet but imperative interruption came from Miss Diana. Excitement was overpowering Bridget. "It was Mr. Rupert, ma'am; Jim saw him fire it."

"Diana! Diana! I feel ill," gasped Mrs. Chattaway, in faint tones. "Let me go to him; I cannot breathe under this suspense."

She meant her husband. Pressing across the crowded rick-yard—for people, aroused by the sight of the flames, were coming up now in numbers—she succeeded in reaching Mr. Chattaway. Maude, scared to death, followed her closely. She caught him just as he had taken a bucket of water to hand on to some one standing next him in the line, causing him to spill it. Mr. Chattaway turned with a passionate word.

"What do you want here?" he roughly asked, although he saw it was his wife.

"James, tell me," she whispered. "I felt sick with suspense, and could not wait. What did Cris mean by saying it was Rupert?"

"There's not a shadow of doubt that it was Rupert," answered Mr. Chattaway. "He has done it out of revenge."

"Revenge for what?"

"For the horsewhipping I gave him. When I joined you upstairs just now, I came straight from it. I horsewhipped him on this very spot," continued Mr. Chattaway, as if it afforded him satisfaction to repeat the avowal. "He had a torch with him, and I—like a fool—left it with him, never thinking of consequences, or that he might use it in the service of felony. He must have fired the rick in revenge."

Mrs. Chattaway had been gradually drawing away from the heat of the blaze; from the line formed to pass buckets for water on to the flames, which crackled and roared on high; from the crowd and confusion prevailing around the spot. Mr. Chattaway had drawn with her, leaving his place in the line to be filled by another. She fell against a distant rick, sick unto death.

"Oh, James! Why did you horsewhip him? What had he done?"

"I horsewhipped him for insolence; for bearding me to my face. I bade him tell me who let him in last night when he returned home, and he set me at defiance by refusing to tell. One of my servants must be a traitor, and Rupert is screening him."

A great cry escaped her. "Oh, what have you done? It was I who let him in."

"*You!*" foamed Mr. Chattaway. "It is not true," he added, the next moment. "You are striving also to deceive me—to defend him."

"It is true," she answered. "I saw him come to the house from my dressing-room window, and I went down the back-stairs and opened the door for him. If he refused to betray me, it was done in good feeling, out of love for me, lest you should reproach me. And you have horsewhipped him for it!—you have goaded him on to this crime! Oh, Rupert! my darling Rupert!"

Mr. Chattaway turned impatiently away; he had no time to waste on sentiment when his ricks were burning. His wife detained him.

"It has been a wretched mistake altogether, James," she whispered. "Say you will forgive him—forgive him for my sake!"

"Forgive him!" repeated Mr. Chattaway, his voice assuming quite a hissing angry sound. "Forgive this? Never. I'll prosecute him to the extremity of the law; I'll try hard to get him condemned to penal servitude. Forgive *this*! You are out of your mind, Madam Chattaway."

Her breath was coming shortly, her voice rose amidst sobs, and she entwined her arms about him caressingly, imploringly, in her agony of distress and terror.

"For my sake, my husband! It would kill me to see it brought home to him. He must have been overcome by a fit of the Trevlyn temper. Oh, James! forgive him for my sake."

"I never will," deliberately replied Mr. Chattaway. "I tell you that I will prosecute him to the utmost limit of the law; I swear it. In an hour's time from this he shall be in custody."

He broke from her; she staggered against the rick, and but for Maude might have fallen. Poor Maude, who had stood and listened, her face turning to stone, her heart to despair.

CHAPTER XXXVII
A NIGHT SCENE

Alas for the Trevlyn temper! How many times has the regret to be repeated! Were the world filled with lamentations for the unhappy state of mind to which some of its mortals give way, they could not atone for the ill inflicted. It is not a pleasant topic to enlarge upon, and I have lingered in my dislike to approach it.

When Rupert leaped the palings and flew away over the field, he was totally incapable of self-government for the time being. I do not say this in extenuation. I say that such a state of things is lamentable, and ought not to be. I only state that it was so. The most passionate temper ever born with man *may* be kept under, where the right means are used—prayer, ever-watchful self-control, stern determination; but how few there are who find the means! Rupert Trevlyn did not. He had no clear perception of what he had done; he probably knew he had thrust the blazing torch into the rick; but he gave no thought whatever to consequences, whether the hay was undamaged or whether it burst forth into a flame.

He flew over the field as one possessed; he flew over a succession of fields; the high-road intervened, and he was passing over it in his reckless career, when he was met by Farmer Apperley. Not, for a moment, did the farmer recognise Rupert.

"Hey, lad! What in the name of fortune has taken you?" cried he, laying his hand upon him.

His face distorted with passion, his eyes starting with fury, Rupert tore on. He shook the farmer's hand off him, and pressed on, leaping the low dwarf hedge opposite, and never speaking.

Mr. Apperley began to doubt whether he had not been deceived by some strange apparition—such, for instance, as the Flying Dutchman. He ran to a stile, and stood there gazing after the mad figure, which seemed to be rustling about without purpose; now in one part of the field, now in another: and Mr. Apperley rubbed his eyes and tried to penetrate more clearly the obscurity of the night.

"It *was* Rupert Trevlyn—if I ever saw him," decided he, at length. "What can have put him into this state? Perhaps he's gone mad!"

The farmer, in his consternation, stood he knew not how long: ten minutes possibly. It was not a busy night with him, and he would as soon linger as go on at once to Bluck the farrier—whither he was bound. Any time would do for his orders to Bluck.

"I can't make it out a bit," soliloquised he, when at length he turned away. "I'm sure it was Rupert; but what could have put him into that state? Halloa! what's that?"

A bright light in the direction of Trevlyn Hold had caught his eye. He stood and gazed at it in a second state of consternation equal to that in which he had just gazed after Rupert Trevlyn. "If I don't believe it's a fire!" ejaculated he.

Was every one running about madly? The words were escaping Mr. Apperley's lips when a second figure, white, breathless as the other, came flying over the road in the selfsame track. This one wore a smock-frock, and the farmer recognised Jim Sanders.

"Why, Jim, is it you? What's up?"

"Don't stop me, sir," panted Jim. "Don't you see the blaze? It's Chattaway's rick-yard."

"Mercy on me! Chattaway's rick-yard! What has done it? Have we got the incendiaries in the county again?"

"It was Mr. Rupert," answered Jim, dropping his voice to a whisper. "I see him fire it. Let me go on, please, sir."

In very astonishment, Mr. Apperley loosed his hold of the boy, who went speeding off in the direction of Barbrook. The farmer propped his back against the stile, that he might gather his scared senses together.

Rupert Trevlyn had set fire to the rick-yard! Had he really gone mad?—or was Jim Sanders mad when he said it? The farmer, slow to arrive at conclusions, was sorely puzzled. "The one looked as mad as the other, for what I saw," deliberated he. "Any way, there's the fire, and I'd better make my way to it: they'll want hands if they are to put that out. Thank God, it's a calm night!"

He took the nearest way to the Hold; another helper amidst the many now crowding the busy scene. What a babel it was!—what a scene for a painting!—what a life's remembrance! The excited workers as they passed the buckets; the deep interjections of Mr. Chattaway; the faces of the lookers-on turned up to the lurid flames. Farmer Apperley, a man more given to deeds than words, rendered what help he could, speaking to none.

He had been at work some time, when a shout broke simultaneously from the spectators. The next rick had caught fire. Mr. Chattaway uttered a despairing word, and the workers ceased their efforts for a few moments—as if paralysed with the new evil.

"If the fire-engines would only come!" impatiently exclaimed Mr. Chattaway.

Even as he spoke a faint rumbling was heard in the distance. It came nearer and nearer; its reckless pace proclaiming it a fire-engine. And Mr. Chattaway, in spite of his remark, gazed at its approach with astonishment; for he knew there had not been time for the Barmester engines to arrive.

It proved to be the little engine from Barbrook, one kept in the village. A very despised engine indeed; from its small size, one rarely called for; and which Mr. Chattaway had not so much as thought of, when sending to Barmester. On it came, bravely, as if it meant to do good service, and the crowd in the rick-yard welcomed it with a shout, and parted to make way for it.

Churlish as was Mr. Chattaway's general manner, he could not avoid showing pleasure at its arrival. "I am glad you have come!" he exclaimed. "It never occurred to me to send for you. I suppose you saw the flames, and came of your own accord?"

"No, sir, we saw nothing," was the reply of the man addressed. "Mr. Ryle's lad, Jim Sanders, came for us. I never see a chap in such commotion; he a'most got the engine ready himself."

The mention of Jim Sanders caused a buzz around. Bridget's assertion that the offender was Rupert Trevlyn had been whispered and commented upon; and if some were found to believe the whisper, others scornfully rejected it. There was Mr. Chattaway's assertion also; but Mr. Chattaway's ill-will to Rupert was remembered that night, and the assertion was doubtfully received. A meddlesome voice interrupted the fireman.

"Jim Sanders! why 'twas he fired it. There ain't no doubt he did. Little wonder he seemed frighted."

"Did he fire it?" interrupted Farmer Apperley, eagerly. "What, Jim? Why, what possessed him to do such a thing? I met him just now, looking frightened out of his life, and he laid the guilt on Rupert Trevlyn."

"Hush, Mr. Apperley!" whispered a voice at his elbow, and the farmer turned to see George Ryle. The latter, with an almost imperceptible movement, directed his attention to the right: the livid face of Mrs. Chattaway. As one paralysed stood she, her hands clasped as she listened.

"Yes, it was Mr. Rupert," protested Bridget, with a sob. "Jim Sanders told me he watched Mr. Rupert thrust the lighted torch into the rick. He seemed not to know what he was about, Jim said; seemed to do it in madness."

"Hold your tongue, Bridget," interposed a sharp commanding voice. "Have I not desired you already to do so? It is not upon the hearsay evidence of Jim Sanders that you can accuse Mr. Rupert."

The speaker was Miss Diana Trevlyn. In good truth, Miss Diana did not believe Rupert could have been guilty of the act. It had been disclosed that the torch in the rick-yard belonged to Jim Sanders, had been brought there by him, and she deemed that fact suspicious against Jim. Miss Diana had arrived unwillingly at the conclusion that Jim Sanders had set the rick on fire by accident; and in his fright had accused Rupert, to screen himself. She imparted her view of the affair to Mr. Apperley.

"Like enough," was the response of Mr. Apperley. "Some of these boys have no more caution in 'em than if they were children of two years old. But what could have put Rupert into such a state? If anybody ever looked insane, he did to-night."

"When?" asked Miss Diana, eagerly, and Mrs. Chattaway pressed nearer with her troubled countenance.

"It was just before I came up here. I was on my way to Bluck's and someone with a white face, breathless and panting, broke through the hedge right across my path. I did not know him at first; he didn't look a bit like Rupert; but when I saw who it was, I tried to stop him, and asked what was the matter. He shook me off, went over the opposite hedge like a wild animal, and there tore about the field. If he had been an escaped lunatic from the county asylum, he couldn't have run at greater speed."

"Did he say nothing?" a voice interrupted.

"Not a word," replied the farmer. "He seemed unable to speak. Well, before I had digested that shock, there came another, flying up in the same mad state, and that was Jim Sanders. I stopped *him*. Nearly at the same time, or just before it, I had seen a light shoot up into the sky. Jim said as well as he could speak for fright, that the rick-yard was on fire, and Mr. Rupert had set it alight."

"At all events, the mischief seems to lie between them," remarked some voices around.

There would have been no time for this desultory conversation—at least, for the gentlemen's share in it—but that the fire-engine had put a stop to their efforts. It had planted itself on the very spot where the line had been formed, scattering those who had taken part in it, and was rapidly getting itself into working order. The flames were shooting up terribly now, and Mr. Chattaway was rushing here, there, and everywhere, in his frantic but impotent efforts to subdue them. He was not insured.

George Ryle approached Mrs. Chattaway, and bent over her, a strange tone of kindness in his every word: it seemed to suggest how conscious he was of the great sorrow that was coming upon her. "I wish you would let me take you indoors," he whispered. "Indeed it is not well for you to be here."

"Where is he?" she gasped, in answer. "Could you find him, and remove him from danger?"

A sure conviction had been upon her from the very moment that her husband had avowed his chastisement of Rupert—the certainty that it was he, Rupert, and no other who had done the mischief. Her own brothers—but chiefly her brother Rupert—had been guilty of one or two acts almost as mad in their passion. He could not help his temper, she reasoned—some, perhaps, may say wrongly; and if Mr. Chattaway had provoked him by that sharp, insulting punishment, he, more than Rupert, was in fault.

"I would die to save him, George," she whispered. "I would give all I am worth to save him from the consequences. Mr. Chattaway says he will prosecute him to the last."

"I am quite sure you will be ill if you stay here," remonstrated George, for she was shivering from head to foot; not, however, with cold, but with emotion. "I will go with you to the house, and talk to you there."

"To the house!" she repeated. "Do you suppose I could remain in the house to-night? Look at them; they are all out here."

She pointed to her children; to the women-servants. It was even so all were out there. Mr. Chattaway, in passing, had once or twice sharply demanded what they, a pack of women, did in such a scene, and the women had drawn away at the rebuke, but only to come forward again. Perhaps it was not in human nature to keep wholly away from that region of excitement.

A half-exclamation of fear escaped Mrs. Chattaway's lips, and she pressed a few steps onwards.

Holding a close and apparently private conference with Mr. Apperley was Bowen, the superintendent of the very slight staff of police stationed in the place. As a general rule, these rustic districts are too peaceable to require much supervision from the men in blue.

"Mr. Apperley, you will not turn against him!" she implored, from between her fevered and trembling lips; and in good truth, Mrs. Chattaway gave indications of being almost as much beside herself that night as the unhappy Rupert. "Is Bowen asking you where you saw Rupert, that he may go and search for him? Do not *you* turn against him!"

"My dear, good lady, I haven't a thing to tell," returned Mr. Apperley, looking at her in surprise, for her manner was strange. "Bowen heard me say, as others heard, that Mr. Rupert was in the Brook field when I came from it. But I have nothing else to tell of him; and he may not be there now. It's hardly likely he would be."

Mrs. Chattaway lifted her white face to Bowen. "You will not take him?" she imploringly whispered.

The man shook his head—he was an intelligent officer, much respected in the neighbourhood—and answered her in the same low tone. "I can't help myself, ma'am. When charges are given to us, we are obliged to take cognisance of them, and to arrest, if need be, those implicated."

"Has this charge been given you?"

"Yes, this half-hour ago. I was up here almost with the breaking out of the flames, for I happened to be close by, and Mr. Chattaway made his formal complaint to me, and put it in my care."

Her heart sank within her. "And you are looking for him?"

"Chigwell is," replied the superintendent, alluding to a constable. "And Dumps has gone after Jim Sanders."

"Thank Heaven!" exclaimed a voice at her elbow. It was that of George Ryle; and Mrs. Chattaway turned in amazement. But George's words had not borne reference to her, or to anything she was saying.

"It is beginning to rain," he exclaimed. "A fine, steady rain would do us more good than the engines. What does that noise mean?"

A murmur of excitement had arisen on the opposite side of the rick-yard, and was spreading as fast as did the flame. George looked in vain for its cause: he was very tall, and raised himself on tiptoe to see the better: as yet without result.

But not for long. The cause soon showed itself. Pushing his way through the rick-yard, pale, subdued, quiet now, came Rupert Trevlyn. Not in custody; not fettered; not passionate; only very worn and weary, as if he had undergone some painful amount of fatigue. It was only that the fit of passion had left him; he was worn-out, powerless. In the days gone by it had so left his uncle Rupert.

Mr. Bowen walked up, and laid his hand upon his shoulder. "I am sorry to do it, sir," he said, "but you are my prisoner."

"I can't help it," wearily responded Rupert.

But what brought Rupert Trevlyn back into the very camp of the Philistines? In his terrible passion, he had partly fallen to the ground, partly flung himself down in the field where Mr. Apperley saw him, and there lay until the passion abated. After a time he sat up, bent his head upon his knees, and revolved what had passed. How long he might have stayed there, it is impossible to say, but that shouts and cries in the road aroused him, and he looked up to see that red light, and men running in its direction. He went and questioned them. "The rick-yard at the Hold was on fire!"

An awful consciousness came across him that it was *his* work. It is a fact, that he did not positively remember what he had done: that is, had no clear recollection of it. Giving no thought to the personal consequences—any more than an hour before he had measured the effects of his work—he began to hasten to the Hold as fast as his depressed physical state would permit. If he had created that flame, it was only fair he should do what he could towards putting it out.

The clouds cleared, and the rain did not fulfil its promise as George Ryle had fondly hoped. But the little engine from Barbrook did good service, and the flames were not spreading over the whole rick-yard. Later, the two great Barmester engines thundered up, and gave their aid towards extinguishing the fire.

And Rupert Trevlyn was in custody for having caused it!

CHAPTER XXXVIII
NORA'S DIPLOMACY

Amidst all the human beings collected in and about the burning rick-yard of Trevlyn Hold, perhaps no one was so utterly miserable, not even excepting the unhappy Rupert, as its mistress, Mrs. Chattaway. *He* stood there in custody for a dark crime; a crime for which the punishment only a few short years before would have been the extreme penalty of the law; he whom she had so loved. In her chequered life she had experienced moments of unhappiness than which she had thought no future could exceed in intensity; but had all those moments been concentrated into one dark and dreadful hour, it could not have equalled the trouble of this. Her vivid imagination leaped over the present, and held up to view but one appalling picture of the future—Rupert working in chains. Poor, unhappy, wronged Rupert! whom they had kept out of his rights; whom her husband had now by his ill-treatment goaded to the ungovernable passion which was the curse of her family: and this was the result.

Every pulse of her heart beating with its sense of terrible wrong; every chord of love for Rupert strung to its utmost tension; every fear that an excitable imagination can depict within her, Mrs. Chattaway leaned against the palings in utter faintness of spirit. Her ears took in with unnatural quickness the comments around. She heard some hotly avowing their belief that Rupert was not guilty, except in the malicious fancy of Mr. Chattaway; heard them say that Chattaway was scared and startled that past day when he found Rupert was alive, instead of dead, down in the mine: even the more moderate observed that after all it was only Jim Sanders's word for it; and if Jim did not appear to confirm it, Mr. Rupert must be held innocent.

The wonder seemed to be, where was Jim? He had not reappeared on the scene, and his absence certainly looked suspicious. In moments of intense fear, the mind receives the barest hint vividly and comprehensively, and Mrs. Chattaway's heart bounded within her at that whispered suggestion. *If Jim Sanders did not appear Rupert must be held innocent.* Was there no possibility of keeping Jim back? By persuasion—by stratagem—by force, even, if necessary? The blood mounted to her pale cheek at the thought, red as the lurid flame which lighted up the air. At that moment she saw

George Ryle hastening across the yard near to her and glided towards him. He turned at her call.

"You see! They have taken Rupert!"

"Do not distress yourself, dear Mrs. Chattaway," he answered. "I wish you could have been persuaded not to remain in this scene: it is altogether unfit for you."

"George," she gasped, "do *you* believe he did it?"

George Ryle did believe it. He had heard about the horsewhipping; and aware of that mad passion called the Trevlyn temper, he could not do otherwise than believe it.

"Ah, don't speak!" she interrupted, perceiving his hesitation. "I see you condemn him, as some around us are condemning him. But," she added, with feverish eagerness, "there is only the word of Jim Sanders against him. They are saying so."

"Very true," replied George, heartily desiring to give her all the comfort he could. "Mr. Jim must make good his words before we can condemn Rupert."

"Jim Sanders has always been looked upon as truthful," interposed Octave Chattaway, who had drawn near. Surely it was ill-natured to say so at that moment, however indisputable the fact might be!

"It has yet to be proved that Jim made the accusation," said George, replying to Octave. "Although Bridget asserts it, it is not obliged to be fact. And even if Jim did say it, he may have been mistaken. He must show that he was not mistaken before the magistrates to-morrow, or the charge will fall to the ground."

"And Rupert be released?" added Mrs. Chattaway eagerly.

"Certainly. At least, I suppose so."

He passed on his way; Octave went back to where she had been standing, and Mrs. Chattaway remained alone, buried in thought.

A few minutes, and she glided out of the yard. With stealthy steps, and eyes that glanced fearfully around her, she escaped by degrees beyond the crowd, and reached the open field. Then, turning an angle at a fleet pace, she ran against some one who was coming as swiftly up. A low cry escaped her. It seemed to her that the mere fact of being encountered like this, was sufficient to betray the wild project she had conceived. Conscience is very suggestive.

But it was only Nora Dickson: and Nora in a state of wrath. When the alarm of fire reached Trevlyn Farm, its inmates had hastened to the scene with one accord, leaving none in the house but Nora and Mrs. Ryle. Mrs. Ryle, suffering from some temporary indisposition, was in bed, and Nora, consequently, had to stay and take care of the house, doing violence to her curiosity. She stood leaning over the gate, watching the people hasten by to the excitement from which she was excluded; and when the Barbrook engine thundered past, Nora's anger was unbounded. She felt half inclined to lock up the house, and start in the wake of the engine; the fierce if innocent anathemas she hurled at the head of the truant Nanny were something formidable; and when that damsel at length returned, Nora would have experienced the greatest satisfaction in shaking her. But the bent of her indignation changed; for Nanny, before Nora had had time to say so much as a word, burst forth with the news she had gathered at the Hold. Rupert Trevlyn fired the hay-rick because Mr. Chattaway had horsewhipped him.

Nora's breath was taken away: wrath for her own grievance merged in the greater wrath she felt for Rupert's sake. Horsewhipped him? That brute of a Chattaway had horsewhipped Rupert Trevlyn? A burning glow rushed over her as she listened; a resentful denial broke from her lips: but Nanny persisted in her statement. Chattaway had locked out Rupert the previous night, and Madam, unknown to her husband, admitted him: Chattaway had demanded of Rupert who let him in, but Rupert, fearing to compromise Madam, refused to tell, and then Chattaway used the horsewhip.

Nora waited to hear no more. She started off to the Hold in her indignation; not so much now to take part in the bustling scene, or to indulge her curiosity, as to ascertain the truth of this shameful story. Rupert could scarcely have felt more indignant pain at the chastisement, than Nora at hearing it. Close to the outer gate of the fold-yard, she encountered Mrs. Chattaway.

A short explanation ensued. Nora, forgetting possibly that it was Mrs. Chattaway to whom she spoke, broke into a burst of indignation at Mr. Chattaway, a flood of sympathy for Rupert. It told Mrs. Chattaway that she might trust her, and her delicate fingers entwined themselves nervously around Nora's stronger ones in her hysterical emotion.

"It must have been done in a fit of the Trevlyn temper, Nora," she whispered imploringly, as if beseeching Nora's clemency. "The temper was born with him, you know, and he could not help that—and to be horsewhipped is a terrible thing."

If Nora felt inclined to doubt the report before, these words dispelled the doubt, and brought a momentary shock. Nora was not one to excuse or extenuate a crime so great as that of wilfully setting fire to a rick-yard: to all who have to do with farms, it is especially abhorrent, and Nora was no exception to the rule; but in this case by some ingenious sophistry of her own, she did shift the blame from Rupert's shoulders, and lay it on

Mr. Chattaway's; and she again expressed her opinion of that gentleman's conduct in very plain terms.

"He is in custody, Nora!" said Mrs. Chattaway with a shiver. "He is to be examined to-morrow before the magistrates, and they will either commit him for trial, or release him, according to the evidence. Should he be tried and condemned for it, the punishment might be penal servitude for life!"

"Heaven help him!" ejaculated Nora in her dismay at this new feature presented to her view. "That would be a climax to his unhappy life!"

"But if they can prove nothing against him to-morrow, the magistrates will not commit him," resumed Mrs. Chattaway. "There's nothing to prove it but Jim Sanders's word: and—Nora,"—she feverishly added—"perhaps we can keep Jim back?"

"Jim Sanders's word!" repeated Nora, who as yet had not heard of Jim in connection with the affair. "What has Jim to do with it?"

Mrs. Chattaway explained. She mentioned all that was said to have passed, Bridget's declaration, and her own miserable conviction that it was but too true. She just spoke of the suspicion cast on Jim by several doubters, but in a manner which proved the suspicion had no weight with her: and she told of his disappearance from the scene. "I was on my way to search for him," she continued; "but I don't know where to search. Oh, Nora, won't you help me? I would kneel to Jim, and implore him not to come forward against Rupert; I will be ever kind to Jim, and look after his welfare, if he will only hear me! I will try to bring him on in life."

Nora, impulsive as Mrs. Chattaway, but with greater calmness of mind and strength of judgment, turned without a word. From that moment she entered heart and soul into the plot. If Jim Sanders could be kept back by mortal means, Nora would keep him. She revolved matters rapidly in her mind as she went along, but had not proceeded many steps when she halted, and laid her hand on the arm of her companion.

"I had better go alone about this business, Madam Chattaway. If you'll trust to me, it shall be done—if it can be done. You'll catch your death, coming out with nothing on, this cold night: and I'm not sure that it would be well for you to be seen in it."

"I must go on, Nora," was the earnest answer. "I cannot rest until I have found Jim. As to catching cold, I have been standing in the open air since the fire broke out, and have not known whether it was cold or hot. I am too feverish to-night for any cold to affect me."

Nevertheless, she untied her black silk apron, and folded it over her head, concealing all her fair falling curls. Nora made no further remonstrance.

The most obvious place to look for Jim was his own home; at least so it occurred to Nora. Jim had the honour of residing with his mother in a lonely three-cornered cottage, which boasted two rooms and a loft. It was a good step to it, and they walked swiftly, exchanging a sentence now and then in hushed tones. As they came within view of it, Nora's quick sight detected the head (generally a very untidy one) of Mrs. Sanders, airing itself at the open door.

"You halt here, Madam Chattaway," she whispered, pointing to a friendly hedge, "and let me go on and feel my way with her. She'll be a great deal more difficult to deal with than Jim; and the more I reflect, the more I am convinced it will not do for you to be seen in it."

So far, Mrs. Chattaway acquiesced. She remained under cover of the hedge, and Nora went on alone. But when she had really gained the door, it was shut; no one was there. She lifted the old-fashioned wooden latch, and entered. The door had no other fastening; strange as that fact may sound to dwellers in towns. The woman had backed against the further wall, and was staring at the intruder with a face of dread. Keen Nora noted the signs, drew a very natural deduction, and shaped her tactics accordingly.

"Where's Jim?" began she, in decisive but not unkindly tones.

"It's not true what they are saying, Miss Dickson," gasped the woman. "I could be upon my Bible oath that he never did it. Jim ain't of that wicked sort, he'd not harm a fly."

"But there are such things as accidents, you know, Mrs. Sanders," promptly answered Nora, who had no doubt as to her course now. "It's certain that he was in the rick-yard with a lighted torch, and boys, as everyone knows, are the most careless animals on earth. I suppose you have Jim in hiding?"

"I haven't set eyes on Jim since night fell," the woman answered.

"Look here, Mrs. Sanders, you had better avow the truth to me. I have come as a friend to see what can be done for Jim; and I can tell you that I would rather keep him in hiding—or put him into hiding, for the matter of that—than betray him to the police, and say, 'You'll find Jim Sanders so-and-so.' Tell me the whole truth, and I'll stand Jim's friend. He has been about our place from a little chap in petticoats, when he was put to hurrish the crows, and it's not likely we should want to harm him."

Her words reassured the woman, but she persisted in her denial. "I declare to goodness, ma'am, that I know nothing of him," she said, pushing back her untidy hair. "He come in here after he left work, and tidied hisself a bit, and went off with one of them puppies of his; and he has never been back since."

"Yes," said Nora. "He took the puppy to the Hold, and was showing it to Bridget when the fire broke out—that's the tale that's told to me. But Jim had a torch, they say; and torches are dangerous things in rick-yards—"

"Jim's a fool!" was the complimentary interruption of Jim's mother. "His head's running wild over that flighty Bridget, as ain't worth her salt. I asked him what he was bringing on that puppy for, and he said for Bridget—and I told him he was a simpleton for his pains. And now this has come of it!"

"How did you hear of Jim's being connected with the fire?"

"I have had a dozen past here, opening their mouths," resentfully spoke the woman. "Some of 'em said Mr. Rupert was mixed up in it, and the police were after him as well as after Jim."

"It is true that Mr. Rupert is said to be mixed up in it," said Nora, speaking with a purpose. "And he is taken into custody."

"Into custody?" echoed Mrs. Sanders, in a scared whisper.

"Yes; and Jim must be hidden away for the next four and twenty hours, or they'll take him. Where's he to be found?"

"I couldn't tell you if you killed me for't," protested Mrs. Sanders; and her tones were earnestly truthful. "Maybe he is in hiding—has gone and put himself into 't in his fear of Chattaway and the police. Though I'll take my oath he never did it wilful. If he *had* a torch, why, a spark of it might have caught a loose bit of hay and fired it: but he never did it wilful. It ain't a windy night, either," she added reflectively. "Eh! the fool that there Jim has been ever since he was born!"

Nora paused. In the uncertainty as to where to look for Jim, she did not see her way very clearly to accomplishing the object in view, and took a few moments' rapid counsel with herself.

"Listen, Mrs. Sanders, and pay attention to what I say," she cried impressively. "I can't do for Jim what I wanted to do, because he is not to be found. But now mind: should he come in after I am gone, send him off instantly to the farm. Tell him to dodge under the trees and hedges on his way, and take care that no one catches sight of him. When he gets to the farm, he must come to the front-door, and knock gently with his knuckles: I shall be in the room."

"And then?" questioned Mrs. Sanders, looking puzzled.

"I'll take care what then; I'll take care of *him*. Now, do you understand?"

"Yes, yes," said the woman. "I'll be sure to do it, Miss Dickson."

"Mind you do," said Nora. "And now, good-night to you."

Mrs. Sanders was officiously coming to the door with the candle, to light her visitor; but Nora peremptorily sent her back, giving her at the same time a piece of advice in rather sharp tones—to keep her cottage dark and silent that night, lest the attention of passers-by might be drawn to it.

It was not cheering news to carry back to poor Mrs. Chattaway. That timid, trembling, unhappy lady had left the shelter of the hedge—where she probably found her crouching position not a very easy one—and was standing behind the trunk of a tree at a little distance, her whole weight leaning upon it. To stand long, unaided, was almost a physical impossibility to her, for her spine was weak. She saw Nora, and came forward.

"Where is he?"

"He is not at home. His mother does not know where he is. She had heard—Hush! Who's this?"

Nora's voice dropped, and they retreated behind the tree. To be seen in the vicinity of Jim Sanders's cottage would not have furthered the object they had in view—that of burying the gentleman for a time. The steps advanced, and Nora, stealing a peep, recognised Farmer Apperley.

He was coming from the direction of the Hold; and they rightly judged, seeing him walking leisurely, that the danger must be over. At the same moment they became conscious of footsteps approaching from another direction. They were crossing the road, bearing rather towards the Hold, and in another moment would meet Mr. Apperley. Footsore, weary, yet excited, and making what haste he could, their owner came into view, disclosing the person of Mr. Jim Sanders. Mrs. Chattaway uttered an exclamation, and would have started forward; but Nora, with more caution, held her back.

The farmer heard the cry, and looked round, but seeing nothing, probably thought his ears had deceived him. As he turned his head again, there, right in front of him, was Jim Sanders. Quick as lightning his grasp was laid upon the boy's shoulder.

"Now then! Where have you been skulking?"

"Lawk a mercy! I han't been skulking, sir," returned Jim, apparently surprised at the salutation. "I be a'most ready to drop with the speed I've made."

Poor, ill-judged Jim! In point of fact he had done more, indirectly, towards putting out the fire, than Farmer Apperley and ten of the best men at his back. Jim's horror and consternation when he saw the flames burst forth had taken from him all thought—all power, as may be said—except instinct. Instinct led him to Barbrook, to warn the fire-engine there: he saw it off, and then hastened all the way to Barmester, and actually gave notice to the engines and urged their departure before the arrival of Cris

Chattaway on horseback. From Barmester Jim started to Layton's Heath—a place standing at an acute angle between Barmester and Barbrook—and posted off the engines from there also. And now Jim was toiling back again, footsore and weary, but bending his course to Trevlyn Hold to render his poor assistance in putting out the flames. Rupert Trevlyn had always been a favourite of Jim's. Rupert in his good-natured way had petted Jim, and the boy in his unconscious gratitude was striving to amend the damage which Rupert had caused. In after-days, this night's expedition of Jim's was talked of as a marvel verging on the impossible. Men are apt to forget the marvels that may be done under the influence of great emotion.

Something of this—of where he had been and for what purpose—Jim explained to the farmer, and Mr. Apperley released his hold upon him.

"They are saying up there, lad"—indicating the Hold—"that you had a torch in the rick-yard."

"So I had," replied Jim. "But I didn't do no damage with it."

"You told me it was Rupert Trevlyn who had fired the rick."

"And so it was," replied Jim. "He was holding that there torch of mine, when Mr. Chattaway came up; looking at the puppy, we was. And Chattaway had a word or two with him, and then horsewhipped him; and Mr. Rupert caught up the torch, which he had let fall, and pushed it into the rick. I see him," added Jim, conclusively.

Mr. Apperley stroked his chin. He also liked Rupert, and very much condemned the extreme chastisement inflicted by Mr. Chattaway. He did not go so far as Nora and deem it an excuse for the mad act; but it is certain he did not condemn it as he would have condemned it in another, or if committed under different circumstances. He felt grieved and uncomfortable; he was conscious of a sore feeling in his mind; and he heartily wished the whole night's work could be blotted out from the record of deeds done, and that Rupert was free again and guiltless.

"Well, lad, it's a bad job altogether," he observed; "but you don't seem to have been to blame except for taking a lighted torch into a rick-yard Never you do such a thing again. You see what has come of it."

"We warn't nigh the ricks when I lighted the torch," pleaded Jim. "We was yards off 'em."

"That don't matter. There's always danger. I'd turn away the best man have on my farm, if I saw him venture into the rick-yard with a torch. Don't you be such a fool again. Where are you off to now?" for Jim was passing on

"Up to the Hold, sir, to help put out the fire."

"The fire's out—or nigh upon it; and you'd best stop where you are. If you show your face there, you'll get taken up by the police—they are looking out for you. And I don't see that you've done anything to merit a night's lodging in the lock-up," added the farmer, in his sense of justice. "Better pass it in your bed. You'll be wanted before the Bench to-morrow; but it's as good to go before them a free lad as a prisoner. The prisoner they have already taken, Rupert Trevlyn, is enough. Never you take a torch near ricks again."

With this reiterated piece of advice, Mr. Apperley departed. Jim stood in indecision, revolving in a hazy kind of way the various pieces of information gratuitously bestowed upon him. He himself suspected; in danger of being taken up by the police!—and Mr. Rupert a prisoner! and the fire out, or almost out! It might be better, perhaps, that he went in to his cottage, and got to sleep as Mr. Apperley advised, if he was not too tired to sleep.

But before Jim saw his way clearly out of the maze, or had come to any decision, he found himself seized from behind with a grasp fast and firm as Mr. Apperley's. A vision of a file of policemen brought a rush of fear to Jim's mind, hot blood to his face. But the arms proved to be only Nora Dickson's, and a soft, gentle voice of entreaty was whispering a prayer into his ear, almost as the prayer of an angel. Jim started in amazement, and looked round.

"Lawk a mercy!" ejaculated he. "Why, it's Madam Chattaway!"

CHAPTER XXXIX ANOTHER VISITOR FOR MRS. SANDERS

A few minutes after his encounter with Jim Sanders, to which interview Mrs. Chattaway and Nora had been unseen witnesses, Farmer Apperley met Policeman Dumps, to whom, you may remember, the superintendent had referred as having been sent after Jim. He came up from the direction of Barbrook.

"I can't find him nowhere," was his salutation to Mr. Apperley. "I have been a'most all over Mr. Ryle's land, and in every hole and corner of Barbrook, and he ain't nowhere. I'm going on now to his own home, just for form's sake; but that's about the last place he'd hide in."

"Are you speaking of Rupert Trevlyn?" asked Mr. Apperley, who knew nothing of the man's search for Jim.

"No, sir; Jim Sanders."

"Oh, you need not look after him," replied the farmer. "I have just met him. Jim's all right. It was not he who did the mischief. He has been after all the fire-engines on foot, and is just come back, dead-beat. He was going on to the Hold to help put out the fire, but I told him it was out, and he could go home. There's not the least necessity to look after Jim."

Mr. Dumps—whose clearness of vision was certainly not sufficient to set the Thames on fire—received the news without any doubt. "I thought it an odd thing for Jim Sanders to do. He haven't daring enough," he remarked. "That kitchenmaid was right, I'll be bound, as to its being Mr. Rupert in his passion. Gone in home, did you say, sir?"

"In bed by this time, I should say," replied the farmer. "They have got Mr. Rupert, Dumps."

"Have they?" returned Dumps. "It's a nasty charge, sir. I shouldn't be sorry that he got off it."

The farmer continued his road towards Barbrook; the policeman went the other way. As he came to the cottage inhabited by the Sanders family, it occurred to him that he might as well ascertain the fact of Jim's safety, and he went to the door and knocked. Mrs. Sanders opened it instantly, believing it to be the wanderer. When she saw policeman Dumps standing there, she thought she should have died with fright.

"Your son has just come in all right, I hear, Madge Sanders. Farmer Apperley have told me."

"Yes, sir," replied she, dropping a curtsey. The untruthful reply was spoken in her terror, almost unconsciously; but there may have been some latent thought in her heart to mislead the policeman.

"Is he gone to bed? I don't want to disturb him if he is."

"Yes, sir," replied she again.

"Well, they have got Mr. Rupert Trevlyn, so the examination will take place to-morrow morning. Your son had better go right over to Barmester the first thing after breakfast; tell him to make for the police-station, and stop there till he sees me. He'll have to give evidence, you know."

"Very well, sir," repeated the woman, in an agony of fear lest Jim should make his appearance. "Jim ain't guilty, sir: he wouldn't harm a fly."

"No, he ain't guilty; but somebody else is, I suppose; and Jim must tell what he knows. Mind he sets off in time. Or—stop. Perhaps he had better come to the little station at Barbrook, and go over with us. Yes, that'll be best."

"To-night, sir?" asked she timidly.

"To-night?—no. What should we do with him to-night? He must be there at eight o'clock in the morning; or a little before it. Good night."

"Good night, sir."

She watched him off, quite unable to understand the case, for she had seen nothing of Jim, and Nora Dickson had not long gone. Mr. Dumps made his way to the headquarters at Barbrook; and when, later on, Bowen came in with Rupert Trevlyn, Dumps informed him that Jim Sanders was all right, and would be there by eight o'clock.

"Have you got him—all safe?"

"I haven't got him," replied Dumps. "There wasn't no need for that. He was a-bed and asleep," he added, improving upon his information. "It was him that went for all the injines, and he was dead tired."

"Your orders were to take him," curtly returned Bowen, who believed in Jim's innocence as much as Dumps did, but would not tolerate disobedience to orders. "He was seen with a lighted torch in the rick-yard, and that's enough."

Rupert Trevlyn looked round quickly. This conversation had occurred as Bowen was going through the room with his prisoner to consign the latter to a more secure one. "Jim Saunders did no harm with the torch, Bowen. He lighted it to show me a little puppy of his; nothing more. There is no need to accuse Jim—"

"I beg your pardon, Mr. Trevlyn, but I'd rather not hear anything from you one way or the other," interrupted Bowen. "Don't as much as open your mouth about it, sir, unless you're obliged; and I speak in your interest when I give you this advice. Many a prisoner has brought the guilt home to himself through his own tongue."

Rupert took the hint, and subsided into silence. He was consigned to his quarters for the night, and no doubt passed it as agreeably as was consistent with the circumstances.

The fire had not spread beyond a rick or two. It was quite out before midnight; and the engines, which had done effectual service, were on their way home again. At eight o'clock the following morning a fly was at the door to convey Rupert Trevlyn to Barmester. Bowen, a cautious man, deemed it well that the chief witness—it may be said, the only witness to any purpose—should be transported there by the same conveyance. But that witness, Mr. Jim Sanders, delayed his appearance unwarrantably, and Dumps, in much wrath, started in search of him. Back he came—it was not more than a quarter-of-a-mile to the mother's cottage.

"He has gone on, the stupid blunderer," cried he to Bowen; "Mrs. Sanders says he's at Barmester by this time. He'll be at the station there, no doubt."

So the party started in state: Bowen, Dumps, and Rupert Trevlyn inside; and Chigwell, who had been sent to capture him, on the box. There was just as much necessity for the presence of the two men as for yours or mine; but they would not have missed the day's excitement for the world: and Bowen did not interpose his veto.

The noise and bustle at the fire had been great, but it was scarcely greater than that which prevailed that morning at Barmester. As a matter of course, various contradictory versions were afloat; it is invariably the case. All that was certainly known were the bare facts; Mr. Chattaway had horsewhipped Rupert Trevlyn; a fire had almost immediately broken out in the rick-yard; and Rupert was in custody on the charge of causing it.

Belief in Rupert's guilt was accorded a very limited degree. People could not forget the ill-feeling supposed to exist towards him in the breast of Mr. Chattaway; and the flying reports that it was Jim Sanders who had been the culprit, accidentally, if not wilfully, obtained far more credence than the other. The curious populace would have subscribed a good round sum to be allowed to question Jim to their hearts' content.

But a growing rumour, freezing the very marrow in the bones of their curiosity, had come abroad. It was said that Jim had disappeared: was not to be found under the local skies; and it was this caused the chief portion of the public excitement. For in point of fact, when Bowen and the rest arrived at Barmester, Jim Sanders could not be seen or heard of. Dumps was despatched back to Barbrook in search of him.

The hearing was fixed for ten o'clock; and before that hour struck, the magistrates—a full bench of them—had taken their places. Many familiar faces were to be seen in the crowded court—familiar to you, my readers; for the local world was astir with interest and curiosity. In one part of the crowd might be seen the face of George Ryle, grave and subdued; in another, the dark flashing eyes of Nora Dickson; yonder the red cheeks of Mr. Apperley; nearer, the pale concerned countenance of Mr. Freeman. Just before the commencement of the proceedings, the carriage from Trevlyn Hold drove up, and there descended from it Mr. and Madam Chattaway, and Miss Diana Trevlyn. A strange proceeding, you will say, that the ladies should appear; but it was not deemed strange in the locality. Miss Diana had asserted her determination to be present in tones quite beyond the power of Mr. Chattaway to contradict, even had he wished to do so; and thus he had no plea for refusing his wife. How ill she looked! Scarcely a heart but ached for her. The two ladies sat in a retired spot, and Mr. Chattaway—who was in the commission of the peace, but did not exercise the privilege once in a dozen years—took his place on the bench.

Then the prisoner was brought in, civilly conducted by Superintendent Bowen. He looked pale, subdued, gentlemanly—not in the least like one who would set fire to a hay-rick.

"Have you all your witnesses, Bowen?" inquired the presiding magistrate.

"All but one, sir, and I expect him here directly; I have sent after him," was the reply. "In fact, I'm not sure but he is here," added the man, standing on tiptoe, and stretching his neck upwards; "the crowd's so great one can't see who's here and who isn't. If he can be heard first, his evidence may be conclusive, and save the trouble of examining the others."

"You can call him," observed the magistrate. "If he is here, he will answer. What's the name?"

"James Sanders, your worship."

"Call James Sanders," returned his worship, exalting his voice.

The call was made in obedience, and "James Sanders!" went ringing through the court; and walls and roof echoed the cry.

But there was no other answer.

CHAPTER XL
THE EXAMINATION

The morning sun shone upon the crowded court, as the Bench waited for the appearance of Mr. Jim Sanders. The windows, large, high, and guiltless of blinds, faced the south-east, and the warm autumn rays poured in, to the discomfort of those on whom they directly fell. They fell especially on the prisoner; his fair hair, his winning countenance. They fell on the haughty features of Miss Diana Trevlyn, leaning forward to speak to Mr. Peterby, who had been summoned in haste by herself, that he might watch the interests of Rupert. They fell on the sad face of Mrs. Chattaway, bent downwards until partly hidden under its falling curls; and they fell on the red face of Farmer Apperley, who was in a brown study, gently flicking his top-boot with his riding-whip.

One, who had come pressing through the crowd, extended her hand, and touched the farmer on the shoulder. He turned to behold Nora Dickson.

"Mr. Apperley, did your wife make those inquiries for me about that work-woman at the upholsterer's, whether she goes out by the day or not?" asked Nora, as though speaking for the benefit of the court in general.

Mr. Apperley paused to collect his thoughts upon the subject. "I *did* hear the missis say something about that woman," he remarked at length. "I can't call to mind what, though. Brown, isn't her name?"

"We must have her, or somebody else," continued Nora, in the same tones. "Our drawing-room winter-curtains must be turned top for bottom; and as to the moreen bed-furniture—"

"Silence there!" interrupted an authoritative voice. And then there came again the same call which had already been echoed through the court twice before—

"James Sanders!"

"Just step here to the back, and I'll send your wife a message for the woman," resumed Nora, in defiance of the mandate just issued.

The farmer did not see why the message could not have been given to him where he was; but we are all apt to yield to a ruling power, and he followed Nora.

She struggled through the crowded doorway of the court into a comparatively empty stone hall. The farmer contrived to follow her; but he was short and stout, and emerged purple with the exertion. Nora cast her cautious eyes around, and then bent towards him with the softest whisper.

"Look here, Mr. Apperley. If they examine *you*, you have no need to tell everything, you know."

Mr. Apperley, none of the keenest at taking a hint, stared at Nora. He could not understand. "Are you talking about the upholstering woman?" asked he, in his perplexity.

"Rubbish!" retorted Nora. "Do you suppose I brought you here to talk about her? You have not a bit of gumption—as everybody knows. Jim Sanders is not to be found; at least, it seems so," continued Nora, with a short cough; "for that's the third time they have called him. Now, if they examine you—as I suppose they will, by Bowen saying you might be wanted, there's no need to go and repeat what Jim said about Rupert Trevlyn's guilt when you met him last night down by his cottage."

"Why! how did you know I met Jim last night?" cried the farmer, staring at Nora.

"There's no time to explain now: I didn't dream it. You liked Joe Trevlyn: I have heard you say it."

"Ay, I did," replied the farmer, casting his thoughts back.

"Well, then, just bring to your mind how that poor lad, his son, has been wronged and put upon through life; think of the critical position he stands in now; before a hundred eyes—brought to it through that usurper, Chattaway. Don't *you* help on the hue and cry against him, I say. You didn't see him fire the rick; you only heard Jim Sanders say that he fired it; and you are not called upon to repeat that hearsay evidence. *Don't do it,* Mr. Apperley."

"I suppose I am not," assented he, after digesting the words.

"Indeed you are not. If Jim can't be found, and you don't speak, I think it's not much of a case they'll make out against him. After all, Jim *may* have done it himself, you know."

She turned away, leaving the farmer to follow her, and he, slow at coming to conclusions, stopped where he was, pondering all sides of the question in his mind.

But there's a word to say about Policeman Dumps. Nothing could exceed the consternation experienced by that functionary at the non-appearance of Jim Sanders. On their arrival at Barmester, they had searched for him in vain. Dumps would not believe that he had been purposely deceived, although the stern eyes of his superior were bent on him with a very significant look. "Get the fleetest conveyance you can, and be off to Barbrook and see about it," were the whispered commands of the latter. "A pretty go, this is! I shall have the Bench blowing me up in public!"

The Bench, vexed at the fruitless calls for Jim Sanders, looked much inclined to blow some one up. They were better off in regard to the sun than their audience, since they had their backs to it. The chairman, who sat in the middle, was a Mr. Pollard, a kindly, but hasty and opinionated man. He ordered the case to proceed, while the principal witness, Jim Sanders, was being looked for.

Mr. Flood, the lawyer from Barmester, acting for Mr. Chattaway, stated the case shortly and concisely. And the first witness called upon was Mr. Chattaway, who descended from the bench to give his evidence.

He was obliged to confess to his shame. He stood there before the condemning faces around, and acknowledged that the chastisement spoken to was a fact—that he *had* laid his horsewhip on the shoulders of Rupert Trevlyn. He was pressed for the why and wherefore—Chattaway was no favourite with his brother-magistrates, and they did not show him any remarkable favour—and he had further to confess that the provocation was totally inadequate to the punishment.

"State your grounds for charging your nephew, Rupert Trevlyn, with the crime," said the Bench.

"There is not the slightest doubt that he did it in a fit of passion," said Mr. Chattaway. "There was no one but him in the rick-yard, so far as I saw, and he had a lighted torch in his hand. This torch he dropped for a moment, but I suppose picked it up again."

"It is said that James Sanders was also in the rick-yard; and the torch was his."

"I did not see James Sanders. I saw only Rupert Trevlyn, and he had the torch in his hand when I went up. Not many minutes after I quitted the rick-yard the flames broke out."

Apparently this was all Mr. Chattaway knew of the actual facts. The man Hatch was called, and testified to the fact that Jim Sanders was in the rick-yard. Bridget, the kitchenmaid, in a state of much tremor, confirmed this, and confessed she was there subsequently with Jim, that he had a torch, and they saw the flames break out. She related her story pretty circumstantially, winding up with the statement that Jim told her Mr. Rupert had set it on fire.

"Stop a bit, lass," interrupted Mr. Peterby. "You have just stated to their worships that Jim Sanders flew off the moment he saw the flames burst forth, never stopping to speak a word. *Now* you say he told you it was Mr. Rupert who fired it. How do you reconcile the contradiction?"

"He had told me first, sir," answered the girl. "He said he saw the master horsewhip Mr. Rupert, and Mr. Rupert in his passion caught up the torch which had fell, thrust it into the rick, and then leaped over the palings and got away. Jim pulled the torch out of the rick, and all the hay that had caught, as he thought; he told me all this when he was showing me the puppy. I suppose a spark must have been left in to smoulder, unknown to him."

"Now don't you think that you and he and the torch and the puppy, between you, managed to get the spark there, instead of its having 'smouldered,' eh, girl?" sarcastically asked Mr. Peterby.

Bridget burst into tears. "No, I am sure we did not," she answered.

"Don't you likewise think that this pretty little bit of news regarding Mr. Rupert may have been a fable of Mr. Jim's invention, to excuse his own carelessness?" went on the lawyer.

"I am certain it was not, sir," she sobbed. "When Jim told me about Mr. Rupert, he never thought the rick was on fire."

They could not get on at all without Jim Sanders. Mr. Peterby's insinuations were pointed; nay, more; for he boldly asserted that the rick was far more likely to have been fired by Jim than Rupert—that is, by a spark from that gentleman's torch, whilst engaged with two objects so exacting as a puppy and Bridget. Jim himself could alone clear up the knotty question, and the Court gave vent to its impatience, and wished they were at the heels of Policeman Dumps who had gone in search of him.

But the heels of Policeman Dumps could not by any means have flown more quickly over the ground, had the whole court been after him in full cry. In point of fact, they were not his own heels that were at work, but those of a fleet little horse, drawing the light gig in which the policeman sat. So effectually did he whip up this horse, that in considerably less time than half-an-hour, Mr. Dumps was nearing Jim's dwelling. As he passed the police-station at Barbrook, the only solitary policeman left to take care of the interests of the district was fulfilling his duty by taking a lounge against the door-post.

"Have you seen anything of Jim Sanders?" called out Mr. Dumps, partially checking his horse. "He has never made his appearance yonder, and I'm come after him."

"I hear he's off," answered the man.

"Off! Off where?"

"Cut away," was the explanatory reply. "He hasn't been seen since last night."

Allowing himself a whole minute to take in the news, Mr. Dumps whipped on his horse, and gave utterance to a very unparliamentary word. When he burst into Mrs. Sanders's cottage, which was full of steam, and she before a washing-tub, he seized that lady's arm in so emphatic a manner that perceiving what was coming, she gave a scream, and very nearly plunged her head into the soap-suds.

Mr. Dumps ungallantly shook her. "Now, you just answer me," cried he; "and if you speak a word of a lie this time you'll get transported, or something as bad. What made you tell me last night Jim had come home and was in bed? Where is he?"

She supposed he knew all—all the wickedness of her conduct in screening him; and it had the effect of hardening her. She was, as it were, at bay; and deceit was no longer possible.

"If you did transport me I couldn't tell where he is. I don't know. I never set eyes on him all the blessed night, and that's the naked truth. Let me go, Mr. Dumps: it's no good choking me."

Mr. Dumps looked ready to choke himself. He had been deceived, and turned aside from the execution of his duty, his brother constables would have the laugh against him, Bowen would blow up, the Bench at Barmester was waiting, Jim was off—and that wretched woman had done it all! Mr. Dumps ground his teeth in impotent rage.

"I'll have you punished as sure as my name's what it is, Madge Sanders, if you don't tell me the truth," he foamed. "Is Jim in this here house?"

"You be welcome to search the house," she replied, throwing open the staircase door, which led to the loft. "I'm telling nothing but truth now, though I was frighted into doing summit else last night; frighted to death a'most, and so I was this morning when I said he'd gone on to Barmester."

Mr. Dumps felt inclined to shake her again: we are sure to be more angry with others when we have ourselves to blame; how could he have been fool enough to place such blind confidence in Farmer Apperley? One thing forced itself on his conviction; the woman was stating nothing but fact now.

"You persist in it to my face that you don't know where Jim is?" he cried.

"I swear I don't. There! I swear I have never set eyes on him since last night when he came home after work, and went out to take his black puppy to Trevlyn Hold. He never came in after that."

"You just dry those soap-suddy arms of yours, put your bonnet on, and come straight off, and tell that to the magistrates," commanded Mr. Dumps, in sullen tones.

She did not dare resist. Putting on her bonnet, flinging her old shawl across her shoulders, she was marshalled by Mr. Dumps to the gig. To look after Jim was a secondary consideration. To make his own excuse good was the first; and if Jim had had a matter of twelve-hours' start, he might be at twelve-hours' distance.

Not to be found! Jim Sanders had made his escape, and was not to be found! reiterated the indignant Bench, when Mrs. Sanders and her escort appeared. What did Bowen mean, by asserting that Jim was ready to be called upon?

Bowen shifted the blame from his own shoulders to those of Dumps; and Dumps, with a red face, shifted it on to Mrs. Sanders. She was sternly questioned, and made the same excuse she had made to Dumps—it was his saying to her that Jim had returned, and was in bed, that caused her in her fright to agree with it, and reply that he was. But she had not seen Jim, and he had never been a-nigh home since he went out with the puppy in the earlier part of the evening. She knew no more where Jim was than Dumps himself knew.

That she told the truth appeared to be pretty clear to the magistrates, and to punish her for having so far used deceit to screen her son, might have been neither just nor legal. They turned back on Dumps.

"What induced you to put such a leading question to the woman, assuming the boy was at home and in bed?" they severely asked.

Dumps began rather to excuse himself than to explain. Such a thing hadn't never happened to him before; and it was Mr. Apperley's fault, for he met that gentleman nigh Meg Sanders's door, who told him Jim was all right, and gone home to bed.

This was the first time Mr. Apperley's name had been mentioned in connection with the affair, and the magistrates ordered him before them. Nora insinuated her way to the front, and Mrs. Chattaway's face bent lower, to conceal its anxious expression, the wild beating of her heart.

"Did you meet James Sanders last night, Mr. Apperley?" inquired the chairman.

"Yes; I did, sir. I was going home, when the danger was over, and the fire had got low, and I came upon Jim Sanders near his cottage, coming from the direction of Layton's Heath. Knowing he had been wanted, I laid hold of him: but the boy told me, simply enough, where he had been,—to Barbrook, Barmester, and Layton's Heath after the engines. He was then hastening to the Hold to help at the fire. I told him the fire was out, and he might get to bed."

"And you told Dumps that he had gone to bed?"

"I did. I never supposed but Jim went home then and there; and when I met Dumps a few minutes afterwards, I told him so. I can't understand it at all. The boy seemed almost too tired to move, and no wonder—and where he could have gone instead, is uncommon odd to me. It's to know whether his mother speaks truth in saying he did not go in," added the farmer, gratuitously imparting a little of his mind to the Bench.

"What did he say to you?"

"He said where he had been, and that he was going up to the Hold," replied the witness, in tones of palpable hesitation, as if weighing his words.

"You are sure it was Jim Sanders?" asked a very silent magistrate who sat at the end of the bench.

Mr. Apperley opened his eyes at this. "Sure it was Jim Sanders? Why, of course I'm sure of it?"

"Well, it appears that only you, so far as can be learnt, saw Jim Sanders at all near the spot after the alarm went out."

"Like enough," answered the farmer. "If the boy went to all these places, one after the other, he couldn't be at the Hold. But there's no mistake about my having seen him, and talked to him."

The danger appeared to be over. The Bench seemed to have no intention of asking further questions of Mr. Apperley, and Nora breathed freely again. But it often happens that when we deem ourselves most secure, hidden danger is all the nearer. As the witness was turning round to retire, Flood, the lawyer, stepped forward.

"A moment yet, if you please, Mr. Apperley. I must ask you a question or two, with the permission of the Bench. I believe you had met Jim Sanders before that, last night—soon after the breaking out of the fire?"

"Yes," replied the farmer; "it was at the bend of the road between the Hold and Barbrook. I had that minute caught sight of the flame, not knowing rightly where it was or what it was, and Jim came running up and said, as well as he could speak for his hurry and agitation, that it was in Mr. Chattaway's rick-yard."

"Agitated, was he?" asked the Bench; and a keen observer might have noticed Mr. Flood's brow contract with a momentary annoyance.

"So agitated as hardly to know what he was saying, as it appeared to me," returned the witness. "He went away at great speed in the direction of Barbrook; on his way—as I learnt afterwards—to fetch the fire-engines."

"And very laudable of him to do so," spoke up the lawyer. "But I have a serious question to put to you now, Mr. Apperley; be so good as to attend to me, and speak up. Did not Jim Sanders distinctly tell you that it was Rupert Trevlyn who had fired the rick?"

Mr. Apperley paused in indecision. On the one hand, he was a plain, straightforward, honest man, possessing little tact, no cunning; on the other, he shrank from harming Rupert. Nora's words had left a strong impression upon him, and the mysterious absence of Jim Sanders was also producing its effect, as it was on three-parts of the people in court. He and they were beginning to ask why Jim should run away unless he had been guilty.

"Have you lost your voice, Mr. Apperley?" resumed the lawyer. "Did or did not Jim Sanders say it was Rupert Trevlyn who fired the rick?"

"I cannot say but he did," replied Mr. Apperley, as an unpleasant remembrance came across him that he had proclaimed this fact the previous night to as many as chose to listen, to which incaution Mr. Flood no doubt owed his knowledge. "But Jim appeared so flustered and wild," he continued, "that my belief is—and I have said this before—that he didn't rightly know what he was saying."

"Unless I am misinformed, you had just before met Rupert Trevlyn," continued Mr. Flood. "*He* was wild and flustered, was he not?"

"He was."

"Were both coming from the same direction?"

"Yes. As if they had run straight from the Hold."

"From the rick-yard, eh?"

"It might be that they had; 'twas pretty straight, if they leaped a hedge or two."

"Just so. You were walking soberly along the high-road, on your way to Bluck the farrier's, when you were startled by the apparition of Rupert Trevlyn flying from the direction of the rick-yard like a wild animal—I only quote your own account of the fact, Mr. Apperley. Rupert was pale and breathless; in short, as you described him, he must have been under the influence of some great terror, or *guilt*. Was this so? Tell their worships."

"It was so," replied Mr. Apperley.

"You tried to stop him, and you could not; and as you stood looking after him, wondering whether he was mad, and, if not mad, what could have put him into such a state, Jim Sanders came up and told you a piece of news that was sufficient to account for any amount of agitation—namely, that Rupert Trevlyn had just set fire to one of the ricks in the yard at the Hold."

It was utterly impossible that Mr. Apperley in his truth could deny this, and a faint cry broke from the lips of Mrs. Chattaway. But when Mr. Flood had done with the farmer, it was Mr. Peterby's turn to question him. He had not much to ask him, but elicited the positive avowal—and the farmer seemed willing to make as much of it as did Mr. Peterby—that Jim Sanders was in as great a state of agitation as Rupert Trevlyn, or nearly so. He, Mr. Apperley, summed up the fact by certain effective words.

"Yes, they were both agitated—both wild; and if those signs were any proof of the crime, the one looked as likely to have committed it as the other."

The words told with the Bench. Mr. Flood exerted his eloquence to prove that Rupert Trevlyn, and he alone, must have been guilty. Not that he had any personal ill-feeling towards Rupert; he only spoke in his lawyerly instinct, which must do all it could for his client's cause. Mr. Peterby, on the other hand, argued that the circumstances were more conclusive of the guilt of James Sanders. Mr. Apperley had testified that both were nearly equally agitated; and if Rupert was the most so, it was only natural, for a gentleman's feelings were more easily stirred than an ignorant day-labourer's. In point of fact, this agitation might have proceeded from terror alone in each of them. Looking at the case dispassionately, what real point was there against Rupert Trevlyn? None. Who dared to assert that he was guilty? No one but the runaway, James Sanders, who most probably proffered the charge to screen himself. Where was James Sanders, Mr. Peterby continued, looking round the court. Nowhere: he had decamped; and this, of itself, ought to be taken by all sensible people as conclusive of guilt. He asked the Bench, in their justice, not to remand Rupert Trevlyn, as was urged by Mr. Flood, but to discharge him, and issue a warrant for the apprehension of James Sanders.

Ah, what anxious hearts were some of those in court as the magistrates consulted with each other. Mr. Chattaway had had the grace not to return to his seat, and waited, as did the rest of the audience. Presently the chairman spoke—and it is very possible that the general disfavour in which Mr. Chattaway was held had insensibly influenced their decision.

It appeared to the Bench, he said, that there were not sufficient facts proved against Rupert Trevlyn to justify their keeping him in custody, or in remanding the case. That he may have smarted in passion under the personal chastisement inflicted by Mr. Chattaway was not unlikely, and that gentleman had proved that, when he left the rick-yard, the lighted torch was, so to say, in possession of the prisoner. Mr. Apperley had likewise testified to meeting Rupert Trevlyn soon afterwards in a state of wild agitation. In the opinion of the Bench, these facts were not worth much: the lighted torch was proved to be in the possession of James Sanders in the rick-yard after this, as it had been before it; and the prisoner's agitation might have been solely the effect of the beating inflicted on him by Mr. Chattaway. Except the assertion of the boy, James Sanders, as spoken to by Mr. Apperley and the servant-maid, Bridget Sanders, there was nothing to connect the prisoner with the actual crime. It had been argued by Mr. Peterby that James Sanders himself had probably committed it, wilfully or accidentally, and that his absence might be regarded as pretty conclusive proof of this. Be that as it might, the Bench had come to the decision that there were not sufficient grounds for detaining the prisoner, and therefore he was discharged.

He was discharged! And the shout of approbation that arose in court made the very walls ring.

CHAPTER XLI
NIGHT ENCOUNTER

The first to press up to Rupert Trevlyn after his restored liberty was George Ryle. George held a very decided opinion upon the unhappy case; but strove to bury it five-fathom deep in his heart, and he hated Mr. Chattaway for the inflicted horsewhipping. Holding his arm out to Rupert, he led him towards the exit; but the sea of faces, of friendly voices, of shaking hands, was great, and somehow he and Rupert were separated.

"It is a new lease of life for me, George," whispered a soft, sweet voice in his ear, and he turned to behold the glowing cheeks of Mrs. Chattaway, glowing with thanksgiving and unqualified happiness.

Unqualified? Ah, if she could only have looked into the future, as George did in his forethought! Jim Sanders would probably not remain absent for ever. But he suffered his face to become radiant as Mrs. Chattaway's, as he stayed to talk with her.

"Yes, dear Mrs. Chattaway, was it not a shout! I will drive Rupert home. I have my gig here. Treve shall walk. I wonder—I have been wondering whether it would not be better for all parties if Rupert came and stayed a week with Treve at the Farm? It might give time for the unpleasantness to blow over between him and Mr. Chattaway."

"How good you are, George! If it only might be! I'll speak to Diana."

She turned to Miss Diana Trevlyn and George saw Rupert talking with Mr. Peterby. At that moment, some one took possession of George.

It was Mr. Wall, the linen-draper. He had been in court all the time, his sympathies entirely with the prisoner, in spite of his early friendship with the master of Trevlyn Hold. Ever since that one month passed at Mr. Wall's house, which George at the time thought the blackest month that could have fallen to the lot of mortal, Mr. Wall and George had been great friends.

"This has been a nasty business," he said in an undertone. "Where *is* Jim Sanders?"

George disclaimed, and with truth, all knowledge on the point. Mr. Wall resumed.

"I guess how it was; an outbreak of the Trevlyn temper. Chattaway was a fool to provoke it. Cruel, too. He had no more right to take a whip to Rupert Trevlyn than I have to take one to my head-shopman. Were the ricks insured?"

"No. There's the smart. Chattaway never would insure his ricks; never has insured them. It is said that Miss Diana has often told him he deserved to have his ricks burnt down for being penny wise and pound foolish."

"How many were burnt?"

"Two: and another damaged by water. It is a sharp loss."

"Ay. One he won't relish. Rupert is not *secure*, you know," continued Mr. Wall in a spirit of friendly warning. "He can be taken up again."

"I am aware of that. And this time I think it will be very difficult to lay the spirit of anger in Mr. Chattaway. Good evening. I am going to drive Rupert home. Where has he got to?"

George had cause to reiterate the words "Where has he got to?" for he could not see him anywhere. His eyes roved in vain in search of Rupert. Mr. Peterby was alone now.

George went hunting everywhere. He inquired of every one, friend and stranger, if they had seen Rupert, but all in vain; he could not meet or hear of him. At last he gave up the search, and started for home, Treve occupying the place in the gig he had offered to Rupert.

Where was Rupert? In a state of mind not to be described, he had stolen away in the dusky night from the mass of faces, the minute he was released by Mr. Peterby, and made the best of his way out of Barmester, taking the field way towards the Hold. He felt in a sea of guilt and shame. To stand there a prisoner, the consciousness of guilt upon him—for he knew he had set fire to the rick—was as the keenest agony. When his previous night's passion cooled down, it was replaced by an awful sense—and the word is not misplaced—of the enormity of his act. It was a positive fact that he could not remember the details of that evil moment; but an innate conviction was upon him that he did thrust the burning brand into the rick and had so revenged himself on Mr. Chattaway. He turned aghast as he thought of it: in his sober senses he would be one of the last to commit so great a wickedness—would shudder at its bare thought. Not only was the weight of the guilt upon his mind, but a dread of the consequences. Rupert was no hero, and the horror of the punishment that might follow was working havoc in his brain. If he had escaped it for this day, he knew sufficient of our laws to be aware that he might not escape it another, and that Chattaway would prove implacable. The disgrace of a trial, the brand of felon—all might be his. Perhaps it was fear as much as shame which took Rupert alone out of Barmester.

He knew not where to go. He reached the neighbourhood of the Hold, passed it, and wandered about in the moonlight, sick with hunger, weary with walking. He began to wish he had gone home with George Ryle; and he wished he could see George Ryle then, and ask his advice. To the Hold, to face Chattaway, he dared not yet go; nay, with that consciousness of guilt upon him, he shrank from facing his kind aunt Edith, his sister Maude, his aunt Diana. A sudden thought flashed into his mind—and for the moment it seemed like an inspiration—he would go after Mr. Daw and beg a shelter with him.

But to get to Mr. Daw, who lived in some unknown region in the Pyrenees, and had no doubt crossed the Channel, would take money, time, and strength. As the practical views of the idea came up before him, he abandoned it in utter despair. Where should he go and what should he do? He sat down on the stile forming the entrance to a small grove of trees, through which a near road led to Barbrook; in fact, it was at the end of that very field in which Mr. Apperley had seen him the previous evening. Some subtle instinct, perhaps, took his wandering steps to it. As he leaned against the stile, he became conscious of the advance of some one along the narrow path leading from Barbrook—a woman, by her petticoats.

It was a lovely night. The previous night had been dull, but on this one the moon shone in all her splendour. Rupert did not fear a woman, least of all the one approaching, for he saw that it was Ann Canham. She had been at work at the parsonage. Mrs. Freeman, taking advantage of the departure of their guest, had instituted the autumn cleaning, delayed on his account; and Ann had been there to-day, helping Molly, and was to go also on the morrow. A few happy tears dropped from her eyes when she saw him.

"The parson's already home with the good news, sir. But why ever do you sit here, Master Rupert?"

"Because I have nowhere to go to," returned Rupert.

Ann paused, and then spoke timidly. "Isn't there the Hold, as usual, sir?"

"I can't go there. Chattaway might horsewhip me again, you know, Ann."

The bitter mockery with which he spoke brought pain to her. "Where shall you go, sir?"

"I don't know. Lie down under these trees till morning. I am awfully hungry."

Ann Canham opened a basket which she carried, and took out a small loaf, or cake. She offered it to Rupert, curtseying humbly.

"Molly has been baking to-day, sir; and the missis, she gave me this little loaf for my father. Please take it, sir."

Rupert's impulse was to refuse, but hunger was strong within him. He took a knife from his pocket, cut it in two, and gave one half back to Ann Canham.

"Tell Mark I had the other, Ann. He won't grudge it to me. And now go home. It's of no use your stopping here."

She made as if she would depart, but hesitated. "Master Rupert, I don't like to leave you here so friendless. Won't you come to the lodge, sir, and shelter there for the night?"

"No, that I won't," he answered. "Thank you, Ann; but I am not going to get you and Mark into trouble as I have got myself."

She sighed as she finally went away. Would this unhappy trouble touching Rupert ever be over?

Perhaps Rupert was asking the same. He ate the bread, and sat on the stile afterwards, ruminating. He was terribly bitter against Chattaway; but for his wicked conduct he should not now be the outcast he was. All the wrongs of his life rose up before him. The Hold that ought to be his, the rank he was deprived of, the wretched humiliations that were his daily portion. They assumed quite an exaggerated importance to his mind. He worked himself into—not the passion of the previous night, but into an angry, defiant temper; and he wished he could meet Chattaway face to face, and return the blows, the pain of which was still upon him.

With a cry that almost burst from his lips in terror, with a feeling verging on the supernatural, he suddenly saw Chattaway before him. Rupert recovered himself, and though his heart beat pretty fast, he kept his seat on the stile in his defiant humour.

And Mr. Chattaway? Every drop of blood in that gentleman's body had bubbled up with the unjust leniency shown by the magistrates, and had remained at fever heat. Never, never had his feelings been so excited against Rupert as on this night. As he came along he was plotting with himself how Rupert could be recaptured on the morrow—on what pretext he could apply for a warrant against him. That miserable, detested Rupert! He made his life a terror through that latent dread, he was a burden on his pocket, he brought him into disfavour with the neighbourhood, he treated him with cavalier insolence, and now had set his ricks on fire. And—there he was! Before him in the moonlight. Mr. Chattaway bounded forward, and seized him by the shoulder.

A struggle ensued. Blows were given on either side. But Mr. Chattaway was the stronger: he flung Rupert to the ground; and a dull, heavy human sound went forth on the still night air.

Did the sound come from Rupert, or from Chattaway? No; Rupert was lying motionless, and Chattaway knew he had made no sound himself. He looked up in the trees; but it had not been the sound of a night-bird. A rustling caught his ear behind the narrow grove, and Chattaway bounded towards it, just in time to see a man's legs flying over the ground in the direction of Barbrook.

Who had been a witness to the scene?

CHAPTER XLII
NEWS FOR TREVLYN HOLD

When Mr. and Mrs. Chattaway and Miss Diana had driven home from Barmester, they were met with curious faces, and eager questions, the result of the day's proceedings not having reached the Hold. It added to the terrible mortification gnawing the heart of Mr. Chattaway to confess that Rupert was discharged. He had been too outspoken that morning before his children and household of the certain punishment in store for Rupert—his committal for trial.

And the mortification was destined to be increased on another score. Whilst they were seated at a sort of high tea—Cris came in from Blackstone with some news. The Government inspectors had been there that day, and chosen to put themselves out on account of the absence of Mr. Chattaway, whom they had expected at the office.

"They mean mischief," observed Cris. "How far *can* they interfere?" he asked, turning to his father. "Could they force you to go to the expense they hint at?"

Mr. Chattaway really did not know. He sat looking surly and gloomy, buried in rumination, and by-and-by rose and left the room. Soon after this, George Ryle entered, to take Rupert to the farm. George knew now that Rupert had walked home: Bluck, the farrier, had told him so. But Rupert, it appeared, was not yet come in.

So George waited: waited and waited. It was a most uncomfortable evening. Mrs. Chattaway was palpably nervous and anxious, and Maude, who sat apart, as if conscious that Rupert's fault in some degree reflected upon her, was as white as a sheet. When George rose to leave it was nearly eleven. Rupert, it must be supposed, had taken shelter somewhere for the night, and Mr. Chattaway did not appear in a hurry to return. None had any idea where Mr. Chattaway was to be found: when he left the house, they only supposed him to be going to the out-buildings.

The whole flood of moonlight came flushing on George Ryle, as he stood for a moment at the door of the Hold. He lifted his face to it, thinking how beautiful it was, when the door was softly opened behind him, and Maude came out, pale and shivering.

"Forgive my following you, George," she whispered, in pleading tones. "I could not ask you before them, but I am ill with suspense. Tell me, is the danger over for Rupert?"

George took her hand in his. He looked down with tender fondness upon the unhappy girl; but hesitated in his answer.

She bent her head, and there came a half-breathed whisper of pain. "Do you believe he did it?"

"Maude, my darling, I do believe he did it; you ask me for the truth, and I will not give you anything else. But I believe that he must have been in a state of madness, irresponsible for his actions."

"What can be done?" she gasped.

"Nothing. Nothing, except that we must endeavour to conciliate Mr. Chattaway. If he can be appeased, the danger will pass."

"Never will he be appeased!" she answered. "He will think of the value of the ricks, the money lost to him. George, if it comes to the worst—if they try Rupert, I shall die."

"Hush, my dear, hush! Try and look on the bright side of things, Maude; your grieving cannot influence Rupert, and will harm you. Nothing shall be left undone on my part to serve him. I wish I had more influence with Mr. Chattaway."

"No one has any influence with him,—no one in the world; unless it is Aunt Diana."

"She has—and I can talk to her as I could not to Chattaway. I intend to see her privately in the morning. Maude, how you shiver!"

George bent to take his farewell, and went on his way. Ere he was quite out of sight, he turned to take a last look at her. She was standing in the white moonlight, her hands clasped, her face one sad expression of distress and despair. A vague feeling came over George that this despondency of Maude's bore ill omen for poor Rupert. But he could not have told why the feeling should come to him, and he put it from him as absurd and foolish.

The night wore on at the Hold, and its master did not return. All sat up, ladies, children, and servants; wondering where he could be. It was close upon midnight when his ring sounded at the locked door.

Mr. Chattaway came in with his face scratched and a bruise over one eye. The servant stared in astonishment, and noticed, as his master unbuttoned a light overcoat, that the front of his shirt was torn. Mr. Chattaway was not one to be questioned by his servants, and the man went off to the kitchen and reported the news.

"Good Heavens, papa! what have you done to your face?"

The exclamation came from Octave, who was the first to catch sight of him as he entered the room. Mr. Chattaway responded by an angry demand why they were not in bed, what they did sitting up at that hour: and he began to light the bed-candles.

"What *have* you done to your face?" reiterated Miss Diana, coming close to take a nearer view.

"Nothing," was his curt response.

"What's the use of saying that?" retorted Miss Diana. "It looks as though you had been fighting. And your shirt's torn!"

"I tell you there's nothing the matter with it; or with my shirt either," he said testily. "Can't you take an answer?" And, as if to put an end to questioning, he took a candle and went up to his room.

The scratches were less apparent in the morning, and the bruise was only a slight one. Cris, in his indifferent manner, said the Squire must have walked into the branches of a thorny tree.

By tacit consent they avoided all mention of Rupert. It is possible that even Miss Diana did not care to mention his name to Mr. Chattaway. Whilst they were at breakfast, Hatch came and put his head inside the door.

"Jim Sanders is back, sir."

Mr. Chattaway started up, a certain flashing light in his dull eyes that boded no good to Jim. "Where is he?" he cried. "How do you know?"

"Ted, the cow-boy, has just seen him at work at Mr. Ryle's as usual, sir. I thought you might like to know it, and made bold to come in and tell ye. Ted asked him where he had runned away to yesterday, and Jim answered he had not runned away at all; only overslep' hisself."

Mr. Chattaway hastened from the room, followed by Cris; and Mrs. Chattaway took the opportunity to ask Hatch if he had seen or heard anything of Mr. Rupert. But Hatch only stood stolidly in the middle of the carpet, and made no reply.

"Did you not hear Madam's question, Hatch?" sharply asked Miss Diana. "Why don't you answer it?"

"Because I don't like to," responded stolid Hatch. "Happen Madam mayn't like to hear the answer, Miss Diana."

"Nonsense!" quickly cried Miss Trevlyn. "Have you heard of him?"

"Well, yes, I have," answered Hatch. "They be talking of it now in the sheep-pen."

"What are they saying?" asked Mrs. Chattaway, in eager tones.

But the man remained silent, staring at his mistress.

"What are they saying?—do you hear?" imperatively repeated Miss Diana.

Hatch could not hold out longer. "They be saying that he's dead, ma'am."

"That he is—*what*?"

"They be saying that Mr. Rupert's dead," equably repeated Hatch; "he was killed down in the little grove last night, as you go through the fields to Barbrook. I didn't like to tell the Squire, because they be saying that if he be killed, happen the Squire have killed him."

Only for a moment did Miss Diana Trevlyn lose her self-possession. She raised her hands to still the awestruck terror around her, and glanced at Mrs. Chattaway's blanched face. "Hatch, where did you hear this?"

"In the sheep-pen, ma'am. The men be a-talking on't. They say he was killed last night—murdered."

Her own face for once in her life was turning white. "Be still, all of you, and remain here," she said. "Edith, if ever you had need of self-command, it is now."

She went straight off to the sheep-pen, bidding Hatch follow her. From the first moment Hatch had spoken, there had risen up before her, as an ugly picture—a dream to be shunned—the scratched and bruised face of Mr. Chattaway.

The sheep-pen was empty: the men had dispersed. Cris came out of the stables, and she signed to him. He advanced to meet her. "Where is your father?" she asked.

"Off to Barbrook," returned Cris. "Sam wasn't long getting his horse ready, was he? He has gone to order Bowen to look after Mr. Jim Sanders."

"Have you heard this report about Rupert?" she resumed, her hushed tones imparting to Cris a vague sense of something unpleasant.

"I have not heard any report about him. What is the report? That he's dead?"

"Yes; that he is dead."

Cris had spoken in a half-jesting, half-sneering tone; but his face changed at the answer, consternation in every feature, "What on earth do you mean, Aunt Diana? Rupert—"

"Good morning, Miss Diana."

They turned to behold George Ryle. He had come up thus early to know if they had news of Rupert. The scared expression of their faces struck him that something was wrong.

"You have bad news, I see. What is it?"

Miss Diana rapidly turned over a question in her mind. Should she mention this report to George? Yes; he was thoroughly trustworthy; and might be of use.

"Hatch came in a few minutes ago, and frightened us very greatly," she said. "I was just telling Cris about it. The man says there's a report going about that Rupert is—is"—she scarcely liked to bring out the word—"is dead."

"What?" uttered George.

"That he has been killed—murdered," continued Miss Diana. "George, I want to get at the truth of it."

He could not rejoin just at first. News, such as that, takes time to revolve. He could only look at them alternately; his heart, for Rupert's sake, beating fast. Miss Diana repeated what Hatch had said. "George," she concluded, "I cannot go after these men, examining into the truth or falsehood of the report, but you might."

George started away impulsively ere she had well spoken. Hatch mentioned the names of the men who had been talking, and George hastened to look for them over the fields. Cris was following, but Miss Diana caught him by the arm.

"Not you, Cris; stop where you are."

"Stop where I am?" returned Cris, indignantly, who had a very great objection to being interfered with by Miss Diana. "I shall not, indeed. I don't pretend to have had much love for Rupert, but I'm sure I shall look into it if there's such a report as that about. He must have killed himself, if he is dead."

But Miss Diana kept her hand upon him. "Remain where you are, I say. They are connecting your father's name with it in a manner I do not understand, and it will be better you should be quiet until we know more."

She went on to the house as she spoke. Cris stared after her in blank dismay, wondering what the words meant, yet sufficiently discomposed to give up his own will for once, and remain quiet, as she had suggested.

Meanwhile, Mr. Chattaway, unconscious of the commotion at the Hold, was galloping towards Barbrook. He reined in at the police-station, and Bowen came out to him.

"I know what you have come about, Mr. Chattaway," cried the man, before that gentleman could speak. "It's to tell us that Jim Sanders has turned up. We know all about it, and Dumps has gone after him. Hang the boy! giving us all this bother."

"I'll have him punished, Bowen."

"Well, sir, it's to know whether he won't get enough punishment as it is. His going off looks uncommonly suspicious—as I said yesterday: looks as if he had had a finger in the pie."

"Is Dumps going to bring him on here?"

"Right away, as fast as he can march him. Impudent monkey, going to work this morning, just as if nothing had happened! Dumps'll be on to him. They won't be long, sir."

"Then I'll wait," decided Mr. Chattaway.

CHAPTER XLIII
JAMES SANDERS

George Ryle speedily found the men spoken of by Hatch as having held the conversation in the sheep-pen. But he could gather nothing more certain from them than Miss Diana had gathered from Hatch. Upon endeavouring to trace the report to its source he succeeded in finding out that one man alone had brought it to the Hold. This man declared he heard it from his wife, and his wife had heard it from Mrs. Sanders.

Away sped George Ryle to the cottage of Mrs. Sanders: passing through the small grove of trees, spoken of in connection with this fresh report, the nearest way to Barbrook and the cottage from the upper road, but lonely and unfrequented. He found the woman busy at the work Mr. Dumps had interrupted the previous day—washing. With some unwillingness on her part and much circumlocution, George drew her tale from her. And to that evening we may as well return for a few minutes, for we shall arrive at the conclusion much more quickly than Mrs. Sanders.

It was dark when the woman walked home from Barmester—Dumps not having had the politeness to drive her, as in going,—and she found her kitchen as she had left it. Her children—she had three besides Jim—were out in the world, Jim alone being at home with her. Mrs. Sanders lighted a candle, and surveyed the scene: grate black and cold; washing-tub on the bench, wet clothes lying over it; bricks sloppy. "Drat that old Dumps!" ejaculated she. "I'd serve him out if I could. And I'd like to serve out that Jim, too. This comes of dancing up to the Hold after Bridget with that precious puppy!"

She put things tolerably straight for the night, made herself some tea, and began to think. What had become of Jim? And did he or did he not have anything to do with the fire? Not wilfully; she could answer for that, but accidentally? She looked into vacancy, and shook her head in a timid, doubtful manner, for she knew that torches in rick-yards might prove dangerous adjuncts to suspicion.

"I wonder what they could do to him, happen they proved it were a spark from his torch?" she deliberated. "Sure they'd never transport for an accident! Dumps said transportation were too good for Jim, but—"

The train of thought was interrupted, the door burst open, and by no less a personage than Jim himself. Jim, as it appeared, in a state of fear and agitation. His breath came fast, and his eyes had a wild, terrified stare in them.

With his presence, Mrs. Sanders's maternal apprehensions for his safety merged into anger. She laid hold of Jim and shook him—kindly, as she expressed it; but poor Jim found little kindness in it.

"Mother, what's that for?"

"That's what it's for," retorted his mother, giving him a sound box on the ear. "You'll dance out with puppies again up to that good-for-nothing minx of a Bridget!—and you'll set rick-yards a-fire!—and you'll go off and hide yourself, and let the place be searched by the police!—and me drawn into trouble, and took off by that insolent Dumps in a stick-up gig to Barmester, and lugged afore the court! Now, where have you been?"

Jim made no return in kind. All the spirit the boy possessed seemed to have gone out of him. He sat down meekly on a broken chair, and began to shiver. "Don't, mother," said he. "I've got a fright."

"A fright!" indignantly responded Mrs. Sanders. "And what sort of a fright do you suppose you have given others? Happen Madam Chattaway might have died of it, they say. *You* talk of a fright! Who hasn't been in a fright since you took the torch into the yard and set the ricks alight?"

"It isn't that," said Jim. "I ain't afraid of that; I didn't do it. Nora knows I didn't, and Mr. Apperley knows, and Bridget knows. I've no cause to be afeard of that."

"Then what are you quaking for?" angrily demanded Mrs. Sanders.

"I've just got a fright," he answered. "Mother, as true as we be here, Mr. Rupert's dead. I've just watched him killed."

Mrs. Sanders's first proceeding on receipt of this information was to stare; her second to discredit it, believing Jim was out of his mind, or dreaming. "Talk sense, will you?" cried she.

"I'm not a-talking nonsense," he answered. "Mother, as sure as us two be living here, I see it. It were in the grove, up by the field. I saw him struck down."

The woman began to think there must be something in the tale. "It's Mr. Rupert you be talking of?"

"Yes, and it was him as set the rick a-fire. And now he's murdered! Didn't I run fast! I was in mortal fear."

"Who killed him?"

Jim looked round timorously, as if thinking the walls might have ears. "I daren't say," he shivered.

"But you must say."

He shook his head. "No, I'll never tell it—unless I'm forced. He might be for killing *me*. When the hue and cry goes about to-morrow, and folks is asking who did it, there'll be nobody to answer. I shall keep dark, because I must. But if Ann Canham had waited and seen it, I wouldn't ha' minded saying; she'd ha' been a witness as I told the truth."

"If you don't speak plainer I'll box your ears again," was the retort. "What about Ann Canham?"

"Well, I met her at the top o' the field as I was turning into 't. That were but a few minutes afore. She'd been to work at the parson's, she said. I say, mother, you don't think they'll come after me here?" he questioned, his tone full of doubt.

"They *did* come after ye, to some purpose," wrathfully responded Mrs. Sanders. "My belief is you've come home with your head turned. I'd like to know where you've been hiding."

"I've been nowhere but up in the tallet at master's," replied Jim. "I crep' in there last night, dead tired, and never woke this morning. Hay do make one sleep; it's warmer than bed."

We need not follow the interview any further. At the close of the night she knew little more than she had known at its commencement beyond the assertion that Rupert Trevlyn was killed. Jim went off in the morning to his work as usual, and she resumed her labours of the day before. Nora had scarcely shown her wisdom in releasing Jim so quickly; but it may be that to keep him longer concealed in the "tallet" was next door to impossible.

Mrs. Sanders was interrupted in her work by George Ryle. She smoothed down the coarse towel pinned before her, and put her untidy hair behind her ears as her master entered. He questioned her as to the report which had been traced to her, and she disclosed what she had heard from Jim. Not much in itself, but it wore an air of mystery George could not understand and did not like. He left her to go in search of Jim.

But another, as we have heard, had taken precedence of him in searching for that gentleman—Policeman Dumps. Mr. Dumps found him in the out-buildings at Trevlyn Farm, working as unconcernedly as though nothing had happened. The man's first move, fearing perhaps a second escape, was to clap a pair of handcuffs on him.

"There, you young reptile! You'll go off again, will you, after committing murder!"

Now, in point of fact, Mr. Dumps had really no particular reason for using the word. He only intended to imply that Mr. Jim's general delinquency deserved a strong name. Jim took it in a different light.

"It wasn't me murdered him!" he said, terrified almost out of his life at the handcuffs. "I only see it done. Why should I murder him, Mr. Dumps?"

"Who's talking about murder?" cynically returned Dumps, forgetting probably that he had used the word. "The setting of the rick-yard on fire was enough for you, warn't it, without anything else added on to it?"

"Oh, you mean the fire," said Jim, considerably relieved. "I didn't do that, neither, and there'll be plenty to prove it. I thought you meant the murder."

Dumps surveyed his charge critically, uncertain what to make of him. He proceeded to questioning; setting about it in an artistic manner that was perhaps characteristic of his calling.

"Which murder might be you meaning of, pray?"

"Mr. Rupert's."

"Mr.—What be you talking of?" uttered Dumps, staring at Jim in the utmost astonishment.

And now Jim Sanders found he had been caught in a trap, one not expressly laid for him. He could have bitten his tongue out with vexation. That the death of Rupert Trevlyn would become public property, he had never doubted, but he had intended to remain silent upon the subject.

It was too late to retract now, and he must make the best of it, and put up with the consequences.

"Who says Mr. Rupert's murdered?" persisted Dumps.

"So he is," sullenly answered Jim. "But I didn't do it."

Mr. Dumps's rejoinder was to seize Jim by the collar, and march him off in the direction of the station as fast as he could walk. The farming men, who had been collecting since the policeman's arrival, followed to the fold-yard gate, and stood staring, supposing he was taken on suspicion of having caused the fire. Nora, shut up in her dairy, had seen nothing, or there's no knowing but she might have flown out to the rescue.

Not another word was spoken; indeed the pace at which Mr. Dumps chose to walk prevented it. When they reached the station, Mr. Chattaway was talking to Bowen. Jim went into a shivering fit at the sight of Chattaway, and strove to hide behind Policeman Dumps.

"So you have turned up!" exclaimed Bowen. "And now, where did you get to yesterday?"

Jim did not answer; he appeared to wish to avoid Mr. Chattaway, and trembled visibly. Bowen was on the point of inquiring what made him quake in that fashion, when Mr. Chattaway's voice broke in like a peal of thunder.

"How dared you be guilty of suppressing evidence? How dared you run away?"

Bowen turned the boy round to face him. "Just state where you got to, Jim Sanders."

"I didn't run away," replied Jim. "I lay down in the tallet at the farm atop o' the hay, and never woke all day yesterday. Miss Dickson can say I was there, for she come and found me there at night, and sent me off. There warn't no cause for me to run away," he somewhat fractiously repeated, as if weary of having to harp upon the same string. "It wasn't me that fired the rick."

"But you saw it fired?" cried Mr. Chattaway.

Jim stole round, so as to put Dumps between him and the questioner. Mr. Bowen brought him to again. "There's no need to dodge about like that," cried he, repeating Jim's words. "Just speak up the truth; but you are not forced to say anything to criminate yourself."

"I can tell 'em," thought Jim to himself; "it won't hurt him, now he's dead. It was Mr. Rupert," he said aloud. "After he got the horsewhipping, he caught up the torch and pushed it into one o' the ricks; and that's as true as I be living."

"You saw him do this?"

"I was watching all the while, round the pales. He seemed like one a'most mad, and it frighted me. I pulled the burning hay out o' the rick, and thought I pulled it all out, but suppose a spark must ha' stopped in. I was frighted worse afterwards when the flames burst out, and I ran off for the engines. I telled Mr. Apperley I'd been for 'em when I met him at night."

The boy's earnest tones and honest eyes, lifted to Bowen's, convinced that experienced officer that it was the truth. But he chose to gaze implacably at the culprit, never relaxing his sternness of voice.

"Then what made you go and hide yourself? Out with the truth!"

Jim's eyes fell now. "I was tired to death," he said, "and crep' up into the tallet at master's, and went to sleep. And I never woke in the morning, when I ought to ha' woke."

This was so far probable that it *might* be true. But before Bowen could go on questioning he was interrupted by Mr. Chattaway.

"He has confessed sufficient, Bowen—it was Rupert Trevlyn. But he deserves punishment for the trouble he has put everyone to; and there must be a fresh examination. Keep him safely here, and take care he's not tampered with. I am obliged to go to Blackstone to-day, but the hearing can take place to-morrow, if you'll apprise the magistrates. And—Bowen—mind you accomplish that other matter to-day that I have charged you with."

The last sentence, spoken emphatically and slowly, Mr. Chattaway turned round to deliver as he was going out. Bowen nodded in acquiescence; and Chattaway mounted his horse and rode off in the direction of Blackstone.

Jim Sanders, looking the picture of misery in his handcuffs, stood awkwardly in a corner of the room; it was a square room with a boarded floor; and a railed-off desk. Bowen had gone within these rails as Mr. Chattaway departed, and was busy writing a few detached words or sentences, that looked like memoranda. Dumps was gazing after the retreating figure of Mr. Chattaway.

"Call Chigwell," said Bowen, glancing at the small door which led into the inner premises. "There's work for both of you to-day."

But before Dumps could do this, he was half-knocked over by some one entering. It was George Ryle. He took in a view of affairs at a glance: Bowen writing; Dumps doing nothing; Mr. Jim Sanders handcuffed.

"So you have come to grief?" said George to the latter. "You are just the man I wanted, Jim. Bowen," he added, going within the railings and lowering his voice, "have you heard this report about Rupert Trevlyn?"

"I have heard he is probably off, sir," was Bowen's answer. "Two of the men are going out now to look after him. Mr. Chattaway has signed a warrant for his apprehension."

George paused. "There is a report that he is dead," he resumed.

"Dead!" echoed Bowen, aghast. "Rupert Trevlyn dead! Who says it?"

George looked round at Jim. The boy stood white and shivery; but before any questions could be asked, Dumps came forward and spoke.

"*He* was talking of that," he said to Bowen, indicating Jim. "When I clapped the handcuffs on him, he turned scared, and began denying it was him that did the murder. I asked him what he meant, and who was murdered, and he said it was Mr. Rupert Trevlyn."

Bowen looked thunderstruck, little as it is in the way of police officers to show emotion of any kind. "What grounds has he for saying that?" he exclaimed, gazing keenly at Jim. "Mr. Ryle, where did you hear the report?"

"I heard it just now at Trevlyn Hold. It would have alarmed them very much had they believed it. Mr. Chattaway was away, and Miss Trevlyn requested me to inquire into it, and bring back news—as she assumed I should—of its absurdity. I believe we must go to Jim for information," added George, "for I have traced the report to him."

Bowen beckoned Jim within the railings; where there was just sufficient space for the three. Dumps stood outside, leaning on the bars. "Have you been doing mischief to Mr. Rupert Trevlyn?" asked the superintendent.

"Me!" echoed Jim—and it was evident that his astonishment was genuine. "I wouldn't have hurt a hair of his head," he added, bursting into tears. "I couldn't sleep for vexing over it. It wasn't me."

Bowen quietly took off the handcuffs, and laid them on the desk. "There," said he, in a kindlier tone; "now you can talk at your ease. Let us hear about this."

"I'm afeard, sir," responded Jim.

"There's nothing to be afeard of, if you are innocent. Do you know of any ill having happened to Mr. Rupert Trevlyn?"

"I know he's dead," answered Jim. "They blowed me up for saying it was him set the rick a-fire, and I was sorry I had said it; but now he's gone, it don't matter, and I can say still that it was him fired it."

"Who blew you up?"

"Some on 'em," answered Jim, doing his best to evade the question.

"Well, what is this about Mr. Rupert? If you are afraid to tell me, tell your master there," suggested Bowen. "I'm sure he is a kind master to you; all the parish knows that."

"It *must* be told, Jim," said George Ryle, impressively, as he laid his hand upon the boy's shoulder. "What are you afraid of?"

"Mr. Chattaway might kill me for telling, sir," said unwilling Jim.

"Nonsense! Mr. Chattaway would be as anxious to know the truth as we are."

"But if it was him did it?" whispered Jim, glancing fearfully round the whitewashed walls of the room, as he had glanced around those of his mother's cottage.

A blank pause. Mr. Bowen looked at George, whose face had turned hectic with the surprise, the *dread* the words had brought. "You must speak out, Jim," was all he said.

"It was in the little grove last night," rejoined the boy. "I was running home after Nora Dickson turned me out o' the tallet, and when I got up to 'em they was having words—"

"Who were having words?"

"Mr. Chattaway and Master Rupert. I was scared, and crep' in amid the trees, and they never saw me. And then I heard blows, and I looked out and saw Mr. Rupert struck down to the earth, and he fell as one who hasn't got no life in him, and I knew he was dead."

"And what happened next?" asked Bowen.

"I don't know, sir. I come off then, and got into mother's. I didn't dare tell her it was Chattaway killed him. I wouldn't tell now, only you force me."

Bowen was revolving things in his mind, this and that. "Not five minutes ago Chattaway gave me orders to have Rupert Trevlyn searched for and taken up to-day," he muttered, more to himself than to George Ryle. "He knew he was skulking somewhere in the neighbourhood, he said; skulking, that was the word. I don't know what to think of this."

Neither did his hearers know, Mr. Jim Sanders possibly excepted. "I wonder," slowly resumed Bowen, a curious light coming into his eyes, "what brought those scratches on the face of Mr. Chattaway?"

CHAPTER XLIV
FERMENT

Strange rumours were abroad in the neighbourhood of Trevlyn Hold, and the excitement increased hourly. Mr. Chattaway had murdered Rupert Trevlyn—so ran the gossip—and Jim Sanders was in custody. Before the night of the day on which you saw Jim in the police-station, these reports, with many wild and almost impossible additions, were current, and spreading largely.

With the exception of the accusation made by Jim Sanders, the only corroboration to the tale appeared to rest in the fact that Rupert Trevlyn was not to be found. Dumps and his brother-constable scoured the locality high and low, and could find no traces of him. Sober lookers-on (but it is rare to find them in times of great excitement) regarded this as a favourable fact. Had Rupert really been murdered, or even accidentally killed by a chance blow from Mr. Chattaway, surely his body would be forthcoming to confirm the tale. But there were not wanting others who believed, and did not shrink from the avowal, that Mr. Chattaway was quite capable of suppressing all signs of the affray, including the dead body itself; though by what sleight-of-hand the act could have been accomplished seemed likely to remain a mystery.

Before Mr. Chattaway got home from Blackstone in the evening, all the rumours, good and bad, were known at Trevlyn Hold.

Mr. Chattaway was not unprepared to find this the case. In returning, he had turned his horse to the police-station, and reined in. Bowen, who saw him, came out.

"Has he been taken?" demanded Mr. Chattaway.

He put the question in an earnest tone, some impatience dashed with it, that was apparently genuine. "No, he has not," replied Bowen, stroking his chin, taking note of Mr. Chattaway's face. "Dumps and Chigwell have been at it all day; are at it still; but as yet without result."

"Then they are laggards at their work!" retorted Mr. Chattaway, his countenance darkening. "He was wandering about the place last night, and is sure to be not far off it to-day. By Heaven, he shall be unearthed! If there's any screening going on, as I know there was yesterday with regard to Jim Sanders, I'll have the actors brought to justice!"

Bowen came out of a reverie. "Would you be so good as to step inside for a few minutes, Mr. Chattaway? I have a word to say to you."

Mr. Chattaway got off his horse, hooked the bridle to the rails, as he had hooked it in the morning, and followed Bowen. The man saw that the doors were closed, and then spoke.

"There's a tale flying about, Mr. Chattaway, that Rupert Trevlyn has come to some harm. Do you know anything of it?"

"Not I," slightingly answered Mr. Chattaway. "What harm should come to him?"

"It is said that you and he met last night, had some sort of encounter by moonlight, and that Rupert was—in short, that some violence was done him."

For a full minute they remained looking at each other. The policeman appeared intent on biting the feathers of his pen; in reality, he was studying the face of Mr. Chattaway with a critical acumen his apparently careless demeanour imparted little idea of. He saw the blood mount under the dark skin; he saw the eye lighten with emotion: but the emotion was more like that called forth by anger than guilt. At least, so the police officer judged; and habit had rendered him a pretty correct observer. Mr. Chattaway was the first to speak.

"How do you know anything of the sort took place?—any interview?"

"It was watched—that is, accidentally seen. A person was passing at the time, and has mentioned it to-day."

"Who was the person?"

Bowen did not reply to the question. The omission may have been accidental, since he was hastening to put one on his own account.

"Do you deny this, Mr. Chattaway?"

"No. I wish I had the opportunity of acknowledging it to Mr. Rupert Trevlyn in the manner he deserves," continued Mr. Chattaway, in what looked like a blaze of anger.

"It is said that after the—the encounter, Rupert Trevlyn was left as one dead," cautiously resumed Bowen.

"Psha!" was the scornful retort. "Dead! He got up and ran away."

A very different account from that of Jim Sanders. Bowen was silent for a minute, endeavouring, most likely, to reconcile the two. "Have you any objection to state what took place, sir?"

"I don't know that I have," was the reply, somewhat sullenly delivered. "But I can't see what business it is of yours."

"People are taking up odd notions about it," said Bowen.

"People be hanged! It's no concern of theirs."

"But if they come to me and oblige me to make it my concern?" returned the officer, in significant tones. "If it's all fair and above-board, you had better tell me, Mr. Chattaway. If it's not, perhaps the less you say the better."

It was a hint not calculated to conciliate a chafed spirit, and Mr. Chattaway resented it. "How dare you presume to throw out insinuations to me?" he cried, snatching his riding-whip off the desk, where he had laid it, and stalking towards the door. "I'll tell you nothing; and you may make the best and the worst of it. Find Rupert Trevlyn, if you must know, and get it out of him. I ask you who has been spreading the rumour that I met Rupert Trevlyn last night?"

Bowen saw no reason why he should not disclose it. "Jim Sanders," he replied.

"Psha!" contemptuously ejaculated Mr. Chattaway: and he mounted his horse and rode away.

So that after this colloquy, Chattaway was in a degree prepared to find unpleasant rumours had reached the Hold. When he entered he could not avoid seeing the shrinking, timid looks cast on him by his children; the haughty, questioning face of Miss Diana; the horror in that of Mrs. Chattaway. He took the same sullen, defiant tone with them that he had taken with Bowen, denying the thing by implication more than by direct assertions. He asked them all whether they had gone out of their minds, that they should listen to senseless tales; and threatened the most dire revenge against Rupert when he was found.

Thus matters went on for a few days. But the rumours did not die away: on the contrary, they gathered strength and plausibility. Things were in a most uncomfortable state at the Hold: the family were tortured by dread and doubt they dared not give utterance to, and strove to hide; the very servants went about with silent footsteps, casting covert glances at their master from dark corners, and avoiding a direct meeting with him. Mr. Chattaway could not help seeing all this, and it did not tend to give him equanimity.

The only thing that could clear up this miserable doubt was to find Rupert. But Rupert was not found. Friends and foes, police and public, put out their best endeavours to accomplish it; but no more trace could be discovered of Rupert than if he had never existed—or than if, as many openly said, he were buried in some quiet corner of Mr. Chattaway's grounds. To do Mr. Chattaway justice, he appeared the most anxious of any for Rupert's discovery: not with a view to clearing himself from suspicion; *that* he trampled under foot, as it were; but that Rupert might be brought to justice for burning the ricks.

Perhaps Mr. Chattaway's enemies may be pardoned for their doubts. It cannot be denied that there were apparent grounds for them: many a man has been officially accused of murder upon less. There was the well-known ill-feeling which had long existed on Mr. Chattaway's part towards Rupert; there was the dread of being displaced by him, which had latterly arisen through the visit of Mr. Daw; there was the sore feeling excited on both sides by the business of the rick-yard and the subsequent examination; there was the night contest spoken of by Jim Sanders, which Mr. Chattaway did not deny; there were the scratches and bruises visible on that gentleman's face; and there was the total disappearance of Rupert. People could remember the blank look which had passed over Mr. Chattaway's countenance when Rupert ran into the circle gathered round the pit at Blackstone. "He'd ha' bin glad that he were dead," they had murmured then, one to another. "And happen he have put him out o' the way," they murmured now.

Perhaps they did not all go so far as to suspect Mr. Chattaway of the crime of premeditated murder: he might have killed him wilfully in the passion of the moment; or killed him accidentally by an unlucky blow that had done its work more effectually than he had intended. The fruitless search was no barrier to these doubts; murdered men had been hidden away before, and would be again.

I have not yet mentioned the last point of suspicion, but it was one much dwelt upon—the late return of Mr. Chattaway to his home on the night in question. The servants had not failed to talk of this, and the enemies outside took it up and discussed it eagerly. It was most unusual for Mr. Chattaway to be away from home at night. Unsociable by nature, and a man whose company was not sought by his neighbours—for they disliked him—it was a rare thing for Mr. Chattaway to spend his evenings out. He attended evening parties now and then in the company of his wife and Miss Trevlyn, but not once a year was he invited out alone. His absence therefore on this night, coupled with his late entrance, close upon midnight, was the more remarkable. Where had he been until that hour? Everyone wondered: everyone asked it. Mr. Chattaway carelessly answered his wife and Miss Diana that he had been on business at Barbrook, but condescended to give no reply whatever to any other living mortal amongst the questioners.

As the days went on without news of Rupert, Mr. Chattaway expressed a conviction that he had made his way to Mr. Daw, and was being sheltered there. A most unsatisfactory conviction, if he really and genuinely believed it. With those two hatching plots against him, he could never know a moment's peace. He was most explosive against Rupert; at home and abroad he never ceased to utter threats of prosecution for the crime of which he had been guilty. He rode every other day to the station, worrying Bowen, asking whether any traces had turned up: urged—this was in the first day or so of the disappearance—that houses and cottages should be searched. Bowen quite laughed at the suggestion. If Mr. Chattaway had reason to suspect any particular house or cottage, they might perhaps go the length of getting a search warrant; but to enter dwellings indiscriminately would be an intolerable and unjustifiable procedure.

Mr. Chattaway was unable to say that he had especial cause to suspect any house or cottage: unless, he added in his temper, it might be Trevlyn Farm. Jim Sanders had, it appeared, hidden there in an outbuilding: why not Rupert Trevlyn? But Bowen saw and knew that Mr. Chattaway had only spoken in exasperation. Trevlyn Farm was not more likely to conceal Rupert Trevlyn than any other house of its standing—in fact less; for Mrs. Ryle would not have permitted it. Her dislike to any sort of underhand dealing was so great, that she would not have concealed Rupert, or countenanced his being concealed, had it been to save him from hanging. In that she resembled Miss Diana Trevlyn. Miss Diana would have spent her last shilling nobly to defend Rupert on his trial—had it come to a trial—but ignominiously conceal him from the reach of the law, that she would never have done. Chattaway's remark travelled to George Ryle: George happened to meet Bowen the same day, not an hour after, and spoke of it. He told Bowen that the bare idea of Rupert's being concealed on their premises was absurd, and added, on his word of honour, not only that he did not know where Rupert was, but where he was likely to be: the thing was to him a complete mystery. Bowen nodded. In Bowen's opinion the idea of his being concealed in any house was all moonshine.

The days went on and on, and it did appear very mysterious where Rupert could be, or what his fate. His clothes, his effects, remained unclaimed at Trevlyn Hold. When Mrs. Chattaway came unexpectedly upon anything that had belonged to him, she turned sick with the fears that darted across her heart. A faint hope arose within her at times that Rupert had gone, as Mr. Chattaway loudly, and perhaps others more secretly, surmised, to Mr. Daw in his far-off home, but it was rejected the next moment. She knew, none better, that Rupert had no means to take him there. Oh, how often did she wish, in her heart of hearts, that they had never usurped Trevlyn Hold! It seemed they were beginning to reap all the bitter fruits, which had been so long ripening.

But this supposition was soon to be set aside. Two letters arrived from Mr. Daw: one to Mr. Freeman, the other to Rupert himself; and they completely did away with the idea that Rupert Trevlyn had found his way to the Pyrenees.

It appeared that Rupert had written an account to Mr. Daw of these unhappy circumstances; his setting the rick on fire in his passion, and his arrest. He had written it on the evening of the day he was discharged from custody. And by the contents of his letter, it was evident that he then contemplated returning to the Hold.

"These letters from Mr. Daw settle the question: Rupert has not gone there," observed Mr. Freeman. "But they only make the mystery greater."

Yes, they did. And the news went forth to the neighbourhood that Rupert Trevlyn had written a letter subsequent to the examination at Barmester, wherein he stated that he was going straight home to the Hold. Gossip never loses in the carrying, you know.

Jim Sanders, who was discharged and at work again, became quite the lion of the day. He had never been made so much of in his life. Tea here, supper there, ale everywhere. Everyone was asking Jim the particulars of that later night, and Jim, nothing loth, gave them, with the addition of his own comments.

And the days went on, and the ferment and the doubts increased.

CHAPTER XLV
AN APPLICATION

The ferment increased. The arguments in the neighbourhood were worthy of being listened to, if only from a logical point of view. If Rupert Trevlyn had stated that he was going back to the Hold after the proceedings at Barmester; and if Rupert Trevlyn never reached the Hold, clearly Mr. Chattaway had killed and buried him. Absurd as the deduction may be from a dispassionate point of view, to those excited gentry it appeared not only a feasible but a certain conclusion. The thing could not rest; interviews were held with Mr. Peterby, who was supposed to be the only person able to take up the matter on the part of the missing and ill-used Rupert; and that gentleman bestirred himself to make secret inquiries.

One dark night, between eight and nine, the inmates of the lodge were disturbed by a loud imperative knocking at their door. Ann Canham—trying her poor eyes over some dark sewing by the light of the solitary candle—started from her chair, and remarked that her heart had leaped into her mouth.

Which may have been a reason, possibly, for standing still, face and hands uplifted in consternation, instead of answering the knock. It was repeated more imperatively.

Old Canham turned his head and looked at her, as he smoked his last evening pipe over the fire. "Thee must open it, Ann."

Seeing no help for it, she went meekly to the door, wringing her hands. What she feared was best known to herself; but in point of fact, since Bowen, the superintendent, had pounced upon her a few days before, as she was going past the police-station, handed her inside, and put her through sundry questions as we put a boy through his catechism, she had lived in a state of tremor. She may have concluded it was Bowen now, with the fellow handcuffs to those which had adorned Jim Sanders.

It proved to be Mr. Peterby. Ann looked surprised, but lost three parts of her fear. Dropping her humble curtsey, she was about to ask his pleasure, when he brushed past her without ceremony, and stepped into the kitchen.

"Shut the door," were his first words to her. "How are you, Canham?"

Mark had risen, and stood with doubtful gaze, wondering, no doubt, what the visit could mean. "I be but middlin', sir," he answered, putting his pipe in the corner of the hearth. "We ain't none of us too well, I reckon, with this uncertainty hanging over our minds, as to poor Master Rupert."

"It is the business I have come about. Sit down, Ann," Mr. Peterby added, settling himself on the bench opposite Mark. "I want to ask you a few questions."

"Yes, sir," she meekly answered. But her hands shook, and she nearly dropped the work she had taken up.

"There's nothing to be afraid of," cried Mr. Peterby, noticing the emotion. "I am not going to accuse you of putting him out of sight, as it seems busy tongues are accusing somebody else. On the night the encounter took place between Mr. Chattaway and Rupert Trevlyn, you were passing near the spot, I believe. You must tell me all you saw. First of all, as I am told, you encountered Rupert."

Ann Canham raised her shaking hand to her brow. Mr. Peterby had begun his questioning in a hard, matter-of-fact tone, as if he were examining a witness in court, and it did not tend to reassure her. Ann was often laughed at for her timidity. She gave him the account of her interview with Rupert as correctly as she could remember it.

"He said nothing of his intention of going off anywhere?" asked Mr. Peterby, when she had finished.

"Not a word, sir. He said he had nowhere to go to; if he went to the Hold, Mr. Chattaway might be for horsewhipping him again. He thought he should lie under the trees till morning."

"Did you leave him there?"

"I left him sitting on the stile, sir, eating the bread. He had complained of hunger, and I got him to take a part of a cake Mrs. Freeman had given me for my father."

"You told Bowen, the superintendent of the police-station, that you asked him to take refuge in the lodge for the night?"

"Yes, sir," after a slight pause. "Mr. Bowen put a heap of questions to me, and what with being confused, and the fright of his calling me into the place, I didn't well know what I said to him."

"But you did ask Rupert Trevlyn?"

"I asked him if he'd be pleased to take shelter in the lodge till the morning, as he seemed to have nowhere to go to. But he spoke out quite sharp, at my asking it, and said, did I think he wanted to get me and father into trouble with Mr. Chattaway? So I went away, leaving him there."

"Well, now, just tell me whom you met afterwards."

"I hadn't got above three-parts up the field, sir, when I met Mr. Chattaway. I stood off the narrow path to let him pass, and wished him good night, but he didn't answer me: he went on. Just as I came close to the road-stile, I see Jim Sanders coming over it, so I asked him where he had been, and how he had got back again, having heard he'd not been found all day, and he answered rather impertinently that he'd been up in the moon. The moon was uncommon bright that night, sir," she simply added.

"Was that all Jim Sanders said?"

"Yes, sir, every word. He went on down the path as if he was in a hurry."

"In the direction Mr. Chattaway had taken?"

"The very same. There is but that one path, sir."

"And that was the last you saw of them?"

Ann Canham stopped to snuff the candle before she answered. "That was all, sir. I was hastening to get back to father, knowing he'd be wanting me, for I was late. Mr. Bowen kep' on telling me it was strange I heard nothing of the encounter, but I never did. I must ha' been out of the field long before Mr. Chattaway could get up to Master Rupert."

"Pity but you had waited and gone back," observed Mr. Peterby, musingly. "It might have prevented what occurred."

"Pity, perhaps, but I had, sir. It never entered my head that anything bad would come of their meeting. Since, after I came to know what did happen, I wondered I had not thought of it. But if I had, sir, I shouldn't have dared go back after Mr. Chattaway. It wouldn't have been my place."

Mr. Peterby sat looking at Ann, as she imagined. In point of fact he was so buried in thought as to see nothing. He rose from the settle. "And this is all you know about it! Well, it amounts to nothing beyond establishing the fact that all three—Rupert Trevlyn, Mr. Chattaway, and the boy—were on the spot at that time. Good night, Canham. I hope your rheumatism will get easier."

Ann Canham opened the door, and wished him good night. When he was fairly gone she slipped the bolt, and stood with her back against it, to recover her equanimity.

"Father, my heart was in my mouth all the time he was here," she repeated. "I be all of a twitter."

"More stupid you!" was the sympathising answer of old Canham.

The public ferment, I say, did not lessen, and the matter was at length carried before the magistrates; so far as that the advice of one of them was asked by Mr. Peterby. It happened that Mr. Chattaway had gone this very day to Barmester. He was standing at the entrance to the inn-yard where he generally put up, when his solicitor, Flood, approached, evidently in a state of excitement.

"What a mercy I found you!" he exclaimed, quite out of breath. "Jackson told me you were in town. Come along!"

"Why, what's the matter?" asked Chattaway.

"Matter? There's matter enough. Peterby's before the magistrates at this very moment preferring a charge against you for having murdered Rupert Trevlyn. I got word of it in the oddest manner, and—"

"*What* do you say?" interrupted Chattaway, his face blazing, as he stood stock still, and refused to stir another step without an answer.

"Come along, I say. There's some application being made to the magistrates about you, and my advice is—Mr. Chattaway," added the lawyer, in a deeper, almost an agitated tone, as he abruptly broke off his words, "I assume that you are innocent of this. You *are*?"

"Before Heaven, I am innocent!" thundered Chattaway. "What do you mean, Flood?"

"Then make haste. My advice to you is, go right into the midst of it, and confront Peterby. Don't let the magistrates hear only one side of the question. Make your explanation and set these nasty rumours at rest. It is what you ought to have done at first."

Apparently eager as himself now, Mr. Chattaway strode along. They found on reaching the courts that some trifling cause was being heard by the magistrates, nothing at all connected with Mr. Chattaway. But the explanation was forthcoming, Mr. Peterby was in a private room with one of the Bench only—a Captain Mynn. With scant ceremony the interview was broken in upon by the intruders.

There was no formal complaint being made, no accusation lodged, or warrant applied for. Mr. Peterby, who was on terms of intimacy with Captain Mynn, was laying the case before him unofficially, and asking his advice as a friend. A short explanation on either side ensued, and Mr. Peterby turned to Mr. Chattaway.

"This has been forced upon me," he said. "For days and days past I have been urged to apply for a warrant against you, and have declined. But public opinion is becoming so urgent, that if I don't act it will be taken out of my hands, and given to those who have less scruple than I. Therefore I resolved to adopt a medium course; and came here asking Captain Mynn's opinion as a friend—not as a magistrate—whether I should have sufficient grounds for acting. For myself, I honestly confess I think them very slight;

and assure you, Mr. Chattaway, that I am no enemy of yours, although it may look like it at this moment."

"By whom have you been urged to this?" coldly asked Mr. Chattaway.

"By more than I should care to name: the public, to give them a collective term. But how you obtained cognisance of my being here, I can't make out," he added, turning to Mr. Flood. "Not a soul knew I was coming."

"As we have met here, we had better have it out," was Mr. Flood's indirect answer. "It is my advice to Mr. Chattaway, and he wishes it. If Captain Mynn hears your side unofficially he must, in justice, hear ours. That's fair, all the world over."

It was, doubtless, a very unusual, perhaps unorthodox, mode of proceeding; but things far more unorthodox than that are done in local courts every day. Captain Mynn knew all the doubts and rumours just as well as Mr. Peterby could state them, but he listened attentively, as in duty bound. Mr. Chattaway did not deny the encounter with Rupert: never had denied it. He acknowledged they were neither of them very cool; Rupert was the first to strike, and Rupert fell or was knocked down. Immediately upon that, he, Chattaway, heard a sound, went to see what it was, and found they had had an eavesdropper, who was then making off across the field, on the other side of the grove. Chattaway, angry at the fact, gave pursuit, in the hope of identifying the intruder (whom he had since discovered to be Jim Sanders), but was unable to catch him. When he got back to the spot, Rupert was gone.

"How long were you absent?" inquired Captain Mynn of Mr. Chattaway.

"About six or seven minutes, I think. I ran to the other end of the field, and looked into the lane, but the boy had escaped out of sight, and I walked back again. It would take about seven minutes; the field is large."

"And after that?"

"Finding, as I tell you, that Rupert had disappeared, I re-traversed the ground over the lower field, and went on to Barbrook, where I had business. I never saw Rupert Trevlyn after I left him on the ground. The inference, therefore—nay, the absolute certainty—is, that he got up and escaped."

A pause. "You did not reach home, I believe, until midnight, or thereabouts," remarked Captain Mynn. "Some doubts have been raised as to where you could have spent your time."

And this question led to the very core of the suspicion. Mr. Chattaway appeared to feel that it did, and hesitated. So far he had spoken freely and openly enough, not with the ungracious, sullen manner that generally characterised him, but he hesitated now.

"Strange to say," he resumed, "I could not account for the whole of my time that evening. That is, if I were asked for proof, I am not sure that it could be furnished. I was anxious to see Hurnall, the agent for the Boorfield mines, and that's where I went. My son had brought home news from Blackstone, that they were going to force me to make certain improvements in my pit, and I wanted to consult Hurnall about it. He is up to every trick and turn, and knows what they can compel an owner to do and what they can't. When I reached Hurnall's house, he was out; might return immediately, the servant said, or might not be home till late. She asked me if I would go in and wait; but I had no fancy for a close room, after being boxed up all day in the court *here,* and said I would walk about. I walked about for two mortal hours before Hurnall came; and then went indoors with him. That's the whole truth, I'll swear."

"Then I would have avowed it before, had I been you," cried Mr. Peterby. "It's your silence has done half the mischief, and given colouring to the rumours."

"Silence!" cried Mr. Chattaway, angrily. "When a man's accused of murder by a set of brainless idiots it is punishment he'd like to give them, not self-defence."

"Ah!" said the lawyer, "but we can't always do as we like; if we could, the world might be better worth living in."

Mr. Chattaway turned to the magistrate. "I have told you the whole truth, so far as I know it; and you may judge whether these unneighbourly reports have not merited all my contempt. You can question Hurnall, who will tell you where he met me, and how long I stayed with him. As to Rupert Trevlyn, I have no more idea where he is than Mr. Peterby himself has. He will turn up some time, there's not the least doubt about it; and I solemnly declare that I'll then bring him to justice, should it be ten years hence."

There was nothing more for Mr. Chattaway to wait for, and he went out with his solicitor. Mr. Peterby turned to Captain Mynn with a questioning glance.

The magistrate shook his head. "My opinion is that you cannot proceed with this, Mr. Peterby. Were you to bring the matter officially before the Bench, I for one would not entertain it; neither, I am sure, would my brother-magistrates. Mr. Chattaway is no favourite of ours, but he must receive justice. That there are suspicious points connected with the case, I can't deny; but every one may be explained away. If what he says be true, they are explained now."

"All but the two hours, when he says he was walking about, waiting for Hurnall."

"It may have been so. No; upon these very slight grounds, it is of no use to press for a warrant against Mr. Chattaway. The very enormity of the crime would almost be its answer. A man of position and property, a county magistrate, guilty of the crime of murder in these enlightened days! Nonsense, Peterby!"

And Mr. Peterby mentally echoed the words; and went forth prepared to echo them to those who had urged him to make the charge.

CHAPTER XLVI
A FRIGHT FOR ANN CANHAM

So the magistrates declined to interfere, and Mr. Chattaway went about a free man. But not untainted; for the neighbourhood was still free in its comments, and openly accused him of having made away with Rupert. Mr. Chattaway had his retaliation; he offered a reward for the recovery of the incendiary, Rupert Trevlyn, and the walls for miles round were placarded with handbills. Urged by him, the police recommenced their search, and Mr. Chattaway actually talked of sending for an experienced detective. One thing was indisputable—if Rupert were in life he must keep from the neighbourhood of Trevlyn Hold. Nothing could save him from the law, if taken the second time. Jim Sanders would not be kidnapped again; he had already testified to it officially; and Mr. Chattaway thirsted for vengeance.

Take it for all in all, it was breaking the heart of Mrs. Chattaway. Looked at in any light, it was bad enough. The fear touching her husband, not the less startling from its improbability, was over, for he had succeeded in convincing her that so far he was innocent; but her fears for Rupert kept her in a constant state of terror. Miss Diana publicly condemned Rupert. This hiding from justice (if he was hiding) she regarded as only a degree less reprehensible than the crime itself; as did Mrs. Ryle; and had Miss Diana met Rupert returning some fine day, she would have laid her hand upon him as effectually as Mr. Dumps himself, and said, "You shall not escape again." Do not mistake Miss Diana; it would not have pleased her to see Rupert standing at the bar of justice to be judged by the laws of his country. She would have taken Rupert home to the Hold, and said to Chattaway, "Here he is, but you must and shall forgive him: you must forgive him, because he is a Trevlyn; and a Trevlyn cannot be disgraced." Miss Diana had full confidence in her own power to command this. Others wisely doubted whether any amount of interference on any part would now avail with Mr. Chattaway. His wife felt that it would not. She felt that were poor Rupert to venture home, even twelve months hence, trusting that time and mercy had effected his pardon, he would be sacrificed; between Miss Diana's and Mr. Chattaway's opposing policies, he would inevitably be sacrificed. Altogether, Mrs. Chattaway's life was more painful now Rupert had gone than it had been when he was at the Hold.

Cris was against Rupert; Octave was bitterly against him; Maude went about the house with a white face and beating heart, health and spirits giving way under the tension. Suspense is, of all evils, the worst to bear: and they who loved Rupert, Maude and her Aunt Edith, were hourly victims to it. The bow was always strung. On the one hand was the latent doubt that he had come to some violent end that night, in spite of Mr. Chattaway's denial; on the other hand, the lively dread that he was concealing himself, and might be discovered by the police every new day the sun rose. They had speculated so much upon where he could be, that the ever-recurring thought now brought only its heart-sickness; and Maude had the additional pain of hearing petty shafts launched at her because she was his sister. Mrs. Chattaway prayed upon her bended knees that, hard to be borne as the suspense was, Rupert might not return until time should have softened the heart of Mr. Chattaway, and the grievous charge be done away with for want of a prosecutor.

Nora was in the midst of bustle at Trevlyn Farm. And Nora was also in a temper. It was the annual custom there, when the busy time of harvest was over, to institute a general house-renovating: summer curtains were taken down, winter ones were put up, carpets were shaken, floors and paint scoured; and the place, in short, to use an ordinary expression, was turned inside out.

There was more than usual to be done this year: for mendings and alterations had to be made in sundry curtains, and the upholstering woman, named Brown, had been at Trevlyn Farm the last day or two, getting forward with her work. Nora's *ruse* in the court at Barmester, to wile Farmer Apperley to a private conference, had really some point in it, for negotiations were going on with that industrious member of the upholstering society through Mrs. Apperley, who had recommended her.

Mrs. Brown sat in the centre of a pile of curtains, steadily plying her needle: the finishing stitches were being put to the work; at least, they would be before night closed in. Mrs. Brown, a sallow woman with a chronic cold in her head, preferred to work in outdoor costume; a black poke bonnet and faded woollen shawl crossed over her shoulders. Nora stood by her in a very angry mood, her arms folded, just as though she had nothing to do: a circumstance to be recorded in these cleaning times.

For Nora never let the grass grow under her feet, or under any one else's feet, when there was work in hand. By dint of beginning hours before daylight, and keeping at it hours after nightfall, she succeeded in getting it all over in one day. Herself, Nanny, and Ann Canham put their best energies into it, one or two of the men were set to rub up the mahogany furniture, and Mrs. Ryle had almost entirely to dispense with being waited upon. And Nora's present anger arose from the fact that Ann Canham, by some extraordinary mischance, had not made her appearance.

It was bringing things almost to a standstill, as Nora complained to Mrs. Brown. The two cleaners were Nanny and Ann Canham. Nanny was doing her part, but what was to become of the other part? And where was Ann Canham? Nora kept her eyes turned to the window, as she talked and grumbled, watching for the return of Jim Sanders, whom she had despatched to see after Ann.

Presently she saw him approaching, went to the door and threw it open long before the lad reached it. "She can't come," he called out at length.

"Not come!" echoed Nora, in wrathful consternation, looking as if she felt inclined to beat Jim for bringing the message. "What on earth does she mean by that?"

"She said her father was ill, and she couldn't leave him," returned Jim.

Nora could scarcely speak from indignation. Old Canham, as was known to the neighbourhood, had been ailing for years, and it had never kept Ann at home before. "I don't believe it," said she, in her perplexity.

"I don't think I do, neither," returned Jim. "I'm a'most sure old Canham was right afore the fire, smoking his pipe as usual. She put the door to behind her, all in a hurry, while she talked to me, but not afore I see old Canham there. I be next to certain of it."

Nora could not understand the state of affairs. Ann Canham, humble, industrious, grateful for any day's work offered to her, had never failed to come, when engaged, in all Barbrook's experience. What was to be done? The morrow was Saturday, and to have the cleaning extended to that day would have upset the farm's regularity and Nora's temper for a month.

Nora took a sudden resolution. She put on her bonnet and shawl and set off for the lodge, determined to bring Ann Canham back willing or unwilling, or know the reason why. This *contretemps* would be quite a life-long memory for Nora.

Without any superfluous knocking, Nora turned the handle of the door when she reached the lodge. But the door was locked. "What can that be for?" ejaculated Nora—for she had never known the lodge locked in the day-time. "She expects I shall come after her, and thinks she'll keep me out!"

Without an instant's delay, Nora's face was at the window, to reconnoitre the interior. She saw the smock-frock of old Mark disappearing through the opposite door as quickly as was consistent with his rheumatism. Nora rattled the handle of the door with one hand, and knocked sharply on its panel with the other. Ann opened it.

"Now, Ann Canham, what's the meaning of this?" she began, pushing past Ann, who stood in the way, almost as if she would have kept her out.

"I beg a humble pardon, ma'am, a hundred times," was the low, deprecating answer. "I'd do anything rather than disappoint you—such a thing has never happened to me yet—but I'm obliged. Father's too poorly for me to leave him."

Nora surveyed her critically. The woman was evidently in a state of discomfort, if not terror. She trembled visibly, and her lips were white.

"I got a boy to run down to Mrs. Sanders's this morning at daylight, and ask her to take my place," resumed Ann Canham. "Until Jim came up here a short while ago, I never thought but she had went."

"What's the reason *you* can't come?" demanded Nora, uncompromisingly stern.

"I'd come but for father."

"You needn't peril your soul with deliberate untruths," interrupted angry Nora. "There's nothing the matter with your father; nothing that need hinder your coming out. If he's well enough to be in the house-place, smoking his pipe, he's well enough to be left. He *was* smoking. And what's that?"—pointing to the pipe her eyes had detected in the corner of the hearth.

Ann Canham stood the picture of helplessness under the reproach. She stammered out that she "daredn't leave him: he wasn't himself to-day."

"He was sufficiently himself to make off on seeing me," said angry Nora. "What's to become of my cleaning? Who's to do it if you don't? I insist upon your coming, Ann Canham."

It appeared almost beyond Ann Canham's courage to bring out a second refusal, and she burst into tears. She had never failed before, and hoped, if forgiven this time, never to fail again: but to leave her father that day was impossible.

And Nora had to make the best of the refusal. She went away searching the woman's motive, and came to the conclusion that she must have some sewing in hand she was compelled to finish: that Mark's illness was detaining her, she did not believe. Still, she could not comprehend it. Ann had always been so eager to oblige, so simple and straightforward. Had sewing really detained her, she would have brought it out to Nora; would have told the truth, not making her father's health the excuse. Nora was puzzled, and that was a thing she hated. Ruminating upon all this as she walked along, she met Mrs. Chattaway. Nora, who, when suffering under a grievance, must dilate upon it to everyone, favoured Mrs. Chattaway with an account of Ann Canham's extraordinary conduct and ingratitude.

"Rely upon it, her father is ill," answered Mrs. Chattaway. "I will tell you why I think so, Nora. Yesterday I was at Barmester with my sister, and as we pulled up at the chemist's where I had business, Ann Canham came out with a bottle of medicine in her hand. I asked her who was ill, and she said it was her father. I remarked to the chemist afterwards that I supposed Mark Canham had a fresh attack of rheumatism, but he replied that it was fever."

"Fever!" echoed Nora.

"I exclaimed as you do: but the chemist persisted that Mark must be suffering from a species of low fever. As we returned, my sister stopped the pony carriage at the lodge, and Ann came out to us. She explained it differently from the chemist. What she had meant to imply when she went for the medicine was, that her father was feverish—but he was better then, she said. Altogether, I suppose he is worse than usual, and she is afraid to leave him to-day."

"Well," said Nora, "all I can say is that I saw old Canham stealing out of the room when I knocked at it, just as though he did not want to be seen. He was smoking, too. I can't make it out."

Mrs. Chattaway was neither so speculative nor so curious as Nora; perhaps not so keen: she viewed it as nothing extraordinary that Mark Canham should be rather worse than usual, or that his daughter should decline to leave him.

Much later in the day—in fact, when the afternoon was passing—Ann Canham, with a wild look in her face, turned out of the lodge and took the road towards Trevlyn Farm. Not openly, as people do who have nothing to fear, but in a timorous, uncertain, hesitating manner. Plunging into the fields when she was nearing the farm, she stole along under cover of the hedge, until she reached the one which skirted the fold-yard. Cautiously raising her head to see what might be on the other side, it almost came into contact with another head, raised to see anything that might be on this—the face of Policeman Dumps.

Ann Canham uttered a shrill scream, and flew away as fast as her legs could carry her. Perhaps of all living beings, Mr. Dumps was about the last she would wish to encounter just then. That gentleman made his way to a side-gate, and called after her.

"What be you afeard of, Ann Canham? Did you think I was a mad bull looking over at you?"

It occurred to Ann Canham that to start away in that extraordinary fashion could only be regarded as consistent with a guilty conscience, and the policeman might set himself to discover her motive—as it lay in the nature of a policeman to do. That or some other thought made her turn slowly back again, and confront Mr. Dumps.

"What was you afeard of?" he repeated.

"Of nothing in particular, please, sir," she answered. "It was the suddenness like of seeing a face that startled me."

Mr. Dumps thought she looked curiously startled still. But that complacent official, accustomed to strike terror to the hearts of boys and other scapegraces, did not give it a second thought. "Were you looking for anyone?" he asked, simply as an idle question.

"No, sir. I just put my head over the hedge without meaning. I didn't want nothing."

Mr. Dumps loftily turned on his heel without condescending so much as a "good afternoon." Ann Canham pursued her way along the hedge which skirted the fold-yard. Any one observing her closely might have detected indications of fear about her still. In a cautious and timid manner, she at length turned her head, to obtain a glimpse of Mr. Dumps's movements.

Dumps had turned into the road, and was pursuing his way slowly down it. Every step carried him farther from her; and when he was fairly out of sight, her sigh of relief was long and deep.

But of course there was no certainty that he would not return. Possibly that insecurity caused Ann to take stolen looks into the fold-yard, and then dive under the hedge, as if she had been at some forbidden play. But Dumps did not return; and yet she continued her game.

A full hour had she been at it: and by her countenance, and the occasional almost despairing movement of her hands, it might be inferred that she was growing sadly anxious and weary: when Jim Sanders emerged from one of the out-buildings at the upper end of the fold-yard, and began to make for the other end. To do this he had to pass within a few yards of the hedge where the by-play was going on; and somewhat to his surprise he heard himself called to in hushed tones. Casting his eyes to the spot whence the voice proceeded, he saw the care-worn brow and weak eyes of Ann Canham above the hedge. She beckoned to him mysteriously, and then all signs of her disappeared.

"If ever I see the like o' that!" soliloquised Jim. "What's up with Ann Canham?" He approached the hedge, and bawled out to know what she wanted.

"Hush—sh—sh—sh!" came the warning from the other side. "Come here, Jim."

Considerably astonished, thinking perhaps Ann Canham had a litter of puppies to show him—for, if Jim had a weakness for anything on earth, it was for those charming specimens of the animal world—he made his way through the gate. Ann had no puppies; nothing but a small note in her hand wafered and pressed with a thimble.

"Is the master anywhere about, Jim?"

"He's just gone into the barn now. The men be thrashing."

Ann paused a moment. Jim stared at her.

"Could you just do me a service, Jim?"

Jim, good-natured at all times, replied that he supposed he could if he tried. But he stared, still puzzled by this extraordinary behaviour on the part of quiet Ann Canham.

"I want this bit of a letter given to him," she said, pointing to what she held. "I want it given to him when he's by himself, so that it don't get seen. Could you manage it, Jim?"

"I dare say I could," replied Jim. "What is the letter? What's inside it?"

"It concerns Mr. Ryle," said Ann, after a perceptible hesitation. "Jim, if you'll do this faithful, I won't forget it. Watch your opportunity; and keep the letter inside your smock-frock, for fear anybody should see it."

"I'll do it," said Jim. He took the note from her, put it in his trousers pocket, and went back towards the barn whistling. Ann turned homewards, flying over the ground as if she were running a race.

Jim had not to wait for an opportunity. He met his master coming out of the barn. The doorway was dark; the thrashing men were at the upper end of the barn, and no eyes were near. Jim could not help some of the mystery which had appeared in Ann Canham's manner extending to his own.

"What's this?" asked George.

"Ann Canham brought it, sir. She was hiding t'other side the hedge and called to me, and telled me to be sure give it when nobody was by."

George took the missive to the door and looked at it. A piece of white paper, which had apparently served to wrap up tea or something of that sort, awkwardly folded and wafered. No direction.

He opened it; and saw a few words in a sprawling hand:

"Don't betray me, George. Come to me in secret as soon as you can. I think I am dying."

And in spite of its being without signature; in spite of the scrawled characters, and blotted words, George Ryle recognised the handwriting of Rupert Trevlyn.

CHAPTER XLVII
SURPRISE

On the hard flock bed in the upper back room at the lodge, he lay. As George Ryle stood there bending over him, he could have touched each of the surrounding walls. The remark of Jim Sanders that Ann Canham had brought the note, guided George naturally to the lodge; otherwise he would not have known where to look for him. One single question to old Canham as he entered—"Is he here?"—and George bounded up the stairs.

Ann Canham, who was standing over the bed—her head just escaping the low ceiling—turned to George: trouble and pain on her countenance as she spoke.

"He is in delirium now, sir. I was afeared he would be."

George Ryle was too astonished to make any reply. Never had he cast a shadow of suspicion to Rupert's being concealed at the lodge. "Has he been here long?" he whispered.

"All along, sir, since the night he was missed," was the reply. "After I had got home that night, and was telling father about Master Rupert's having took the half-loaf in his hunger, he come knocking at the door to be let in. Chattaway and him had met and quarrelled, and he was knocked down, his shoulder was hurt, and he felt tired and sick; and he said he'd stop with us till morning, and be away afore daylight, so that we should not get into trouble for sheltering him. He got me to lend him my pen and ink, and wrote a letter to that there foreign gentleman, Mr. Daw. After that, with a dreadful deal of pressing, sir, I got him to come up to bed here, and I lay on the settle downstairs for the night. Before daylight I was up, and had the fired lighted, and the kettle on, to make him a cup o' tea before starting, but he did not come down. I came up here and found him ill. His shoulder was stiff and painful, he was bruised and sore all over, and thought he couldn't get out o' bed. Well, sir, he stopped, and have been here ever since, getting worse, and me just frightened out of my life, for fear he should be found by Mr. Chattaway or the police, and took off to prison. I was sick for the whole day after, sir, that time Mr. Bowen called me into his station-house and set on to question me."

George was looking at Rupert. There could not be a doubt that he was in a state of partial delirium. George feared there could not be a doubt that he was in danger. The bed was low and narrow, evidently hard; the bolster small and thin. Rupert's head lay on it quietly enough; his hair, which had grown long since his confinement, fell around him in wavy masses; his cheeks wore the hectic of fever, his blue eyes were unnaturally bright. There was no speculation in those eyes. They were partially closed, and though at the entrance of George they were turned to him, there was no recognition in them. His arms were flung outside the bed, the wristbands pushed up as if from heat.

"I have put him on a shirt o' father's, sir, when his have wanted washing," explained Ann Canham, to whom it was natural to relate minute details.

"How long has he been without consciousness?" inquired George.

"Just for the last hour, sir. He wrote the letter I brought to you, and when I come back he was like this. Maybe he'll come to himself again presently; he's been as bad as this at times in the last day or two. I'm so afeard of its going on to brain-fever or some other fever. If he should get raving, we could never keep his being here a secret; he'd be heard outside."

"He ought to have had a doctor before this."

"But how is one to be got here?" debated Ann Canham. "Once a doctor knew where Mr. Rupert was, he might betray it—there's the reward, you know, sir. And how could we get a doctor in without its being known at the Hold? What mightn't Chattaway suspect?"

George remained silent, revolving the matter. There were difficulties undoubtedly in the way.

"Nobody knows the trouble I've been in, sir, especially since he grew worse. At first, he just lay here quiet, more as if glad of the rest, and my chief care was to keep folks as far as I could out o' the lodge, bathe his shoulder, and bring him up a share of our poor meals. But since the fever came upon him, I've been half dazed, wondering what I ought to do. There were two people I thought I might speak to—you, sir, and Madam. But Mr. Rupert was against it, and father was dead against it. They were afraid, you see, that if only one was told, it might come to be known he was here. Father's old now, and helpless; he couldn't do a stroke towards getting his own living. If I be out before daylight at any of my places, it's as much as he can do to open the gate and fasten it back: and he knows Mr. Chattaway would turn us right off the estate if it come to be known we had sheltered Mr.

Rupert. But yesterday Mr. Rupert found he was getting worse and worse, and I said to father what would become of us if he should die? And they both said that you should be told to-day if he was no better. We did think him a trifle better this morning, but later the fever came on again, and Mr. Rupert himself said he'd write you a word, and I found a bit o' paper and brought him the big Bible, and held it while he wrote the letter on it."

She ceased. George, as before, was looking at Rupert. It seemed to Ann Canham that he could not gaze sufficiently, but in truth he was lost in thought; fairly puzzled with the difficulties encompassing the case.

"Is it anything more than low fever?" he asked.

"I don't think it is, sir, yet. But it may go on to more, you know."

George did know. He knew that assistance was necessary in more ways than one, if worse was to be avoided. Medical attendance, a more airy room, generous nourishment; and how was even one of them to be accomplished, let alone all? The close closet—it could scarcely be called more—had no chimney in it; air and light could come in only through a small pane ingeniously made to open in the roof. The narrow bed and one chair occupied almost all the space, leaving very little for George and Ann Canham as they stood. George, coming in from the fresh air, felt half-stifled with the closeness of the room: and this must be dangerous for the invalid. It is a mercy that these inconveniences are soothed to those who have to endure them—as most inconveniences and trials are in life. To an outsider they appear unbearable, but to the sufferers they are tempered. George Ryle felt as if a day in that atmosphere would half kill him; but Rupert, lying there always, was sensible of no discomfort. It was not, however, the less injurious; and it appeared that there was no remedy; could be no removal.

"What have you given him?" inquired George.

"I have made him some herb tea, sir, but it didn't seem to do him good, and then I went over to Barmester and got a bottle o' physic. I had to say it was for father, and the druggist told me I ought to call in a doctor, when I described the illness. Coming out of the shop there was Miss Diana's pony-carriage at the door, and Madam met me and asked who the physic was for: I never was so took aback. But the physic didn't seem to do him good neither."

"I meant as to food," returned George.

"Ah! sir—what could I give him but our poor fare? milk porridge and such like. I went up to the Hold one day and begged a basin o' curds-and-whey, and he eat it all and drank up the whey quite greedy; but I didn't dare go again, for fear of their suspecting something. It's meat and wine he ought to have had from the first, sir, but we can't get such things as that. Why, sir, I shouldn't dare be seen cooking a bit o' meat: it would set Mr. Chattaway wondering at once. What's to be done?"

What, indeed? There was the question. Idea after idea shot through George Ryle's brain; wild fancies, because impossible to be acted upon. It might be dangerous to call in a doctor. Allowing that the man of medicine proved true and kept the secret, the very fact of his attendance would cause a stir at the Hold. Miss Diana would come down, questioning old Canham; and would inevitably find that he was *not* ill enough to need a doctor. A doctor might venture there once: but regularly? George did not see the way by any means clear.

But Rupert must not be left to die. George took up his delicate hand—Rupert's hands had always been delicate—and held it as he spoke to him. It was hot; fevered; the dry lips were parched; the hectic cheeks, the white brow, all burning with fever. "Don't you know me, Rupert?" he bent lower to ask.

The words were so far heard that Rupert moved his head on the bolster; perhaps the familiar name struck some chord in his memory; but there was no recognition, and he began to twitch at the bed-clothes with one of his hands.

George turned away. He went down the ladder of a staircase, feeling that little time was to be lost. Old Canham stood in his tottering fashion, leaning upon his crutch, watching the descent.

"What do you think of him, Mr. George?"

"I hardly know what to think, Mark. Or rather, I know what to think, but I don't know what to do. A doctor must be got here; and without loss of time."

Old Canham lifted his hands with a gesture of despair. "Once the secret is give over to a doctor, sir, there's no telling where it'll travel, or what'll be the consequence to us all."

"I think King would be true," said George. "Nay, I feel sure he would be. The worst is, he's simple-minded, and might betray it through sheer inadvertency. I would a great deal rather bring Mr. Benage to him; I *know* we might rely on Benage, and he is more skilful than King; but it is not practicable. To see the renowned Barmester doctor in attendance on you might create greater commotion at the Hold than would be desirable. No, it must be King."

"Sir, couldn't you go to one o' the gentlemen yourself and describe what's the matter with Master Rupert. You needn't say who's ill."

George shook his head. "It would not do, Mark; the responsibility is too great. Were anything to happen to Rupert—and I believe he is in danger—you and I should blame ourselves for not having called in advice at all risks. I shall get King here somehow."

He went out as he spoke, partly perhaps to avoid further opposition to what he felt *must* be done. Yet he did not see the surrounding difficulties the less, and halted in thought outside the lodge door.

At that moment, Maude Trevlyn came into view, walking slowly down the avenue. George advanced to meet her, and could not help noticing her listless step, her pale, weary face.

"Maude, what is the trouble now?"

That she had been grieving, and recently, her eyes betrayed. Struggling for a brief moment with her feelings, she gave way to a burst of tears.

George drew her into the trees. "Maude, Maude, if you go on like this you will be ill. What is it?"

"This suspense!—this agony!" she breathed. "Every day, almost every hour, something or other occurs to renew the trouble. If it could only end! I cannot bear it much longer. I feel as if I must go off to the ends of the earth in search of him. If I only knew he was living, it would be something."

George took rapid counsel with himself. Surely Maude would be safe; surely it would be a charity, nay, a duty, to tell her! He drew her hand in his, and bent his face near to hers.

"Maude! what will you give me for news I have heard? I can give you tidings of Rupert. He is not dead; not even very far away!"

For an instant her heart stood still. But George glanced round as with fear, and his tones were sad.

"He is taken!" she exclaimed, her pulses bounding on.

"No. But care must be observed if we would prevent it. In that sense, he is at liberty. But it is not all sunshine, Maude; he is very ill."

"Where is he?" she gasped.

"Will you compose yourself if I take you to him? But we have need of great caution; we must make sure no prying eyes are spying at us."

Her very agitation proved how great had been the strain upon her nervous system; for a few minutes he thought she would faint, as she stood leaning against the tree. "Only take me to him, George," she murmured. "I will bless you forever."

Into the lodge and up old Canham's narrow staircase he led her. She entered the room timidly, not with the eager bound of hope, but with slow and hesitating steps, almost as she had once entered into the presence of the dead, that long past night at Trevlyn Farm.

He lay as he had lain when George went out: the eyes fixed, the head beginning to turn restlessly, one hand picking at the coarse brown sheet. "Come in, Maude; there is nothing to fear; but he will not know you."

She went in and stood for a moment gazing at him who lay there, as though it required time to take in the scene; then she fell on her knees in a strange burst, half joy, half grief, and kissed his hands and fevered lips.

"Oh, Rupert, Rupert! My brother Rupert!"

CHAPTER XLVIII
DANGER

The residence of Mr. King, the surgeon, was situated on the road to Barbrook, not far from the parsonage: a small, square, red-brick house, two storeys high, with a great bronze knocker on the particularly narrow and modest door. If you wanted to enter, you could either raise this knocker, which would most likely bring forth Mr. King himself; or, ignoring ceremony, turn the handle and walk in of your own accord, as George Ryle did, and admitted himself into the narrow passage. On the right was the parlour, quite a fashionable room, with a tiger-skin stretched out by way of hearth-rug; on the left a small apartment fitted up with bottles and pill-boxes, where Mr. King saw his patients. One sat there as George Ryle entered, and the surgeon turned round, as he poured some liquid from what looked like a jelly-glass, into a green bottle.

Now, of all the disagreeable *contretemps* that could have occurred, to meet that particular patient was about the worst. Ann Canham had not been more confounded at the sight of Policeman Dumps's head over the hedge, than George was at Policeman Dumps himself—for it was no other than that troublesome officer who sat in the patient's chair, the late afternoon's sun streaming on his head. George's active mind hit on a ready excuse for his own visit.

"Is my mother's medicine ready, Mr. King?"

"The medicine ready! Why, I sent it three good hours ago!"

"Did you? I understood them to say—But there's no harm done; I was coming down this way. A nice warm afternoon!" he exclaimed, throwing himself into a chair as if he would take a little rest. "Are you having a tooth drawn, Dumps?"

"No, sir, but I've got the face-ache awful," was Dumps's reply, who was holding a handkerchief to his right cheek. "It's what they call tic-douloureux, I fancy, for it comes on by fits and starts. I'm out of sorts altogether, and thought I'd ask Doctor King to make me up a bottle of physic."

So the physic was for Dumps. Mr. King seemed a long time over it, measuring this liquid, measuring that, shaking it all up together, and gossiping the while. George, in his impatience, thought it would never come to an end. Dumps seemed to be in no hurry to depart, Mr. King in no hurry to dismiss him. They talked over half the news of the parish. They spoke of Rupert Trevlyn and his prolonged absence, and Mr. Dumps gave it as his opinion that "if he wasn't in hiding somewhere, he was gone for good." Whether Mr. Dumps meant gone to some foreign terrestrial country, or into a celestial, he did not explain.

Utterly out of patience he rose and left the room, standing outside against the door-post, as if he would watch the passers-by. Perhaps the movement imparted an impetus to Mr. Dumps, for he also rose and took his bottle of medicine from the hands of the surgeon. But he lingered yet: and George thought he never would come forth.

That desirable consummation arrived at last. The man departed, and paced away on his beat with his official tread. George returned indoors.

"I fancied you were waiting to see me," observed Mr. King. "Is anything the matter?"

"Not with me. I want to put you upon your honour, doctor," continued George, a momentary smile crossing his lips.

"To put me upon my honour!" echoed the surgeon, staring at George.

"I wish to let you into a secret: but you must give me your word of honour that you will be a true man, and not betray it. In short, I want to enlist your sympathies, your kindly nature, heartily in the cause."

"I suppose some of the poor have got into trouble?" cried Mr. King, not very well knowing what to make of the words.

"No," said George. "Let me put a case to you. One under the ban of the law and his fellow-men, whom a word could betray to years of punishment—lies in sore need of medical skill; if he cannot obtain it he may soon die. Will you be a good Samaritan, and give it; and faithfully keep the secret?"

Mr. King regarded George attentively, slowly rubbing his bald head: he was a man of six-and-sixty now. "Are you speaking of Rupert Trevlyn?" he asked.

George paused, perhaps rather taken back; but the surgeon's face was kindly, its expression benevolent. "What if I were? Would you be true to *him*?"

"Yes, I would: and I am surprised that you thought it necessary to ask. Were the greatest criminal on earth lying in secret, and wanting my aid, I would give it and be silent. I go as a healing man; not in the name of the law. Were a doctor taken to a patient under such circumstances, to betray trust, he would violate his duty. Medical men are not informers."

"I felt we might trust you," said George. "It is Rupert Trevlyn. He took refuge that night at old Canham's, it seems, and has been ill ever since, growing worse and worse. But they fear danger now, and thought fit this afternoon to send for me. Rupert scrawled a few lines himself, but before I could get there he was delirious."

"Is it fever?"

"Low fever, Ann Canham says. It may go on to worse, you know, doctor."

Mr. King nodded his head. "Where can they have concealed him at Canham's?"

"Upstairs in a bed-closet. The most stifling hole you can imagine! I felt ill as I stood there. It is a perplexing affair altogether. The place itself is enough to kill any one in a fever, and there's no chance of removing him from it; hardly a chance of getting you in to see him: it must be accomplished in the most cautious manner. Were Chattaway to see you entering, who knows what it might lead to? If he should, by ill luck, see you," added George, after a pause, "your visit is to old Canham, remember."

Mr. King gave a short, emphatic nod; his frequent substitute for an answer. "Rupert Trevlyn at Canham's!" he exclaimed. "Well, you have surprised me!"

"I cannot tell you how surprised I was," returned George. "But we had better be going; I fear he is in danger."

"Ay. Delirious, you say?"

"I think so. He was quiet, but evidently did not know me. He did not know Maude. I met her as I was leaving the lodge, and thought it only kind to tell her of the discovery. It has been an anxious time for her."

"There's another it's an anxious time for; and that's Madam Chattaway," remarked the surgeon. "I was called in to her a few days ago. But I can do nothing; the malady is on the mind. Now I am ready."

He had been putting one or two papers into his pocket, probably containing some cooling powder or other remedy for Rupert. George walked with him; he wished to go in with him if it could be managed, anxious to hear his opinion. They pursued their way unmolested, meeting no one of more consequence than Mr. Dumps, who appeared to be occupied in nursing his cheek.

"So far so good," cried George, as they came in sight of the lodge. "But now for the tug of war; my walking with you is nothing; but to be seen entering the lodge with you might be a great deal. There seems no one about."

Ah! unlucky chance! By some untoward fatality the master of Trevlyn Hold emerged in sight, coming quickly down the avenue, at the moment Mr. King had his feet on the lodge steps to enter. George suppressed a groan of irritation.

"There's no help for it; you must have your wits about you," he whispered. "I shall go straight on as if I had come to pay a visit to the Hold."

Mr. King was not perhaps the best of men to "have his wits about him" on a sudden emergency, and almost as the last word left George's lips, Mr. Chattaway was upon them.

"Good afternoon, Mr. Chattaway," said George. "Is Cris at home?"

George continued his way as he spoke, brushing past Mr. Chattaway. You know what a very coward is self-consciousness. The presence of Chattaway at that ill-omened moment set them all inwardly quaking. George, the surgeon, old Canham sitting inside, and Ann peeping from the window, felt one and all as if Chattaway must divine some part of the great secret locked within their breasts.

"Cris? I don't think Cris is at home," called out Chattaway. "He went out after dinner."

"I am going to see," replied George, looking back.

The little delay had given the doctor time to collect himself, and he strove to look and speak as much at ease as possible. He stood on the lodge step, waiting to greet Mr. Chattaway. It would never do to make believe he was not going into the lodge, as George did, for Mr. Chattaway had seen him step up to it.

"How d'ye do, Mr. Chattaway? Fine weather this!"

"We shall have a change before long; the glass is shifting. Anyone ill here?" continued Chattaway.

"Not they, I hope!" returned the surgeon with a laugh. "I give old Canham a look in now and then, when I am passing and can spare the time, just for a dish of gossip and to ask after his rheumatism. I suppose you thought I had quite forgotten you," he added, turning to the old man, who had risen and stood leaning on his crutch, looking, if Mr. Chattaway could but have understood it, half frightened to death. "It's a long time since I was here, Mark."

He sat down on the settle as he spoke, as if to intimate that he intended to take a dish of gossip then. Chattaway—ah! can he suspect? thought old Mark as he entered the lodge; a thing he did not do once in a year. Conscience does make cowards of us all—and it need not be altogether a guilty conscience to do this—and it was rendering Ann Canham as one paralysed. She would have given the whole world to leave the room, go up to Rupert, and guard as far as possible against noise; but she feared to excite suspicion. Foolish fears! Had Rupert not been there, Ann Canham would have passed in and out of the room twenty times without thinking of Mr. Chattaway.

"Madam Chattaway said you were ill, I remember," said he to Mark Canham. "Fever, I understood. She said something about seeing your fever mixture at the chemist's at Barmester."

Ann Canham turned hot and cold. She did not dare to even glance at her father, still less prompt him; but it so happened that, willing to spare him unnecessary worry, she had not mentioned the little episode of meeting Mrs. Chattaway at Barmester. Old Mark was cautious, however.

"Yes, Squire. I've had a deal o' fever lately, on and off. Perhaps Doctor King could give me some'at better for't than them druggists gives."

"Perhaps I can," said Mr. King. "I'll have a talk with you presently. How is Madam to-day, Mr. Chattaway?"

"As well as usual, except in the matter of grumbling," was the ungracious answer. And the master of the Hold, perhaps not finding it particularly lively there, went out as he delivered it, giving a short adieu to Mr. King.

Meanwhile, George Ryle reached the Hold. Maude saw his approach from the drawing-room window, and came to the hall-door. "I want to speak to you," she whispered.

He followed her into the room; there was no one in it. Maude closed the door, and spoke in a gentle whisper.

"May I tell Aunt Edith?"

George looked dubious. "That is a serious question, Maude."

"It would give her renewed life," returned Maude, her tone intensely earnest. "George, if this suspense is to continue, she will sink under it. It was very, very bad for me to bear, and I am young and strong. I fear, too, that my aunt gets the dreadful doubt upon her now and then whether—whether—what was said of Mr. Chattaway is not true; and Rupert was killed that night. Oh, let me tell her!"

"Maude, I should be glad for her to know it. My only doubt is, whether she would *dare* keep the secret from her husband, Rupert being actually within the precincts of the Hold."

"She can be braver in Rupert's cause than you imagine. I am sure that she will be as safe as you or I."

"Then let us tell her."

Maude's eyes grew bright with gladness. Taking all circumstances into view, there was not much cause for congratulation; but, compared with what had been, it seemed as joy to Maude, and her heart grew light.

"I shall never repay you, George," she cried, with enthusiasm, lifting her eyes gratefully to his.

George laughed, and made a prisoner of her. "I can repay myself, Maude."

And Mrs. Chattaway was told.

In the twilight of that same evening, when the skies were grey, and the trees in the lonely avenue were gloomy, there glided one beneath them with timid and cautious step. It was Mrs. Chattaway. A soft black shawl was thrown over her head and shoulders, and her gown was black; precautions rendering her less easy to be observed; and curious eyes might be about. She kept close to the trees as she stole along, ready to conceal herself amidst them if necessary.

And it was necessary. Surely there was a fatality clinging to the spot this evening, or Mr. Chattaway was haunting it in suspicion. One moment more, and he would have met his wife; but she heard the footsteps in time.

Her heart beating, her hands pressed upon her bosom, she waited in her hiding-place until he had gone past: waited until she believed him safe at home, and then she went on.

The shutters were closed at the lodge, and Mrs. Chattaway knocked softly at them. Alas! alas! I tell you there was some untoward fate in the ascendant. In the very act of doing so she was surprised by Cris running in at the gate.

"Goodness, mother! who was to know you in that guise? Why, what on earth are you trembling at?"

"You have startled me, Cris. I did not know you; I thought it some strange man running in upon me."

"What are you doing down here?"

Ah! what was she doing? What was she to say? what excuse to make?

"Poor old Canham has been so ailing, Cris. I must just step in to see him."

Cris tossed his head in scorn. To make friendly visits to sick old men was not in *his* line. "I'm sure I should not trouble myself about old Canham if I were you, mother," cried he.

He ran on as he spoke, but had not gone many steps when he found his mother's arm gently laid on his.

"Cris, dear, oblige me by not saying anything of this at home. Your father has prejudices, you know; he thinks as you do; and perhaps would be angry with me for coming. But I like to visit those who are ill, to say a kind word to them; perhaps because I am so often ill myself."

"I sha'n't bother myself to say anything about it," was Cris's ungracious response. "I'm sure you are welcome to go, mother, if it affords you any pleasure. Fine fun it must be to sit with that rheumatic old Canham! But as to his being ill, he is not that—if you mean worse than usual: I have seen him about to-day."

Cris finally went off, and Mrs. Chattaway returned to the door, which was opened about an inch by Ann Canham. "Let me in, Ann! let me in!"

She pushed her way in; and Ann Canham shut and bolted the door. Ann's course was uncertain: she was not aware whether or not it was known to Mrs. Chattaway. That lady's first words enlightened her, spoken as they were in the lowest whisper.

"Is he better to-night? What does Mr. King say?"

Ann lifted her hands in trouble. "He's no better, Madam, but seems worse. Mr. King said it would be necessary that he should visit him once or twice a day: and how can he dare venture? It passed off very well his saying this afternoon that he just called in to see old father; but he couldn't make that excuse to Mr. Chattaway a second time."

"To Mr. Chattaway!" she quickly repeated. "Did Mr. Chattaway see Mr. King here?"

"Worse luck, he did, Madam. He came in with him."

A fear arose to the heart of Mrs. Chattaway. "If we could only get him away to a safe distance!" she exclaimed. "There would be less danger then."

But it could not be; Rupert was too ill to be moved. Mrs. Chattaway was turning to the stairs, when a gentle knocking was heard at the outer door.

It was only Mr. King. Mrs. Chattaway eagerly accosted him with the one anxious question—was Rupert in danger?

"Well I hope not: not in actual danger," was the surgeon's answer. "But—you see—circumstances are against him."

"Yes," she said, hesitatingly, not precisely understanding to what circumstances he alluded. Mr. King resumed.

"Nothing is more essential in these cases of low fever than plenty of fresh air and generous nourishment. The one he cannot get, lying where he does; to obtain the other may be almost as difficult. If these low fevers cannot be checked, they go on very often to—to—"

"To what?" a terrible dread upon her that he meant to say, "to death."

"To typhus," quietly remarked the surgeon.

"Oh, but that is dangerous!" she cried, clasping her hands. "That sometimes goes on to death."

"Yes," said Mr. King; and it struck her that his tone was significant.

"You must try and prevent it, doctor—you must save him," she cried; and her imploring accents, her trembling hands, proved to the surgeon how great was her emotion.

He shook his head: the issues of life and death were not in his power. "My dear lady, I will do what I am enabled to do; more, I cannot. We poor human doctors can only work under the hand of God."

CHAPTER XLIX
A RED-LETTER DAY

There are some happy days in the most monotonous, the least favoured life; periods on which we can look back always, even to the life's end, and say, "That was a red-letter day!"

Such a day had arisen for Trevlyn Farm. Perhaps never, since the unhappy accident which had carried away its master, had so joyful a day dawned for Mrs. Ryle and George—certainly never one that brought half the satisfaction; for George Ryle was going up to the Hold to clear off the last instalment of Mr. Chattaway's debt.

It was the lifting of a heavy tax; the removal of a cruel nightmare—a nightmare that had borne them down, had all but crushed them with its weight. How they had toiled, striven, persevered, saved, George and Nora alone knew. They knew it far better than Mrs. Ryle; she had joined in the saving, but little in the work. To Mrs. Ryle the debt seemed to have been cleared off quickly—far more quickly than had appeared likely at the time of Mr. Ryle's death. And so it had been. George Ryle was one of those happy people who believe in the special interposition and favour of God; and he believed that God had shown favour to him, and helped him with prosperity. It could not be denied that Trevlyn Farm had been blessed with remarkable prosperity since George's reign there. Season after season, when other people complained of short returns, those of Trevlyn Farm had flourished. Harvests had been abundant; cattle, sheep, poultry—all had richly prospered. It is true George brought keen intelligence, ever-watchful care to bear upon it; but returns, even with these, are not always satisfactory. They had been so with him. His bargains in buying and selling stock had been always good, yielding a profit—for he had entered into them somewhat largely—never dreamt of by his father. The farmers around, seeing how all he put his hand to seemed to flourish, set it down to his superior skill, and talked one to another, at their fairs and markets, of "young Ryle's cuteness." Perhaps the success might be owing to a very different cause, as George believed—and nothing could have shaken that belief—the special blessing of Heaven!

Yes, in spite of Mr. Chattaway's oppression, they had flourished. It had seemed like magic to that gentleman how they had kept up and increased the payments to him, in addition to their other expenses. That the debt should be ready to be finally cancelled he scarcely believed, although he had received intimation to that effect.

It did not please him. Dear as money was to the master of Trevlyn Hold, he had been better pleased to keep George Ryle still under his thumb. *He* had not been favoured with the same success: his corn had, some seasons, been thin in the ear; his live stock unhealthy; his bargains had turned out losses instead of gains; he had made bad debts; his coal-mine had exploded; his ricks had been burnt. Certainly no extraordinary luck had followed Mr. Chattaway—rather the contrary; and he regarded George Ryle with anger and envy; a great deal more than would have pleased George, had he known it. Not that George cared, in the abstract, whether he had Mr. Chattaway's anger or good will; but George wanted to stand so far well with him as to obtain the lease of his best farm. A difficult task!

Mr. Chattaway sat in what was called the steward's room that fine autumn morning—but autumn was merging into winter now. When rents were paid to him, it was here he sat to receive them. It was where the steward, in the old days of Squire Trevlyn, sat to receive them; see the tenants and work-people upon other matters; transact business generally—for it was not until the advent of Mr. Chattaway that Trevlyn Hold had been without its steward or bailiff. In the estimation of Miss Diana, it ought not to be without one now.

Mr. Chattaway was not in a good humour that morning—which is not saying much: but he was in an unusually bad one. A man who rented a small farm of fifty acres under him had come in to pay his annual rent. That is, he had paid part of it, pleading unavoidable misfortune for not being able to make up the remainder, and begging time and grace. It did not please Mr. Chattaway—never a more exacting man than he with his tenants—and the unhappy defaulter wound up the displeasure to a climax by inquiring, innocently and simply, really not meaning any offence, whether any news of the poor young Squire had come to light.

Mr. Chattaway had not done digesting the unpalatable remark when George entered. "Good morning, Mr. Chattaway," was his greeting. And perhaps of all his tenants George Ryle was the only one who did not on these occasions, when they met face to face as landlord and tenant, address him by his coveted title of "Squire."

"Good morning," returned Mr. Chattaway, shortly and snappishly. "Take a seat."

George drew a chair to the table at which Mr. Chattaway sat. Opening a substantial bag, he counted out notes and gold, and a few shillings in silver, which he divided into two portions; then, with his hands, he pushed each nearer Mr. Chattaway, one after the other.

"This is the year's rent, Mr. Chattaway; and this, I am happy to say, is the last instalment of the debt and interest which my father owed—or was said to owe—to Squire Trevlyn. Will you be so good as to give me a receipt in full?"

Mr. Chattaway swept towards him the heap designated as the rent, apparently ignoring the other. "What have you deducted?" he asked, in angry tones, as he counted it over, and found that it came somewhat short of the sum expected.

"Not much," replied George; "only what I have a right to deduct. The fences, and—But I have the accounts with me," he continued, taking three or four papers from his pocket. "You can look them over."

Mr. Chattaway scrutinised the papers one by one, but he was unable to find anything to object to in the items. George Ryle knew better than to deduct money for anything that did not fall legally to the landlord. But it was in Mr. Chattaway's nature to dispute.

"If I brought this matter of the fences into court I believe it would be given against you."

"I don't think you believe anything of the sort," returned George, good-humouredly. "If you have any great wish to try it, you can do so: but the loss would be yours."

Probably Mr. Chattaway knew that it would be. He said no more, but proceeded to count the other money. It was all there, both principal and interest. In vain Mr. Chattaway opened his books of the days gone by, and went over old figures; he could not claim another fraction. The long-pending two thousand pounds, the disputed loan, which had caused so much heart-burning, and had led in a remote degree to Mr. Ryle's violent death, was at length paid off.

"As I have paid former sums under the same protest that my father did, so I now pay this last and final one," said George, in a civil but straightforward and business-like tone. "I believe that Squire Trevlyn cancelled the debt on his death-bed; I and my mother have lived in that belief; but there was no document to prove it, and we have had to bear the consequences. It is all, however, honourably paid now."

Mr. Chattaway could not demur to this, and gave a receipt—in full, as George expressed it—for that and the year's rent. As George put the former safely in his pocket-book, he felt like a bird released from a long and cruel imprisonment. He was a free man and a joyous one.

"That farm of yours has turned out well of late years," observed Mr. Chattaway.

"Very well: there's the proof," pointing to the money. "To tell you the truth, I gave myself two more years to pay it off in, and Mrs. Ryle thought it would take longer. But I have prospered in my bargains with stock. Would you be afraid to try me on a farm on my own account?"

Had it been any eligible person except George Ryle, Mr. Chattaway would probably have said he should not be afraid; but Chattaway did not like George Ryle. He disliked him, as a mean, ill-principled man will dislike and shun an honourable one.

"I should think that when you are making Trevlyn Farm answer so well, you would be loth to leave it," he remarked ungraciously.

"So I might be, were Trevlyn Farm mine alone. Of all the returns which have accrued from my care and labour, not a shilling has found its way to me: I have worked entirely for others. But for the heavy costs which have been upon us, the chief of which were Treve's expenses and this old debt of Squire Trevlyn's, there would have been a fair sum to put by yearly, and I imagine my mother would have allowed me to take my portion. I believe she intends to do so by Treve, and I hope Treve will make as good a thing of the farm as I have made."

"That's not likely," slightingly spoke Mr. Chattaway.

"He may do well if he chooses; there's no doubt about it, and he can always come to me for advice. I shall not be far off—at least, if I can settle as I hope. My mother wishes the lease transferred into Trevlyn's name. I suppose there will be no objection to it."

"I'll consider it," shortly replied Mr. Chattaway.

"And now, Mr. Chattaway," George continued, with a smile, "I want you to promise me the lease of the Upland Farm. It will be vacant in spring."

"You are mad to ask it," said Chattaway. "A man without a shilling—and you have just informed me you don't possess one—can't undertake the Upland Farm. That farm's only suited to a gentleman"—and he laid an offensive stress upon the word: "one whose pockets are lined with money. I have had an application for the Upland Farm, which I think I shall accept. In fact, for the matter of that, I had some thought of retaining it in my own hands, and putting in a bailiff to manage it."

"You had better let it to me," returned George, not losing his good humour. "Was the application made to you by Mr. Peterby?"

Mr. Chattaway stared in surprise at his knowing so much. "What if it was?" he returned resentfully.

"Why, then, I can tell you that it will not be repeated. Mr. Peterby's client—I am not sure that I am at liberty to mention his name—has given up the idea. Partly because I have told him I want the farm myself, and he says he won't oppose me, out of respect to my father's memory; partly because Mr. Peterby has heard of another likely to suit him as well, if not better. All the neighbours would be glad to see me take the Upland Farm."

Mr. Chattaway's breath was almost taken away with the insolence. "Had you not better constitute yourself manager of my estate, and let my farms to whom you please?" he cried sarcastically. "How dare you interfere with my tenants, or with those who would become my tenants?"

"I have not interfered with them. This client of Mr. Peterby's happened to mention to me that he had asked the firm to make inquiries about the Upland Farm. I immediately rejoined that it was the very farm I was hoping to take myself; and he determined of his own goodwill not to oppose me."

"Who was it?"

"One who would not have suited you, if you have set your mind upon a gentleman," freely answered George. "He is an honest man, and a man whose coffers are well lined through his own industry; but he could not by any stretch of imagination be called a gentleman. It is Cope, the butcher—I may as well tell you. Since he retired from his shop, he finds time hangs on his hands, and has resolved to turn farmer. Mr. Chattaway, I hope you will let me have it."

"It appears to me nothing less than audacity to ask it," was the chilling retort. "Pray, where's your money to come from to stock it?"

"It's all ready," said George.

Mr. Chattaway looked at him, thinking the assertion a joke. "If you have nothing better to do with your time than to jest it away, I have with mine," was the delicate hint he gave in reply.

"I repeat that the money is ready," continued George. "Mr. Chattaway, I do not wish to conceal anything from you: to be otherwise than quite open with you. The money to stock the Upland Farm is going to be lent to me; you will be surprised when I tell you by whom—Mr. Apperley."

Mr. Chattaway was very much surprised. It was not much in Farmer Apperley's line to lend money: he was too cautious a man.

"It's quite true," said George, laughing. "He has so good an opinion of my skill as a farmer, or of the Upland Farm's capabilities, that he has offered to lend me sufficient money to take it."

"I should have thought you had had enough of farming land upon borrowed money," ungenerously retorted Chattaway.

"So I have—from one point of view," was the composed answer. "But I have managed to clear off the debt, you see, and don't doubt I shall be able to do the same again. Apperley proposes only a fair rate of interest; considerably less than I have been paying you."

"It is strange that you, a young and single man, should raise your ambitious eyes to the Upland Farm."

"Not at all. If I don't take the Upland, I shall take some other equally large. But I should have to go a greater distance, and I don't care to do that. As to being a single man—perhaps that might be remedied if you will let me have the Upland."

He spoke with a laugh; yet Mr. Chattaway detected a serious meaning in the tone, and he gazed hard at George. It may be that his thoughts glanced at his daughter Octave.

There was a long pause. "Are you thinking of marrying?"

"As soon as circumstances will allow me to do so."

"And who is the lady?"

George shook his head; a very decisive shake, in spite of the smile on his lips. "I cannot tell you now; you will know sometime."

"I suppose I shall, if the match ever comes off," returned Chattaway, in a very cross-grained manner. "If it has to wait until you rent the Upland Farm, it may wait indefinitely."

"You will promise me the lease of it, Mr. Chattaway. You cannot think but I shall do the land justice, or be anything but a good tenant."

"I won't promise anything of the sort," was the dogged reply. "I'll promise you, if you like, that you never shall have the lease of it."

And, talk as George would, he could not get him into a more genial frame of mind. At length he rose, good-humoured and gay; as he had been throughout the interview.

"Never mind for the present, Mr. Chattaway. I shall not let you alone until you promise me the farm. There's plenty of time between now and spring."

As he was crossing the hall on his way to the door, he saw Miss Diana Trevlyn, and stopped to shake hands with her. "You have been paying your rent, I suppose," she said.

"My rent and something else," replied George, in high spirits—the removal of that incubus which had so long lain on him had sent them up to fever heat. "I have handed over the last instalment of the debt and interest, Miss Diana, and have the receipt here"—touching his breast-pocket. "I have paid it under protest, as I have always told Mr. Chattaway; for I fully believe Squire Trevlyn cancelled it."

"If I thought my father cancelled it, Mr. Chattaway should never have had my approbation in pressing it," severely spoke Miss Diana. "Is it true that you think of leaving Trevlyn Farm? Rumour says so."

"Quite true. It is time I began life on my own account. I have been asking Mr. Chattaway to let me have the Upland."

"The Upland! You!" There was nothing offensive in Miss Diana's exclamation: it was spoken in simple surprise.

"Why not? I may be thinking of getting a wife; and the Upland is the only farm in the neighbourhood I would take her to."

Miss Diana smiled in answer to his joke, as she thought it. "The house on the Upland Farm is quite a mansion," she returned, keeping up the jest. "Will no lesser one suffice her?"

"No. She is a gentlewoman born and bred, and must live as one."

"George, you speak as if you were in earnest. Are you really thinking of being married?"

"If I can get the Upland Farm. But—"

George was startled from the conclusion of his sentence. Over Miss Diana's shoulder, gazing at him with a strangely wild expression, was the face of Octave Chattaway, her lips parted, her face crimson.

CHAPTER L
DILEMMAS

About ten days elapsed, and Rupert Trevlyn, lying in concealment at the lodge, was both better and worse. The prompt remedies applied by Mr. King had effected their object in abating the fever; it had not developed into brain-fever or typhus, and the tendency to delirium was arrested; so far he was better. But these symptoms had been replaced by others that might prove not less dangerous in the end: great prostration, alarming weakness, and what appeared to be a settled cough. The old tendency to consumption was showing itself more plainly than it had ever shown itself before.

He had had a cough often enough, which had come and gone again, as coughs come to a great many of us; but the experienced ear of Mr. King detected a difference in this one. "It has a nasty sound in it," the doctor privately remarked to George Ryle. Poor Ann Canham, faint at heart lest this cough should betray his presence, pasted up all the chinks, and kept the door hermetically closed when any one was downstairs. Things usually go by contrary, you know; and it seemed that the lodge had never been so inundated with callers.

Two great cares were upon those in the secret: to keep Rupert's presence in the lodge from the knowledge of the outside world, and to supply him with proper food. Upon none did the first press so painfully as upon Rupert himself. His dread lest his place of concealment should be discovered by Mr. Chattaway was never ceasing. When he lay awake, his ears were on the strain for what might be happening downstairs, who might be coming in; if he dozed—as he did several times in the course of the day—his dreams were haunted by pursuers, and he would start up wildly in bed, fancying he saw Mr. Chattaway entering with the police at his heels. For twenty minutes afterwards he would lie bathed in perspiration, unable to get the fright or the vision out of his mind.

There was no doubt that this contributed to increase his weakness and keep him back. Let Rupert Trevlyn's future be what it might; let the result be the very worst; one thing was certain—any actual punishment in store for him could not be worse than this anticipation. Imagination is more vivid than reality. He would lie and go through the whole ordeal of his future trial: would see himself in the dock, not before the magistrates of

Barmester, but before a scarlet-robed judge; would listen to the evidence of Mr. Chattaway and Jim Sanders, bringing home the crime to him; would hear the irrevocable sentence from those grave lips—that of penal servitude. Nothing could be worse for him than these visions. And there was no help for them. Had Rupert been in strong health, he might have shaken off some of these haunting fears; lying as he did in his weakness, they took the form of morbid disease, adding greatly to his bodily sickness.

His ear strained, he would start up whenever a footstep was heard to enter the downstairs room, breathing softly to Ann Canham, or whoever might be sitting with him, the question: "Is it Chattaway?" And Ann would cautiously peep down the staircase, or bend her ear to listen, and tell him who it really was. But sometimes several minutes would elapse before she could find out; sometimes she would be obliged to go down upon some plausible errand, and then come back and tell him. The state that Rupert would fall into during these moments of suspense no pen could describe. It was little wonder that Rupert grew weaker.

And the fears of discovery were not misplaced. Every hour brought its own danger. It was absolutely necessary that Mr. King should visit him at least once a day, and each time he ran the risk of being seen by Chattaway, or by some one equally dangerous. Old Canham could not feign to be on the sick list for ever; especially, sufficiently sick to require daily medical attendance. George Ryle ran the risk of being seen entering the lodge; as well as Mrs. Chattaway and Maude, who *could not* abandon their stolen interviews with the poor sufferer. "It is my only happy hour in the four-and-twenty; you must not fail me!" he would say to them, imploringly holding out his fevered hands. Some evenings Mrs. Chattaway would steal there, sometimes Maude, now and then both together.

Underlying it all in Rupert's mind was the sense of guilt for having committed so desperate a crime. Apart from those moments of madness, which the neighbourhood had been content for years to designate as the Trevlyn temper, few living men were so little likely to commit the act as Rupert. Rupert was of a mild, kindly temperament, a very sweet disposition; one of those inoffensive people of whom we are apt to say they would not hurt a fly. Of Rupert it was literally true. Only in these rare fits was he transformed; and never had the fit been upon him as on that unhappy night. It was not so much repentance for the actual crime that overwhelmed him, as surprise that he had perpetrated it. "I was not conscious of the act," he would groan aloud; "I was mad when I did it." Perhaps so; but the consequences remained. Poor Rupert! Remorse was his portion, and he was in truth repenting in sackcloth and ashes.

The other care upon him—supplying Rupert with appropriate nourishment—brought almost as much danger and difficulty in its train as concealing him. A worse cook than Ann Canham could not be found. It was her misfortune, rather than her fault. Living in extreme poverty all her life, no opportunity for learning or improving herself in cooking had ever been afforded her. The greatest luxury that ever entered old Canham's lodge was a bit of toasted or boiled bacon.

It was not invalid dishes that Rupert wanted now. As soon as the fever began to leave him, his appetite returned. Certain cases of incipien consumption are accompanied by a craving for food difficult to satisfy, anc this unfortunately became the case with Rupert. Had he been at the Hold or in a plentiful home, he would have played his full part at the daily meals and assisted their digestion with interludes besides.

How was he to get sufficient food at the lodge? Mr. King said he must have full nourishment, with wine, strong broths, and other things in addition. It was the only chance, in his opinion, to counteract the weakness that was growing upon him, and which bid fair soon to attain an alarming height. Mrs. Chattaway, George Ryle, even the doctor himself would have been quite willing to supply the cost; but even so, where was the food to be dressed?—who was to do it?—how was it to be smuggled in? This may appear a trifling difficulty in theory, but in practice it was found almos insurmountable.

"Can't you dress a sweetbread?" Mr. King testily asked Ann Canham when she was timidly confessing her incapability in the culinary art. "I'd easily manage to get it up here."

This was the first day Rupert's appetite had come back to him, just afte the turn of the fever. Ann Canham hesitated. "I'm not sure, sir," she said meekly. "Could it be put in a pot and boiled?"

"Put in a pot and boiled!" repeated Mr. King, nettled at the question "Much goodness there'd be in it when it came out! It's just blanched and dipped in egg crumbs, and toasted in the Dutch oven. That's the best way of doing them."

Egg crumbs were as much of a mystery to Ann Canham as sweetbread themselves. She shook her head. "And if, by ill-luck, Mr. Chattaway came in and saw a sweetbread in our Dutch oven before our fire, sir; or smelt th savour of it as he passed—what then?" she asked. "What excuse could w make to him?"

This phase of the difficulty had not before presented itself to th surgeon's mind. It was one that could not well be got over; the more h dwelt upon it the more he became convinced of this. George Ryle, Mrs Chattaway, Maude, all, when appealed to, were of the same opinion. Ther was too much at stake to permit the risk of exciting any suspicions on th part of Mr. Chattaway.

But it was not only Chattaway. Others who possessed noses were in the habit of passing the lodge: Cris, his sisters, Miss Diana, and many more: and some of them were in the habit of coming into it. Ann Canham was giving mortal offence, causing much wonder, in declining her usual places of work; and many a disappointed housewife, following Nora Dickson's example, had come up, in consequence, to invade the lodge and express her sentiments upon the point. Ann Canham was driven to the very verge of desperation in trying to frame plausible excuses, and had serious thoughts of making believe to take to her bed herself—had she possessed just then a bed to take to.

In the dilemma Mrs. Chattaway came to the rescue. "I will contrive it," she said: "the food shall be supplied from the Hold. My sister does not personally interfere, giving her orders in the morning, and I know I can manage it."

But Mrs. Chattaway found she had undertaken what it would scarcely be possible to perform. What had flashed across her mind when she spoke was, "The cook is a faithful, kind-hearted woman, and I know I can trust her." Mrs. Chattaway did not mean trust her with the secret of Rupert, but trust her to cook a few extra dishes quietly and say nothing about them. Yes, she might, she was sure; the woman would be true. But it now struck Mrs. Chattaway with a sort of horror, to ask herself how she was to get them away when cooked. She could not go into the kitchen herself, have meat, fowl, or jelly put into a basin, and carry it off to the lodge. However, that was an after-care. She spoke to the cook, who was called Rebecca, told her she wanted some nice things dressed for a poor pensioner of *her own*, and nothing said about it. The woman was pleased and willing; all the servants were fond of their mistress; and she readily undertook the task and promised to be silent.

CHAPTER LI
A LETTER FOR MR. CHATTAWAY

Although an insignificant place, Barbrook and its environs receive their letters early. The bags were dropped by the London mail train a Barmester in the middle of the night; and as the post-office arrangement were well conducted—which cannot be said for all towns—by eight o'cloc Barbrook had its letters.

Rather before that hour than after it, they were delivered at Trevly Hold. Being the chief residence in the neighbourhood, the postman was i the habit of beginning his round there; it had been so in imperious old Squir Trevlyn's time, and was so still. Thus it generally happened that breakfas would be commencing at the Hold when the post came in.

It was a morning of which we must take some notice—a mornin which, as Mr. Chattaway was destined afterwards to find, he would hav cause to remember to his dying day. If Miss Diana Trevlyn happened t see the postman approaching the house, she would most likely walk to th hall-door and receive the letters into her own hands. And it was so on thi morning.

"Only two, ma'am," the postman said, as he delivered them to her.

She looked at the addresses. The one was a foreign letter, bearing he own name, and she recognised the handwriting of Mr. Daw; the other bor the London postmark, and was addressed "James Chattaway, Esquir Trevlyn Hold, Barmester."

With an eager movement, somewhat foreign to the cold and statel motions of Miss Diana Trevlyn, she broke the seal of the former; there, a the hall-door as she stood. A thought flashed into her mind that Rupe might have found his way at length to Mr. Daw, and that gentleman wa intimating the same—as Miss Diana by letter had requested him to do. was just the contrary, however. Mr. Daw wrote to beg a line from Mis Diana, as to whether tidings had been heard of Rupert. He had visited hi father and mother's grave the previous day, he observed, and did not kno whether that had caused him to think more than usual of Rupert; but, all th past night and again to-day, he had been unable to get him out of his hea a feeling was upon him (no doubt a foolish one, he added in a parenthesi that the boy was taken, or that some other misfortune had befallen him, or was about to befall him, and he presumed to request a line from Miss Diana Trevlyn to end his suspense.

She folded the letter when read; put it into the pocket of her black silk apron, and returned to the breakfast-room, with the one for Mr. Chattaway. As she did so, her eyes happened to fall upon the reverse side of the letter, and she saw it was stamped with the name of a firm—Connell, Connell, and Ray.

She knew the firm by name; they were solicitors of great respectability in London. Indeed, she remembered to have entertained Mr. Charles Connell at the Hold for a few days in her father's lifetime, that gentleman being at the time engaged in some legal business for Squire Trevlyn. They must be old men now, she knew, those brothers Connell; and Mr. Ray, she believed to have heard, was son-in-law to one of them.

"What can they have to write to Chattaway about?" marvelled Miss Diana; but the next moment she remembered they were the agents of Peterby and Jones, of Barmester, and concluded it was some matter connected with the estate.

Miss Diana swept to her place at the head of the breakfast-table. It was filled, with the exception of two seats: the armchair opposite to her own, Mr. Chattaway's; and Cris's seat at the side. Cris was not down, but Mr. Chattaway had gone out to the men. Mrs. Chattaway was in her place next Miss Diana. She used rarely to be down in time to begin breakfast with the rest, but that was altered now. Since these fears had arisen concerning Rupert, it seemed that she could not rest in her bed, and would quit it almost with the dawn.

Mr. Chattaway came in as Miss Diana was pouring out the tea, and she passed the letter down to him. Glancing casually at it as it lay beside his plate, he began helping himself to some cold partridge. Cris was a capital shot, and the Hold was generally well supplied with game.

"It is from Connell and Connell," remarked Miss Diana.

"From Connell and Connell!" repeated Mr. Chattaway, in a tone of bewilderment, as if he did not recognise the name. "What should they be writing to me about?" But he was too busy with the partridge just then to ascertain.

"Some local business, I conclude," observed Miss Diana. "They are Peterby's agents, you know."

"And what if they are?" retorted Mr. Chattaway. "Peterby's have nothing to do with me."

That was so like Chattaway! To cavil as to what might be the contents o the letter, rather than put the question at rest by opening it. However, wher he looked up from his plate to stir his tea, he tore open the envelope.

He tore it open and cast his eyes over the letter. Miss Diana happenec to be looking at him. She saw him gaze at it with an air of bewilderment she saw him go over it again—there were apparently but some half-dozer lines—and then she saw him turn green. You may cavil at the expression, bu it is a correct one. The leaden complexion with which nature had favourec Mr. Chattaway did assume a green tinge in moments of especial annoyance

"What's the matter?" questioned Miss Diana.

Mr. Chattaway replied by a half-muttered word, and dashed the lette down. "I thought we had had enough of that folly," he presently said.

"What folly?"

He did not answer, although the query was put by Miss Diana Trevlyn She pressed it, and Mr. Chattaway flung the letter across the table to her "You can read it, if you choose." With some curiosity Miss Diana took it up and read as follows:—

> "Sir,
>
> "We beg to inform you that the true heir of Trevlyn Hold, Rupert Trevlyn, is about to put in his claim to the estate, and will shortly require to take possession of it. We have been requested to write this intimation to you, and we do so in a friendly spirit, that you may be prepared to quit the house, and not be taken unawares, when Mr. Trevlyn—henceforth Squire Trevlyn—shall arrive at it.
>
> "We are, sir, your obedient servants,
>
> "Connell, Connell, and Ray.
>
> "James Chattaway, Esquire."

"Then Rupert's not dead!" were the first words that broke from Mis Diana's lips. And the exclamation, and its marked tone of satisfactior proved of what nature her fears for Rupert had been.

Mrs. Chattaway started up with white lips. "What of Rupert?" sh gasped; believing nothing else than that discovery had come.

Miss Diana, without in the least thinking it necessary to consult M Chattaway's pleasure first, handed her the letter. She read it rapidly, an her fears calmed down.

"What an absurdity!" she exclaimed. Knowing as she did the helpless position of Rupert, the contents sounded not only absurd, but impossible. "Some one must have written it to frighten you, James."

"Yes," said Mr. Chattaway, compressing his thin lips; "it comes from the Peterby quarter. A felon threatening to take possession of Trevlyn Hold!"

But in spite of the scorn he strove to throw into his manner; in spite of his indomitable resolution to bring Rupert to punishment when he appeared; in spite of even his wife, Rupert's best friend, acknowledging the absurdity of this letter, it disturbed him in no measured degree. He stretched out his hand for it, and read it again, pondering over every word; he pushed his plate from him, as he gazed on it. He had had sufficient breakfast for one day; and gulping down his tea, declined to take more. Yes, it was shaking his equanimity to its centre; and the Miss Chattaways and Maude, only imperfectly understanding what was amiss, looked at each other, and at him.

Mrs. Chattaway began to feel indignant that poor Rupert's name should be thus made use of; only, so far as she could see, for the purpose of exciting Mr. Chattaway further against him. "But Connells' is a most respectable firm," she said aloud, following out her thoughts; "I cannot comprehend it."

"I say it comes from Peterby," roared Mr. Chattaway. "He and Rupert are in league. I dare say Peterby knows where he's concealed."

"Oh no, no; you are mistaken," broke incautiously from the lips of Mrs. Chattaway.

"No! Do you know where he is, pray, that you speak so confidently?"

The taunt recalled her to a sense of the danger. "James, what I meant was this: it is scarcely likely Rupert would be in league with any one against you," she said in low tones. "I think he would rather try to conciliate you."

"If you think this letter emanates from Peterbys' why don't you go down and demand what they mean by writing it?" interposed Miss Diana Trevlyn, in her straightforward, matter-of-fact tone.

He nodded his head significantly. "I shall not let the grass grow under my feet before I am there."

"I cannot think it's Peterby and Jones," resumed Miss Diana. "They are quite as respectable as the Connells, and I don't believe they would ally themselves with Rupert, after what he has done. I don't believe they would work mischief secretly against any one. Anything they may have to do, they'd do openly."

Had Mr. Chattaway prevailed with himself so far as to put his temper and prejudices aside, this might not have been far from his own opinion.

He had always, in a resentful sort of way, considered Mr. Peterby an honourable man. But if Peterby was not at the bottom of this, who was? Connell, Connell, and Ray were his town agents.

The very uncertainty only made him the more eager to get to them and set the matter at rest. He knew it was of no use attempting to see Mr. Peterby before ten o'clock, but he would see him then. He ordered his horse to be ready, and rode into Barmester attended by his groom. As ten o'clock struck, he was at their office-door.

A quarter-of-an-hour's detention, and then he was admitted to Mr. Peterby's room. That gentleman was sweeping a pile of open letters into a corner of the table at which he sat, and the master of Trevlyn Hold shrewdly suspected that his waiting had been caused by Mr. Peterby's opening and reading them. He proceeded at once to the business that brought him there, and taking his own letter out of his pocket, handed it to Mr. Peterby.

"Connell, Connell, and Ray are your agents in London, I believe? They used to be."

"And are still," said Mr. Peterby. "What is this?"

"Be so good as to read it," replied Mr. Chattaway.

The lawyer ran his eyes over it carelessly, as it seemed to those eyes watching him. Then he looked up. "Well?"

"In writing this letter to me—I received it, you perceive, by post this morning, if you'll look at the date—were Connell and Connell instructed by you?"

"By me!" echoed Mr. Peterby. "Not they. I know nothing at all about it. I can't make it out."

"You are a friend of Rupert Trevlyn's, and they are your agents," remarked Mr. Chattaway, after a pause.

"My good sir, I tell you I know nothing whatever of this. Connells are our agents; but I never sent any communication to them with regard to Rupert Trevlyn in my life; never had cause to send one. If you ask me my opinion, I should say that if the lad—should he be still living—entertains hopes of coming into Trevlyn Hold after this last escapade of his, he must be a great simpleton. I expect you'd prosecute him, instead of giving him up the Hold."

"I should," quietly answered Mr. Chattaway. "But what do Connell and Connell mean by sending me such a letter as this?"

"It is more than I can tell you, Mr. Chattaway. We have received a communication from them ourselves this morning upon the subject. I was opening it when you were announced to me as being here."

He bent over the letters previously spoken of, selected one, and held it out to Mr. Chattaway. Instead of being written by the firm, it was a private letter from Mr. Ray to Mr. Peterby. It merely stated that the true heir of Squire Trevlyn, Rupert, was about shortly to take possession of his property, the Hold, and they (Connell, Connell, and Ray) should require Mr. Peterby to act as local solicitor in the proceedings, should a solicitor be necessary.

Mr. Chattaway began to feel cruelly uneasy. Rupert had committed that great fault, and was in danger of punishment—*would* be punished by his country's laws; but in this new uneasiness that important fact seemed to lose half its significance. "And you have not instructed them?" he repeated.

"Nonsense, Mr. Chattaway! it is not likely. I cannot make out what they mean, any more than you can. The nearest conclusion I can come to is, that they must be acting from instructions received from that semi-parson who was over here, Mr. Daw."

"No," said Mr. Chattaway, "I think not. Miss Trevlyn heard from that man this morning, and he appears to know nothing about Rupert. He asks for news of him."

"Well, it is a curious thing altogether. I shall write by to-night's post to Ray, and inquire what he means."

Mr. Chattaway, suspicious Mr. Chattaway, pressed one more question. "Have you any idea at all where Rupert is likely to be? That he is in hiding, and accessible to some people, is evident from these letters.

"I have already informed you that I know nothing whatever of Rupert Trevlyn," was the lawyer's answer. "Whether he is alive or whether he is dead, I know not. You cannot know less of him yourself than I do."

Mr. Chattaway was obliged to be contented with the answer. He went out and proceeded direct to Mr. Flood's, and laid the letter—his letter—before him. "What sort of thing do you call that?" he intemperately uttered, when it was read. "Connell and Connell must be infamous men to write it."

"Stop a bit," said Mr. Flood, who had his eyes strained on the letter. "There's more in this than meets the eye."

"You don't think it's a joke—done to annoy me?"

"A joke! Connell and Connell would not lend themselves to a joke. No, I don't think it's that."

"Then what do you think?"

Mr. Flood was several minutes before he replied, and his silence drove Mr. Chattaway to the verge of exasperation. "It is difficult to know what to think," said the lawyer presently. "I should be inclined to say they have been brought into personal communication with Rupert Trevlyn, or with somebody acting for him: perhaps the latter is the more probable. And I should also say they must have been convinced, by documentary or other evidence, that a good foundation exists for Rupert's claims to the Hold. Mr. Chattaway—if I may speak the truth to you—I should dread this letter."

Mr. Chattaway felt as if a bucket of cold water had been suddenly flung over him, and was running down his back. "Why is it that you turn against me?"

"*Turn* against you! I don't know what you mean. I don't turn against you; quite the opposite. I am willing to act for you; to do anything I legally can to meet the fear."

"Why *do* you fear?"

"Because Connell, Connell, and Ray are keen and cautious practitioners as well as honourable men, and I do not think they would write so decided a letter as this, unless they knew they were fully justified in doing so, and were prepared to follow it out."

"You are a pretty Job's comforter," gasped Mr. Chattaway.

CHAPTER LII
A DAY OF MISHAPS

Rebecca the servant was true and crafty in her faithfulness to her mistress, and contrived to get various dainties prepared and conveyed unsuspiciously under her apron, watching her opportunity, to the sitting-room of Madam, where they were hidden away in a closet, and the key turned upon them. So far, so good. But that was not all: the greatest difficulty lay in transporting them to Rupert.

The little tricks and *ruses* that the lodge and those in its secret learnt to be expert in at this time were worthy of a private inquiry office. Ann Canham, at a given hour, would be standing at the open door of the lodge; and Mrs. Chattaway, with timid steps, and eyes that wandered everywhere lest witnesses were about, would come down the avenue: opposite the lodge door, by some sleight of hand, a parcel, or basket, or bottle would be transferred from under her shawl to Ann Canham's hands. The latter would close the door and slip the bolt, whilst the lady would walk swiftly on through the gate, for the purpose of taking exercise in the road. Or perhaps it would be Maude that went through this little rehearsal, instead of Madam. But at the best it was all difficult to accomplish for many reasons, and might at any time be stopped. If only the extra cooking came to the knowledge of Miss Diana Trevlyn, it would be quite impossible to venture to continue it, and next to impossible any longer to conceal Rupert's hiding place.

One day a disastrous *contretemps* occurred. It happened that Miss Diana Trevlyn had arranged to take the Miss Chattaways to a morning concert at Barmester. Maude might have gone, but excused herself: whilst Rupert's fate hung in the balance, it was scarcely seemly, she thought, that she should be seen at public festivals. Cris had gone out shooting that day; Mr. Chattaway, as was supposed, was at Barmester; and when dinner was served, only Mrs. Chattaway and Maude sat down to it. It was a plain sirloin; and during a momentary absence of James, who was waiting at table, Maude exclaimed in a low tone:

"Aunt Edith, if we could only get some of this to Rupert!"

"I was thinking so," said Mrs. Chattaway.

The servant returned to the room, and the conversation ceased. But his mistress, under some plea, dismissed him, saying she would ring. And then the thought was carried out. A sauce-tureen which happened to be on the table was made the receptacle for some of the hot meat, and Maude put on her bonnet and stole away with it.

An unlucky venture. In her haste to reach the lodge unmolested, she spilt some of the gravy on her dress, and was stopping to wipe it with her handkerchief, when she was interrupted by Mr. Chattaway. It was close to the lodge. Maude's heart, as the saying runs, came into her mouth.

"What's that? Where are you taking it to?" he demanded, for his eyes had caught the tureen before she could slip it under her mantle.

He peremptorily took it from her unresisting hand, raised the cover, and saw some tempting slices of hot roast beef, and part of a cauliflower. Had Maude witnessed the actual discovery of Rupert, she could not have felt more utterly terrified.

"I ask you, to whom were you taking this?"

His resolute tones, coupled with her own terror, were more than poor Maude could brave. "To Mark Canham," she faltered. There was no one she could mention with the least plausibility: and she could not pretend to be merely taking a walk with a tureen of meat in her hand.

"Was it Madam's doings to send this?"

Again she could only answer in the affirmative. Chattaway stalked off to the Hold, carrying the tureen.

His wife sat at the dinner-table, and James was removing some pastry as he entered. Regardless of the man's presence, he gave vent to his anger, reproaching her in no measured terms for what she had done. Meat and vegetables from his own table to be supplied to that profitless, good-for-nothing man, Canham, who already enjoyed a house and half-a-crown a week for doing nothing! How dared she be guilty of extravagance so great, of wilful waste?

The scene was prolonged but came to an end at last; all such scenes do, it is to be hoped; and the afternoon went on. Mr. Chattaway went out again, Cris had not come in, Miss Diana and the girls did not return, and Mrs. Chattaway and Maude were still alone. "I shall go down to see him, Maude," the former said in low tones, breaking an unhappy silence. "And I shall take him something to eat; I will risk it. He has had nothing from us to-day."

Maude scarcely knew what to answer: her own fright was not yet over. Mrs. Chattaway dressed herself, took the little provision-basket and went out. It was all but dark; the evening was gloomy. Meeting no one, she gained the lodge, opened its door with a quick hand, and—stole away again silently and swiftly, with perhaps greater terror than she had ever felt rushing over her heart.

For the first figure she saw there was that of her husband, and the first voice she heard was his. She made her way amidst the trunks of the almost leafless trees, and concealed herself as she best could.

In returning that evening, it had struck Mr. Chattaway as he passed the lodge that he could not do better than favour old Canham with a piece of his mind, and forbid him, under pain of instant dismissal, to rob the Hold (as he phrased it) of so much as a scrap of bread. Old Canham, knowing what was at stake, took it patiently, never denying that the food (which Mr. Chattaway enlarged upon) might have been meant for him. Ann Canham stood against Rupert's door, shivering and shaking; and poor Rupert himself, who had not failed to recognise that loud voice, lay as one in agony.

Mr. Chattaway was in the midst of his last sentence, when the front-door was suddenly opened, and as suddenly shut again. He had his back to it, but turned just in time to catch a glimpse of somebody's petticoats before the door closed.

It was a somewhat singular proceeding, and Mr. Chattaway, always curious and suspicious, opened the door after a minute's pause, and looked out. He could see no one. He looked up the avenue, he looked down; he stepped out to the gate, and gazed up and down the road. Whoever it was had disappeared.

"Did you see who it was opened the door in that manner?" he demanded of old Canham.

Old Canham had stood deferentially during the lecture, leaning on his stick. He had not seen who it was, and therefore could answer readily, but he strongly suspected it to be Mrs. Chattaway. "Maybe 'twas some woman bringing sewing up for Ann, Squire. They mostly comes at dusk, not to hinder their own work."

"Then why couldn't they come in?" retorted Mr. Chattaway. "Why need they run away as if caught at some mischief?"

Old Canham wisely declined an answer: and Mr. Chattaway, after a parting admonition, finally quitted the lodge, and took his way towards the Hold. But for her dark attire, and the darker shades of evening, he might have detected his wife there, watching for him to pass.

It seemed an unlucky day. Mrs. Chattaway, her heart beating, came out of her hiding-place as the last echoes of his steps died away and almost met the carriage as it turned into the avenue, bringing her daughters and Miss Diana from Barmester. When she did reach the lodge, Ann Canham had the door open an inch or two. "Take it," she cried, giving the basket to Ann as she advanced to the stairs. "I have not a minute to stop. How is he to-night?"

"Madam," whispered Ann Canham, in her meek voice, but meek though it was, there was that in its tones to-night which arrested Mrs. Chattaway, "if he continues to get worse and weaker, if he cannot be got away from here and from these frights, I fear me he'll die. He has never been as bad as he is to-night."

She untied her bonnet, and stole upstairs to Rupert's room. By the rushlight she could see the ravages of illness on his wasting features; features that seemed to have changed for the worse even since she had seen him that time last night. He turned his blue eyes, bright and wild with disease, on her as she entered.

"Oh, Aunt Edith! Is he gone? I thought I should have died with fright, here as I lay."

"He is gone, darling," she answered, bending over him, and speaking with reassuring tenderness. "You look worse to-night, Rupert."

"It is this stifling room, aunt; it is killing me. At least, it gives me no chance to get better. If I only had a large, airy room at the Hold—where I could lie without fear, and be waited on—I might get better. Aunt Edith, I wish the past few weeks could be blotted out. I wish I had not been overtaken by that fit of madness?"

Ah! he could not wish it as she did. Her tears silently fell, and she began in the desperate need to debate in her own heart whether the impossible might not be accomplished—disarming the anger of Mr. Chattaway, and getting him to pardon Rupert. In that case only could he be removed. Perhaps Diana might effect it? If she could not, no one else could. As she thought of its utter hopelessness, there came to her recollection that recent letter from Connell and Connell, which had so upset the equanimity of Mr. Chattaway. She had not yet mentioned it to Rupert, but must do so now. Her private opinion was, that Rupert had written to the London lawyers for the purpose of vexing Mr. Chattaway.

"It is not right, Rupert, dear," she whispered. "It can only do harm. If it does no other harm, it will by increasing Mr. Chattaway's anger. Indeed, dear, it was wrong."

He looked up in surprise from his pillow.

"I don't know what you mean, Aunt Edith. Connell and Connell? What should I do, writing to Connell and Connell?"

She explained about the letter, reciting its contents as accurately as she remembered them. Rupert only stared.

"Acting for me!—I to take possession of the Hold! Well, I don't know anything about it," he wearily answered. "Why does not Mr. Chattaway go up and ask them what they mean? Connell and Connell don't know me, and I don't know them. Am I in a fit state to write letters, Aunt Edith?"

"It seemed to me the most unlikely thing in the world, Rupert, but what else was I to think?"

"They'd better have written to say I was going to take possession of the grave," he resumed; "there'd be more sense in that. Perhaps I am, Aunt Edith."

More sense in it? Ay, there would be. Every pulse in Mrs. Chattaway's heart echoed the words. She did not answer, and a pause ensued only broken by his somewhat painful breathing.

"Do you think I shall die, Aunt Edith?"

"Oh, my boy, I hope not; I hope not! But it is all in God's will. Rupert, darling, it seems a sad thing, especially to the young, to leave this world; but do you know what I often think as I lie and sigh through my sleepless nights: that it would be a blessed change both for you and for me if God were to take us from it, and give us a place in heaven."

Another pause. "You can tell Mr. Chattaway you feel sure I had nothing to do with the letter, Aunt Edith."

She shook her head. "No, Rupert; the less I say the better. It would not do; I should fear some chance word on my part might betray you: and all I could say would not make any impression on Mr. Chattaway."

"You are not going!" he exclaimed, as she rose from her seat on the bed.

"I must. I wish I could stay, but I dare not; indeed it was not safe to-night to come in at all."

"Aunt Edith, if you could only stay! It is so lonely. Four-and-twenty hours before I shall see you or Maude again! It is like being left alone to die."

"Not to die, I trust," she said, her tears falling fast. "We shall be together some time for ever, but I pray we may have a little happiness on earth first!"

Very full was her heart that night, and but for the fear that her red eyes would betray her, she could have wept all the way home. Stealing in at a side door, she gained her room, and found that Mr. Chattaway, fortunately, had not discovered her absence.

A few minutes after she entered, the house was in a commotion. Sounds were heard proceeding from the kitchen, and Mrs. Chattaway and others hastened towards it. One of the servants was badly scalded. Most unfortunately, it happened to be the cook, Rebecca. In taking some calve's-foot jelly from the fire, she had inadvertently overturned the boiling liquid.

Miss Diana, who was worth a thousand of Mrs. Chattaway in an emergency, had the woman placed in a recumbent position, and sent one of the grooms on horseback for Mr. King. But Miss Diana, while sparing nothing that could relieve the sufferer, did not conceal her displeasure at the awkwardness.

"Was it *jelly* you were making, Rebecca?" she sternly demanded.

Rebecca was lying back in a large chair, her feet raised. Everyone was crowding round: even Mr. Chattaway had come to ascertain the cause of the commotion. She made no answer.

Bridget did; rejoicing, no doubt, in her superior knowledge. "Yes, ma'am, it was jelly: she had just boiled it up."

Miss Diana wheeled round to Rebecca. "Why were you making jelly? It was not ordered."

Rebecca, not knowing what to say, glanced at Mrs. Chattaway. "Yes, it was ordered," murmured the latter. "I ordered it."

"You!" returned Miss Diana. "What for?" But Miss Diana spoke in surprise only; not objecting: it was so very unusual for Mrs. Chattaway to interfere in the domestic arrangements. It surprised them all, and her daughters looked at her. Poor Mrs. Chattaway could not put forth the plea that it was being made for herself, for calve's-foot jelly was a thing she never touched. The confusion on his wife's face attracted the notice of Mr. Chattaway.

"Possibly you intended to regale old Canham?" he scornfully said, alluding to what had passed that day. Not that he believed anything so improbable.

"Madam knows the young ladies like it, and she told me to make some," good-naturedly spoke up Rebecca in the midst of her pain.

The excuse served, and the matter passed. Miss Diana privately thought what a poor housekeeper her sister would make, ordering things when they were not required, and Mr. Chattaway quitted the scene. When the doctor arrived and had attended to the patient, Mrs. Chattaway, who was then in her room, sent to request him to come to her before he left, adding to the message that she did not feel well.

He came up immediately. She put a question or two about the injury to the girl, which was trifling, he answered, and would not keep her a prisoner long; and then Mrs. Chattaway lowered her voice, and spoke in the softest whisper.

"Mr. King, you must tell me. Is Rupert worse?"

"He is very ill," was the answer. "He certainly grows worse instead of better."

"Will he die?"

"I do believe he will die unless he can be got out of that unwholesome place. The question is, how is it to be done?"

"It cannot be done; it cannot be done unless Mr. Chattaway can be propitiated. That is the only chance."

"Mr. Chattaway never will be," thought Mr. King. "Everything is against him where he is," he said aloud: "the air of the room, the constant fear upon him, the want of proper food. The provisions conveyed to him at chance times are a poor substitute for the meals he requires."

"And they will be stopped now," said Mrs. Chattaway. "Rebecca has prepared them privately, but she cannot do so now. Mr. King, *what* can be done!"

"I don't know, indeed. It will not be safe to attempt to move him. In fact, I question if he would consent to it, his dread of being discovered is so great."

"Will you do all you can?" she urged.

"To be sure," he replied. "I *am* doing all I can. I got him another bottle of port in to-day. If you only saw me trying to dodge into the lodge unperceived, and taking observations before I whisk out again, you would say that I am as anxious as you can be, my dear lady. Still—I don't hesitate to avow it—I believe it will be life or death, according as we can manage to get him away from that hole and set his mind at rest."

He wished her good night, and went out.

"Life or death!" Mrs. Chattaway stood at the window, and gazed into the dusky night, recalling over and over again the ominous words. "Life or death!" There was no earthly chance, except the remote one of appeasing Mr. Chattaway.

CHAPTER LIII
A SURPRISE FOR MR. CHATTAWAY

George Ryle by no means liked the uncertainty in which he was kept as to the Upland Farm. Had Mr. Chattaway been any other than Mr. Chattaway, had he been a straightforward man, George would have said, "Give me an answer, Yes or No." In point of fact, he did say so; but was unable to get a reply from him, one way or the other. Mr. Chattaway was pretty liberal in his sneers as to one with no means of his own taking so extensive a farm as the Upland; but he did not positively say, "I will not lease it to you." George bore the sneers with equanimity. He possessed that very desirable gift, a sweet temper; and he was, and could not help feeling that he was, so really superior to Mr. Chattaway, that he could afford that gentleman's evil tongue some latitude.

But the time was going on; it was necessary that a decision should be arrived at; and one morning George went up again to the Hold, determined to receive a final answer. As he was entering the steward's room, he met Ford, the Blackstone clerk, coming out of it.

"Is Mr. Chattaway in there?" asked George.

"Yes," replied Ford. "But if you want any business out of him this morning, you won't get it. I have tramped all the way up here about a hurried matter and have had my walk for my pains. Chattaway won't do anything or say anything; doesn't seem capable; says he shall be at Blackstone by-and-by. And that's all I've got to go back with."

"Why won't he?"

"Goodness knows. He seems to have had a shock or fright: was staring at a letter when I went in, and I left him staring at it when I came out, his wits evidently wool-gathering. Good morning, Mr. Ryle."

The young man went his way, and George entered the room. Mr. Chattaway was seated at his desk; an open letter before him, as Ford had said. It was one that had been delivered by that morning's post, and it had brought the sweat of dismay upon his brow. He looked at George angrily.

"Who's this again? Am I never to be at peace? What do you want?"

"Mr. Chattaway, I want an answer. If you will not let me the Upland Farm—"

"I will give you no answer this morning. I am otherwise occupied, and cannot be bothered with business."

"Will you give me an answer—at all?"

"Yes, to-morrow. Come then."

George saw that something had indeed put Mr. Chattaway out; he appeared incapable of business, as Ford had intimated, and it would be policy, perhaps, to let the matter rest until to-morrow. But a resolution came into George's mind to do at once what he had sometimes thought of doing—make a friend, if possible, of Miss Diana Trevlyn. He went about the house until he found her, for he was almost as much at home there as poor Rupert had been. Miss Diana happened to be alone in the breakfast-room, looking over what appeared to be bills, but she laid them aside at his entrance, and—it was a most unusual thing—condescended to ask after the health of her sister, Mrs. Ryle.

"Miss Diana, I want you to be my friend," he said, in the winning manner that made George Ryle liked by everyone, as he drew a chair near to her. "Will you whisper a word for me into Mr. Chattaway's ear?"

"About the Upland Farm?"

"Yes. I cannot get an answer from him. He has promised me one to-morrow morning, but I do not rely upon it. I must be at some certainty. I have my eye on another farm if I cannot get Mr. Chattaway's; but it is at some distance, and I shall not like it half as well. Whilst he keeps me shilly-shallying over this one, I may lose both. There's an old proverb, you know, about two stools."

"Was that a joke the other day, the hint you gave about marrying?" inquired Miss Diana.

"It was sober earnest. If I can get the Upland Farm, I shall, I hope, take my wife home to it almost as soon as I am installed there myself."

"Is she a good manager, a practical woman?"

George smiled. "No. She is a lady."

"I thought so," was the remark of Miss Diana, delivered in very knowing tones. "I can tell you and your wife, George, that it will be uphill work for both of you."

"For a time; I know that. But, Miss Diana, ease, when it comes, will be all the more enjoyable for having been worked for. I often think the prosperity of those who have honestly earned it must be far sweeter than the monotonous abundance of those who are born rich."

"True. The worst is, that sometimes the best years of life are over before prosperity comes."

"But those years have had their pleasure, in working on for it. I question whether actual prosperity ever brings the pleasure we enjoy in anticipation. If we had no end to work for, we should not be happy. Will you say a word for me, Miss Diana?"

"First of all, tell me the name of the lady. I suppose you have no objection—you may trust me."

George's lips parted with a smile, and a faint flush stole over his features. "I shall have to tell you before I win her, if only to obtain your consent to taking her from the Hold."

"*My* consent! I have nothing to do with it. You must get that from Mr. and Madam Chattaway."

"If I have yours, I am not sure that I should care to ask—his."

"Of whom do you speak?" she rejoined, looking puzzled.

"Of Maude Trevlyn."

Miss Diana rose from her chair, and stared at him in astonishment. "Maude Trevlyn!" she repeated. "Since when have you thought of Maude Trevlyn?"

"Since I thought of any one—thought at all, I was going to say. I loved Maude—yes, *loved* her, Miss Diana—when she was only a child."

"And you have not thought of anyone else?"

"Never. I have loved Maude, and I have been content to wait for her. But that I was so trammelled with the farm at home, keeping it for Mrs. Ryle and Treve, I might have spoken before."

Maude Trevlyn was evidently not the lady upon whom Miss Diana's suspicions had fallen, and she seemed unable to recover from her surprise or realise the fact. "Have you never given cause to another to—to—suspect any admiration on your part?" she resumed, breaking the silence.

"Believe me, I never have. On the contrary," glancing at Miss Diana with peculiar significance for a moment, his tone most impressive, "I have cautiously abstained from doing so."

"Ah, I see." And Miss Trevlyn's tone was not less significant than his.

"Will you give her to me?" he pleaded, in his softest and most persuasive voice.

"I don't know, George, there may be trouble over this."

"Do you mean with Mr. Chattaway?"

"I mean—No matter what I mean. I think there will be trouble over it."

"There need be none if you will sanction it. But that you might misconstrue me, I would urge you to give her to me for Maude's own sake. This escapade of poor Rupert's has rendered Mr. Chattaway's roof an undesirable one for her."

"Maude is a Trevlyn, and must marry a gentleman," spoke Miss Diana.

"I am one," said George quietly. "Forgive me if I remind you that my ancestors are equal to those of the Trevlyns. In the days gone by—"

"You need not enter upon it," was the interruption. "I do not forget it. But gentle descent is not all that is necessary. Maude will have money, and it is only right that she should marry one who possesses it in an equal degree."

"Maude will not have a shilling," cried George, impulsively.

"Indeed! Who told you so?"

George laughed. "It is what I have always supposed. Where is her money to come from?"

"She will have a great deal of money," persisted Miss Diana. "The half of my fortune, at least, will be Maude's. The other half I intended for Rupert. Did you suppose the last of the Trevlyns, Maude and Rupert, would be turned penniless into the world?"

So! It had been Miss Diana's purpose to bequeath them money! Yes; loving power though she did; acquiescing in the act of usurping Trevlyn Hold as she had, she intended to make it up in some degree to the children. Human nature is full of contradictions. "Has Maude learnt to care for you?" she suddenly asked. "You hesitate!"

"If I hesitate it is not because I have no answer to give, but whether it would be quite fair to Maude to give it. The truth may be best, however; she *has* learnt to care for me. Perhaps you will answer me a question—have you any objection to me personally?"

"George Ryle, had I objected to you personally, I should have ordered you out of the room the instant you mentioned Maude's name. Were your position a better one, I would give you Maude to-morrow—so far as my giving could avail. But to enter the Upland Farm upon borrowed money?—no; I do not think that will do for Maude Trevlyn."

"It would be a better position for her than the one she now holds, as Mr. Chattaway's governess," replied George, boldly. "A better, and a far happier."

"Nonsense. Maude Trevlyn's position at Trevlyn Hold is not to be looked upon as that of governess, but as a daughter of the house. It was well that both she and Rupert should have some occupation."

"And on the other score?" resumed George. "May I dare to say the truth to you, that in quitting the Hold for the home I shall make for her, she will be leaving misery for happiness?"

Miss Diana rose. "That is enough for the present," said she. "It has come upon me with surprise, and I must give it some hours' consideration before I can even realise it. With regard to the Upland Farm, I will ask Mr. Chattaway to accord you preference if he can do so; the two matters are quite distinct and apart one from the other. I think you might prosper at the Upland Farm, and be a good tenant; but I decline—and this you must distinctly understand—to give you any hope now with regard to Maude."

George held out his hand with his sunny smile. "I will wait until you have considered it, Miss Diana."

She took her way at once to Mrs. Chattaway's room. Happening, as she passed the corridor window, to glance to the front of the house, she saw George Ryle cross the lawn. At the same moment, Octave Chattaway ran after him, evidently calling to him.

He stopped and turned. He could do no less. And Octave stood with him, laughing and talking rather more freely than she might have done, had she been aware of what had just taken place. Miss Diana drew in her severe lips, changed her course, and sailed back to the hall-door. Octave was coming in then.

"Manners have changed since I was a girl," remarked Miss Diana. "It would scarcely have been deemed seemly then for a young lady to run after a gentleman. I do not like it, Octave."

"Manners do change," returned Miss Chattaway, in tones she made as slighting as she dared. "It was only George Ryle, Aunt Diana."

"Do you know where Maude is?"

"No; I know nothing about her. I think if you gave Maude a word of reprimand instead of giving one to me, it might not be amiss, Aunt Diana. Since Rupert turned runagate—or renegade might be a better word—Maude has shamefully neglected her duties with Emily and Edith. She passes her time in the clouds and lets them run wild."

"Had Rupert been your brother you might have done the same," curtly rejoined Miss Diana. "A shock like that cannot be lived down in a day. Allow me to give you a hint, Octave; should you lose Maude for the children, you will not so efficiently replace her."

"We are not likely to lose her," said Octave, opening her eyes.

"I don't know that. It is possible that we shall. George Ryle wants her."

"Wants her for what?" asked Octave, staring very much.

"He can want her but for one thing—to be his wife. It seems he has loved her for years."

She quitted Octave as she said this, on her way up again to Mrs. Chattaway's room; never halting, never looking back at the still, white face, that seemed to be turning into stone as it was strained after her.

In Mrs. Chattaway's sitting-room she found that lady and Maude. She entered suddenly and hastily, and had Miss Diana been of a suspicious nature it might have arisen then. In their close contact, their start of surprise, the expression of their haggard countenances, there was surely evidence of some unhappy secret. Miss Diana was closely followed by Mr. Chattaway.

"Did you not hear me call?" he inquired of his sister-in-law.

"No," she replied. "I only heard you on the stairs behind me. What is it?"

"Read that," said Mr. Chattaway.

He tossed an open letter to her. It was the one which had so put him out, rendering him incapable of attending to business. After digesting it alone in the best manner he could, he had now come to submit it to the keen and calm inspection of Miss Trevlyn.

"Oh," said she carelessly, as she looked at the writing, "another letter from Connell and Connell."

"Read it," repeated Mr. Chattaway, in low tones. He was too completely shaken to be anything but subdued.

Miss Diana proceeded to do so. It was a letter shorter, if anything, than the previous one, but even more decided. It simply said that Mr. Rupert Trevlyn had written to inform them of his intention of taking immediate possession of Trevlyn Hold, and had requested them to acquaint Mr. Chattaway with the same. Miss Diana read it to herself, and then aloud for the general benefit.

"It is the most infamous thing that has ever come under my notice," said Mr. Chattaway. "What *right* have those Connells to address me in this strain? If Rupert Trevlyn passes his time inventing such folly, is it the work of a respectable firm to perpetuate the jokes on me?"

Mrs. Chattaway and Maude gazed at each other, perfectly confounded. It was next to impossible that Rupert could have thus written to Connell and Connell. If they had only dared defend him! "Why suffer it to put you out, James?" Mrs. Chattaway ventured to say. "Rupert *cannot* be writing such letters; he *cannot* be thinking of attempting to take possession here; the bare idea is absurd: treat it as such."

"But these communications from Connell and Connell are not the less disgraceful," was the reply. "I'd as soon be annoyed with anonymous letters."

Miss Diana Trevlyn had not spoken. The affair, to her keen mind, began to wear a strange appearance. She looked up from the letter at Mr. Chattaway. "Were Connell and Connell not so respectable, I should say they have lent themselves to a sorry joke for the purpose of the worst sort of annoyance: being what they are, that view falls to the ground. There is only one possible solution to it: but—"

"And what's that?" eagerly interrupted Mr. Chattaway.

"That Rupert is amusing himself, and has contrived to impose upon Connell and Connell—"

"He never has," broke in Mrs. Chattaway. "I mean," she more calmly added, "that Connell and Connell could not be imposed upon by any foolish claim put forth by a boy like Rupert."

"I wish you would hear me out," was the composed rejoinder of Miss Diana. "It is what I was about to say. Had Connell and Connell been different men, they might be so imposed upon; but I do not think they, or any firm of similar standing, would presume to write such letters to the master of Trevlyn Hold, unless they had substantial grounds for doing so."

"Then what can they mean?" cried Mr. Chattaway, wiping his hot face.

Ay, what could they mean? It was indeed a puzzle, and the matter began to assume a serious form. What had been the vain boastings of Mr. Daw, compared with this? Cris Chattaway, when he reached home, and this second letter was shown to him, was loudly indignant, but all the indignation Mr. Chattaway had been prone to indulge in seemed to have gone out of *him*. Mr. Flood wrote to Connell and Connell to request an explanation, and received a courteous and immediate reply. But it contained no further information than the letters themselves—or than even Mr. Peterby had elicited when he wrote up, on his own part, privately to Mr. Ray: nothing but that Mr. Rupert Trevlyn was about to take possession of his own again, and occupy Trevlyn Hold.

CHAPTER LIV
A GHOST FOR OLD CANHAM

Trevlyn Hold was a fine place, the cynosure and envy of the neighbourhood around; and yet it would perhaps be impossible in all that neighbourhood to find any family so completely miserable as that which inhabited the house. The familiar saying is a very true one: "All is not gold that glitters."

Enough has been said of the trials and discomforts of Mrs. Chattaway; they had been many and varied, but never had trouble accumulated upon her head as now. The terrible secret that Rupert was within hail, wasting unto death, was torturing her brain night and day. It seemed that the whole weight of it lay upon her; that she was responsible for his weal and woe: if he died would reproach not lie at her door, remorse be her portion for ever? It might be that she should have disclosed the secret, and not have left him there to die.

But how disclose it? Since the second letter received from Connell, Connell, and Ray, Mr. Chattaway had been doubly bitter against Rupert—if that were possible; and to disclose Rupert's hiding-place would only be to consign him to prison. Mr. Chattaway was another who was miserable in his home. Suspense is far worse than reality; and the present master would never realise in his own heart the evils attendant on being turned from the Hold as he was realising them now. His days were one prolonged scene of torture. Miss Diana Trevlyn partook of the general discomfort: for the first time in her life a sense of ill oppressed her. She knew nothing of the secret regarding Rupert; somewhat scornfully threw away the vague ideas imparted by the letters from Connell and Connell; and yet Miss Diana was conscious of being oppressed with a sense of ill, which weighed her down, and made life a burden.

The evil had come at last. Retribution, which they too surely invoked when they diverted God's laws of right and justice from their direct course years ago, was working itself just now. Retribution is a thing that *must* come; though tardy, as it had been in this case, it is sure. Look around you, you who have had much of life's experience, who may be drawing into its "sear and yellow leaf." It is impossible but that you have gathered up in the garner of your mind instances you have noted in your career. In little things and in great, the working of evil inevitably brings forth its reward. Years, and years, and years may elapse; so many, that the hour of vengeance seems to have rolled away under the glass of time; but we need never hope that, for it cannot be. In your day, ill-doer, or in your children's, it will surely come.

The agony of mind, endured now by the inmates of Trevlyn Hold, seemed sufficient punishment for a whole lifetime and its misdoings. Should they indeed be turned from it, as these mysterious letters appeared to indicate, that open, tangible punishment would be as nothing to what they were mentally enduring now. And they could not speak of their griefs one to another, and so lessen them in ever so slight a degree. Mr.

Chattaway would not speak of the dread tugging at his heart-strings—for it seemed to him that only to speak of the *possibility* of being driven forth, might bring it the nearer; and his unhappy wife dared not so much as breathe the name of Rupert, and the fatal secret she held.

She, Mrs. Chattaway, was puzzled more than all by these letters from Connell and Connell. Mr. Chattaway could trace their source (at least he strove to do so) to the malicious mind and pen of Rupert; but Mrs. Chattaway knew that Rupert it could not well be. Nevertheless, she had been staggered on the arrival of the second to find it explicitly stated that Rupert Trevlyn had written to announce his speedy intention of taking possession of the Hold. "Rupert had written to them!" What was she to think? If it was not Rupert, someone else must have written in his name; but who would be likely to trouble themselves now for the lost Rupert?—regarded as dead by three parts of the world. Had Rupert written? Mrs. Chattaway determined again to ask him, and to set the question so far at rest.

But she did not do this for two days after the arrival of the letter. She waited the answer which Mr. Flood wrote up to Connell and Connell, spoken of in the last chapter. As soon as that came, and she found that it explained nothing, then she resolved to question Rupert at her next stolen visit. That same afternoon, as she returned on foot from Barmester, she contrived to slip unseen into the lodge.

Rupert was sitting up. Mr. King had given it as his opinion that to lie constantly in bed, as he was doing, was worse than anything else; and in truth Rupert need not have been entirely confined to it had there been any other place for him. Old Canham's chamber opposite was still more stifling, inasmuch as the builder had forgotten to make the small window to open. Look at Rupert now, as Mrs. Chattaway enters! He has managed to struggle into his clothes, which hang upon him like sacks, and he sits uncomfortably on a small rush-bottomed chair. Rupert's back looks as if it were broken; he is bent nearly double with weakness; his lips are white, his cheeks hollow, and his poor, weak hands tremble with joy as they are feebly raised to greet Mrs. Chattaway. Think what it was for him! lying for long hours, for days, in that stifling room, a prey to his fears, sometimes seeing no one for two whole days—for it was not every evening that an opportunity could be found of entering the lodge. What with the Chattaways' passing and repassing the lodge, and Ann Canham's grumbling visitors, an entrance for those who might not be seen to enter it was not always possible. Look at poor Rupert; the lighting up of his eye, the kindling hectic of his cheek!

Mrs. Chattaway contrived to squeeze herself between Rupert and the door, and sat down on the edge of the bed as she took his hand in hers. "I am so glad to see you have made an effort to get up, Rupert!" she whispered.

"I don't think I shall make it again, Aunt Edith. You have no conception how it has tired me. I was a good half-hour getting into my coat and waistcoat."

"But you will be all the better for it."

"I don't know," said Rupert, in a spiritless tone. "I feel as if there would never be any 'better' for me again."

She began telling him of what she had been purchasing for him at Barmester—a dressed tongue, a box of sardines, potted meats, and similar things found in the provision shops. They were not precisely the dishes suited to Rupert's weakly state; but since the accident to Rebecca he had been fain to put up with what could be thus procured. And then Mrs. Chattaway opened gently upon the subject of the letters.

"It seems so strange, Rupert, quite inexplicable, but Mr. Chattaway has had another of those curious letters from Connell and Connell."

"Has he?" answered Rupert, with apathy.

Mrs. Chattaway looked at him with all the fancied penetration she possessed—in point of fact she was one of those persons who possess none—but she could not detect the faintest sign of consciousness. "Was there anything about me in it?" he asked wearily.

"It was all about you. It said you had written to Connell and Connell stating your intention of taking immediate possession of the Hold."

This a little aroused him. "Connell and Connell have written that to Mr. Chattaway! Why, what queer people they must be!"

"Rupert! You have *not* written to them, have you?"

He looked at Mrs. Chattaway in surprise; for she had evidently asked the question seriously. "You know I have not. I am not strong enough to play jokes, Aunt Edith. And if I were, I should not be so senseless as to play *that* joke. What end would it answer?"

"I thought not," she murmured; "I was sure not. Setting everything else aside, Rupert, you are not well enough to write."

"No, I don't think I am. I could hardly scrawl those lines to George Ryle some time ago—when the fever was upon me. No, Aunt Edith: the only letter I have written since I became a prisoner was the one I wrote to Mr. Daw, the night I first took shelter here, just after the encounter with Mr. Chattaway, and Ann Canham posted it at Barmester the next day. What on earth can possess Connell and Connell?"

"Diana argues that Connell and Connell must be receiving these letters, or they would not write to Mr. Chattaway in the manner they are doing. For my part, I can't make it out."

"What does Mr. Chattaway say?" asked Rupert, when a fit of coughing was over. "Is he angry?"

"He is worse than angry," she seriously answered; "he is troubled. He thinks you are writing them."

"No! Why, he might know that I shouldn't dare do it: he might know that I am not well enough to write them."

"Nay, Rupert, you forget that Mr. Chattaway does not know you are ill."

"To be sure; I forgot that. But I can't believe Mr. Chattaway is *troubled*. How could a poor, weak, friendless chap, such as I, contend for the possession of Trevlyn Hold? Aunt Edith, I'll tell you what it must be. If Connells are not playing this joke themselves, to annoy Mr. Chattaway, somebody must be playing it on them."

Mrs. Chattaway acquiesced: it was the only conclusion she could come to.

"Oh, Aunt Edith, if he would only forgive me!" sighed Rupert. "When I get well—and I should get well, if I could go back to the Hold and get this fear out of me—I would work night and day to repay him the cost of the ricks. If he would only forgive me!"

Ah! none knew better than Mrs. Chattaway how vain was the wish; how worse than vain any hope of forgiveness. She could have told him, had she chosen, of an unhappy scene of the past night, when she, Edith Chattaway, urged by the miserable state of existing things and her tribulation for Rupert, had so far forgotten prudence as to all but kneel to her husband and beg him to forgive that poor culprit; and Mr. Chattaway, excited to the very depths of anger, had demanded of his wife whether she were mad or sane, that she should dare ask it.

"Yes, Rupert," she meekly said, "I wish it also, for your sake. But, my dear, it is just an impossibility."

"If I could be got safely out of the country, I might go to Mr. Daw for a time, and get up my strength there."

"Yes, *if* you could. But in your weak state discovery would be the result before you were clear from these walls. You cannot take flight in the night. Everyone knows you: and the police, we have heard, are keeping their eyes open."

"I'd bribe Dumps, if I had money—"

Rupert's voice dropped. A commotion had suddenly arisen downstairs, and, his fears ever on the alert touching the police and Mr. Chattaway, he put up his hand to enjoin caution, and bent his head to listen. But no strange voice could be distinguished: only those of old Canham and his daughter. A short time, and Ann came up the stairs, looking strange.

"What's the matter?" panted Rupert, who was the first to catch sight of her face.

"I can't think what's come to father, sir," she returned. "I was in the back place, washing up, and heard a sort o' cry, as one may say, so I ran in. There he was standing with his hair all on end, and afore I could speak he began saying he'd seen a ghost go past. He's staring out o' window still. I hope his senses are not leaving him!"

To hear this assertion from sober-minded, matter-of-fact old Canham, certainly did impart a suspicion that his senses were departing. Mrs. Chattaway rose to descend, for she had already lingered longer than was prudent. She found old Canham as Ann had described him, with that peculiarly scared look on the face some people deem equivalent to "the hair standing on end." He was gazing with a fixed expression towards the Hold.

"Has anything happened to alarm you, Mark?"

Mrs. Chattaway's gentle question recalled him to himself. He turned towards her, leaning heavily on his stick, his eyes full of vague terror.

"It happened, Madam, as I had got out o' my seat, and was standing to look out o' window, thinking how fine the a'ternoon was, when he come in at the gate with a fine silver-headed stick in his hand, turning his head about from side to side as if he was taking note of the old place to see what changes there might be in it. I was struck all of a heap when I saw his figure; 'twas just the figure it used to be, only maybe a bit younger; but when he moved his head and looked full at me, I felt turned to stone. It was his face, ma'am, if I ever saw it."

"But whose?" asked Mrs. Chattaway, smiling at his incoherence.

Old Canham glanced round before he spoke; glanced at Mrs. Chattaway, with a half-compassionate, half-inquiring look, as if not liking to speak. "Madam, it was the old Squire, my late master."

"It was—who?" demanded Mrs. Chattaway, less gentle than usual in her great surprise.

"It was Squire Trevlyn; Madam's father."

Mrs. Chattaway could do nothing but stare. She thought old Canham's senses were decidedly gone.

"There never was a face like his. Miss Maude—that is, Mrs. Ryle now—have his features exact; but she's not as tall and portly, being a woman. Ah, Madam, you may smile at me, but it was Squire Trevlyn."

"But, Mark, you know it is impossible."

"Madam, 'twas him. He must ha' come out of his grave for some purpose, and is visiting his own again. I never was a believer in them things afore, or thought as the dead come back to life."

Ghosts have gone out of fashion; therefore the enlightened reader will not be likely to endorse old Canham's belief. But when Mrs. Chattaway, turning quickly up the avenue on her way to the Hold, saw, at no great distance from her, a gentleman standing to talk to some one whom he had encountered, she stopped, as one in sudden terror, and seemed about to fall or faint. Mrs. Chattaway did not believe in "the dead coming back" any more than old Canham had believed in it; but in that moment's startled surprise she did think she saw her father.

She gazed at the figure, her lips apart, her bright complexion fading to ashy paleness. Never had she seen so extraordinary a likeness. The tall, fine form, somewhat less full perhaps than of yore, the distinctly-marked features with their firm and haughty expression, the fresh clear skin, the very manner of handling that silver-headed stick, spoke in unmistakable terms of Squire Trevlyn.

Not until they parted, the two who were talking, did Mrs. Chattaway observe that the other was Nora Dickson. Nora came down the avenue towards her; the stranger went on with his firm step and his firmly-grasped stick. Mrs. Chattaway was advancing then.

"Nora, who is that?" she gasped.

"I am trying to collect my wits, if they are not scared away for good," was Nora's response. "Madam Chattaway, you might just have knocked me down with a feather. I was walking along, thinking of nothing, except my vexation that you were not at home—for Mr. George charged me to bring this note to you, and to deliver it instantly into your own hands, and nobody else's—when I met him. I didn't know whether to face him, or scream, or turn and run; one doesn't like to meet the dead; and I declare to you, Madam Chattaway, I believed, in my confused brain, that it was the dead. I believed it was Squire Trevlyn."

"Nora, I never saw two persons so strangely alike," she breathed, mechanically taking the note from Nora's hand. "Who is he?"

"My brain's at work to discover," returned Nora, dreamily. "I am trying to put two and two together, and can't do it; unless the dead have come to life—or those we believed dead."

"Nora! you cannot mean my father!" exclaimed Mrs. Chattaway, gazing at her with a strangely perplexed face. "You know he lies buried in Barbrook churchyard. What did he say to you?"

"Not much. He saw me staring at him, I suppose, and stopped and asked me if I belonged to the Hold. I answered, no; I did not belong to it; I was Miss Dickson, of Trevlyn Farm. And then it was his turn to stare at me. 'I think I should have known you,' he said. 'At least, I do now that I have the clue. You are not much altered. Should you have known me?' 'I don't know you now,' I answered: 'unless you are old Squire Trevlyn come out of his grave. I never saw such a likeness.'"

"And what did he say?" eagerly asked Mrs. Chattaway.

"Nothing more. He laughed a little at my speech, and went on. Madam Chattaway, will you open the note, please, and see if there's any answer. Mr. George said it was important."

She opened the note, which had lain unheeded in her hand, and read as follows:

"Do not attempt further visits. Suspicions are abroad.

"G. B. R."

She had just attempted one, and paid it. Had it been watched? A rush of fear bounded within her for Rupert's sake.

"There's no answer, Nora," said Mrs. Chattaway: and she turned homewards, as one in a dream. Who *was* that man before her? What was his name? where did he come from? Why should he bear this strange likeness to her dead father? Ah, why, indeed! The truth never for one moment entered the mind of Mrs. Chattaway.

He went on: he, the stranger. When he came to the lawn before the house, he stepped on to it and halted. He looked to this side, he looked to that; he gazed up at the house; just as one loves to look on returning to a beloved home after an absence of years. He stood with his head thrown back; his right hand stretched out, the stick it grasped planted firm and upright on the ground. How many times had old Squire Trevlyn stood in the selfsame attitude on that same lawn!

There appeared to be no one about; no one saw him, save Mrs. Chattaway, who hid herself amidst the trees, and furtively watched him. She would not have passed him for the world, and she waited until he should be gone. She was unable to divest her mind of a sensation akin to the supernatural, as she shrank from this man who bore so wonderful a resemblance to her father. He, the stranger, did not detect her behind him, and presently he walked across the lawn, ascended the steps, and tried the door.

But the door was fastened. The servants would sometimes slip the bolt as a protection against tramps, and they had probably done so to-day. Seizing the bell-handle, the visitor rang such a peal that Sam Atkins, Cris Chattaway's groom, who happened to be in the house and near the door, flew with all speed to open it. Sam had never known Squire Trevlyn; but in this stranger now before him, he could not fail to remark a great general resemblance to the Trevlyn family.

"Is James Chattaway at home?"

To hear the master of the Hold inquired for in that unceremonious manner, rather took Sam back; but he answered that he was at home. He had no need to invite the visitor to walk in, for the visitor had walked in of his own accord. "What name, sir?" demanded Sam, preparing to usher the stranger across the hall.

"Squire Trevlyn."

This concluded Sam Atkins's astonishment. "*What* name, sir, did you say?"

"Squire Trevlyn. Are you deaf, man? Squire Trevlyn, of Trevlyn Hold."

And the haughty motion of the head, the firm pressure of the lips, might have put a spectator all too unpleasantly in mind of the veritable old Squire Trevlyn, had one who had known him been there to see.

CHAPTER LV
THE DREAD COME HOME

Nothing could well exceed Mr. Chattaway's astonishment at hearing that George Ryle wished to make Maude Trevlyn his wife. And nothing could exceed his displeasure. Not that Mr. Chattaway had higher views for Maude, or deemed it an undesirable match in a pecuniary point of view, as Miss Diana Trevlyn had intimated. Had Maude chosen to marry without any prospect at all, that would not have troubled Mr. Chattaway. But what did trouble Mr. Chattaway was this—that a sister of Rupert Trevlyn should become connected with George Ryle. In Mr. Chattaway's foolish and utterly groundless prejudices, he had suspected, as you may remember, that George Ryle and Rupert had been ever ready to hatch mischief against him; and he dreaded for his own sake any bond of union that might bring them closer together.

There was something else. By some intuitive perception Mr. Chattaway had detected that misplaced liking of his daughter's for George Ryle: and *this* union would not have been unpalatable to Mr. Chattaway. Whatever may have been his ambition for his daughter's settlement in life, whatever his dislike to George Ryle, he was willing to forego it all for his own sake. Every consideration was lost sight of in that one which had always reigned paramount with Mr. Chattaway—self-interest. You have not waited until now to learn that James Chattaway was one of the most selfish men on the face of the earth. Some men like, as far as they can, to do their duty to God and to their fellow-creatures; the master of Trevlyn Hold had made self the motive-spring through life. And what sort of a garner for the Great Day do you suppose he had been laying up for himself? He was soon to experience a little check here, but that was little, in comparison. The ills our evil conduct entails upon ourselves here, are as nothing to the dread reckoning we must render up hereafter.

Mr. Chattaway would have leased the Upland Farm to George Ryle with all the pleasure in life, provided he could have leased his daughter with it. Were George Ryle his veritable son-in-law, he would fear no longer plotting against himself. Somehow, he did fear George Ryle, feared him as a good man, brave, upright, honourable, who might be tempted to make common cause with the oppressed against the oppressor. It may be, also, that Miss Chattaway did not render herself as universally agreeable at home as she might have done, for her naturally bad temper did not improve with years; and for this reason Mr. Chattaway was not sorry that the Hold should be rid of her. Altogether, he contemplated with satisfaction, rather than the contrary, the connection of George Ryle with his family. And he could not be quite blind to certain predilections shown by Octave, though no hint or allusion had ever been spoken on either side.

And on that first day when George Ryle, after speaking to Mr. Chattaway about the lease of the Upland Farm, said a joking word or two to Miss Diana of his marriage, Octave had overheard. You saw her with her scarlet face looking over her aunt's shoulder: a face which seemed to startle George, and caused him to take his leave somewhat abruptly.

Poor Octave Chattaway! When George had remarked that his coveted wife was a gentlewoman, and must live accordingly, the words had imparted to her a meaning George himself never gave them. *She* was the gentlewoman to whom he alluded.

Ere the scarlet had faded, her father entered the room. Octave bent over the table drawing a pattern. Mr. Chattaway stood at the window, his hands in his pockets, a habit of his when in thought, and watched George Ryle walking away in the distance.

"He wants the Upland Farm, Octave."

Mr. Chattaway presently remarked, without turning round. "He thinks he can get on in it."

Miss Chattaway carried her pencil to the end of the line, and bent her face lower. "I should let him have it, papa."

"The Upland Farm will take money to stock and carry on; no slight sum," remarked Mr. Chattaway.

"Yes. Did he say how he should manage to get it?"

"From Apperley. He will have his work cut out if he is to begin farming on borrowed money; as his father had before him. It is only this very day that he has paid off that debt, contracted so many years ago."

"And no wonder, on that small Trevlyn Farm. The Upland is different. A man would grow rich on the one, and starve on the other."

"To take the best farm in the world on borrowed money, would entail uphill work. George Ryle will have to work hard; and so must his wife, should he marry."

Octave paused for a moment, apparently mastering some intricacies in her pattern. "Not his wife; I do not see that. Aunt Maude is a case in point; she has never worked at Trevlyn Farm."

"She has had her cares, though," returned Mr. Chattaway. "And she would have had to work—but for Nora Dickson."

"The Upland Farm could afford a housekeeper if necessary," was Octave's answer.

Not another word was spoken. Mr. Chattaway's suspicions were confirmed, and he determined when George Ryle again asked for the farm lease and for Octave, to accord both with rather more graciousness than he was accustomed to accord anything.

Things did not turn out, however, quite in accordance with his expectations. The best of us are disappointed sometimes, you know. George Ryle pressed for the farm, but did not press for Octave. In point of fact, he never mentioned her name, or so much as hinted at any interest he might feel in her; and Mr. Chattaway, rather puzzled and very cross, abstained from promising the farm. He put off the question, very much to George's inconvenience, who set it down to caprice.

But the time came for Mr. Chattaway's eyes to be opened, and he awoke to the cross-purposes which had been at work. On the afternoon of the day mentioned in the last chapter, during Mrs. Chattaway's stolen visit to Rupert, Mr. Chattaway was undeceived. He had been at home all day, busy over accounts and other matters in the steward's room; and Miss Diana, mindful of her promise to George Ryle, to speak a word in his favour relative to the Upland Farm, entered that room for the purpose, deeming it a good opportunity. Mr. Chattaway had been so upset since the receipt of the second letter from Connell and Connell, that she had hitherto abstained from mentioning the subject. He was seated at his desk, and looked up with a start as she abruptly entered; the start of a man who lives in fear.

"Have you decided whether George Ryle is to have the Upland Farm?" she asked, plunging into the subject without circumlocution, as it was the habit of Miss Diana Trevlyn to do.

"No, not precisely. I shall see in a day or two."

"But you promised him an answer long before this."

"Ah," slightingly spoke Mr. Chattaway. "It's not always convenient to keep one's promises."

"Why are you holding off?"

"Well, for one thing, I thought of retaining that farm in my own hands, and keeping a bailiff to look after it."

"Then you'll burn your fingers, James Chattaway. Those who manage the Upland Farm should live at the Upland Farm. You can't properly manage both places, that and Trevlyn Hold; and you live at Trevlyn Hold. I don't see why you should not let it to George Ryle."

Mr. Chattaway sat biting the end of his pen. Miss Diana waited; but he did not speak, and she resumed.

"I believe he will do well on it. One who has done so much with that small place, Trevlyn Farm, and its indifferent land, will not fail to do well on the Upland. Let him have it, Chattaway."

"You speak as if you were interested in the matter," remarked Mr. Chattaway, resentfully.

"I am not sure but I am," equably answered Miss Diana. "I see no reason why you should not let him the farm; for there's no doubt he will prove a good tenant. He has spoken to me about its involving something more, should he obtain it," she continued, after a pause.

"Ah," said Mr. Chattaway, without surprise. "Well?"

"He wants us to give him Maude."

Mr. Chattaway let fall his pen and it made a dreadful blot on his account-book, as he turned his head sharply on Miss Diana.

"Maude! You mean Octave."

"Pooh!" cried Miss Diana. "Octave has been spending her years looking after a mare's nest: people who do such foolish things must of necessity meet disappointment. George Ryle has never cared for her, never cast a thought to her."

Mr. Chattaway's face was turning its disagreeable colour; and his lips were drawn as he glared at Miss Trevlyn. "He has been always coming here."

"Yes. For Maude—as it turns out. I confess I never thought of it."

"How do you know this?"

"He has asked for Maude, I tell you. His hopes for years have been fixed upon her."

"He shall never have her," said Mr. Chattaway, emphatically. "He shall never have the Upland Farm."

"It was the decision—with regard to Maude—that crossed me in the first moment. I like him; quite well enough to give him Maude, or to give him Octave, had she been the one sought; but I do not consider his position suitable—"

"Suitable! Why, he's a beggar," interrupted Mr. Chattaway, completely losing sight of his own intentions with regard to his daughter. "George Ryle shall smart for this. Give him Maude, indeed!"

"But if Maude's happiness is involved in it, what then?" quietly asked Miss Diana.

"Don't be an idiot," was the retort of Mr. Chattaway.

"I never was one yet," said Miss Diana, equably. "But I have nearly made up my mind to give him Maude."

"You cannot do it without my consent. She is under my roof and guardianship, and I tell you that she shall never leave it for that of George Ryle."

"You should bring a little reason to your aid before you speak," returned Miss Diana, with that calm assumption of intellectual superiority which so vexed Mr. Chattaway whenever it peeped out. "What are the true facts? Why, that no living being, neither you nor any one else, can legally prevent Maude from marrying whom she will. You have no power to prevent it. She and Rupert have never had a legally-appointed guardian, remember. But for the loss of that letter, written at the instance of their mother when she was dying, and which appears to have vanished so mysteriously, *I* should have been their guardian," pointedly concluded Miss Diana. "And might have married Maude as I pleased."

Mr. Chattaway made no reply, except that he nervously bit his lips. If Diana Trevlyn turned against him, all seemed lost. That letter was upon his conscience as he sat there; for he it was who had suppressed it.

"And therefore, as in point of fact we have no power whatever vested in us, as Maude might marry whom she chose without consulting us, and as I like George Ryle on his own account, and *she* likes him better than the whole world, I consider that we had better give a willing consent. It will be making a merit of necessity, you see, Chattaway."

Mr. Chattaway saw nothing of the sort; but he dared not too openly defy Miss Trevlyn. "You would marry her to a beggar!" he cried. "To a man who does not possess a shilling! You must have a great regard for her!"

"Maude has no money, you know."

"I do know it. And that is all the more reason why her husband should possess some."

"They will get on, Chattaway, at the Upland Farm."

"I dare say they will—when they have it. I shall not lease the Upland Farm to a man who has to borrow money to go into it."

"I might be brought to obviate that difficulty," rejoined Miss Diana, in her coldest and hardest manner, as she gazed full at Mr. Chattaway. "Since I learnt that their mother left the children to me, I have felt a sort of proprietary right in them, and shall perhaps hand over to Maude, when she leaves us, sufficient money to stock the Upland Farm. The half at least of what I possess will some time be hers."

Was *this* the result of his having suppressed that dying mother's letter? Be very sure, Mr. Chattaway, that such dealings can never prosper! So long as there is a just and good God above us, they can but bring their proper recompense.

Mr. Chattaway did not trust himself to reply. He drew a sheet of paper towards him, and dashed off a few lines upon it. It was a peremptory refusal to lease the Upland Farm to George Ryle. Folding it, he placed it in an envelope, directed it, and rang the bell.

"What's that?" asked Miss Diana.

"My reply to Ryle. He shall never rent the Upland Farm."

In Mr. Chattaway's impatience, he did not give time for the bell to be answered, but opened the door and shouted. It was no one's business in particular to answer that bell; and Sam Atkins, who was in the kitchen, waiting for orders from Cris, ran forward at Mr. Chattaway's call.

"Take this letter down to Trevlyn Farm instantly," was the command. "Instantly, do you hear?"

But in the very act of the groom's taking it from Mr. Chattaway's hand, there came that violent ringing at the hall-door of which you have heard. Sam Atkins, thinking possibly the Hold might be on fire, as the ricks had been not so long ago, flew to open it, though it was not his place to do so.

And Mr. Chattaway, disturbed by the loud and imperative summons, stood where he was, and looked and listened. He saw the entrance of the stranger, and heard the announcement: "Squire Trevlyn, of Trevlyn Hold."

Miss Diana Trevlyn heard it, and came forth, and they stood like two living petrifactions, gazing at the apparition. Miss Diana, strong-minded woman that she was, did think for the moment that she saw her father. But her senses came to her, and she walked slowly forward to meet him.

"You must be my brother, Rupert Trevlyn!—risen from the dead."

"I am; but not risen from the dead," he answered, taking the hands she held out. "Which of them are you? Maude?"

"No; Diana. Oh, Rupert! I thought it was my father."

It was indeed him they had for so many years believed to be dead; Rupert Trevlyn, the runaway. He had come home to claim his own; come home in his true character; Squire Trevlyn, of Trevlyn Hold.

But Mr. Chattaway, in his worse and wildest dreams, had never bargained for this!

CHAPTER LVI
DOUBTS CLEARED AT LAST

Many a painting has been handed down to posterity whose features bore not a tithe of the interest presented at that moment in the old hall of the Trevlyns. The fine figure of the stranger, standing with the air of a chieftain, conscious of his own right; the keen gaze of Miss Diana, regarding him with puzzled equanimity; and the slow horror of conviction that was rising to the face of Mr. Chattaway. Behind all, stealing in by a side-door, came the timid steps, the pale questioning looks of Mrs. Chattaway, not yet certain whether the intruder was an earthly or a ghostly visitor.

Mr. Chattaway was the first to recover himself. He looked at the stranger with a face that strove to be haughty, and would have given the whole world to possess the calm equanimity of the Trevlyns, the unchanged countenance of Miss Diana; but his leaden face wore its worst and greenest tinge, his lips quivered as he spoke—and he was conscious of it.

"*Who* do you say you are? Squire Trevlyn? He has been in his grave long ago. We do not tolerate impostors here."

"I hope you do not," was the reply of the stranger, turning his face full on the speaker. "*I* will not in future, I can tell you that. True, James Chattaway: one Squire Trevlyn is in his grave; but he lives again in me. I am Rupert Trevlyn, and Squire of Trevlyn Hold."

Yes, it was Rupert Trevlyn. The young Rupert Trevlyn of the old days; the runaway heir. He, whom they had so long mourned as dead (though perhaps none had mourned very greatly), had never died, and now had come home, after all these years, to claim his own.

Mr. Chattaway backed against the wall, and stood staring with his livid face. To contend was impossible. To affect to believe that it was not Rupert Trevlyn and the true heir, next in legal succession to his father, the old Squire, would have been child's play. The well-remembered features of Rupert grew upon his memory one by one. Putting aside that speaking likeness to the Squire, to the Trevlyns generally, Mr. Chattaway, now that the first moments of surprise were over, would himself have recognised him. He needed not the acknowledgment of Miss Diana, the sudden recognition of his wife, who darted forward, uttering her brother's name, and fell sobbing into his arms, to convince him that it was indeed Rupert Trevlyn, the indisputable master from henceforth of Trevlyn Hold.

He leaned against the wall, and took in all the despair of his position. The latent fear so long seated in his heart, that he would some time lose Trevlyn Hold, had never pointed to *this*. In some far-away mental corner Chattaway had vaguely looked forward to lawsuits and contentions between him and its claimant, poor Rupert, son of Joe. He had fancied that the lawsuits might last for years, he meanwhile keeping possession, perhaps up to the end. Never had he dreamed that it would suddenly be wrested from him by indisputable right; he had never believed that he himself was the usurper; that a nearer and direct heir, the Squire's son, was in existence. The Squire's will, leaving Trevlyn Hold to his eldest son, had never been cancelled.

And this was the explanation of the letters from Connell, Connell and Ray, which had so annoyed Mr. Chattaway and puzzled his wife. "Rupert Trevlyn was about to take up his own again—as Squire of Trevlyn Hold." True; but it was this Rupert Trevlyn, not that one.

The explanation he might have entered into is of little moment to us; the bare fact is sufficient. It was an explanation he gave only partially to those around, descending to no details. He had been shipwrecked at the time of his supposed death, and knew that an account of his death had been sent home. That was true. Why he had suffered it to remain uncontradicted he did not explain; and they could only surmise that the crime of which he had been suspected kept him silent. However innocent he knew himself to be, whilst others at home believed him guilty he was not safe, and he had never known until recently that his reputation had been cleared. So much he did say. He had been half over the world, he told them, but had lived chiefly in South America, where he had made a handsome fortune.

"And whose children are these?" he asked, as he passed into the drawing-room, where the sea of wondering faces was turned upon him. "*You* should be James Chattaway's daughter," he cried, singling out Octave, "for you have the face of your father over again."

"I am Miss Chattaway," she answered, drawing from him with a scornful gesture. "Papa," she whispered, going up to the cowed, shrinking figure, who had followed in the wake of the rest, "who is that man?"

"Hush, Octave! He has come to turn us out of our home."

Octave gazed as one suddenly blinded. She saw the strange likeness to the Trevlyns, and it flashed into her mind that it must be the Uncle Rupert, risen from the supposed dead, of whom she had heard so much. She saw him notice her two sisters; saw him turn to Maude, and gaze earnestly into her face.

"You should be a Trevlyn. A softer, fairer face than Joe's, but the same outlines. What is your name, my dear?"

"Maude Trevlyn, sir."

"Ay. Joe's child. Have you any brothers or sisters?"

"One brother."

Squire Trevlyn—we must give him his title henceforth—looked round the room, as if in search of the brother. "Where is he?"

Maude shivered; but he waited for an answer, and she gave it. "He is not here, sir."

"And now tell me a little of the past," he cried, wheeling round on his sister Diana. "Who is the reigning master of Trevlyn Hold?"

She indicated Chattaway with her finger. "He is."

"He! Who succeeded my father—in my place?"

"He did. James Chattaway."

"Then where was Joe?"

"Joe was dead. He had died a few months previously."

"Leaving—how many children did you say—two?"

"Two—Maude and Rupert."

"The latter still an infant, I presume, at the time of my father's death?"

"Quite an infant."

"Nevertheless, he was Squire of Trevlyn Hold, failing me. Why did he not succeed?"

There came no answer. He looked at them all in succession; but even Miss Diana Trevlyn's undisturbable equanimity was shaken for the moment. It was Mr. Chattaway who plucked up courage to reply, and he put on as bold a front as he could.

"Squire Trevlyn judged it well to will the estate to me. What would a child in petticoats do, reigning at Trevlyn Hold?"

"He might have reigned by deputy. Where is Rupert? I must see him!"

But had they been keen observers they might have detected that Squire Trevlyn put the questions not altogether with the tone of a man who seeks information. In point of fact he was as wise as they were as to the principal events which had followed on the Squire's death. He had remained in

London two or three weeks since landing; had gathered all the information that could be afforded him by Connell and Connell, and had himself dictated the letters which had so upset Mr. Chattaway; more than that, he had, this very morning, halted at Barmester, on his way to Trevlyn Hold, had seen Mr. Peterby, and gleaned many details. One thing Mr. Peterby had not been able to tell him, whether the unfortunate Rupert was living or dead.

"Where is Maude?" he suddenly asked.

Maude stepped forward, somewhat surprised.

"Not you, child. One who must be thirty good years older than you. My sister, Maude Trevlyn."

"She married Thomas Ryle, of the Farm," answered Miss Diana, who had rapidly determined to be the best of friends with her brother. "It was not a fitting match for her, and she entered upon it without our consent; nay, in defiance of us all. She lives there still; and—and—here she is!"

For once in her life Miss Diana was startled into betraying surprise. There, coming in at the door, was her sister Maude, Mrs. Ryle; and she had not been at the Hold for years and years.

Nora, keen-witted Nora, had fathomed the mystery as she walked home. One so strangely resembling old Squire Trevlyn must be very closely connected with him, she doubted not, and worked out the problem. It must be Rupert Trevlyn, come (may it not be said?) to life again. Before she entered, his features had been traced on her memory, and she hastened to acquaint Mrs. Ryle.

That lady lost no time in speeding to the Hold. George accompanied her. There was no agitation on her face; it was a true Trevlyn's in its calm and quiet, but she greeted her brother with words of welcome.

"I have not entered this house, Rupert, my brother, since its master died; I would not enter it whilst a usurper reigned. Thank Heaven, you have come. It will end all heart-burnings."

"Heart-burnings? of what nature? But who are you?" he broke off, looking at George. Then he raised his hand, and laying it on his shoulder, gazed into his face. "Unless I am mistaken, you are your father's son."

George laughed. "My father's son, I believe, sir, and people tell me I am like him; yet more like my mother. I am George Berkeley Ryle."

"Is he here? I and Tom Ryle were good friends once."

"Here!" uttered George, with emotion he could not wholly suppress. "He has been dead many years. He was killed."

Squire Trevlyn lifted his hands. "It will all come out, bit by bit, I suppose: one record of the past after another. Maude"—turning to his sister—"I was inquiring of the days gone by. If the Trevlyns have held a name for nothing else in the county, they have held one for justice; and I want to know how it was that my father—my father and yours—willed away his estate from poor Joe's boy. Good Heavens," he broke off abruptly, as he caught sight of her face in the red light of the declining sun, "how wonderfully you have grown like my father! More so even than I have!"

It was so. As Mrs. Ryle stood there, haughty and self-possessed, they might have deemed it the old Squire over again. "You want to know why my father willed away his estate from Joe's son?" she said. "Ask Chattaway; ask Diana Trevlyn," with a sweep of the hand to both. "Ask them to tell you who kept it from him that a son was born to Joe. *They* did. The Squire made his will, went to his grave, never knowing that young Rupert was born. Ask them to tell you how it was that, when in accordance with this fact the will was made, my father constituted his second daughter's husband his heir, instead of my husband; mine, his eldest daughter's. Ask them, Rupert."

"Heart-burnings? Yes, I can understand," murmured Squire Trevlyn.

"Ask *him*—Chattaway—about the two thousand pounds debt to Mr. Ryle," she continued, never flinching from her stern gaze, never raising her voice above its calm tones of low, concentrated indignation. "You have just said that you and Tom Ryle were friends, Rupert. Yes, you were friends; and had you reigned after my father, he, my husband, would not have been hunted to his death."

"Maude! What are you saying?"

"The truth. Wherever that man Chattaway could lay his oppressive hand, he has laid it. He pursued my husband incessantly during life; it was through that pursuit—indirectly, I admit—that he met his death. The debt of two thousand pounds, money which had been lent to Mr. Ryle, he, my father, cancelled on his death-bed; he made my husband a present of it; he would have handed him the bond then and there, but it was in Chattaway's possession, and he said he would send it to him. It never was sent, Rupert; and the first use Chattaway made of his new power when he came into the Hold, was to threaten to sue my husband upon the bond. The Squire had given my husband his word to renew the lease on the same terms, and *you* know that his word was never broken. The second thing Chattaway did was to raise the rent. It has been nothing but uphill work with us."

"I'll right it now, Maude," he cried, with all the generous impulse of the Trevlyns. "I'll right that, and all else."

"We have righted it ourselves," she answered proudly. "By dint of perseverance and hard work, not on my part, but on *his*"—pointing to George—"we have paid it off. Not many days ago, the last instalment of the debt and interest was handed to Chattaway. May it do him good! *I* should not like to grow rich upon unjust gains."

"But where is Rupert?" repeated Squire Trevlyn. "I must see Rupert."

Ah, there was no help for it, and the whole tale was poured into his ear. Between Mrs. Ryle's revelations on the one side, and Chattaway's denials on the other, it was all poured into the indignant but perhaps not surprised ear of the new master of Trevlyn. The unkindness and oppression dealt out to Rupert throughout his unhappy life, the burning of the rick, the strange disappearance of Rupert. He gave no token that he had heard it all before. Mrs. Ryle spared nothing. She told him of the suspicion so freely dealt out by the neighbourhood that Chattaway had made away with Rupert. Even then the Squire returned no sign that he knew of the suspicion as well as they did.

"Maude," he said, "where is Rupert? Diana, *you* answer me—where is Rupert?"

They were unable to answer. They could only say that he was absent, they knew not how or where.

It may be that Squire Trevlyn feared the suspicion might be too true a one; for he turned suddenly on James Chattaway, his eye flashing with a severe light.

"Tell me where the boy is."

"I don't know," said Mr. Chattaway.

"He may be dead!"

"He may—for all I can say to the contrary."

Squire Trevlyn paused. "Rupert Trevlyn is my heir," he slowly said, "and I will have him found. James Chattaway, I insist on your producing Rupert."

"Nobody can insist upon the impossible."

"Then listen. You don't know much of me, but you knew my father; and you may remember that when he *willed* a thing, he did it: that same spirit is mine. Now I register a vow that if you do not produce Rupert Trevlyn, or tell me where I may find him, dead or alive, I will publicly charge you with the murder."

"I have as much reason to charge you with it, as you have to charge me," returned Mr. Chattaway, his anger rising. "You have heard them tell you of my encounter with Rupert on the evening following the examination before the magistrates. I declare on my sacred word of honour—"

"*Your* word of honour!" scornfully apostrophised Mrs. Ryle.

"That I have never seen Rupert Trevlyn since the moment I left him on the ground," he continued, turning his dark looks on Mrs. Ryle, but never pausing. "I have sought in vain for him since; the police have sought; and he is not to be found."

"Very well," said the Squire. "I have given you the alternative."

Mr. Chattaway opened his lips to reply; but to the surprise of all who knew him, suddenly closed them again, and left the room. To describe the trouble the man was in would be impossible. Apart from the general perplexity brought by this awful arrival of a master for Trevlyn Hold, there was the lesser doubt as to what should be his own conduct. Should it be abject submission, or war to the knife? Mr. Chattaway's temper would have inclined him to the latter; but he feared it might be bad policy for his own interest; and self-interest had always been paramount with James Chattaway. He stood outside the house, where he had wandered, and cast his eyes on the fine old place, the fair domain stretching around. Facing him was the rick-yard, which had given rise to so much discomfort, trouble, and ill-feeling. Oh, if he could only dispute successfully, and retain possession! But a conviction lay on his heart that even to attempt such would be the height of folly. That he, thus returned, was really the true Rupert Trevlyn, who had decamped in his youth, now a middle-aged man, was apparent as the sun at noon-day. It was apparent to him; it would be apparent to the world. The returned wanderer had remarked that his identity would be established by proof not to be disputed; but Mr. Chattaway felt no proof was necessary. Of what use then to hold out? And yet! to quit this fine possession, to sink into poverty and obscurity in the face and eyes of the local world—that world which had been ready enough, as it was, to cast contempt on the master of Trevlyn Hold—would be as the bitterest fate that ever fell upon man. In that cruel moment, when all was pressing upon his imagination with fearfully vivid colours, it seemed that death would be as a boon in comparison.

Whilst he was thus standing, torn with contending emotions, Cris ran up in excitement from the direction of the stables. He had left his horse there on his return from Blackstone, and some vague and confused version of the affair had been told him. "What's this, father?" he asked, in loud anger. "They are saying that Rupert Trevlyn has come boldly back, and claims the Hold. Have you given him into custody?"

Mr. Chattaway raised his dull eyes. The question only added to his misery. "Yes, Rupert Trevlyn has come back," he said; "but—"

"Is he in custody?" impatiently interrupted Cris. "Are the police here?"

"It is another Rupert Trevlyn, Cris; not that one."

Something in his father's manner struck unpleasantly on the senses of Cris Chattaway, subduing him considerably. "Another Rupert Trevlyn!" he repeated, in hesitating tones. "What are you saying?"

"The Rupert Trevlyn of old; the Squire's runaway son; the heir," said Mr. Chattaway, as if it comforted him to tell out all the bitter truth. "He has come back to claim his own, Cris—Trevlyn Hold."

And Mr. Cris fell against the wall, side by side with his father, and stared in dismayed consternation.

CHAPTER LVII
A VISIT TO RUPERT

And what were the emotions of Mrs. Chattaway? They were of a mixed nature. In spite of the very small comfort which possession of the Hold had brought her individually; in spite of the feeling of usurpation, of *wrong*, which had ever rested unpleasantly upon her; she would have been superior to frail human nature, had not a sense of dismay struck upon her at its being thus suddenly wrested from them. She knew not what her husband's means might be: whether he had anything or nothing, by saving or otherwise, that he could call his own, apart from the revenues of the Hold: but she did know sufficient to be sure that it could not be a tithe of what was needed to keep them; and where were they to go with their helpless daughters? That these unpleasant considerations floated through her mind in a vague, confused vision was true; but far above them came a rush of thought, of care, closer to the present hour. Her brother had said—and there was determination not to be mistaken in his tones—that unless Mr. Chattaway produced Rupert Trevlyn, he would publicly charge him with the murder. Nothing but the strongest self-control had restrained Mrs. Chattaway from avowing all when she heard this. Mr. Chattaway was a man not held in the world's favour, but he was her husband; and in her eyes his faults and failings had ever appeared in a venial light. She would have given much to stand out and say, "You are accusing my husband wrongfully; Rupert is alive, and I am concealing him."

But she did not dare do this. That very husband would have replied, "Then I order Rupert into custody—how dared you conceal him?" She took an opportunity of asking George Ryle the meaning of the warning despatched by Nora. George could not explain it. He had met Bowen accidentally, and the officer had told him in confidence that they had received a mysterious hint that Rupert Trevlyn was not far off—hence George's intimation. It was to turn out that the *other* Rupert Trevlyn had been spoken of: but neither Bowen nor George knew this.

George Ryle rapidly drew his own conclusion from this return of Squire Trevlyn: it would be the preservation of Rupert; was the very best thing that could have happened for him. It may be said, the only thing. The tether had been lengthened out to its extreme limits, and to keep him much longer where he was, would be impossible; or, if they so kept him, it would mean death. George Ryle saw that a protector for Rupert had arisen in Squire Trevlyn.

"He must be told the truth," he whispered to Mrs. Chattaway.

"Yes, perhaps it may be better," she answered; "but I dare not tell him. Will you undertake it?"

He nodded, and began to wonder what excuse he could invent for seeking a private conference with the newly-returned Squire. But while he plotted and planned, Maude rendered it unnecessary.

By a sense of the fitness of things, the state-rooms at the Hold, generally kept for visitors, were assigned by Miss Diana to her brother. He was shown to them, and was in the act of gazing from the window at the well-remembered features of the old domain when there stole in upon him one, white and tearless, but with a terrified imploring despair in her countenance.

"Maude, my child, what is it? I like your face, my dear, and must have you henceforth for my very own child!"

"Not me, Uncle Rupert, never mind me," she said, the kindly tones telling upon her breaking heart and bringing forth a gush of tears. "If you will only love Rupert!—only get Mr. Chattaway to forgive him!"

"But he may be dead, child."

"Uncle Rupert, if he were not dead—if you found him now, to-day," she reiterated—"would *you* deliver him up to justice? Oh, don't blame him; don't visit it upon him! It was the Trevlyn temper, and Mr. Chattaway should not have provoked it by horsewhipping him."

"*I* blame him! *I* deliver a Trevlyn up to justice!" echoed Squire Trevlyn, with a threatening touch of the Trevlyn temper at that very moment. "What are you saying, child? If Rupert is in life he shall have his wrongs righted from henceforth. The cost of a burnt rick? The ricks were mine, not Chattaway's. Rupert Trevlyn is my heir, and he shall so be recognised and received."

She sank down before him crying softly with the relief his words brought her. Squire Trevlyn placed his hand on her pretty hair, caressingly. "Don't grieve so, child; he may not be dead. I'll find him if he is to be found. The police shall know they have a Squire Trevlyn amongst them again."

"Uncle Rupert, he is very near; lying in concealment—ill—almost dying. We have not dared to betray it, and the secret is nearly killing us."

He listened in amazement, and questioned her until he gathered the outlines of the case. "Who has known of this, do you say?"

"My aunt Edith, and I, and the doctor; and—and—George Ryle."

The consciousness with which the last name was brought out, the sudden blush, whispered a tale to keen Squire Trevlyn.

"Halloa, Miss Maude! I read a secret. *That* will not do, you know. I cannot spare you from the Hold for all the George Ryles in the world. You must be its mistress."

"My aunt Diana will be that," murmured Maude.

"That she never shall be whilst I am master," was the emphatic rejoinder. "If Diana could look quietly on and see her father deceived, help to deceive him; see Chattaway usurp the Hold to the exclusion of Joe's son, and join in the wickedness, she has forfeited all claim to it: she shall neither reign nor reside in it. No, my little Maude, you must live with me, as mistress of Trevlyn Hold."

Maude's tears were flowing in silence. She kept her head down.

"What is George Ryle to you?" somewhat sternly asked Squire Trevlyn. "Do you love him?"

"I had no one else to love: they were not kind to me—except my aunt Edith," she murmured.

He sat lost in thought. "Is he a good man, Maude? Upright, honourable, just?"

"That, and more," she whispered.

"And I suppose you love him? Would it quite break your heart were I to issue my edict that you should never have him; to say you must turn him over to Octave Chattaway?"

It was only a jest. Maude took it differently, and lifted her glowing face. "But he does not like Octave! It is Octave who likes—"

She had spoken impulsively, and now that recollection came to her she hesitated. Squire Trevlyn, undignified as it was, broke into a subdued whistle.

"I see, young lady. And so, Mr. George has had the good taste to like some one better than Octave. Well, perhaps I should do so, in his place."

"But about Rupert?" she pleaded.

"Ah, about Rupert. I must go to him at once. Mark Canham stared as I came through the gate just now, as one scared out of his wits. He must have been puzzled by the likeness."

Squire Trevlyn went down to the hall, and was putting on his hat when they came flocking around, asking whether he was going out, offering to accompany him, Diana requesting him to wait whilst she put on her bonnet. But he waved them off: he preferred to stroll out alone, he said; he might look in and have a talk with some of his father's old dependants—if any were left.

George Ryle was standing outside, deliberating as to how he should convey the communication, little thinking it had already been done. Squire Trevlyn came up, and passed an arm within his.

"I am going to the lodge," he remarked. "You may know whom I want to see there."

"You have heard, then!" exclaimed George.

"Yes. From Maude. By-the-by, Mr. George, what secret understanding is there between you and that young lady?"

George looked surprised; but he was not one to lose his equanimity. "It is no longer a secret, sir. I have confided it to Miss Diana. If Mr. Chattaway will grant me the lease of a certain farm, I shall speak to him."

"Mr. Chattaway! The farms don't belong to him now, but to me."

George laughed. "Yes, I forgot. I must come to you for it, sir. I want the Upland."

"And you would like to take Maude with it?"

"Oh, yes! I must take her with it."

"Softly, sir. Maude belongs to me, just as the farms do: and I can tell you for your consolation, and you must make the best of it, that I cannot spare her from the Hold. There; that's enough. I have not come home to have my will disputed: I am a true Trevlyn."

A somewhat uncomfortable silence ensued, and lasted until they reached the lodge. Squire Trevlyn entered without ceremony. Old Mark, who was sitting before the hearth apparently in deep thought, turned his head, saw who was coming in, rose as quickly as his rheumatism allowed him, and stared as if he saw an apparition.

"Do you know me, Mark?"

"To my dazed eyes it looks like the Squire," was Mark's answer, slowly shaking his head, as one in perplexity. "But I know it cannot be. I stood at these gates as he was carried out to his last home in Barbrook churchyard. The Squire was older, too."

"The Squire left a son, Mark."

"Sir—sir!" burst forth the old man, after a pause, as the light flashed upon him. "Sir—sir! You surely are never the young heir, Mr. Rupert, we have all mourned as dead?"

"Do you remember the young heir's features, Mark?"

"Ay, I have never forgot them, sir."

"Then look at mine."

There was doubt no longer; and Mark Canham, in his enthusiastic joy forgetting his rheumatism, would almost have gone down on his knees in thankfulness. He brought himself up with a groan. "I be fit for nothing now but to nurse my rheumatiz, sir. And you be the true Rupert Trevlyn—Squire from henceforth? Oh, sir, say it!"

"I am the Squire, Mark. But I came here to see another Rupert Trevlyn—he who will be Squire after me."

Old Mark shook his head. He glanced towards the staircase as he spoke, and dropped his voice to a whisper, as if fearing that it might penetrate to one who was lying above.

"If he don't get better soon, sir, he'll never live to be the Squire. He's very ill. Circumstances have been against him, it can't be denied; but I fear me it was in his constitution from the first to go off, as his father, poor Mr. Joe, went off afore him."

"Nonsense," said the Squire. "We'll get him well again!"

"And what of Chattaway?" asked old Canham. "He'll never forego his vengeance, sir. I have been in mortal fear ever since Master Rupert's been lying here. The fear had selfishness in it, maybe," he added, ingenuously; "for Chattaway'd turn me right off, without a minute's warning, happen he come to know of it. He's never liked my being at the lodge at all, sir; and would have sent me away times and again but for Miss Diana."

"Ah," said the Squire. "Well, it does not rest with him now. What has he allowed you, Mark?"

"Half-a-crown a week, sir."

"Half-a-crown a week?" repeated Squire Trevlyn, his mouth curling with displeasure. "How have you lived?"

"It have been a poor living at best, sir," was the simple answer. "Ann works hard, at home or out, but she don't earn much. Her eyes be bad, sir; happen you may call to mind they was always weak and ailing. The Squire fixed my pay here at five shillings a week, and Chattaway changed it when he come into power. Miss Diana's good to us; but for her and the bit o' money Ann can earn, I don't see as we could ha' got along at all."

"Would you like the half-a-crown changed back again to five shillings, Mark?"

"I should think it was riches come to me right off, Squire."

"Then you may reckon upon it from this day."

He moved to the staircase as he spoke, leaving the old man in an ecstasy of delight. Ann Canham, who had shrunk into hiding, came forward. Her father turned triumphantly.

"Didn't I tell ye it was the Squire? And you to go on at me, saying I was clean off my wits to think it! I know'd it was no other."

"But you said it was the dead Squire, father," was poor Ann's meek response.

"It's all the same," cried old Canham. "There'll be a Trevlyn at the Hold again; and our five shillings a week is to come back to us. Bless the Trevlyns! they was always open-handed."

"Father, what a dreadful come-down for Chattaway! What will he do? He'll have to turn out."

"Serve him right!" shouted Mark. "How many homes have he made empty in his time! Ann, girl, I have kep' my eyes a bit open through life, in spite of limbs cramped with rheumatiz, and I never failed to notice one thing—them who are fond o' making others' homes desolate, generally find their own desolate afore they die. Chattaway'll get a taste now of what he have been so fond o' dealing out to others. I hope the bells'll ring the day he turns out o' the Hold!"

"But Madam will have to turn out with him!" meekly suggested Ann Canham.

It took Mark back. He liked Madam as much as he disliked her husband. "Happen something'll be thought of for Madam," said he. "Maybe the new Squire'll keep her at the Hold."

George Ryle had gone upstairs, and prepared the wondering Rupert for the appearance of his uncle. As the latter entered, his tall head bowing, he halted in dismay. In the fair face bent towards him from the bed, the large blue eyes, the bright, falling hair, he believed for the moment he saw the beloved brother Joe of his youth. But in the hollow, hectic cheeks, the drawn face, the parched lips, the wasted hands, the attenuated frame, he read too surely the marks of the disease which had taken off that brother; and a conviction seated itself in the Squire's mind that he must look elsewhere for his heir.

"My poor boy! Joe's boy! This place is killing you!"

"No, Uncle Rupert, it is not that at all. It is the fear."

Squire Trevlyn could not breathe. He looked up at the one pane, and pushed it open with his stick. The cold air came in, and he seemed relieved, drawing a long breath. But the same current, grateful to him, found its way to the lungs of Rupert, and he began to cough violently. "It's the draught," panted the poor invalid.

George Ryle closed the window again, and the Squire bent over the bed. "You must come to the Hold at once, Rupert."

The hectic faded on Rupert's face. "It is not possible," he answered. "Mr. Chattaway would denounce me."

"Denounce you!" hotly repeated Squire Trevlyn. "Denounce my nephew and my brother Joe's son! He had better let me see him attempt it."

In the impulse, characteristic of the Trevlyns, the Squire turned to descend the stairs. He was going to have Rupert brought home at once. George Ryle followed him, and arrested him in the avenue.

"Pardon me, Squire Trevlyn. You must first of all make sure of Chattaway. I am not clear also but you must make sure of the police."

"What do you mean?"

"The police have the matter in hand. Are they able to relinquish it, even for you?"

They stood gazing at each other in doubt and discomfort. It was an unpleasant phase of the affair; and one which had certainly not until that moment presented itself to Squire Trevlyn's view.

CHAPTER LVIII
A CONVERSATION WITH MR. CHATTAWAY

They stood together, deep in dispute—Squire Trevlyn of the Hold, and he who had so long reigned at the Hold, its usurper. In that very rick-yard which had recently played so prominent a part in the career of the unhappy Rupert, stood they: the Squire—bold, towering, haughty; Chattaway—cowardly, shrinking, indecisive.

It was of that very Rupert they were talking. Squire Trevlyn hastened home from the lodge, and found Chattaway in the rick-yard: he urged upon him the claims of Rupert for forgiveness, for immunity from the consequences of his crime; urged upon him its *necessity*; for a Trevlyn, he said, must not be disgraced. And Mr. Chattaway appeared to be turning obstinate; to say that he never would forgive him or release him from its consequences. He pointed to the blackened spots, scarcely yet cleared of their *débris*. "Is a crime like that to be pardoned?" he asked.

"What caused the crime? Who drove him to it?" And Mr. Chattaway had no plausible answer at hand.

"When you married into the Trevlyn family, you married into its faults," resumed the Squire. "At any rate, you became fully acquainted with them. You knew as much of the Trevlyn temper as we ourselves know. I ask you, then, how could you be so unwise—to put the question moderately—as to provoke it in Rupert?"

"Evil tempers can be subdued," returned Mr. Chattaway. "And ought to be."

"Just so. They can be, and they ought to be. But unfortunately we don't all of us do as we can and ought to do. Do you? I have heard it said in the old days that James Chattaway's spirit was a sullen one: have you subdued its sullenness?"

"I wish you wouldn't wander from the point, Mr. Trevlyn."

"I am keeping pretty near to the point. But I can go nearer to it, if you please. How could you, James Chattaway, dare to horsewhip a Trevlyn? Your wife's nephew, and her brother's son! Whatever might be the provocation—but, so far as I can learn, there was no just provocation—how came you so far to forget yourself and your temper as to strike him? One, possessing the tamest spirit ever put into man, might be expected to turn at the cruel insult you inflicted on Rupert. Did you do it with the intention of calling up the Trevlyn temper?"

"Nonsense," said Mr. Chattaway.

"It will not do to say nonsense to me, sir. Setting fire to the rick was your fault, not his; the crime was occasioned by you; and I, the actual owner of those ricks, shall hold you responsible for it. Yes, James Chattaway, those ricks were mine; you need not dispute what I say; the ricks were mine then, as they are now. They have been mine, in point of fact, ever since my father's death. You may rely upon one thing—that had I known the injustice that was being enacted, I should have returned long ago."

"Injustice!" cried Mr. Chattaway. "What injustice?"

"What injustice! Has there been anything *but* injustice? When my father's breath left his body, his legitimate successor (in my absence and supposed death) was his grandson Rupert; this very Rupert you have been goading on to ill, perhaps to death. Had my brother Joe lived, would you have allowed *him* to succeed, pray?"

"But your brother Joe did not live; he was dead."

"You evade the question."

"It is a question that will answer no end," cried Mr. Chattaway, biting his thin lips, and feeling very like a man being driven to bay. "Of course he would have succeeded. But he was dead, and Squire Trevlyn chose to make his will in my favour, and appoint me his successor."

"Beguiled by treachery. He was suffered to go to his grave never knowing that a grandson was born to him. Were I guilty of the like treachery, I could not rest in my bed. I should dread that the anger of God would be ever coming down upon me."

"The Squire did well," growled Mr. Chattaway. "What would an infant have done with Trevlyn Hold?"

"Granted for a single moment that it had been inexpedient to leave Trevlyn Hold to an infant, it was not to you it should have been left. If Squire Trevlyn must have bequeathed it to a son-in-law, it should have been to him who was the husband of his eldest daughter, Thomas Ryle."

"Thomas Ryle!" contemptuously ejaculated Mr. Chattaway. "A poor, hard-working farmer—"

"Don't attempt to disparage Thomas Ryle to me, sir," thundered the Squire; and the voice, the look, the rising anger were so like the old Squire of the days gone by, that Mr. Chattaway positively recoiled. "Thomas Ryle was a good and honourable man, respected by all; he was a gentleman by birth and breeding; he was a gentleman in mind and manners—and that could never be said of you, James Chattaway. Work! To be sure he worked; and so did his father. They had to work to live. Their farm was a poor one; and extra labour was needed to make up for the money which ought to have been spent upon it, but which they possessed not, for their patrimony had dwindled away. They might have taken a more productive farm; but they preferred to remain upon that one because it was their own, descended from their forefathers. It had to be sold at last, but they still remained on it, and they worked, always hoping to prosper. You used the word 'work' as a term of reproach! Let me tell you, that if the fact of working is to take the gentle blood out of a man, there will be little gentle blood left for the next generation. This is a working age, sir; the world has grown wise, and we most of us work with hands or head. Thomas Ryle's son is a gentleman, if I ever saw one—and I am mistaken if his looks belie his mind—and he works. Do not disparage Thomas Ryle again to me. I think a sense of the injury you did him, must induce you to do it."

"What injury did I do Thomas Ryle?"

"To usurp Trevlyn Hold over him was an injury. It was Rupert's: neither yours nor his; but had it come to one of you, it should have been to him; *you* had no manner of right to it. And what about the two thousand pounds bond?"

Squire Trevlyn asked the last question in an altered and very significant tone. Mr. Chattaway's green face grew greener.

"I held the bond, and I enforced its payment in justice to my wife and children. I could do no less."

"In justice to your wife and children!" retorted Squire Trevlyn. "James Chattaway, did a thought ever cross you of God's justice? I believe from my very heart that my father cancelled that bond upon his dying bed, died believing Thomas Ryle released from it; and you, in your grasping, covetous nature, kept the bond with an eye to your own profit. Did you forget that the eye of the Great Ruler of all things was upon you, when you pretended to destroy that bond? Did you suppose that Eye was turned away when you usurped Trevlyn Hold to the prejudice of Rupert? Did you think you would be allowed to enjoy it in security to the end? It may look to you, James Chattaway, as it would to any superficial observer, that there has been wondrous favour shown you in this long delay of justice. I regard it differently. It seems to me that retribution has overtaken you at the worst time: not the worse for you, possibly, but for your children. By that inscrutable law which we learn in childhood, a man's ill-doings are visited on his children: I fear the result of your ill-doing will be felt by yours. Had you been deposed from Trevlyn Hold at the time you usurped it, or had you not usurped it, your children must have been brought up to play their parts in the busy walks of life; to earn their own living. As it is, they have been reared to idleness and luxury, and will feel their fall in proportion. Your son has lorded it as the heir of Trevlyn Hold, as the future owner of the works at Blackstone, and lorded it, as I hear, in a very offensive manner. He will not like to sink down to a state of dependency; but he will have to do it."

"Where have you been gathering your account of things?" interposed Mr. Chattaway.

"Never mind where. I have gathered it, and that is sufficient. And now—to go back to Rupert Trevlyn. Will you give me a guarantee that he shall be held harmless?"

"No," growled Mr. Chattaway.

"Then it will be war to the knife between you and me. Mind you—I do not think there's any necessity to ask you this; as the ricks were not yours, but mine, at the time of the occurrence, you could not, as I believe, become the prosecutor. But I prefer to be on the safe side. On the return of Rupert, if you attempt to prosecute him, the first thing that I shall do will be to insist that he prosecutes you for the assault, and I shall prosecute you for the usurpation of Trevlyn Hold. So it will be prosecution and counter-prosecution, you see. Mark you, James Chattaway, I promise you to do this, and you know I am a man of my word. I think we had better let bygones be bygones. What are you going to do about the revenues of the Hold?"

"The revenues of the Hold!" stammered Mr. Chattaway, wiping his hot face, for he did not like the question.

"The past rents. The mesne profits you have received and appropriated since Squire Trevlyn's death. Those profits are mine."

"In law, possibly," was the answer. "Not in justice."

"Well, we'll go by law," complacently returned the Squire, a spice of mischief in his eye. "Which have you gone by all these years? Law, or justice? The law would make you refund all to me."

"The law would be cunning to do it," was the answer. "If I have received the revenues, I have spent them in keeping up Trevlyn Hold."

"You have not spent them all, I suspect; and it would be productive of great trouble and annoyance to you were I to come upon you for them. But now, look you, James Chattaway: I will be more merciful than you have been to others, and say nothing about them, for my sister Edith's sake. In the full sense of the word, I will let bygones be bygones."

The ex-master of Trevlyn Hold gazed out from the depths of his dull gray eyes: gazed upon vacancy, buried in thought. It might be well to make a friend of the Squire. On the one hand was the long-cherished revenge against Rupert; on the other was his own interest. Should he gratify revenge, or study himself? Ah, you need not ask; revenge may be sweet, but with Mr. Chattaway his own interest was sweeter. The scales were not equally balanced.

He saw that Squire Trevlyn's heart was determined on the pardon of Rupert; he knew that the less he beat about the bush the better; and he spoke at once. "I'll forgive him," he said. "Rupert Trevlyn behaved infamously, but—"

"Stop, James Chattaway. Pardon him, or don't pardon him, as you please; but we will have no names over it. Rupert Trevlyn shall have none cast at him in my presence."

"It is of no consequence. He did the wrong in the eyes of the neighbourhood, and they don't need to be reminded of what he is."

"And how have the neighbourhood judged?" sternly asked Squire Trevlyn. "Which side have they espoused—yours, or his? Don't talk to me, sir; I have heard more than you suppose. I know what shame the neighbours have cast on you for years on the score of Rupert; the double shame cast on you since these ricks were burnt. Will you pardon him?"

"I have said so," was the sullen reply.

"Then come and ratify it in writing," rejoined the Squire, turning towards the Hold.

"You are ready to doubt my word," resentfully spoke Mr. Chattaway, feeling considerably aggrieved.

Squire Trevlyn threw back his head. It spoke as plainly as ever motion spoke that he did doubt it. As he strode on to the house, Chattaway in his wake, they came across Cris. Unhappy Cris! His day of authority and assumption had set. No longer was he the son of the master of Trevlyn Hold; henceforth Mr. Cris must set his wits to work, and take his share in the active labour of life. He stood leaning over the palings, biting a bit of straw as he gazed at Squire Trevlyn; but he did not say a word to the Squire or the Squire to him.

With the aid of pen and ink Mr. Chattaway gave an ungracious promise to pardon Rupert. Of course it had nothing formal in it, but the Squire was satisfied, and put it in his pocket.

"Which is Rupert's chamber here?" he asked. "It had better be got ready. Is it an airy one?"

"For what purpose is it to be got ready?" returned Mr. Chattaway.

"In case we find him, you know."

"You would bring him home? Here? to my house?"

"No; I bring him home to mine."

Mr. Chattaway's face went quite dark with pain. In good truth it was Squire Trevlyn's house; no longer his; and he may be pardoned for momentarily forgetting the fact. There are brief intervals even in the deepest misery when we lose sight of the present.

Cris came in. "Dumps, the policeman, is outside," he said. "Some tale has been carried to the police-station that Rupert Trevlyn has returned, and Dumps has come to see about it. The felon Rupert!" pointedly exclaimed Cris.

"Don't call names, sir," said Squire Trevlyn to him as he went out. "Look here, Mr. Christopher Chattaway," he stopped to add. "You may possibly find it to your advantage to be in my good books; but that is not the way to get into them; abuse of my nephew and heir, Rupert Trevlyn, will not recommend you to my favour."

The police-station had certainly heard a confused story of the return of Rupert Trevlyn, but before Dumps reached the Hold he learnt the wondrous fact that it was another Rupert; the one so long supposed to be dead; the real Squire Trevlyn. He had learnt that Mr. Chattaway was no longer master of the Hold, but had sunk down to a very humble individual indeed. Mr. Dumps was not particularly gifted with the perceptive faculties, but the thought struck him that it might be to the interest of the neighbourhood generally, including himself and the station, to be on friendly terms with Squire Trevlyn.

"Did you want me?" asked the Squire.

"I beg pardon, sir. It was the other Mr. Rupert Trevlyn that I come up about. He has been so unfortunate as to get into a bit of trouble, sir."

"Oh, that's nothing," said the Squire. "Mr. Chattaway withdraws from the prosecution. In point of fact, if any one prosecuted it must be myself, since the ricks were mine. But I decline to do so. It is not my intention to prosecute my nephew and heir. Mr. Rupert will be the Squire of Trevlyn Hold when I am gone."

"Will he though, sir?" said Mr. Dumps, humbly.

"He will. You may tell your people at the station that I put up with the loss of the ricks. What do you say—the magistrates? The present magistrates and I were boys together, Mr. Constable: companions; and they'll be glad to see me home again; you need not trouble your head about the magistrates. You are all new at the police-station, I expect, since I left the country—in fact, I forget whether there was such a thing as a police-station then or not—but you may tell your superiors that it is not the custom of the Squires of Trevlyn to proclaim what they cannot carry out. The prosecution of Rupert Trevlyn is at an end, and it never ought to have been instituted."

"Please, sir, I had nothing to do with it."

"Of course not. The police have not been to blame. I shall walk down to-night, or to-morrow morning, to the station, and put things on a right footing. Your name is Dumps, I think?"

"Yes, sir—at your service."

"Well, Dumps, that's for yourself. Hush! not a word. It's not given to you as a constable, but as an honest man to whom I wish to offer an earnest of my future favour. And now come into the Hold, and take something to eat and drink."

The gratified Dumps, hardly knowing whether he stood on his head or his heels, and inwardly vowing eternal allegiance to the new Squire, stepped into the Hold, and was consigned to the hospitality of the lower regions. Mr. Chattaway groaned in agony when he heard the kindly orders echoing through the hall—to put before Mr. Dumps everything that was good to eat and drink. That is, he would have groaned, but for the questionable comfort of recollecting that the Hold and its contents no longer belonged to him.

As the Squire was turning round, he encountered Diana.

"I have been inquiring after my nephew's chamber. Is it an airy one?"

"Your nephew's?" repeated Miss Diana, not understanding. "Do you mean Christopher's?"

"I mean Rupert's. Let me see it."

He stepped up the stairs as he spoke, with the air of a man not born to contradiction. Miss Diana followed, wonderingly. The room she showed him was high up, and very small. The Squire threw his head back.

"*This* his room? I see! it has been all of a piece. This room was a servant's in my time. I am surprised at *you*, Diana."

"It is a sufficiently comfortable room," she answered: "and I used occasionally to indulge him with a fire. Rupert never complained."

"No, poor fellow! complaint would be of little use from him, as he knew. Is there a large chamber in the house unoccupied? one that would do for an invalid."

"The only large spare rooms in the house are the two given to you," replied Miss Diana. "They are the best, as you know, and have been kept vacant for visitors. The dressing-room may be used as a sitting-room."

"I don't want it as a sitting-room, or a dressing-room either," replied the Squire. "I prefer to dress in my bedroom, and there are sufficient sitting-rooms downstairs for me. Let this bed of Rupert's be carried down to that room at once."

"Who for?"

"For one who ought to have occupied the best rooms from the first—Rupert. Had he been properly treated, Diana, he would not have brought this disgrace upon himself."

Miss Diana wondered whether her ears deceived her. "For Rupert!" she repeated. "Where is Rupert? Is he found?"

"He has never been lost," was the curt rejoinder. "He has been all the time within a stone's throw—sheltered by Mark Canham, whom I shall not forget."

She could not speak from perplexity; scarcely knowing whether to believe the words or not.

"Your sister Edith—and James Chattaway may thank fortune that she is his wife, or I should visit the past in a very different manner upon him—and little Maude, and that handsome son of Tom Ryle's, have been in the secret; have visited him in private; stealthily doing for him what they could: but the fear and responsibility have well-nigh driven Edith and Maude to despair. That's where Rupert has been, Diana: where he is. I have not long come from him."

Anger blazed forth from the eyes of Miss Diana Trevlyn. "And why could not Edith have communicated the fact to me?" she cried. "I could have done for him better than they."

"Perhaps not," significantly replied the Squire: "considering that Chattaway was ruler of Trevlyn Hold, and you have throughout upheld his policy. But Trevlyn has another ruler now, and Rupert a protector."

Miss Diana made no reply. She was too vexed to make one. Turning away, she flung a shawl over her shoulders, and marched onwards to the lodge, to pay a visit to the unhappy Rupert.

CHAPTER LIX
NEWS FOR MAUDE

You should have seen the procession going up the avenue. Not that first night; but in the broad glare of the following noon-day. How Squire Trevlyn contrived to make things straight with the superintendent, Bowen, he best knew. Poor misguided Rupert was a free man again, and Policeman Dumps was busiest of all in helping to move him.

The easiest carriage the Hold afforded was driven to the lodge. A shrunken, emaciated object Rupert looked as he tottered down the staircase, Squire Trevlyn standing below to catch him if he made a false step, George Ryle, ready with his protecting arm, and Mr. King, talkative as ever, following close behind. Old Canham stood leaning on his stick, and Ann curtsied behind the door.

"It is the proudest day of my life, Master Rupert, to see you come to your rights," cried old Mark, stepping forward.

"Thank you for all, Mark!" cried Rupert, impulsively, as he held out his hand. "If I live, you shall see that I can be grateful."

"You'll live fast enough now," interposed the Squire in his tone of authority. "If King does not bring you round in no time, he and I shall quarrel."

"Good-bye, Ann," said Rupert. "I owe you more than I can ever repay. She has waited on me night and day, Uncle Rupert; has lain on that hard settle at night, and had no other bed since I have been here. She has offended all her employers, to stop at home and attend on me."

Poor Ann Canham's tears were falling. "I shall get my places back, sir, I dare say. All I hope is, that you'll soon be about again, Master Rupert—and that you'll please excuse the poor accommodation father and me have been obliged to give you."

Squire Trevlyn stood and looked at her. "Don't let it break your heart if the places don't come back to you. What did you earn? ten shillings a week?"

"Oh, no, sir! Poor folks like us couldn't earn such a sum as that."

"Mr. Rupert will settle that upon you from to-day. Don't be overcome, woman. It is only fair, you know, that if he has put your living in peril, he should make it good to you."

She was too overcome to answer; and the Squire stepped out with Rupert and found himself in the midst of a crowd. The incredible news of his return had spread far and wide, and people of all grades were flocking to the Hold to welcome him home. Old men, friends of the late Squire; middle-aged men, who had been hot-headed youths when he, Rupert, went away to exile and supposed death; younger ones, who had been children then and could not remember him, all were there. The chairman of the magistrates' bench himself helped Rupert into the carriage. He shook hands twenty times with the Squire, and linked his arm with that gentleman's to accompany him to the Hold. The carriage went at a foot-pace, Mr. King inside it with Rupert. "Go slowly; he must not be shaken," were the surgeon's orders to the coachman.

The spectators looked on at the young heir as he leaned his head back in the carriage, which had been thrown open to the fine day. The air seemed to revive Rupert greatly. They watched him as he talked with George Ryle, who walked with his arm on the carriage door; they pressed round to get a word with him. Rupert, emancipated from the close confinement, the terrible *dread*, felt as a bird released from its cage, and his spirits went up to fever-heat.

He held out his hands to one and another; and laughingly told them that in a week's time he should be in a condition to run a race with the best of them. "But you needn't expect him," put in Mr. King, by way of warning. "Before he is well enough to run races, I shall order him off to a warmer climate."

As Rupert stepped out of the carriage, he saw, amongst the sea of faces pressing round, one face that struck upon his notice above all others, in its yearning, earnest sympathy, and he held out his hand impulsively. It was that of Jim Sanders, and as the boy sprang forward he burst into tears.

"You and I must be better friends than ever, Jim. Cheer up. What's the matter?"

"It's to see you looking like this, sir. You'll get well, sir, won't you?"

"Oh yes; I feel all right now, Jim. A little tired, that's all. Come up and see me to-morrow, and I'll tell my uncle who you are and all about you."

Standing at the door of the drawing-room, in an uncertain sort of attitude, was Mr. Chattaway. He was evidently undecided whether to receive the offending Rupert with a welcome, burst forth into a reproach, or run away and hide himself. Rupert decided it by walking up to him, and holding out his hand.

"Let us be friends, Mr. Chattaway. I have long repented of my mad passion, and I thank you for absolving me from its consequences. Perhaps you are sorry on your side for the treatment that drove me to it. We will be friends, if you like."

But Mr. Chattaway did not respond to the generous feeling or touch the offered hand. He muttered something about its having been Rupert's fault, not his, and disappeared. Somehow he could not stand the keen eye of Squire Trevlyn that was fixed upon him.

In truth it was a terrible time for Chattaway, and the man was living out his punishment. All his worst dread had come upon him without warning, and he could not rebel against it. There might be no attempt to dispute the claims of Squire Trevlyn; Mr. Chattaway was as completely deposed as though he had never held it.

Rupert was installed in his luxurious room, everything within it that could contribute to his ease and comfort. Squire Trevlyn had been tenderly attached to his brother Joe when they were boys together. He robust, manly; Joe delicate. It may be that the want of strength in the younger only rendered him dearer to the elder brother. Perhaps it was only the old affection for Joe transferred now to the son; certain it was, that the Squire's love had already grown for Rupert, and all care was lavished on him.

But as the days went on it became evident to all that Rupert had only come home to die. The removal over, the excitement of those wonderful changes toned down, the sad fact that he was certainly fading grew on Squire Trevlyn. Some one suggested that a warmer climate should be tried; but Mr. King, on being appealed to, answered that he must get stronger first; and his tone was significant.

Squire Trevlyn noticed it. Later, when he had the surgeon to himself, he spoke to him. "King, you are concealing the danger? Can't we move him?"

"I would have told you before, Squire, had you asked me. As to moving him to a warmer climate—certainly he could be moved, but he would only go there to die; and the very fatigue of the journey would shorten his life."

"I don't believe it," retorted the Squire, awaking out of his dismay. "You are a croaker, King. I'll call in a doctor from Barmeston."

"Call in all the doctors you like, Squire, if it will afford you satisfaction. When they understand his case, they will tell you as I do."

"Do you mean to say that he must die?"

"I fear he must; and speedily. The day before you came home I tried his lungs, and from that moment I have known there was no hope. The disease must have been upon him for some time; I suppose he inherits it from his father."

The same night Squire Trevlyn sent for a physician: an eminent man: but he only confirmed the opinion of Mr. King. All that remained now was to break the tidings to Rupert; and to lighten, as far as might be, his passage to the grave.

But a word must be spoken of the departure of Mr. Chattaway and his family from the Hold. That they must inevitably leave it had been unpleasantly clear to Mr. Chattaway from the very hour of Squire Trevlyn's arrival. He gave a day or two to digesting the dreadful necessity, and then began to turn his thoughts practically to the future.

Squire Trevlyn had promised not to take from him anything he might have put by of his ill-gotten gains. These gains, though a fair sum, were not sufficient to enable him to live and keep his family, and Mr. Chattaway knew that he must do something in the shape of work. His thoughts turned, not unnaturally, to the Upland Farm, and he asked Squire Trevlyn to let him have the lease of it.

"I'll let you have it upon one condition," said the Squire. "I should not choose my sister Edith to sink into obscurity, but she may live upon the Upland Farm without losing caste; it is a fine place both as to land and residence. Therefore, I'll let it you, I say, upon one condition."

Maude Trevlyn happened to be present at the conversation, and spoke in the moment's impulse.

"Oh, Uncle Rupert! you promised—"

"Well, Miss Maude?" he cried, and fixing his eyes on her glowing face. Maude timidly continued.

"I thought you promised someone else the Upland Farm."

"That favourite of yours and of Rupert's, George Ryle? But I am not going to let him have it. Well, Mr. Chattaway?"

"What is the condition?" inquired Mr. Chattaway.

"That you use the land well. I shall have a clause inserted in the lease by which you may cease to be my tenant at any time by my giving you a twelvemonth's notice; and if I find you carrying your parsimonious nature into the management of the Upland Farm, as you have on this land, I shall surely take it from you."

"What's the matter with this land?" asked Mr. Chattaway.

"The matter is, that I find the land impoverished. You have spared money upon it in your mistaken policy, and the inevitable result has followed. You have been penny wise and pound foolish, Chattaway; as you were when you suffered the rick-yard to remain uninsured."

Mr. Chattaway's face darkened, but he made no reply to the allusion. "I'll undertake to do the farm justice, Squire Trevlyn, if you will lease it to me."

"Very well. Let me, however, candidly assure you that, but for Edith's sake, I'd see you starve before you should have had a homestead on this land. It is my habit to be plain-spoken: I must be especially so with you. I suffer from you in all ways, James Chattaway. I suffer always in my nephew Rupert. When I think of the treatment dealt out to him from you, I can scarcely refrain from treating you to a taste of the punishment you inflicted upon him. It is possible, too, that had the boy been more tenderly cared for, he might have had strength to resist this disease which has crept upon him. About that I cannot speak; it must lie between you and God; his father, with every comfort, could not escape it, it seems; and possibly Rupert might not have done so."

Mr. Chattaway made no reply. The Squire, after a pause, during which he had been plunged in thought, continued. "I suffer also in the matter of the two-thousand-pound debt of Thomas Ryle's, and I have a great mind—do you hear me, sir?—I have a great mind that the refunding it should come out of your pocket instead of mine; even though I had to get it from you by suing you for so much of the mesne profits."

"Refunding the debt?" repeated Mr. Chattaway, looking absolutely confounded. "Refunding it to whom?"

"To the Ryles, of course. That money was as surely given by my father to them on his death-bed, as that I am here, talking to you. I feel, I know that it was. I know that Thomas Ryle, ever a man of honour, spoke the truth when he asserted it. Do you think I can do less than refund it? I don't, if you do."

"George Ryle does not want it; he is capable of working for his living," was the only answer Mr. Chattaway in his anger could give.

"I do not suppose he will want it," was the quiet remark of Squire Trevlyn; "I dare say he'll manage to do without it. It is to Mrs. Ryle that I shall refund it, sir. Between you all, I find that she was cut off with a shilling at my father's death."

Mr. Chattaway liked the conversation less and less. He deemed it might be as agreeable to leave details to another opportunity, and withdrew.

Squire Trevlyn looking round for Maude, discerned her at the end of the room, her head bent in sorrow.

"What's this, young lady? Because I don't let Mr. George Ryle the Upland Farm? You great goose! I have reserved a better one for him."

The tone was peculiar, and she raised her timid eyelids. "A better one!" she stammered.

"Yes. Trevlyn Hold."

Maude looked aghast. "What do you mean, Uncle Rupert?"

"My dear, but for this unhappy fiat which appears to have gone forth for your brother Rupert, perhaps I might have let the Upland Farm to George. As it is, I cannot part with both of you. If poor Rupert is to be taken from me, you must remain."

She looked up, utterly unable to understand him.

"And as you appear not to be inclined to part with Mr. George, all that can be done in the matter, so far as I see, is that we must have him at the Hold."

"Oh, Uncle Rupert!" And Maude's head and her joyous tears were hidden in the loving arms that were held out to shelter her.

"Child! Did you think I had come home to make my dead brother's children unhappy? You will know me better by and by, Maude."

CHAPTER LX
A BETTER HEIRSHIP

A short time, and people had settled down in their places. Squire Trevlyn was alone at the Hold with Maude and Rupert, the Chattaways were at the Upland Farm, and Miss Diana Trevlyn had taken up her abode in a pretty house belonging to herself. Circumstances had favoured the removal of Mr. Chattaway from the Hold almost immediately after the arrival of Squire Trevlyn. The occupant of the Upland Farm, who only remained in it because his time was not up until spring, was glad to find it would be an accommodation if he quitted it earlier; he did so, and by Christmas the Chattaways were installed in it.

Mr. Chattaway had set to work in earnest.

Things were changed with him. At the Hold, whether he was up and doing, or lay in bed in idleness, his revenues came in to him. At the Upland Farm he must be up early and in bed late, for the eye of a master was necessary if the land was to yield its increase; and by that increase he and his family had now to live. There was a serious battle with Cris. It was deemed advisable for the interest of both parties—that is, for Mr. Cris and his father—that the younger man should enter upon some occupation of his own; but Cris resolutely refused. He could find plenty to do on the Upland Farm, he urged, and wouldn't be turned out of his home. In fact, Mr. Cris had lived so long without work, that it was difficult, now he was leaving his youth behind him, to begin it. Better, as Squire Trevlyn said, the change had been made years ago. It was certainly hard for Cris; let us acknowledge it. He had been reared to the expectation of Trevlyn Hold and its revenues; had lorded it as the future master. When he rose in the morning, early or late, as inclination prompted him, he had nothing more formidable before him than to ride about attended by his groom. He had indulged in outdoor sports, hunting, shooting, fishing, at will; no care upon him, except how he could most agreeably get through the day. He had been addicted to riding or driving into Barmester, lounging about the streets for the benefit of admiring spectators, or taking a turn in the billiard-rooms. All that was over now; Mr. Cris's leisure and greatness had come to an end; his groom would take service elsewhere, his fine horse must be used for other purposes than pleasure. In short, poor Cris Chattaway had fallen from his high estate, as many another has fallen before him, and must henceforth earn his bread before he ate it. "There's room for both on the Upland Farm, and a good living for both," Cris urged upon his father; and though Mr. Chattaway demurred, he gave way, and allowed Cris to remain. With all his severity to others, he had lost his authority over his children, especially over Cris and Octave, and perhaps he scarcely dared to maintain his own will against that of Cris, or tell him he should go if he chose to stay. Cris had no more love for work than anyone else has brought up to idleness; and Cris knew quite well that the easiest life he could now enter upon would be that of pretending to be busy upon the farm. When the dispute was at its height between himself and his father, as to what the future arrangements should be, Cris so far bestirred himself as to ask Squire Trevlyn to give him the post of manager at Blackstone. But the Squire had heard quite enough of the past doings there, and told Cris, with the plainness that was natural to him, that he would not have either him or his father in power at Blackstone, if they paid him in gold. And so Cris was at home.

There were other changes also in Mr. Chattaway's family. Maude's tuition, that Octave had been ever ready to find fault with, was over for ever, and Octave had taken her place. Amelia was at home, for expenses had to be curtailed. An outlay quite suitable for the master of Trevlyn Hold would be imprudent in the tenant of the Upland Farm. They found Maude's worth now that they had lost her; could appreciate the sweetness of her temper, her gentle patience. Octave, who also liked an idle life, had undertaken the tuition of her sisters with a very bad grace: hating the trouble and labour. She might have refused but for Miss Diana Trevlyn. Miss Diana had not lost her good sense or love of ruling on leaving Trevlyn Hold, and openly told Octave that she must bend to circumstances as well as her parents, and that if she would not teach her sisters, she had better go out as governess and earn her living. Octave could have annihilated Miss Diana for the unwelcome suggestion—but she offered no further opposition to the arrangement.

Life was very hard just then for Octave Chattaway. She had inherited the envious, selfish disposition of her father, and the very fact that Maude and herself had changed positions was sufficient to vex her almost beyond endurance. She had become the drudge whose days must be passed beating grammar into the obtuse minds of her rebellious sisters; Maude, the mistress of Trevlyn Hold. How things would go on it was difficult to say; for the scenes that frequently took place between Octave and her pupils disturbed to a grave degree the peace of the Upland Farm. Octave was impatient, fretful, and exacting; they were tantalising and disobedient. Quarrels were incessant; and now and then it came to blows. Octave's temper urged her to personal correction, and the girls retorted in kind.

It is in human nature to exaggerate, and Octave not only exaggerated her troubles but wilfully made the worst of them. Instead of patiently sitting down to her new duties, and striving to perform them so that in time they might become a pleasure, she steeled herself against them. A terrible jealousy of Maude had taken possession of her; jealousy in more senses than one. There was a gate in their grounds overlooking the highway to Trevlyn Hold, and it was Octave's delight to stand there and watch, at the hour when Maude might be expected to pass. Sometimes in the open carriage—sometimes she would drive in a closed one, but always accompanied by the symbols of wealth and position, fine horses, attendant servants—Miss Maude Trevlyn, of Trevlyn Hold. And Octave would watch stealthily until they were out of sight, and gather fresh food for her unhappy state of mind. It would seem strange she should thus torment herself, but that the human heart is full of such contradictions.

One day that she was standing there, Mrs. Ryle passed. And it may as well be remarked that, Mr. Chattaway excepted, Mrs. Ryle seemed most to resent the changes: not her brother's return, but some of its results. In the certainty of Rupert's not living to succeed—and it was a certainty now—Mrs. Ryle had again cherished hopes for her son Trevlyn. She had been exceedingly vexed when she heard the Upland Farm was leased to Mr. Chattaway, and thought George must have played his cards badly. She allowed her resentment to smoulder for a time, but one day so far forgot herself as to demand of George whether he thought two masters would answer upon the Farm; and hinted that it was time he left, and made room for Treve.

George, though his cheek burnt—for her, not for himself—calmly answered, that he expected shortly to leave it: relieving her of his presence, Treve of his personal advice and help.

"But you did not get the Upland?" she reiterated. "And I have been told this morning that the other farm you thought of is let over your head."

"Stay, mother," was George's answer. "You are ready to blame Squire Trevlyn for letting these farms, and not to me; but my views have altered. I do not now wish to lease the Upland, or any other farm. Squire Trevlyn has proposed something else to me—I am to manage his own land for him."

"Manage his land for him! Do you mean the land attached to Trevlyn?"

"Yes."

"And where shall you live?"

"With him: at Trevlyn Hold."

Mrs. Ryle could scarcely speak from amazement. "I never heard of such a thing!" she exclaimed, staring excessively at the smile hovering on his lips, which he vainly endeavoured to suppress. "What can it mean?"

"It is assured, unhappily, that Rupert cannot live. Had he regained health and strength, he would have filled this place. But he will not regain it. Squire Trevlyn spoke to me, and I am to be with him at the Hold."

George did not add that he at first fought with Squire Trevlyn against going to the Hold, as *its heir*—for indeed it meant nothing less. He would rather make his own fortune than have it made for him, he said. Very well, the Squire answered equably, he could give up the Hold if he liked, but he must give up Maude with it. And you may guess whether George would do that.

But Mrs. Ryle did not recover from her surprise or see things clearly. "Of course, I can understand that Rupert Trevlyn would have held sway on the estate, just as a son would; but what my brother can mean by wanting a 'manager' I cannot understand. You say you are to *live* at Trevlyn Hold?"

The smile grew very conspicuous on George's lips. "It is so arranged," he answered. "And therefore I no longer wish to rent the Upland."

Mrs. Ryle stared as if she did not believe it. She fell into deep thought—from which she suddenly started, put on her bonnet, and went straight to Trevlyn Hold.

A pretty little mare's nest she indulged in as she went along. If Rupert was to be called away from this world, the only fit and proper person to succeed him as the Squire's heir was her son Treve. In which case, George would not be required as manager, and their anticipated positions might be reversed; Treve take up his abode at the Hold, George remain at the farm.

Squire Trevlyn was alone. She gave herself no time to reconsider the propriety of speaking at all, or what she should say; but without circumlocution told him that, failing Rupert, Trevlyn must be the heir.

"Oh, dear, no," said the Squire. "You forget Maude."

"Maude!"

"If poor Rupert is to be taken, Maude remains to me. And she will inherit Trevlyn Hold."

Mrs. Ryle compressed her lips. "Is it well to leave Trevlyn Hold to a woman? Your father would not do it, Rupert."

"I am not bound to adopt the prejudices of my father. I imagine the reason of his disinheriting Maude—whose birth and existence it appears he did know of—was the anger he felt towards Joe and her mother, for having married in opposition to him. But that does not extend to me. Were I capable of leaving the estate away from Joe's children, I should deem myself as bad as Chattaway."

"Maude is a girl; it ought not to be held by a girl," was Mrs. Ryle's reiterated answer.

"Well, that objection need not trouble you; for in point of fact, it will be held by Maude's husband. Indeed, I am not sure but I shall bequeath it direct to him. I believe I shall do so."

"She may never marry."

"She will marry immediately. You don't mean to say he has not let you into the secret?" as he gazed on her puzzled face. "Has George told you nothing?"

"He has just told me that he was coming here as your manager," she replied, not in the least comprehending Squire Trevlyn's drift.

"And as Maude's husband. My manager, eh? He put it in that way, did he? He will come here as my son-in-law—I may say so for I regard Maude as my daughter and recognised successor. George Ryle comes here as the future Squire of Trevlyn Hold."

Mrs. Ryle was five minutes recovering herself. Utterly unable to digest the news, she could do nothing but stare. George Ryle inheritor of Trevlyn Hold! Was she awake or dreaming?

"It ought to be Trevlyn's," she said at length. "He is your direct relative; George Ryle is none."

"I know he is not. I leave it to him as Maude's husband, and he will take the name of Trevlyn. You should have got Maude to fall in love with the other one, if you wished him to succeed."

Perhaps it was the most unhappy moment in all Mrs. Ryle's life. Never had she given up the hope of her son's succession until now. That George should supplant him!—George, whom she had so despised! She sat beating her foot on the carpet, her pale face bent.

"It is not right; it is not right," she said, at length. "George Ryle is not worthy to succeed to Trevlyn Hold: it is reversing the order of things."

"Not worthy!" echoed Squire Trevlyn. "Your judgment must be strangely prejudiced to say so. Of all who have flocked from far and near to welcome me home, I have looked in vain for a second George Ryle. He has not his equal. If I hesitated at the first moment to give him Maude, I don't hesitate now that I know him. I can tell you that had Maude chosen unworthily, as your sister Edith did, her husband should never have come in for Trevlyn Hold."

"Is your decision irrevocable?"

"Entirely so. I wish them to be married immediately; for I should like George to be installed here as soon as possible, and, of course, he cannot come until Maude is his wife. Rupert wishes it."

"It appears to me that this arrangement is very premature," resumed Mrs. Ryle. "You may marry yet, and have children of your own."

A change came over Squire Trevlyn's face. "I shall never marry," he said, with emphasis; and to Mrs. Ryle's ears there was a strange solemnity in his tones. "You need not ask me why, for I shall not enter into reasons; let the assurance suffice—*I shall never marry*. Trevlyn Hold will be as securely theirs as though I bequeathed it to them by deed of gift."

"Rupert, this is a blow for my son."

"If you persist in considering it so, I cannot help that. It must have been very foolish of you ever to cast a thought to your son's succeeding, whilst Joe's children were living."

"Foolish! when one of my sons—my step-son, at any rate—is to succeed, as it seems!"

The Squire laughed. "You must talk to Maude about that. They had settled their plans together before I came home. If Treve turns out all he should be, I may remember him before I die. Trevlyn Farm was originally the birthright of the Ryles; I may possibly make it so again in the person of Treve. Don't let us go on with the discussion; it will only be lost labour. Will you see Rupert?"

She had the sense to see that if it were prolonged until night, it would indeed be useless, and she rose to follow him into the next room. Rupert, not looking very ill to-day, sat near the fire. Maude was reading to him.

"Is it you, Aunt Ryle!" he called out feebly. "You never come to see me."

"I am sorry to hear you are so poorly, Rupert."

"I am not half as ill as I feared I should be," he said. "I thought by this time it—it would have been all over. But I seem better. Where's George?"

"George is at home. I have been talking to your uncle about him. Until to-day I did not know what was in contemplation."

"He'll make a better Squire than I should have made," cried Rupert, lifting his eyes—bluer and brighter than ever, from disease—to her face. Maude made her escape from the room, and Squire Trevlyn had not entered it, so they were alone. "But, Aunt Ryle, I want it to be soon; before I die. I should like George to be here to see the last of me."

"I think I might have been informed of this before," observed Mrs. Ryle.

"It has not been told to any one. Uncle Rupert and I, George and Maude have kept the secret between us. Only think, Aunt Ryle! that after all the hopes, contentions, heart-burnings, George Ryle should succeed to Trevlyn Hold."

She could not bear this repeated harping on the one string. George's conduct to his step-mother had been exemplary, and she was not insensible to the fact; but she was one of those second wives who feel an instinctive dislike to their step-children. Very bitter, for Treve's sake, was her heart-jealousy now.

"I will come in and see you another day, Rupert," she said, rising abruptly. "This morning I am too vexed to remain longer."

"What has vexed you, Aunt Ryle?"

"I hoped that Treve—failing you—would have been the heir."

Rupert opened his eyes in wonder. "Treve?—whilst Maude lives! Not he. I can tell you what I think, Aunt Ryle; that had there been no Maude, Treve would never have come in for the Hold. I don't fancy Uncle Rupert would have left it to him."

"To whom would he have left it, do you fancy?"

"Well—I suppose," slowly turning the matter over in his mind—"I suppose, in that case, it would have been Aunt Diana. But there is Maude, Aunt Ryle, and we need not discuss it. George and Maude will have it, and their children after them."

"Poor boy!" she said, with a touch of compassion; "it is a sad fate for you! Not to live to inherit!"

A gentle smile rose to his face, and he pointed upwards. "There's a better heirship for me, Aunt Ryle."

It was upon returning from this memorable interview with Squire Trevlyn, that Mrs. Ryle met Octave Chattaway and stopped to speak.

"Are you getting settled, Octave?"

"Tolerably so. Mamma says she shall not be straight in six months to come. Have you been to the Hold?"

"Yes," replied Mrs. Ryle, turning her determined gaze on Octave. "Have you heard the news? That the Squire has chosen his heir?"

"No," breathlessly rejoined Octave. "We have heard that Rupert is beyond hope; but nothing else. It will be Maude, I conclude."

"It is to be George Ryle."

"George Ryle!" repeated Octave, in amazement.

"Yes. I believe it will be left to him, not to Maude. But it will be all the same. He is to marry her, and to take the name of Trevlyn. George never told me this. He just said to-day that he was going to live at the Hold; but he never said it was as Maude's husband and the Squire's heir. How prospects have changed!"

Changed! Ay, Octave felt it to her inmost soul, as she leaned against the gate, and gazed in thought after Mrs. Ryle. Gazed without seeing or hearing, deep in her heart's tribulation, her hand pressed upon her bosom, her pale face quivering as it was turned to the winter sky.

CHAPTER LXI
A BETTER HEIRSHIP

Bending in tenderness over the couch of Rupert Trevlyn was Mrs. Chattaway. Madam Chattaway no longer; she had quitted that distinctive title on quitting Trevlyn Hold. It was a warm day early in May, and Rupert had lingered on; the progress of the disease being so gradual, so imperceptible, that even the medical men were deceived; and now that the end had come, they were still saying that he might last until the autumn.

Rupert had been singularly favoured: some, stricken by this dire malady, are so. Scarcely any of its painful features were apparent; and Mr. Daw wrote word that they had not been in his father. There was scarcely any cough or pain, and though the weakness was certainly great, Rupert had not for one single day taken to his bed. Until within two days of this very time, when you see Mrs. Chattaway leaning over him, he had gone out in the carriage whenever the weather permitted. He could not sit up much, but chiefly lay on the sofa as he was lying now, facing the window, open to the warm noon-day sun. The room was the one you have frequently seen before, once the sitting-room of Mrs. Chattaway. When the Chattaways left the Hold, Rupert had changed to their rooms; and would sit there and watch the visitors who came up the avenue.

Mrs. Chattaway had been staying at the Hold since the previous Tuesday, for Maude was away from it. Maude left it with George Ryle on that day, but they were coming home this Saturday evening, for both were anxious not to be long away from Rupert. Rupert sadly wanted to attend the wedding, and the Squire and Mr. Freeman strove to invent all sorts of schemes for warming the church; but it persisted in remaining cold and damp, and Rupert was not allowed to venture. He sat with them, however, at the breakfast afterwards, and but for his attenuated form and the hectic excitement brought to his otherwise white and hollow cheeks, might have passed very well for a guest. George, with his marriage, had taken the name of Trevlyn, for the Squire insisted upon it, and he would come home to the Hold to-day as his permanent abode. Miss Diana received mortal offence at the wedding-breakfast, and sat cold and impenetrable, for the Squire requested his elder sister to preside in right of birth, and Miss Diana had long considered herself far more important than Mrs. Ryle, and had expected to be chief on that occasion herself.

"Shall we invite Edith or Diana to stay with you whilst Maude's away?" the Squire had inquired of Rupert. And a flush of pleasure came into the wan face as he answered, "My aunt Edith. I should like to be again with Aunt Edith."

So Mrs. Chattaway had remained with him, and passed the time as she was doing now—hovering round his couch, giving him all her care, caressing him in her loving, gentle manner, whispering of the happy life on which he was about to enter.

She had some eau-de-cologne in her hand, and was pouring it on a handkerchief to pass it lightly over his brow and temples. In doing this a drop went into his eye.

"Oh, Rupert, I am so sorry! How awkward I am!"

It smarted very much, but Rupert smiled bravely. "Just a few minutes' pain, Aunt Edith. That's all. Do you know what I have got to think lately?"

She put the cork into the long green bottle, and sat down close to his sofa. "What, dear?"

"That we must be blind, foolish mortals to fret so much under misfortunes. A little patience, and they pass away."

"It would be better for us all if we had more patience, more trust," she answered. "If we could leave things more entirely to God."

Rupert lay with his eyes cast upwards, blue as the sky he looked at. "I would have tried to put that great trust in God, had I lived," he said, after a pause. "Do you know, Aunt Edith, at times I do wish I could have lived."

"I wish so, too," she murmured.

"At least, I should wish it but for this feeling of utter fatigue that is always upon me. I sha'n't feel it up there, Aunt Edith."

"No, no," she whispered.

"When you get near to death, knowing that it is upon you, as I know it, I think you obtain clearer views of the reality of things. It seems to me, looking back on the life I am leaving, as if it were of no consequence at what period of life we die; whether young or old; and yet how terrible a calamity death is looked upon by people in general."

"It needs sorrow or illness to reconcile us to it, Rupert. Most of us must be tired of this life ere we can bring ourselves to anticipate another, and wish for it."

"Well, I have not had so happy a life here," he unthinkingly remarked. "I ought not to murmur at exchanging it for another."

No, he had not. The words had been spoken without thought, innocent of intentional reproach; but she was feeling them to the very depths of her long-tried heart. Mrs. Chattaway was not famous for the control of her emotions, and she broke into tears as she rose and bent over him.

"The recollection of the past is ever upon me, Rupert, night and day. Say you forgive me! Say it now, ere the time for it shall have gone by."

He looked surprised. "Forgive you, dear Aunt Edith? I have never had anything to forgive you; and others I have forgiven long ago."

"I lie awake at night and think of it, Rupert," she said, her tones betraying her great emotion. "Had you been differently treated, you might not have died just as your rights are recognised. You might have lived to be the inheritor as well as the heir of Trevlyn."

Rupert lay pondering. "But I must have died at last," he said. "And I might not have been any the better for it. Aunt Edith, it seems to me to be just this. I am twenty-one years old, and a life of some sort is before me, a life *here*, or a life *there*. At my age it is only natural that I should look forward to the life here, and I did so until I grew sick with weariness and pain. But if that life is the better and happier one, does it not seem a favour to be taken to it before my time? Aunt Edith, I say that as death comes on, I believe we see things as they really are, not as they seem. I was to have inherited Trevlyn Hold: but I shall exchange it for a better inheritance. Let this comfort you."

She sat, weeping silently, holding his hand in hers. Rupert said no more, but kept his eyes fixed upwards in thought. Gradually the lids closed, and his breathing, somewhat more regular than when awake, told that he slept. Mrs. Chattaway laid his hand on the coverlet, dried her eyes, and busied herself about the room.

About half-an-hour afterwards he awoke. She was sitting down then, watching him. It almost seemed as if her gaze had awakened him, for she had only just taken her seat.

"Have they come?" were his first words.

"Not yet, Rupert."

"Not yet! Will they be long? I feel sinking."

Mrs. Chattaway hastily called for the refreshment Rupert had until now constantly taken. But he turned his head away as it was placed before him.

"My dear, you said you were sinking!"

"Not *that* sort of sinking, Aunt Edith. Nothing that food will remedy."

A tremor came over Mrs. Chattaway. She detected a change in his voice, saw the change in his countenance. It has just been said, and not for the first time in this history, that she could not boast of much self-control: and she hurried from the room, calling for Squire Trevlyn. He heard her, and came immediately, wondering much. "It is Rupert," she said in irrepressible excitement. "He says he is dying."

Rupert had not said so: though, perhaps, what he did say was almost equivalent to it, and she had jumped to the conclusion. When Squire Trevlyn reached him, he was lying with his eyes closed and the changed look on his white face. A servant stood near the table where the tray of refreshment had been placed, gazing at him.

The Squire hastily felt his forehead, then his hand. "What ails you, my boy?" he asked, subduing his voice as it never was subdued, save to the sick Rupert.

Rupert opened his eyes. "Have they come, uncle? I want Maude."

"They won't be long now," looking at his watch. "Don't you feel so well, Rupert?"

"I feel like—going," was the answer: and as Rupert spoke he gasped for breath. The servant stepped forward and raised his head. Mrs. Chattaway, who had again come in, broke into a cry.

"Edith!" reproved the Squire. "A pretty one you are for a sick room! If you cannot be calm and quiet, better keep out of it."

He quitted it himself as he spoke, called for his own groom, and bade him hasten for Mr. King. Rupert looked better when he returned; the spasm, or whatever it was, had passed, and he was holding the hand of Mrs. Chattaway.

"Aunt Edith was frightened," he said, turning his eyes on his uncle.

"She always was one to be frightened at nothing," cried the Squire. "Do you feel faint, my boy?"

"It's gone now," answered Rupert.

Mrs. Chattaway poured out some cordial, and he drank it without difficulty. Afterwards he seemed to revive, and spoke to them now and then, though he lay so still as to give an idea that all motion had departed from him. Even when the sound of wheels was heard in the avenue he did not stir, though he evidently heard.

"It's only Ralph," remarked the Squire. "I sent him out in the gig."

Rupert slightly shook his head and a half-smile illumined his face. The Squire also became aware of the fact that what they heard was not the noise of gig-wheels. He went down to the hall-door.

It was the carriage bringing back the bride and bridegroom. Maude sprang lightly in, and the Squire took her in his arms.

"Welcome home, my darling!"

Maude laughed and blushed, and the Squire left her and turned to George.

"How is Rupert, sir?"

"He has been famous until half-an-hour ago. Since then there has been a change. You had better go up at once; he has been asking for you and Maude. I have sent for King."

George drew his wife's hand within his arm, and led her upstairs. No one was in the room with Rupert, except Mrs. Chattaway. He never moved or stirred, as they advanced and bent over him, Maude throwing off her bonnet; he only gazed up at their faces with a happy smile.

Maude's eyes were swimming; George was startled. Surely death was even now upon him. It had come closer in this short interval between Squire Trevlyn's departure from the room and his return.

Rupert lay passively, his wasted hands in theirs. Maude was the first to give way. "My darling brother! I did not expect to find you like this."

"I am going on before, Maude," he breathed, his voice so low they had to stoop to catch it. "You will come later."

A cry from Mrs. Chattaway interrupted him. "Oh, Rupert, say you forgive the past! You have not said it. You must not die with unforgiveness in your heart."

He looked at her wonderingly; a look which seemed to ask if she had forgotten his assertion only an hour ago. He laid his hands feebly together holding them raised. "God bless and forgive all who may have been unkind to me, as I forgive them—as I have forgiven them long ago. God bless and forgive us all, and take us when this life is over to our heavenly home; for the sake of our Lord and Saviour Jesus Christ."

"Amen!" said the Squire.

A deep silence fell on them only to be broken by the entrance of Mr. King. He came quietly up to the sofa, glanced at Rupert, and kept his eyes fixed for the space of a minute. Then he turned to the Squire. The face was already the face of the dead. With the sorrows and joys of this world, Rupert Trevlyn had done for ever.

WILD RACES OF SOUTH-EASTERN INDIA